D. H. Mahan

Summary of the course of permanent fortification

And of the Attack and Defence of Permanent Works

SALZWASSER VERLAG

D. H. Mahan

Summary of the course of permanent fortification

And of the Attack and Defence of Permanent Works

Reprint of the original, first published in 1863.

1st Edition 2022 | ISBN: 978-3-37500-509-2

Verlag (Publisher): Salzwasser Verlag GmbH, Zeilweg 44, 60439 Frankfurt, Deutschland
Vertretungsberechtigt (Authorized to represent): E. Roepke, Zeilweg 44, 60439 Frankfurt, Deutschland
Druck (Print): Books on Demand GmbH, In de Tarpen 42, 22848 Norderstedt, Deutschland

SUMMARY

OF THE

COURSE OF PERMANENT FORTIFICATION

AND OF THE

Attack and Defence of Permanent Works.

BY D. H. MAHAN.

RICHMOND:

1863.

PREFACE

HEAD-QUARTERS,

MILITARY DISTRICT SOUTH CAROLINA

Charleston, 1862

The following work is published from the lithographic copy of the treatise on "Permanent Fortification, and Attack and Defence of Fortified Places," taught at the United States Military Academy, under D. H. MAHAN, Professor of Civil and Military Engineering.

It is believed that it contains all which it was in the power of the distinguished compiler to include up to the year 1860, and that it has everything relating to those subjects taught at Metz, in the French School of Engineers, to the same date.

R. S. RIPLEY

Brigadier-General Commanding

TABLE OF CONTENTS.

SUMMARY

OF THE

COURSE OF PERMANENT FORTIFICATIONS

AND OF THE

ATTACK & DEFENCE OF PERMANENT WORKS

System of Fortification Drawing.

1...The method now in general use, among military engineers, for delineating the plans of permanent fortifications, is similar to the one which had been previously employed for representing the natural surface of ground in topographical and hydrographical surveys: which consists in projecting, on a horizontal plane, at any assumed level, the bounding lines of the surfaces and, also, the horizontal lines cut from them by equidistant horizontal planes: the distances of these lines from the assumed plane being expressed numerically in terms of some linear measure, as a yard, a foot, etc

2...PLANE OF REFERENCE, OR COMPARISON. The assumed horizontal plane, upon which the lines are projected, is termed the *plane of comparison* or *plane of reference*, as it is the one to which the distances of all the lines from it are referred, and as it serves to compare these distances with each other, and to determine the relative positions of the lines.

3...REFERENCES. The numbers which express the distances of the lines from the plane of comparison, are termed *references*. The unit in which these distances are expressed, is usually the linear foot and its decimal divisions.

As the position assumed for the plane of comparison is arbitrary, it may be taken either above or below every point of the surface to be projected.

In the French military service, it is usually taken above; in our own, below the surface. The latter seems the more natural and is more convenient, as vertical distances are more habitually estimated from below upward than in the contrary direction. Each of these methods has the advantage of requiring but one kind of symbol to be used, viz: the numerals expressing the references; whereas, if the plane of eomparison were so taken that some of the lines projected should lie on one side of it and some on the other, then it would be necessary to use, in connection with the referenees, the algebraie symbols *plus* or *minus*, to designate those lines above the plane from those below it.

This method of representing objects has given rise to a very useful modification of the ordinary one of orthogonal projections on two planes, and has been denominated *one plane descriptive geometry;* the plane of comparison being the sole plane of projection; the references taking the place of the usual projections on a vertical plane. By this modification, the number of lines to be drawn is greatly decreased; the complication of the drawing lessened; the graphical operations required in the solution of problems, presented by the drawing, simplified; and the relations of the parts more readily seized upon, as the eye is confined to one plane of projection alone. But the chief advantage of it consists in its application to the delineation of objects, like works of permanent fortification, where, from the great disparity of the horizontal extent covered, and the vertical dimensions of the parts, a drawing, made to a scale which would give the horizontal distances with accuracy, could not, in most cases, render the vertical dimensions with any approach to the same degree of accuracy; or, if made to a scale which would admit of the vertical dimensions being accurately determined, would require an area of drawing surface, to render the horizontal dimensions to the same scale, which would exceed the convenient limits of practice.

Taking, for example, an ordinary scale used for drawing the plans of permanent fortifications of *one inch* to *fifty feet*, or the scale $\frac{1}{600}$, the details of all the bounding surfaces can be determined with accuracy to within the fractional part of a foot; whereas, a vertical projection to the same scale would be altogether too small for the same purposes.

The reference of any point or line of the plane of reference will, therefore, be zero; that of any point above it will be expressed in feet, decimal parts of a foot being used whenever the reference is not an entire number. In writing the reference the mark used to designate the linear unit is omitted, in order that the numbers expressing references may not be mistaken for those which may be put upon the drawing to express the horizontal distances between points.

The references of horizontal lines are written upon the projections of these lines. All other references are written, as nearly as practicable, parallel to the bottom border of the drawing, for the convenience of reading them without having to shift the position of the sheet on which the drawing is made.

4...POINT AND RIGHT LINE. To designate the position of a point, Pl. 1, Fig. 1, the projection of the point and its reference are enclosed within a bracket, thus: (28,50). This expresses that the vertical distance of the point from the plane of reference is 28 feet and $\frac{50}{100}$ of a foot. The position of a right line, oblique to the plane of reference, is designated by the projection of the line, and the references of any two of its points. Thus, in Fig. 1, the points *a* and *b*, upon the projection of the right line, with their respective references, (25,15) and (28,50), determine the position of the line with respect to the plane of reference.

When the line is horizontal, or parallel to the plane of reference, its projection, with the reference of one of its points, will be sufficient to designate it, and fix its position with respect to the plane of reference. Thus, in Fig. 1, the reference (25,15) written upon the projection of the line, expresses that the line is horizontal, and 25,15 feet from the plane of reference.

5...For the convenience of numerical calculation, the position of a line, with respect to the plane of reference, is often expressed in terms of the natural tangent of the angle it makes with the plane; but as this angle is the same as that between the line and its projection, its natural tangent can be expressed by the difference of level between any two points of the line, divided by the horizontal distance between the points. Now, as the difference of level between any two points of the line is the same as the difference of the references of the points, and the horizontal distance between them is the same as the horizontal projection of the portion of the line between the same points, it follows, that the natural tangent of the angle which the line makes with the plane of reference is found by dividing the difference of the references of the points by the distance in horizontal projection between them.

The vulgar fraction which expresses this tangent is termed the *inclination*, or *declivity* of the line. Thus, the fraction $\frac{1}{6}$ would express that the horizontal distance between any two points is six times the vertical distance or difference of their references; the fraction $\frac{2}{3}$, that the vertical distance between any two points is two-thirds of the horizontal distance; *the denominator of the fraction*, in all cases, *representing the number of parts in horizontal projection, and the numerator the corresponding number of parts in vertical distance.*

When the position of a line is designated in this way, it is said to be a line whose inclination, or declivity, is one-sixth, two-thirds, ten on one, etc., or simply *a line of one-sixth*, etc.

6...When the projection of a line is divided into equal parts, each of which corresponds to a unit in vertical distance, and the reference of the points of division are written, it is termed *the scale of declivity of the line.* In constructing the scale of declivity of a line, the entire references are alone put down; one of the divisions of the equal parts being subdivided into tenths, or hundredths if necessary, so as to give the fractional parts of the references corresponding to any fractional part of an entire division.

7...Having the inclination of a line, the difference of reference of any two of its points, the projections of which are given, will be found by multiplying the horizontal distance between them by the fraction which expresses this inclination; in like manner, the horizontal distance of any two points will be obtained by dividing the difference of their references by this fraction.

To obtain, therefore, the reference of a point of a line, having its projection, the horizontal distance between it and that of some other known point of the line must be determined, from the scale of the drawing by which the horizontal distances are measured; this distance expressed in numbers, being multiplied by the fraction which expresses the inclination of the line, will give the difference of reference of the two points; the required reference of the point will be found by subtracting this product from the reference of the known point, if it is higher than the one sought, or adding if it is lower. Thus, let (25,15) be the reference of a known point higher than the one sought; the distance between the points being 35,57 feet, and the inclination of the line $\frac{1}{10}$; then, $35{,}75\times\frac{1}{10}=3{,}575$ will be the difference of reference of the points, and $25{,}15-3{,}575=21{,}575$, the required reference. The converse of this shows that the horizontal distance between two points on this line, whose difference of reference is 3,575, will be $3{,}575\div\frac{1}{10}=35{,}75$ feet.

8...The true length of any portion of a line between two

given points is evidently the hypothenuse of a right-angle triangle, of which the other two sides are the difference of reference of the points, and their horizontal distance.

9...PLANE. The position of a plane oblique to the plane of reference, may be determined either by the projections and references of three of its points; by the projections and declivity of two lines in it oblique to the plane of reference; or by the projection of two or more horizontal lines of the plane, with their references.

The more usual method of representing a plane is by the projections on the plane of reference of the horizontal lines determined by intersecting it by equidistant horizontal planes. These lines are termed *horizontals of the plane*, those usually being taken the references of which are entire numbers.

10...If, in a plane given by its horizontals, a line be drawn perpendicular to the horizontals, its projection on the plane of reference will be also perpendicular to the projections of the horizontals. The angle of this line with the plane of reference is evidently the same as that of the given plane with it, and is greater than the angle between any other line drawn in the plane and the plane of reference. This line is, on this account, termed *the line of greatest declivity* of the plane.

11...If the scale of declivity of the line of greatest declivity is constructed, it will alone serve to fix the position of the plane to which it belongs, and to determine the reference of any point of the plane of which the projection is given. For the inclination of this line and that of the plane are the same; and as the horizontals are perpendicular to the line of greatest declivity, the point where the horizontal drawn through the given projection of a point in the plane cuts this line will determine upon the scale the reference of the horizontal, and, therefore, that of the point.

12...The inclination, or declivity of a plane with the plane of reference, may be expressed in the same way as the inclination of its line of greatest declivity. Thus: *a plane of one-fourth, a plane of twenty on one, a plane of two-thirds,* express that the natural tangent of the angle between the planes and the plane of reference are respectively represented by the fractions $\frac{1}{4}$, $\frac{20}{1}$ and $\frac{2}{3}$.

13...The horizontal distance between two horizontals of a plane, the angle of which is given, can be found in the same way as the horizontal distance between two points of a line, the inclination of which is given, Art. 7, by dividing the difference of the reference of the horizontals by the fraction representing the inclination of the plane; in like manner the difference of references of two horizontals will be obtained by multiplying their horizontal distance by the same fraction.

14...To distinguish the scale of declivity, Pl. 1, Fig. 2, from any other line of a plane, it is always represented by two fine parallel lines, drawn near each other, and crossed at the points of division, where the references are written, by short lines, which are portions of the corresponding horizontals.

With the foregoing elements, the usual problems of the right line and plane can be readily solved.

PROBLEMS OF THE RIGHT LINE AND PLANE.

15...Prob. 1, Pl. 1, Fig. 3. *Having the projections and references of two lines that intersect, to find the angle between them.*

Let *a b* be the projection of one of the lines, the references of two of its points (10,30) and (4,90) being given; *c d*, the projection of the other line, (10,30) and (5,0) being the references of two of its points; (10,30) being the point of intersection of the two lines.

Find on each of the lines, Art. 7, a point having the same reference (7,0). The line joining these two points will be horizontal, and projected into its true length; taking this line as the base of the triangle of which the other two sides are respectively the true lengths of the portions of the two given lines projected between (10,30) and (7,0), Art. 7, the angle at the vertex will be the one required.

16...PROB. 2, FIG. 4. *Through a point, to draw a line parallel to a given line.*

Let *c* (7,50) be the projection of the point; *a b* that of the given line of which the two points (7,0) and (9,0) are known.

Through *c* drawing *c d* parallel to *a b*, this will be the projection of the required line; and as its declivity is the same as that of the given line, it will be only necessary to set off from *c* toward *d*, the same distance as between (7,0) and (9,0), to obtain a point (9,50) as far above (7,50) as (9,0) is above (7,0).

17...PROB. 3, FIG. 5. *Through a point in a plane, to draw a line in the plane with a given inclination.*

Let *c d* be the scale of declivity of the given plane, and *a* (5,50) the given point; and suppose, for example, that the declivity of the plane is $\frac{1}{6}$, and that the declivity of the required line is $\frac{1}{10}$.

Draw the horizontal of the plane (5,50) which passes through the point, and any other horizontal as (7,0). The projection of the required line will pass through *a*, and the portion of it between the two horizontals will be equal, Art. 6, to the difference of their references, or 1.5 feet divided by the fraction which represents the inclination of the required line. Describing, therefore, from *a* an arc, with this distance *a c*, or $1.5 \div \frac{1}{10} = 15$ feet as a radius, and joining the point *b*, where it cuts the horizontal (7,0), with *a*, this will be the projection of the required line.

18...PROB. 4, PL. 1, FIG. 6. *Having three points of a plane, to construct its horizontals and scale of declivity.*

Let *a* (12,0), *b* (15,25) and *c* (15,50) be the three points. Join the lowest with the other two, and construct the scales of declivity of the lines of junction, Art. 6. The lines joining the same references on these two lines will be horizontals of the required plane. The scale of its declivity will be found by drawing two parallel lines perpendicular to the horizontals, and writing the references of the points where the scale intersects them.

19.. PROB. 5, PL. 1, FIG. 7. *To find the horizontals of a plane passed through a given line and parallel to another line.*

Let *a b* and *c d* be the projections of the two lines. From a point (10,0) on *c d* draw a line, Prob. 2, parallel to *a b;* and by Prob. 4, find the horizontals of the plane of this line and *c d;* these will be the required horizontals.

20...PROB. 6, PL. 1, FIG. 8. *To find the horizontals of a plane the declivity of which is given, and which passes through a given line.*

Let *b d* be the scale of declivity of the given line, and suppose, for example, the declivity of the line to be $\frac{1}{15}$ and that of the required plane to be $\frac{1}{12}$.

Since the horizontals of the plane must pass through the points of the line having the like references, and as the distance in projection between any two of them, Art 13, will be equal to the difference of their references divided by the fraction of inclination of the plane, it follows that, to find the one drawn through *b* (14,0), for example, it will be simply necessary to describe from any other point, as *a* (12,0), an arc of a circle, with a radius of 12 feet, equal to the quotient just mentioned, and to draw a tangent to this arc from *b*. If any other horizontal, as (16,0), is required, which would not intersect the given line within the limits of the drawing, any two points, as (12,0), and (14,0) for example, may be taken as centres, and two arcs be described from them, with radii of 12 and 24 feet, calculated as above; a line drawn tangent to the arcs will be the required horizontal.

21...PROB. 7, PL. 1, FIG. 9. *Having the horizontals, or the scale of declivity of two planes, to find their intersection.*

Join the points where any two horizontals, as (12,0) and (14,0), in one plane intersect two corresponding horizontals of the other, and the line so found will be the projection of the required intersection.

22...When the horizontals are parallel, or when they are so nearly parallel that their points of intersection cannot be readily found, the following method may be taken: Draw any two parallel lines, as *c d, c' d'*, Pl. 1, Fig. 10.

These may be considered as the horizontals of an arbitrary plane having the same references, (12,0) and (14,0), as the two corresponding horizontals in each of the given planes.

The intersections of the horizontals of the arbitrary plane with those of the given planes will determine two lines, which, being the intersections of the given planes with the arbitrary plane, will, by their intersection *o*, determine a point common to the three planes, and, therefore, a point of the intersection of the two given planes. Assuming any other two parallels, *a b*, *a′ b′*, as the horizontals of another arbitrary plane; finding the point *o′* common to the three planes, and joining *o* and *o′* by a line, this will be the required interseetion.

When the horizontals of the two planes are parallel, one point, as *o*, will be sufficient to determine the intersection, as its projection will be parallel to the horizontals.

23...PROB. 8, PL. 1, Fig. 11. *To find where a given line pierces a given plane.*

Through any two points of the line, having the same references (12,0) (14,0), for example, as two horizontals of the given plane, draw two parallel lines, *a b*, *a′ b′*, which may be taken as the horizontals of an arbitrary plane. The line of intersection, *m n*, of this plane with the given plane being determined, by Prob. 7, the point *o* where it intersects the given line will be the projection of the required point, the reference of which can be found from the scale of the plane.

24...PROB. 9, PL. 1, FIG. 12. *To draw from a given point a perpendicular to a given plane, and find its length.*

Let *a* (12,0) be the given point, and the given plane be represented by its scale of declivity.

The projection of the required perpendicular will pass through *a*, and be parallel to the scale of declivity of the given plane. The angle which it makes with the plane of reference is the complement of that between this plane and the given plane; its tangent, therefore, will be the reciprocal of the tangent of that of the given plane.

Drawing, therefore, through *a*, the line *a c* parallel to the scale of declivity of the plane, and constructing its scale of declivity, Art. 7, this will be the projection of the required perpendicular. The point *o*, where it pierces the given plane, is found by Prob. 8, and its true length by Art. 8.

25... *Curved and Irregular Surfaces.*

All other surfaces may, like the plane, Art. 7, be represented by the projections on the plane of reference of the curves or lines, cut from them by equidistant horizontal planes, together with the references of these curves; as many of these curves being drawn as may be requisite to determine all the points of the surface with accuracy.

In the more simple geometrical surfaces, a single horizontal curve, with the projection of some point or line of the surface, will alone suffice. For example, the cone may be represented by the projection and reference of any curve cut from it by a horizontal plane, with the projection and reference of its vertex; a cylinder by the projection and reference of a like curve, with the projection and reference of one of its right line elements; a sphere by the projection and reference of its centre and that of its great circle parallel to the plane of reference.

26...This method of projection is more particularly advantageous in the representation of irregular surfaces, which, like the natural surfaces of ground, for example, are not submitted to any geometrical law, and in solving the various problems of tangent and secant planes to surfaces of this character. These surfaces can only be represented by the projection of the horizontal curves cut from them by equidistant horizontal planes, and by substituting for the zone of the real surface, contained between any two horizontal curves, an artificial zone, subjected to some geometrical law of generation which shall give an approximation to the real surface sufficiently accurate for the object in view. The usual method of doing this is to take two consecutive horizontal curves, as the directrices of the artificial surface of the zone, and move a right line so as to intersect them, and, in each of its consecutive positions, be perpendicular to the consecutive tangents to one of the curves, the upper curve being usually taken for this last condition.

If, in Pl. 1, Fig. 13, for example, (6,0), (7,0), etc., are the projections of the horizontals of a surface, the zone between the curves (6,0) and (7,0) may be replaced by an artificial surface, the position of the generatrix of which, at any point of the upper curve (7,0), will be determined by constructing the horizontal tangent at that point, as *a*, for example, and drawing *a b* perpendicular to it and intersecting the lower curve. The position of the generatrix *a' b'* at any other point *a'* is constructed in like manner.

27...To obtain any curve of the artificial zone intermediate to the two directrices, it will be only necessary to construct several positions of the generatrix, and to find on these the points having the same reference as the required curve. The horizontal of the surface (6,50), for example, will bisect the projections of the generatrix in its various positions.

PROBLEMS OF IRREGULAR SURFACES AND THE RIGHT LINE AND PLANE.

28...PROB. 10, PL. 1, FIG. 14. *Through a given point, in a vertical plane which intersects a surface, to draw a tangent to the curve of intersection of the plane and surface.*

Let *a* (5,50) be the given point, and *a b* the trace of the plane. The points where this trace intersects the horizontal curves of the surface will be the projections of points of the curve.

Let any arbitrary line, as *a c*, be now drawn through *a*, and its scale of declivity be constructed; and let the horizontal lines be drawn between the points having the same references on *d c* and *a b* where the latter cuts the horizontal curves. These horizontals will generally make different angles with *a c*, and the one, as (7,0), which makes the smallest angle with it, toward the descending portion, will determine on the curve the tangential point. To show this, construct the scale of declivity of the line thus found, of which *a* (5,50) is the projection of one point, and (7,0), on *a b*, the tangent point, another. This is most readily done, by drawing through the points (10,0), (9,0), etc., of *a c*, lines parallel to the horizontal (7,0), and finding where they intersect *a b*, in which the required tangent will be projected. Comparing now the references of the points on the line just found, and assumed as the required tangent, with the references of the points of the curve having the same projection, it will at once be evident that these two lines have only the point projected in (7,0) in common, and that every other point of the right line is exterior to the curve, and, therefore, this line must be tangent to the curve at the point determined as above.

29...PROB. 11, PL. 1, FIG. 15. *To construct the elements of a cone with a given vertex which shall envelop a given surface.*

Let (10,0), etc., be the horizontals of the given surface; and *a* (6,0) the position of the vertex of the cone.

From *a*, draw *a b*, *a b'*, etc., as the traces of vertical planes which pass through the vertex and intersect the surface. Construct, by Prob. 10, the tangents, from *a* to the curves cut from the surface by the planes *a b*, etc. These tangents will be the required elements.

30...PROB. 12, PL. 1, FIG. 15. *To find the curve of intersection of a cone enveloping a given surface by a horizontal plane.*

Having found, by Probs. 11 and 12, the elements of the cone, and constructed the scale of declivity of each one, by joining the points *o*, *o' o''*, having the same reference as the given horizontal plane, as (9,0) for example; this will form a continuous line *mo''o'on*, which will be the projection of the points where these elements pierce the given plane, and, therefore, the projection of the required intersection.

31...PROB. 13, PL. 2, FIG. 1. *A limited extent of surface being given, and a point exterior to it, to find the limits within which planes may be passed through this point and lie above all the given surface.*

Let *a* (8,0) be the given point; (10,0), (9,0), etc., the horizontals of the given surface, the limits of which are the sector contained within the arc *B D C*, and the two radii ***a B*** and *a C*.

Taking a as the vertex of a cone which shall envelop the given surface, the elements of this cone can be found by Probs. 11 and 12. Any plane that can be passed tangent to this cone, and which shall not intersect the surface within the given limits, will satisfy the conditions of the problem.

From the position of the vertex of the cone with respect to the surface, it will be seen that a horizontal plane, passed through the vertex, will cut from the cone two horizontals $a\,b'$, and $a\,b''$ (8,0) [the first of which will be tangent to the horizontal curve (8,0) of the surface, and the second $a\,b''$ will pierce the surface, where the limiting arc $B\,D\,C$ cuts the same horizontal curve]; and that all the elements projected within the angles $B\,a\,b'$ and $C\,a\,b'$ will lie below the horizontal plane (8,0). Now, if the elements within these angles be prolonged beyond the vertex, they will form two portions of cones having the same elements as the portions below the vertex; and it is evident that any plane passed tangent to the lower portion, as $b'\,a\,B$, within one of these angles, will leave this portion below it, and the corresponding portion, formed by the prolonged elements, above it; and, in order that this plane shall satisfy the conditions of the problem, it must also leave the portions of the cone within the angles $b'\,a\,b''$, and $b''\,a\,C$, also below it. The same reasoning applies to planes passed tangent to the portions of the cone within each of the other two angles. It is, therefore, evident that a plane, which shall satisfy the conditions imposed, must leave all that portion of the cone which lies above the horizontal plane (8,0) through the vertex below it, and all the prolonged portions corresponding to the portions below the plane (8,0) above it.

To find any such plane, let the cone be intersected by a horizontal plane, as (9,0), by Prob. 12. This plane will cut, from the portion of the cone within the angle $b'\,a\,b''$, a curve of which $n\,o\,n'$ is the projection; the two extreme points of this curve, within the limits, being at the points where the horizontal (9,0) of the surface cuts the limiting arc; it will also cut, from each of the prolonged portions, a curve, the one $m\,r$, and the other $m'\,r'$; the extreme point m of $m\,r$

being on the prolongation of the extreme element *a C*; that *m'* of the other on the extreme element *a B*, on the other side, prolonged. Having obtained these three curves, let tangent lines be drawn from the points *m* and *m'* to the curve *n o n'* A plane passed through either of these tangents and through the corresponding element of the cone *a s*, or *a s'*, drawn through the tangential point, will be a tangent plane to the cone; and as either of these planes will leave the curve *n o n'* on one side of it, and the two curves *m r* and *m' r'* on the other, it will leave all the portion of the cone corresponding to the first curve below it, and the portions corresponding to the other curves above it; and will, therefore, satisfy the required conditions. The same will hold true for any tangent plane to the cone along any element drawn between the points *s* and *s'*; since the tangent drawn to any point of the curve *n o n'*, between the points *s* and *s'*, will leave this curve on one side of it, and the other two, *m r* and *m' r'*, entirely on the other.

The two horizontal elements, *a b'* and *a b''* of the cone, will be parallel to the assymptotes of the curve *n o n'*; and their lines of prolongation beyond the vertex will be parallel, in like manner, to the assymptotes of the two curves, *m r* and *m' r'*

32...PROB. 14, PL. 1, FIG. 16. *Through a given line, to pass a plane tangent to a surface.*

1st. Let *a b* be the projection of the given line, and (10,0), (9,0), etc., the horizontals of the surface. From the points on the line, as (10,0), etc., draw lines tangent to the horizontal curves having the same references; the tangent which makes with the projection of the line the least angle toward the descending portion will, with the line, determine the required plane.

For, let the horizontal tangent (10,0) be the one which makes with *a b* the least angle; from the other points, (9,0), etc., of *a b*, draw lines parallel to the tangent (10,0); these lines will lie in the plane that contains this tangent and *a b*, and will be horizontals of this plane; they also lie respectively in the planes of the horizontal curves (9,0),

(8,0), etc.; but, since they fall exterior to the curves, it follows that their plane also lies exterior to every horizontal curve of the surface, except at the curve (10,0) where it touches the surface at the point of contact of its horizontal (10,0) with this curve.

2d. When the line *a b*, Pl. 1, Fig. 17, is horizontal, let tangents be drawn to the horizontal curves and parallel to *a b*. These tangents may be regarded as the elements of a cylinder which envelops the surface, the tangent plane to which will be tangent to the surface. To find the element of contact of the plane and cylinder, let the cylinder and given line be intersected by an arbitrary vertical plane, of which *o d* is the trace. From the point *o*, where the line pierces this plane, let a tangent line be drawn to the curve cut from the cylinder by the plane, by Prob. 10. The point of contact will determine the position of the element of the cylinder along which the plane, through *a b*, will be tangent: since the tangent to the curve projected in *o d*, with the line *a b*, will determine the tangent plane to the cylinder.

3d. When the line *a b*, Pl. 1, Fig. 18, is so nearly horizontal that tangents cannot be drawn from its points, within the limits of the drawing, to the horizontal curves, let any point of the line, as *o* (7,0), be taken as the vertex of a cone enveloping the surface; a plane passed through the line and tangent to the cone will be tangent to the surface.

Find, by Probs. 10 and 11, the curve *m r n* cut from this cone by the horizontal plane (8,0); from the point (8,0) of *a b* draw a tangent to this curve. This tangent, with the line *a b*, will determine the required plane.

33...PROB. 15, PL. 1, FIG. 19. *To find, approximately, the point where a given right line pierces a surface.*

Let (8,0), (9,0), etc., be the horizontals of the surface, and *d f* the scale of declivity of the line. Through any two points, as *a* (9,0) and *c* (8,0), draw two parallel lines, as *a m* and *c n*, which may be taken as the horizontals of an arbitrary plane passed through the given line. Joining the points *m n* where the horizontals of the arbitrary plane intersect the corresponding horizontals of the surface, this line *m n* will be the approximate intersection of the plane with the zone of the surface between the horizontals (8,0) and (9,0), and the point *o*, where *m n* intersects *d f*, will be the approximate point required.

34...PROB. 16, PL. 1, FIG. 20. *To find the intersection of a plane and surface.*

Let (10,0), (9,0), etc., be the horizontal curves of the surface, *e f* the scale of declivity of the plane.

Draw the horizontals of the plane having the same references as the horizontal curves; the points of intersection of these lines, in their respective planes, will be points of the required intersection.

When it is desired to find a point of the curve of intersection intermediate to two horizontal curves, if the reference of the required point is fixed, it will be necessary to construct, Art. 27, the horizontal curve of the surface, and the horizontal of the plane having this reference; their intersection will give the required point. If the reference of the required point is not fixed, draw any generatrix, as *a c*, of the zone on which the required point is to be found, and, by Prob. 8, Fig. 11, find the point, as *o*, where *a c* pierces the given plane; this will be the required point.

35...APPLICATION OF PRECEDING PROBLEMS. The following problems will aid as illustrations of the preceding subject in its application to the determination and delineation of lines and surfaces.

36...PROB. 1, PL. 2, FIG. 2. *The plane of site of a work, the exterior line and scale of declivity of its terreplein being given, to construct the plane of the rampart-slope and its foot; also, a ramp of a given inclination along the rampart-slope, leading from the plane of site to the terreplein.*

Let *a* (74,50) and *b* (76,0) be the references of two points on the exterior line of the terreplein, and *m n* its scale of declivity; let the rampart-slope be $\frac{3}{2}$; the declivity of the ramp $\frac{1}{6}$, its width 4.30 yards; and the plane of site be horizontal and at the reference (60,0).

The foot of the rampart-slope lying in the plane of site

will be horizontal, and will be determined, Prob. 6, Fig. 8, by finding the line of the slope at the reference (60,0).

Having the two bounding lines of the rampart-slope, the inner line, *c d*, of the ramp is constructed by assuming a point, *c*, on the foot of the rampart-slope, as the point of departure, and determining the line of $\frac{1}{9}$, drawn from *c*, on the rampart-slope, by Prob. 3, Fig. 5. Having found this line, which is also the line of greatest declivity of the ramp, the exterior line, *ef*, of the ramp is drawn parallel to it, and at a distance 4.30 yards, equal to the width assumed for the ramp. The horizontals of the ramp will be perpendicular to these two lines. The foot of the ramp, *c e*, will be a horizontal line drawn through the point of departure. The top of it, *d f*, will be determined, by Prob. 7, Fig. 9, by finding the intersection of the ramp and the terreplein, one point of which will be the point *d* (76,30), the intersection of the inner line of the ramp and the interior line of the terreplein.

The ramp is terminated on the exterior by passing a plane through its exterior line *e f*, having the same slope as the rampart-slope. This plane will intersect the plane of site in a line parallel to the foot of the rampart-slope, and the terreplein in one parallel to the exterior line of the terreplein.

37...PROB. 18, PL. 2, FIG. 3. *Having given the lines of the parapet of a work, and the scales of declivity of the planes of its interior crest and terreplein, to determine the lines and surfaces of a barbette in its salient for five guns.*

Let *a b* be the scale of declivity of the plane of the interior crest, which, as the terreplein is parallel to the plane of the interior crest and 8 feet below it, estimated vertically, will also serve as the scale of declivity of the terreplein, by subtracting 8 feet from the references of the former to obtain the corresponding references of the latter. Having constructed a pancoupé of 4 yards in the salient, find the intersection of the top surface of the barbette, which is horizontal and assumed on the drawing at the reference (82,75), with the planes of the interior slope, this intersection will determine the foot of the genouillère of the barbette. From this last line at the pancoupé set back along the capital a distance of 8 yards, and from the extremity of this line draw a perpendicular to the interior crest of each face. The pentagonal figure thus marked out will be the space for the gun in the salient. From the foot of each of the perpendiculars set off along the faces distances of 12 yards, for the lengths along the interior crests to be occupied by two guns on each side of the salient. Setting back from the extremities of these two last distances, set off perpendiculars to the interior crest of 8 yards, and drawing lines through the extremities of these perpendiculars parallel to the interior crests, they, with the two perpendiculars, will mark out the exterior bounding lines of the barbette. By passing planes of $\frac{1}{1}$ or 45° through these exterior lines, and finding, by Prob. 7, Fig. 9, their intersections with the terreplein, these lines will be the foot of the barbette-slopes. A ramp, having a slope $\frac{1}{6}$, leads from the terreplein to the top of the barbette; the width of this ramp is 3.30 yards, its interior line in projection being on the prolongation of the foot of the banquette-slope. The ramp is terminated by side-slopes of $\frac{1}{1}$, the intersections of which with the terreplein and the slopes of the barbette and banquette are found by Prob. 7, Fig. 9. The foot of the ramp, or its intersection with the terreplein, is also found by the same problem.

As the top surface of the barbette is horizontal, it may be necessary in some cases to make the interior crest, along the barbette, also horizontal, in which case the superior slope of the parapet along the barbette being higher than the rest of it, the two planes will be connected by a plane of 45°, as at *c*.

38...PROB. 19, PL. 2, FIG. 4. *To determine the bounding surfaces of a ramp leading up an irregular surface, and so placed that its axis or centre line shall nearly coincide with the irregular surface.*

Let (8,0), (9,0), etc., be the horizontal curves of the surface, and let *a* (8,0) be the point of departure or foot of the ramp. Assuming the declivity of the ramp $\frac{1}{9}$, for example, from *a*, with a radius of 9 units, describe an arc, and join by a right line the point *b* where it cuts the horizontal (9,0) with the point. Repeat this construction, from *b* to *c*, on the horizontal (10,0); and so on to the top, *e*, or point of arrival. The broken line *a-b-c-d-e* will be the projection of the axis. But, to avoid the angular changes of direction, the straight portions of the axis may be connected at the angular points, by setting off from *b*, for example, the equal distances *b a'*, *b c'*, and connecting these points by an arc of a circle tangent to the straight portions. The same construction being repeated at the other angular points, the broken line will be replaced by the sinuous line *a a' c'*, etc., as the axis. Having determined the axis, the exterior and interior lines of the top surface are drawn parallel to the axis, and at a distance from it equally to half the assumed width of the ramp. From the position of the axis, the exterior half of the ramp will be in embankment, and the interior in excavation. To determine the side-slopes of the embankment, pass planes through the straight portions of the exterior edge of the ramp, and find, by Prob. 6, Pl. 1, Fig. 8, the horizontals of these planes, and, by Prob. 16, Fig. 20, the intersections of these planes with the irregular surface. The plane surfaces of the side-slopes thus determined, are connected by curved surfaces which pass through the curved lines of the exterior edge. These surfaces may be determined as follows: Take, for example, the point *n* at the foot of the plane side-slope *A*, where it cuts the radius prolonged, of the arc *a' c'*; and the point *O* on the radius through *c'* where it cuts the foot of the plane side-slope *B*. The lines, of which *n v* and *o u* are the projections, will evidently have the same inclination, and they may be assumed as the lines of junction of the plane-slopes *A* and *B* and the curved side-slope *x*. This curved side-slope may then be generated by the motion of a right line, which has the top line of which *v u* is the projection for its directrix, whilst in its motion it makes a constant angle with the plane of comparison, and its projections are constantly normal to the arc $v u$ From the construction comprising these conditions, the foot, $n o$, of the curved portion, x, of the side-slope is determined. The same constructions are repeated to obtain the portions, C, of the plane, and $y z$ of the curved side-slopes, with the line m-n-o-p-q-r-s the foot of these slopes.

The side-slopes of the part in excavation A', B', C' and $x' y'$ with the line m'-n'-o'-p'-q'-r', are determined by like constructions.

The portions of the top surfaces of the ramps, bounded by the arcs of circles, are helicoidal surfaces, of which the axis is the directrix and the plane of comparison the plane director.

The curved surface side-slopes are also evidently helicoidal surfaces, the directrices of which are the curved lines above mentioned; and the vertical lines through the centres of the arcs the projections of these lines.

REMARKS. In the Figure, the declivity of the side-slopes of the embankment is one-half the excavation. The declivities of the curved portions of the top are greater than those of plane surfaces, the difference depending on the angle between the straight portions of the axis.

39...*Plan, Section, Elevation and Profile.*

In delineating permanent fortifications, horizontal projections and horizontal sections, both of which go under the general name of *plans*, are used to represent the relative positions of the parts and their dimensions horizontally Intersections of the parts by vertical planes passed in any required direction, and termed *sections*, show the relative positions and dimensions of all the parts in the plane of section, both horizontally and vertically. Projections on a vertical plane, termed *elevations*, are used to represent the forms of the exterior surfaces of the parts projected and their relative positions vertically. *Profiles* are sections made by vertical planes passed perpendicular to the horizontal projections of the interior crests of the parts where the profiles are taken; they give the vertical and horizontal distances between the points in the plane of the profile. Usually, a profile only shows the bounding lines of the parts intersected, thus presenting nothing more than an outline of the parts.

In giving a horizontal section, it is customary not only to delineate the forms contained in the plane of section, but to project upon this plane all the parts which are seen *below it*, and in some cases parts which are covered by others, the outlines of the latter being shown by broken, or dotted, lines, to distinguish them from the outlines of the parts in view, for which full lines are used. A like method is sometimes employed in sections, the visible parts beyond the plane of section being projected upon it; thus combining an elevation and section in the same figure.

For the perfect comprehension of a fortification, not only will all of the foregoing modes of delineation be requisite, but the references of all the points and lines, as well as the vertical and horizontal distances that determine the relative positions of the points, must be carefully written on each figure.

In Pl. 3, Figs. 1, 2, 3, which show the plan, section and elevation of the end of the face of a work, an illustration is given of the usual manner in which such drawings are made; and the same system will be pursued in the figures which follow these.

40...*Observations on the means for obtaining accuracy in drawings.*

The first requisite in all drawings intended to represent not only the outline of the forms of objects, but to afford the means of determining the exact dimensions of each part, is *minute accuracy*, both in the geometrical constructions, and in writing down all letters and numbers which serve either as references or to give the dimensions.

To attain this end, so far as regards the geometrical part, judgment is to be exercised in the selection of the means for establishing on the drawing the positions of the various points which are either given or to be found; as one method, although in theory as correct as some other, may not, in practice, be found to yield as satisfactory results. Attention to the following remarks will serve both to illustrate the meaning here intended, and to give some simple practical methods:

1st. In setting off several distances along a line, whether equal or unequal, the most accurate method is to commence by first setting off the entire distance, and then the several parts; taking care to verify, from the scale, the aggregate of the several partial distances; thus, in the annexed Pl. 2, Fig. 5, where the aggregate of all the partial distances is 60.33 feet, commence by setting off the entire distance 60′.33 feet; next 50′.33, which is the sum of the two distances, 20′ and 30′.33, then verify the remaining 10′ by the scale.

2d. When a distance to be set off is so small that it cannot be laid down with accuracy by the points of the dividers, the following method may be employed: set back, from the point from which the required distance is to be set off, any arbitrary distance, then set forward, from this last point, a distance equal to the sum of this arbitrary distance and the one required; thus, in Pl. 2, Fig. 6, where 2′ is to be set off from *a* toward *c*, set back from *a* say 30′ to *b*, then from *b* 32′ to *c*.

3d. In setting off a point at a given perpendicular distance from a line, instead of drawing a perpendicular, in the first place, to the line, it will mostly be found more speedy, and more accurate, to take off from the scale the given distance, in the dividers, and, setting one point on the paper, bring the other so that the arc described by it, with the given distance as a radius, shall be tangent to the line; thus, in Pl. 2, Fig. 7, wishing to set off *c* at 20′ from *ab*, take 20′ in the dividers, and, by the eye, find where one point must be placed so that the other describing an arc will touch *ab*. This method will be found convenient in drawing a parallel to a line at a given distance from it by setting off another point in the same way

4th. In setting off several points, for the purpose of drawing several parallels to a given line, as, for example, the lines which bound the planes of a parapet, it will be found most speedy and accurate to draw upon a slip of smooth thin paper two lines perpendicular to each other; mark on one of the lines the respective given distances from the other; then cut the paper close to the line along which the given points are marked off; so that, when the strip is laid upon the drawing, the other line marked upon it being laid upon the line of the drawing to which the parallels are to be drawn can be pricked off, either by a sharp-pointed pencil, or in any other way. In Pl. 2, Fig. 8, *a b* is the line of drawing; *A* the strip of paper, *f c*, *f d*, *f e*, etc., the distances at which the parallels are to be drawn from *a b*, marked off on the edge of *A* perpendicular to the line *f*, which line, when *A* is laid on the drawing, should coincide with *a b*. If the line *a b* is somewhat long, it will be better to set off these points near each of its extremities than to draw the parallels by aid of the ruler and triangle.

5th. When a point is to be constructed by means of the intersection of two lines arbitrarily chosen, such a position should be assumed for the arbitrary lines that they shall not form a very acute angle, as in that case their point of intersection might not be determined by the eye with accuracy. For example, in erecting a perpendicular to a line at a given point, and in like problems, in which points are found by the intersections of arcs of circles, it will be usually most convenient, and best, to take for the radii of the arcs the distance between their centres, as the angle between the tangents to the arcs at their point of intersection will then be 60°, which is sufficient to give accurately the point where the lines cross. In cases like Figs. 10, 11, Arts. 22, 23, the arbitrary lines *a b*, *a′ b′*, etc., should be so chosen as to intersect the horizontals nearly at right angles, and so, also, that the resulting lines, by which the points *o*, *o′* are determined, shall not intersect in too acute an angle.

In all such cases of determining points, and even where a point is pricked into the paper by a sharp point, it will be found well to mark the point thus ⊙, by a small circle drawn around it with the lead pencil, as this will present the point with more distinctness.

6th. In determining a portion of a line, by the construction of two arbitrary points, the points should be so chosen that the portion required may fall between them and not beyond them. In Pl. 1, Fig. 10, for example, if the required portion of the line of intersection of the planes extended on either side, beyond o, or o', or beyond both, the lines $a\,b$, $c\,d$, etc., should be so chosen as to bring o and o' as far apart, at least, as the length of the required portion of the line which they serve to determine.

7th. No means of verifying the accuracy of the construction of points, or lines, should be omitted. In Pl. 1, Fig. 9, for example, other corresponding horizontals should be drawn, and if the line of intersection determined by the two points first found is correct, their points of intersection also will fall upon it. In Pl. 1, Figs. 9, 10, the scale of declivity of the line of intersection being determined, the references of the points, where it intersects the scales of declivity of the planes, should be the same as the same points on the scales, if the line has been accurately determined. A general and minute verification of all the parts of the drawing should be made before any portion of it is put in ink.

8th. Neatness is a not unimportant element in the attainment of accuracy in drawing. A few minutiæ, when attended to, will subserve this end.

That part of the paper on which the draughtsman is not working should be kept covered with clean paper, pasted on the edge of the board so as to fold over the drawing; the parts which are finished should be similarly protected.

Before commencing the daily work the paper should be carefully dusted, and the scales, rules and triangles be carefully wiped with a clean dry rag.

As few lines of construction as possible should be drawn in pencil; and only that part of each which may be strictly necessary to determine the point sought. As, for example, where a point is to be found by the intersection of two arcs of circles; when the position of the point can be approximately judged of by the eye, only a portion of one arc, which will embrace the point, may be drawn, and the point where the second arc would intersect the first be marked without describing the arc. In Pl. 1, Fig. 10, instead of drawing the entire lines *a b*, *c d*, etc., it would be simply necessary to mark the points only where they cut the horizontals, and, in like manner, the points *o* and *o'* might be marked without drawing the entire lines.

No more of any line of the drawing should be made in pencil than what is to remain permanently in ink.

9th. In inking the lines, the following directions will be found useful:

Efface carefully all pencil lines that are not to be inked, and those parts of the permanent lines which are not to remain, before commencing to ink.

When right lines are tangent to curves, put in ink the curve before the right line; draw all arcs of equal radii at once, one after the other; if several arcs are to be described from the same centre, it will be well to put a thin bit of quill over the point for the end of the dividers to rest on, to avoid making a large hole in the drawing.

If the drawing is not to be colored with the brush, all the lines of one color should be put in before commencing on those of another.

If one of the bounding lines of a surface is to be made heavier than the others, its breadth should be taken from the surface they limit and not be added to it; and when the heavy line forms the boundary of two surfaces, its breadth must be taken from the one of greatest declivity.

10th. When the drawing is to be colored, all lines that are not to be black may be put in first with black—making them very faint, so that they may receive their appropriate colors after the drawing is otherwise completed.

No heavy line should be put in until the work with the brush is completed.

When all the lines are in, the drawing should be thoroughly cleaned with stale bread-crumb; and then have several pitchers of water dashed over it, the board being placed in an inclined position to allow the water, colored by the ink lines, to escape rapidly, and not to discolor the paper.

11th. In using the brush, whether for flat tints, or graded, the requisite depth of tint should be reached by a number of faint tints laid over each other; this is especially necessary in laying tints of blacks, browns and reds.

To obtain an even flat, or graded tint, on dry paper, is very difficult for a beginner. The best plan for this is, first to wet with a large brush, or clean rag, the surface on which the tint is to be laid, then, with a slightly moist rag, clear the surface of water, and before the paper has time to dry lay on the tint. With this precaution, the heaviest tints of Chinese ink, the most difficult of all to manage on dry paper, can be neatly laid down.

12th. The lettering and numbering of a drawing should be in ordinary printed character; this is particularly requisite in the numbering, to avoid misapprehensions which might arise from individual peculiarities in writing numbers.

As has been already remarked, references are written in black, within brackets, which, when practicable, embrace the point referred to. When not practicable, a small dotted line may lead from the point to the reference; thus, ⊙......(25,50); but to distinguish references from other numbers the designation of the unit is omitted.

All horizontal distances between points are written upon a dotted line drawn between the points, with an arrow head at each end; where several partial distances in a right line are marked, it will be also well to mark the total distance—the latter may be written above or beneath the former, Pl. 2, Fig. 5.

In writing horizontal distances, the usual designation of the unit is always written thus: *y*, for yards, ′ for feet, etc. All the numbers must be expressed in the same unit; the fractional parts being in decimals.

References and horizontal distances cannot be too much multiplied, in order to avoid misapprehensions, and the results of errors of construction, as well as to save the time that would be taken in applying dividers to the drawing to find, from the scale affixed to it, the dimensions of any part.

A scale very accurately constructed should be affixed to the drawing before it is cut from the board; so that the shrinkage of the paper, which is about $\frac{1}{500}$, may affect all the parts equally, and the scale thus be made to correspond to the real lengths of the lines on the drawing. The scale should be divided according to the decimal system, as being most convenient for counting off.

The first division of the scale should furnish the units, and also their decimal parts, if the scale bears that proportion to the true dimensions of the object represented which will admit of these divisions. This first division is numbered from right to left, Pl. 2, Fig. 9, the zero point being on the right, the 10 point on the left; the succeeding divisions, to 50 inclusive, should each be equal to the first division, containing ten units each. The remaining divisions may contain fifty units each. It will be seen that any number of tens, units, or fractional parts of a unit, can thus be readily taken off from the scale by the dividers. The scale should be long enough to give the dimensions of the longest line on the drawing.

The proportion which the scale bears to the true dimensions of the object should be written above the scale; thus, *scale one inch to ten yards, or* $\frac{1}{360}$. And the designation of the unit of the drawing should be annexed to the last division on the scale, as *yds.* for yards, *ft.* for feet, etc.

PERMANENT FORTIFICATION.

Preliminary Considerations.

41...The term *permanent fortification* is applied to those defences which, constructed of materials of a durable nature, and designed for permanent occupancy by troops, receive such a degree of strength that an enemy will be forced to the operations either of a siege or a blockade to gain possession of them.

42...The object of such defences is to secure the permanent military possession of those points, either on the frontiers or in the interior of a state, which must, at all times, have a well-defined bearing on the operations of a defensive or an offensive war.

43...For the attainment of this object, the following general conditions should be fulfilled in the arrangement of such defences: 1st, they should be of sufficient strength to resist with success all the ordinary means resorted to by an assailant in an open assault; 2d, be provided with suitable shelters to protect the troops, the armament, and the magazines of provisions and munitions of war required for their defence, against the destructive measures of the assailant, of every description; 3d, be so planned that every point exterior to the defences within cannon range shall be thoroughly swept by their fire; 4th, have secure and easy means of communication for the movements of the troops, both within the defences and to the exterior; 5th, and finally, be provided with all such accessory defensive means as the natural features of the position itself may afford, to enable the garrison to dispute with energy the occupancy by the assailant, of every point both within and exterior to the defences.

The defensive branch of the military engineer's art consists in a knowledge of the means which are employed to fulfil the above conditions, and of their suitable adaptation to the natural features of the positions he may be called upon to fortify.

Component Elements of Permanent Works.

GENERAL PROFILE.

44...The first condition laid down for permanent defences, security from open assault, supposes a strength of profile greatly superior to that which is given to temporary works.

45...The usual and most simple form of profile for permanent works consist of a *rampart*, a *parapet*, and a *ditch*, the *scarp* and *counterscarp* of which are faced with *steep walls* of *stone*, or *brick*, and exterior to which a *glacis* is usually thrown up. When the ditch contains at all times a depth of water sufficient to prevent its being forded, the scarp and counterscarp may be simply slopes of earth like those of field works; as the water, with ordinary vigilance on the part of the defence, will give security from surprise, and all the other ordinary means of an open assault.

46...The rampart, *A*, Pl. 3, Figs. 4, 6, is an earthen mound, raised above the natural level of the ground, and upon which the parapet, *B*, is placed. The rampart thus serves to give the troops and armanent, which are placed on top of it and behind the parapet, a commanding view over the ground to be guarded by the fire of the defences; whilst, at the same time, it increases the obstacle to an open assault, by the additional height it gives to the scarp.

47...The top surface of the rampart, *b c*, in rear of the parapet, termed the *terreplein*, affords the troops and armament a convenient position for circulation from point to point, where they are sheltered from the direct views of the assailant's fire.

48...The rampart is usually terminated on the interior, *a b*, by allowing the earth to assume either its natural slope or one somewhat less steep, and which is termed the *rampart-slope*. In cases where this slope would take up too much of the ground within the defences it is replaced by a wall, termed the *parade wall*, which rises from the level of the interior ground, termed the *parade*, to the interior line of the *terreplein*.

49...Inclined planes of earth, termed *ramps*, lead from the parade to the terreplein, being placed against the rampart-slope or the parade wall. The ramps are, in some cases, terminated, inwardly, with the same slope as that of the rampart; in others, this slope is replaced by a wall, which rises to the top surface of the ramp, or a little above it.

50...The parapet, serving the same purposes in permanent as in field works, receives the same general form as in the latter. In some cases, the exterior slope, Pl. 3, Fig. 12, is replaced by a wall, which, resting on the top of the scarp wall, rises to the level of the superior slope. The exterior slope of the parapet usually rises from the top of the scarp wall, leaving a narrow berm between it and the scarp or face of the wall. In some cases, it is thrown so far to the rear of the scarp, Pl. 3, Figs. 9, 10, as to leave sufficient room for a communication, *C*, in front of the parapet, in which the troops can circulate under cover from fire, being masked either by an earthen parapet, or by a wall, *D*. This covered communication, *C*, is termed an *exterior corridor*, or *chemin-de-rondes*.

51...The scarp wall, *C*, Pl. 3, Figs. 4, 6, retains the earth of the rampart and parapet, and forms, by its height and steepness, the chief obstacle to an open assault. The top stone of the wall, *k*, termed the *cordon*, or *coping*, projects beyond its face, and, serving as a *larmier*, or *drip*, protects it from the effects of the rain-water which runs from the parapet upon the coping.

52...The line in which the face of the scarp wall, prolonged, would intersect the coping, is termed the *magistral*. This is a very important line in drawing the plans of permanent works, serving as the directing line to fix (both upon the drawing and upon the ground in setting out the work) the dimensions and relative positions of all the bounding lines of the parapet and other parts.

53...The counterscarp wall, *G*, renders the ditch of more difficult access from without than an earthen slope would; and, when of sufficient height and steepness, it forms a very serious obstacle to an open assault. It receives the same general forms as the scarp wall.

54...The glacis, *F*, is of the same form, and serves the same purposes as in field works; but, besides these, it is indispensable as a mask for the scarp wall, covering it from distant batteries, in cases where it rises above the level of the counterscarp, and thus forcing the assailant to construct his batteries along the crest of the glacis, to obtain a position from which the scarp wall can be breached. When the glacis serves only as a mask, and to bring the assailant, as he rushes forward in an open assault, better under fire, it is brought in so as to rest on top of the counterscarp wall. But in cases where a covered communication is needed beyond the ditch, the glacis is thrown outward far enough to leave the requisite space between it and the counterscarp. This sheltered position is termed the *covered-way*. It serves both for the circulation of the troops, from point to point, and as a defensive position; the part of the glacis facing the covered-way being arranged, for this latter purpose, like an ordinary earthen parapet.

55...Mounds of earth which are formed solely with a view to mask a scarp wall from fire are termed *face covers.* They may be either in the form of a glacis, or receive, on each side, the slope which the earth would naturally take, sufficient height and thickness being given to them to subserve the object to be attained.

56...Among the modifications of the usual profile is the one represented in Pl. 3, Fig. 11, where the scarp wall, rising only to the level of the site, is surmounted by a parapet wall, *D*, which covers a *chemin-de-rondes*, *C*. This part of the work is termed a *fausse-braie.* By dividing the entire height of scarp wall into two parts, thus rendering each more accessible to an open assault, and by exposing the troops in it to injury from the splinters from the scarp wall behind them, caused by the fire of the assailant, the fausse-braie has fallen into disuse.

57...The introduction, within the last thirty years, of the barbette gun-carriage, now in general use for permanent works, has led to a modification in the form of the profile, with a view of better adapting it to the new carriage. This change is shown in Pl. 3, Fig. 4, and consists, mainly, in raising the level, *de*, of the terreplein fifteen inches, placing it thus at six feet nine inches below the interior crest, for a distance of twenty feet back from this crest, and connecting it by a slope, *cd*, of 45° with the level below; the parapet receives an interior slope, *hg*, of 45°, which falls upon a banquette, *fg*, for infantry, the tread of which is two feet, and is placed at four feet six inches below, *h*, the interior crest. The banquette-slope, *ef*, is two base to one perpendicular, and falls upon the raised portion, *de*, of the terreplein. When it is necessary to place guns in battery along any portion of a parapet having this form of profile, the interior slope is cut down, nearly perpendicularly, to the level of the raised portion of the terreplein, and faced with fascines; the earth between this raised portion and the new interior slope being removed, a level and solid bed is ready to receive the carriages. The surplus earth that has to be removed by this operation can be used for ordinary traverses, and for increasing the height of the merlons when the parapet is pierced for embrasures.

58...The dimensions and forms of the different parts of the profile are so established as to afford security against an open assault; sufficient command of the parapet over the exterior ground to sweep it effectually by its fire; cover from the fire of the assailant; and ample room with suitable arrangements for the delivery of the fire of the assailed.

59...SCARP. A scarp wall, 30 feet high, is usually admitted as a sufficient protection in dry ditches against an escalade.

This rule, drawn from the experience of sieges, and the opinions of the most eminent engineers, seems a safe one; since to scale a wall of this height would require ladders of sufficient length to enable the men who ascend to step from the ladder, when planted securely against the wall, on the coping, and of sufficient strength to bear the weight of six or eight men mounting together.

To carry forward ladders of the dimensions requisite for this purpose and place them in position, with that promptitude upon which the success of an open assault must mainly depend, would, of itself, be an operation of no slight difficulty; but, when it is considered that the assailants are exposed to the fire of the defences before reaching the ditch, which from its width and depth alone renders it a serious obstacle, and that after they have entered the ditch they are still under the fire by which it is flanked, it is difficult to imagine how the attempt could succeed if the assailed offer even an ordinary degree of resistance.

60...For wet ditches filled to the depth of six feet, and thus secured from being passed by fording, a height of scarp of 24 feet is considered sufficient security from an open assault.

61...Solid scarp walls, with ordinary counterforts, *D*, receive the thickness requisite to sustain the pressure of the earth resting against their back. The batter given them on their face varies in different services. In Vauban's profiles the batter is $\frac{5}{1}$, or five perpendicular to one base. In Cormontaingne's it is $\frac{6}{1}$. But from the effects of time, as observed in the works built by these engineers, the slopes of their walls are too great. In the French service, a slope of $\frac{20}{1}$ is now usually given. In the Austrian, $\frac{12}{1}$; and in our own, from $\frac{24}{1}$ to $\frac{48}{1}$ In this diversity of practice it is only necessary to remark, that the steeper walls are better protected from the effects of the weather, and this is a very important consideration in structures demanding great durability.

62...PARAPET. The essential properties of the parapet are to afford cover, and facilities for sweeping the ground exterior to it by the artillery and musketry Its form and dimensions are, therefore, so adjusted as to fulfil these requirements.

63...For the service of the artillery, barbettes are constructed behind the parapet, and suitably arranged either for guns mounted on the ordinary travelling carriages, or upon the traversing carriages, which, within some years back, have been introduced for the armament of land and sea-coast fronts; and embrasures are pierced in the parapet for like purposes.

64...As the sole of the embrasure is usually not more than three feet below the superior slope, and generally parallel to it, care must be taken so to adjust its position with respect to the coping of the scarp wall that, when the guns are fired under the same depression as the superior slope, the balls shall clear the edge of the coping sufficiently to prevent its being injured by negligent firing. This requirement will serve to determine the least height of the parapet above the coping, and which may be done by either of the following methods.

65...Supposing the parapet to be formed of earth of the ordinary character, Pl. 4, Fig. 14, in which the natural slope is 45°, or $\frac{1}{1}$; the superior slope, which is the same as that of the embrasure sole, is $\frac{1}{6}$, the one usually adopted as the greatest for the parapets of permanent works; the thickness of the parapet 18 feet, the least given to it to resist the heaviest calibre thus far employed; and that a berm of two feet is allowed on the top of the scarp wall, between the edge of the coping and the foot of the exterior slope: let a horizontal line, *a b*, be first drawn at the level of the coping, and, from its exterior edge, *a*, a second line, *a c*, making an angle of $\frac{1}{6}$ with *a b;* this last line will be the direction of a shot fired under the depression of $\frac{1}{6}$, which would just graze the edge of the coping, and may be assumed as the lowest position that the sole of an embrasure can receive; a line, therefore, drawn parallel to *a c* and 3 feet above it, will be the lowest position also of the superior slope. If a line is now drawn through *e*, the interior edge of the berm and the foot of the exterior slope, making an angle of $\frac{1}{1}$ with *a b*, it will be the direction of the exterior slope; and the point *m*, where it cuts the direction of the superior slope, will be the exterior crest of the parapet. Setting off along the horizontal line through *m* the thickness of the parapet, or 18 feet, and erecting a vertical at the point thus determined, the point *n*, where this vertical cuts the superior slope, will give the position of the interior crest, *n*, and, consequently, will determine its vertical height above the coping.

66...The following simple calculation will, in like manner, give the same result. Denote by x the base $e\,d=d\,m$ of the exterior slope. As the berm $a\,e=2$ feet, the thickness of the parapet $d\,b=18$ feet; the distance $a\,b=a\,e+e\,d+d\,b=2'+x+18'=x+20'$; but since the line *a c* makes an angle of $\frac{1}{6}$ with *a b*, the point *c*, where it cuts the vertical through *d*, will make $b\,c=\frac{1}{6}\,a\,b$, and, as from the position of the superior slope and the thickness, 18 feet, given to the parapet, the point *n* is three feet above the points *m* and *c*, it follows that $b\,c=d\,m=x$. Therefore, from the two preceding equations there obtains $x=\frac{1}{6}\,(x+20')$; hence $x=4$ feet. From this value of x, the height *b c* of *n*, above the point *a*, is 7 feet; which, under the assumed conditions, is the least height of the interior crest above the coping in which a ball, passing in the same line as the sole of the embrasure, would just touch the exterior edge of the coping. In order to secure the coping from damage, the interior crest is placed 8 feet above it.

It should be observed that the result here arrived at, being dependent on the assumed data, will vary by changing the elements of the problem.

67...The height of 8 feet thus determined, as the least which the parapet should receive above the magistral, is advantageous both as to economy and for the defence, and, therefore, should not be exceeded except for good reasons. This will be apparent, when it is considered that the pressure on the scarp wall, from the weight of the parapet, increases with the height of the latter, and that the wall must be made stronger in proportion; and, although an increased height of parapet, by increasing the obstacle to an escalade, is in favor of the defence, still, when it much exceeds 8 feet, the assailant, on reaching the top of the wall, will find shelter from the fire of the parapet, which will pass above his head, and he will be better enabled to reach the top of the parapet than when partly exposed to this fire, as he will be in low parapets.

68...The inclination of $\frac{1}{6}$ has been generally adopted as the greatest inclination of the superior slope, both on account of the greatest depression that guns can be fired under without straining too much the carriages, and to avoid making the portion of the parapet near the interior crest so weak that it could be readily destroyed, and the troops and *materiel* exposed to view Whenever the field of fire will admit of it, it will prove advantageous, under these two points of view, to give a smaller inclination to the superior slope. In cases where it is desirable to reach some point, by the fire requiring a greater slope than $\frac{1}{6}$, it may be done without inconvenience if the parapet is not likely to be exposed to a heavy fire, a suitable inclination being also given to the gun-platform.

69...The exterior slope, for the reasons given in discussing the parapets of field works, should not be less, on land fronts, than the natural slope of the earth of which the parapet is formed. In sea-coast works, where the parapet is high, and can be reached, within cannon range, only by elevating the guns of the ships, the exterior slope may be replaced by a vertical revetement of stone, or one of sods with but a slight inclination, as, from the direction of the fire, this facing, even if partially destroyed, will not cause such weakness in the parapet as to expose the troops. By using a facing of this kind, the parapet will occupy less room and leave more interior space, which, in small works, is often desirable.

70...As a berm of two feet affords a tolerable landing to the assailant in an escalade, it would be better to make it less, particularly on fronts open to such an assault. The usual berm may be given when the work is constructed, and be afterward lessened by increasing the thickness of the parapet when the work is to be placed in a defensive attitude.

71...The thickness of the parapets of ordinary earth seldom exceed 20 feet. This is the dimension usually given in European constructions of important works liable to a long exposure to fire, and has been found, by experience, to afford good cover against a well-nourished and protracted fire of the heaviest calibre thus far used. In our service, a thickness of 18 feet has been more usually given. For less important works, and particularly where parapets are not likely to be systematically battered, the thickness may be safely reduced to 12 or 15 feet.

72...In the form of profile given in Pl. 3, Fig. 4, the portion of the terreplein on which the guns rest in battery is placed at a level below the interior crest, to admit the guns being fired over the parapet; and this difference of level is sufficient to give good cover along the parapet to the men serving the guns. The portion, *b c*, of the terreplein to the rear of this serves as a communication along the line of fortification, and, being further back, should be somewhat lower, to afford good cover from shot just passing over the interior crest. It is usually placed at a level of 8 feet below the interior crest; a slope of one foot inward being given to it, estimating it from the line of the interior crest to the exterior edge of the terreplein, to free it rapidly from the rain-water. This level, however, may be lowered if the irregularity of the site requires it, from the command the exterior ground may have over the work. In all cases it will be rather a question of economy, to be decided by the amount of excavation and embankment. As the space in question serves chiefly the purposes of a communication, it may be reduced, through motives of economy, to a width which will be sufficient for the gun-carriages and other vehicles employed in the defence to pass each other. For this purpose the entire width of the terreplein, estimating it between the verticals through the interior crest of the parapet and the crest of the rampart-slope, has usually received 42 feet in enceintes of importance where a circulation of the kind just mentioned is to be provided for. In other cases it may be reduced to 24, or even 20 feet. It should be remarked, however, that as a wide terreplein facilitates the disposition of troops for an active defence of the breach, it should not be too much reduced along those portions of the enceinte exposed to be opened.

73...The rampart toward the parade usually receives a slope greater than that which the earth would naturally assume where the interior space admits of it. This will offer the means of forming narrow foot-paths along this slope leading from the parade to the terreplein at convenient points, and prevent the slope from being injured, which it is apt to be by the men wearing such short cuts for themselves. Where the interior space would be too much circumscribed, this slope may be replaced by a parade wall.

74...The banquette-tread and the interior slope, as shown in Pl. 3, Fig. 4, will answer sufficiently well for ordinary purposes; but where a warm fire in two ranks is to be sustained, the interior slope should be trimmed down to the same given to it in field works, which will, at the same time, enlarge the banquette-tread so as to receive two ranks. It would be well, also, in making these changes for an active defence, to raise the banquette-tread to within a level of $4\frac{1}{4}$ feet of the interior crest, for the greater convenience of short men in delivering their fire.

75...The *command* of the parapet over the site has a very important bearing in the defence of permanent works, as the assailant meets with the more difficulty, in running forward his trenches, as the fire of the defences becomes more plunging. Motives of economy, however, require the command to be restricted within quite narrow limits. When the work consists of a simple enceinte, enveloped by a covered-way, the command may be reduced to 16 feet, allowing a command of 8 feet to the interior crest of the glacis over the site, and a height of 8 feet to the interior crest above the coping, which, with the rest of the scarp wall, to be masked by the glacis, must not rise above the level of its interior crest. Where there are other outworks besides the covered-way in defensive relations with the enceinte, the latter cannot receive a command over the site of less than about 20 feet, in order to give it a suitable command over the whole of the outworks.

76...COUNTERSCARP WALL. A revetted counterscarp is regarded as adding to the difficulty of descending into the ditch, and as offering greater security against an open assault. For this purpose the wall should not be less than 12 or 15 feet in height, to offer a serious impediment; in any case where motives of economy do not imperiously demand it, the counterscarp wall of the enceinte should be from 18 to 24 feet in height. This height will not only give great security to the ditch, but, as will be seen in the description of the siege works of the assailant, it will delay, considerably, his progress, as the gallery by which he must generally reach the bottom of the ditch from the level of the covered-way terreplein, is one of the slowest and most laborious of his operations.

77...DITCH. The width and depth of the enceinte ditch depends mainly upon the amount of embankment required for the enceinte and the glacis, and, therefore, will result from the calculation for equalizing the excavation and embankment which these demand. A deep and narrow ditch offers the advantage of presenting more difficulty to the assailant in reaching the bottom of it; and, from the position he is obliged to take up for his breach batteries to open the scarp wall, his fire cannot see the wall so near its foot as in a wide ditch, and the breach, therefore, may, from this cause, be less practicable. A wide ditch, on the other hand, requires more labor to construct the trench across it, by which the assailant can reach the foot of the breach under cover. This is a consideration of some importance in wet ditches, where the assailant is obliged to construct a dike, upon which the parapet of his cover is placed. In the practice of engineers the enceinte ditch has received a width of from 20 to 30 yards when dry, and from 30 to 45 yards when wet. These dimensions may be reduced to within 10 or 12 yards, where the embankments are not great and circumstances are unfavorable to an attempt at escalade.

78...The bottom of the ditch usually receives a slight slope from the foot of the scarp and counterscarp to its centre, where a small drain, termed a *cunette*, is dug to receive the surface water and keep the ditch dry. In some cases, from motives of economy, the difference of level between the cunette and the foot of the counterscarp walls is increased, thus giving a less height of wall. This practice, however, can only be followed where the foundations of the wall will be secure from the soil of the bottom of the ditch being of such a nature as not to yield from the effects of the weather upon it.

79...General Remarks. The rules here given with respect to the form and dimensions of the general profile of the enceinte are founded upon reasons growing out of the nature of the question, and as such have served as guides to engineers in the practice of their profession. As they have stood, besides, the test of long experience, it is safe to follow them, whilst at the same time the engineer should not hesitate to vary from them when satisfied, after careful examination, that the case before him requires it. Fortification, it must be remembered, is like all other arts. It has its canons which are founded upon the nature of the question, and its rules of practice based upon these and upon experience. As the latter presents to the engineer new facts, his practice must be made to conform to them, but the general principles of his art must ever remain the same and be his invariable guide.

OPEN DEFENCES.

80...By this term is understood the dispositions made for the action of the troops and armament which are covered from the missiles of the assailed by the parapet alone.

81...To this class belongs the arrangement of the parapet which has already been described; simple *loop-holed walls* for musketry, used as enclosures of gorges, etc.; *exterior corridors* which are covered either by a wall or an earthen parapet; and *barbettes* and *embrasures* for artillery.

82...LOOP-HOLED WALLS. Walls of this class when used as the enclosures of the gorges of lunettes or other isolated works, placed in advance of the enceinte, but within the reach of its artillery fire, should be high enough to secure the work from an open assault, and sufficiently thick to resist the occasional shot which may reach them over the parapet by which they are covered. For these purposes the height, Pl. 4, Fig. 24, should be from 12 to 15 feet, and the thickness from 4 to 5 feet. The loop-holes are not placed nearer to each other than from 3 to 4 feet, estimated between their axes. They should be at least 6 feet above the exterior foot of the wall, and 4¼ feet above the ground or banquette within. The loop-holes are usually placed at regular intervals along the line of the wall; or only opposite that portion of the exterior ground upon which a fire is to be brought to bear.

83...The form and dimensions of the loop-hole will depend upon the thickness of the wall and the field of view, both vertically and horizontally, which is to be covered by its fire. The plan is either trapezoidal, Pl. 4, Figs. 17, 20, widening from the front of the wall inward, or else it widens from the centre each way to the front and back; or, as is the more usual form in our works, the interior portion from the centre widens inward, whilst the exterior part is rectangular in plan. The first form is best adapted to walls not more than 2½ feet thick; the others to heavier walls; the object being to lessen, as far as practicable, the weakness which loop-holes necessarily cause to the wall; this defect increasing as the exterior or interior opening is greater.

84...For thin walls, where the plan of the loop-hole is trapezoidal, the width of the exterior opening may be from 2 to 4 inches, and that of the interior from 15 to 18 inches. These dimensions, however, may vary according to the field of fire to be brought within the range of the loop-hole, the more or less cover to be given to the troops, and the strength of the masonry of which the wall is formed. The vertical dimensions of the loop-hole, both on the interior and the exterior, will depend upon the field of fire to be embraced in this last direction, and they will be regulated accordingly; the slope of the top and sole of the loop-hole receiving a suitable slope or direction for this purpose.

The foregoing details can only be well determined upon from the special object to which the loop-holed defences are to be applied. Care only is to be taken that, in attempting to give cover to the troops, their field of view be not too restricted, by too narrow an opening for the use of the fire-arms.

85...Where the throat or narrowest part of the loop-hole is within the wall, the exterior opening leaves a wider mark for the missiles of the assailed; and when the sides of the loop-hole gradually widen outward a shot striking one of them may glance inward and do injury. To prevent this accident the sides and sometimes the sole are made in offsets. This, however, is not so convenient a mode of constructing the loop-hole, nor one so efficient in arresting the shot which do not directly attain

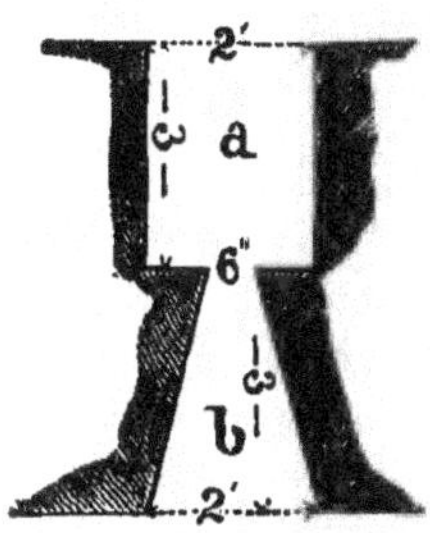

the throat, as the one in the annexed Figure, which is the plan of one, taken from our works, pierced in a wall 6 feet thick. The plan of the exterior portion, *a*, is rectangular, the exterior width 2 feet; the throat is at the centre of the wall, and 6″ wide; the interior portion, *b*, is trapezoidal, and 2 feet wide on the interior.

86...In open exterior corridors the loops are covered in front, either by an earthen parapet, which is usually only musket-proof, the scarp wall being run up to the superior slope, or else the scarp wall serves as the cover, in which case it is pierced either throughout its length or at suitable points with loop-holes. The floor of the corridor, *C*, Pl. 4, Fig. 27, serves as a banquette-tread for the loop-holes, and is, therefore, placed with reference to the direction of the fire from the loop-holes. The height at which the scarp wall rises above the floor of the corridor will depend upon the level of the floor and that of the bottom of the ditch; this height, however, should not be less than 6½ feet, to afford sufficient cover to the troops.

87...Scarp walls of this arrangement are termed *semi-detached*, to distinguish them from the ordinary retaining scarp walls and those in which the wall is entirely separated from the rampart, serving as a simple enclosure to it to prevent an escalade.

88...The preceding Figure is given as an example of a semi-detached scarp, *A*, an earthen counterscarp, and covered-way, *D;* being a section of an outwork of one of our sea-coast forts.

89...Barbette Batteries. For guns mounted on the ordinary field and siege carriages, the barbettes are constructed in the same manner and with the same dimensions as in field works. The arrangement of the ramps and slopes being determined by the position in which the barbette is placed, and its relative position with respect to the terreplein and parapet.

90...For the heavy guns used in forts, both for sea and land fronts, a solid foundation of stone is laid to receive the pintle and rail, upon which the chassis of the gun is made to traverse. This foundation consists of a heavy block, set firmly in a bed of beton, to which the pintle, placed at the centre of motion, is solidly attached; and of stone blocks set in like manner, to which are firmly attached the iron rails, which either form a segment of a circle, as in Pl. 7, Figs. 54, 55, or a complete circle, as in Figs. 56, 57, 58, upon which the traverse-wheels run.

91...In order to afford the gun a wide traverse, a recess is made in the parapet in front of the carriage, of sufficient dimensions to allow the manœuvres of the chassis and top carriage without obstruction; for this purpose it has received a depth of 2 feet, its front 5 feet; its two sides having a slant of 30 inches base to 24 inches perpendicular. The recess, and usually the entire length of the battery front, is faced with a breast-height wall that only rises to within 18 inches of the top of the parapet; its thickness being 2 feet. The Figures referred to give the plan, sections and elevation of the barbette arrangements in question adopted in our service.

92...EMBRASURE BATTERIES. The embrasures cut in the parapets for guns on field and siege carriages, differ in no essential point from those for field works. It is well, however, to observe, as the parapet is weakened by receiving embrasures, the splay given to them should, in all cases, be carefully regulated by the field of fire it is desirable to command, so as to leave as large a mass of merlon between each, as practicable, to resist the assailant's fire.

93...For guns mounted on sea-coast carriages the embrasures are very shallow, merely covering the gun from lateral view. The annexed Figure is a profile of the enceinte through the axis of an embrasure of recent French works, showing the manner in which the profile is modified and revetted for the service of the pieces.

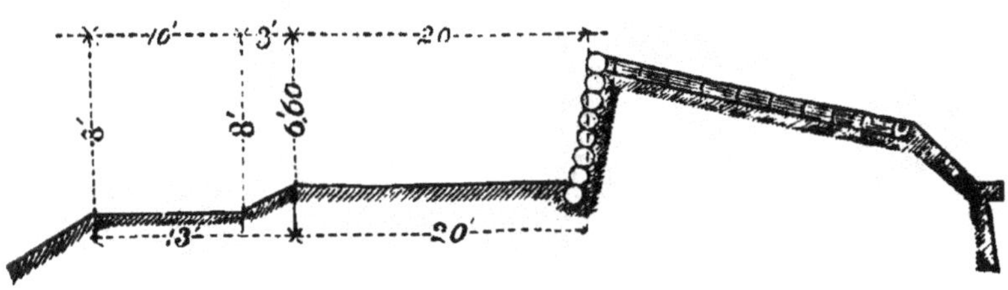

94...MACHICOULIS. For the purpose of attaining, by musketry, the foot of a scarp wall without flank defences, resort must be had to a machicoulated arrangement at the top of the scarp.

95...The usual mode adopted for this purpose, Pl. 8, Figs. 67, 68, is to form a parapet wall, which rests upon a solid horizontal band of stone, near the top of the scarp, which is supported on corbels, or projecting blocks, firmly built into the wall. The back of the parapet wall is placed a few inches in advance of the scarp, leaving room for the slanting loop-holes pierced in the horizontal band through which the fire is to be delivered on the foot of the scarp. The top of the parapet wall is also arranged to admit of firing on more distant points.

96...In the example given, which is from an Austrian authority, Fig. 67 is a front elevation, and Fig. 68 a section through a loop-hole.

Figs. 65, 66, are a front elevation and section through a loop-hole, from the same authority. This is a semi-detached scarp wall, the top portion of which is arranged on the back with loop-holed recesses; the lower portion having very inclined arched recesses in front, with slanting loop-holes to fire on the foot of the scarp from the upper recesses.

97...Where, from the irregularity of the site, the ordinary machicoulis cannot be made efficient, resort may be had to small polygonal chambers of stone, open at top, and having the sides and bottom pierced with loop-holes and machicoulis. These constructions may be made just of sufficient size to hold a single sentinel. They are placed at the angles of the works, where they will not be exposed to artillery, and are supported on a corbel work projecting from the top of the scarp wall.

COVERED DEFENCES.

98...DETACHED SCARP WALLS. When the scarp walls are entirely detached, leaving an open corridor between them and the rampart, they are pierced with one or two tiers of loop-holes from which a fire can be brought from the ditch and upon the terreplein of the covered-way, or any work in front of the enceinte.

99...To give cover to the men at the loop-holes, arched recesses, Pl. 4, Figs. 25, 26, are made in the thickness of wall, or else short counterforts are built back from the wall which serve as the piers of covering arches. The width of the recesses should admit of three or four loop-holes at the usual distance apart; their height and depth be sufficient to give the men shelter from vertical fire, and allow them to handle their arms with convenience.

100...The two Figures above are sections of this description of scarp wall taken through the crowns of the arches, as shown in an Austrian work. *A*, is a section of the wall; *B* and *D*, elevations of the sides of the recess; *C*, an elevation and section of the recess arch.

101...Semi-detached walls, Fig. 28, are also, in some cases, built with recesses. Besides these, traverse walls, *H*, are built back from the scarp wall into the parapet, at intervals, to afford cover to the troops, circulating in the corridor, from enfilading fire, and to admit of a defence of the corridor if the assailant should enter it between any two of these traverses. For this purpose they are pierced with loop-holes, and have door-ways for circulation throughout the corridor.

102...In the more recent fortifications built in Germany and the north of Europe, a frequent use has been made of detached scarps. They present a double obstacle to an escalade, as the assailant, having gained the top of the wall, has still to descend on the other side. They would probably be more easily breached than the ordinary scarp revetements with counterforts; and from some experiments made in England, with a view of ascertaining the resistance of these walls and the cover given them by earthen masks, arranged in a manner similar to some of the German fortifications, it is questionable whether, with the heavier calibre now coming into use in sieges and the improvement of late years in their range, such walls might not be readily breached from a distance.

103...The partly detached scarp wall, with relieving arches, would seem to offer the advantage of more security from escalade than the old scarp wall, as the assailed are in a better position in the corridor to drive the assailant back than when placed behind the parapet. It offers all the difficulties to breaching of the full scarp with relieving arches, and presents, when the breach is rendered practicable, a narrow defile through which the assailant must force his way into the work; whereas, when the wholly detached scarp is overthrown, the assailant may enter with any front he may choose, as the only obstacle then in his way will be that of the height of the rampart and the steepness of its exterior slope.

104...SCARP GALLERIES. In the permanent works of more recent construction in our own country and in Europe, revetement walls, with relieving arches, Pl. 4, Fig. 15, have, in most cases, been introduced instead of the ordinary thick walls, with counterforts, which had been hitherto the usual mode of retaining the earth of the rampart and parapet.

105...The piers of the relieving arches, which also serve as counterforts to the rèvetement wall, are rectangular in plan, and usually run back from 12 to 16 feet. They are from 4 to 6 feet thick, and placed from 12 to 18 feet apart between their centre lines. The arches are usually full centre, and two feet thick, with a roof-shaped capping, which adds an additional thickness from 9 to 12 inches over the crown of the arch.

106...The preceding Figure is a section of a revetement wall of this kind, of one of our forts, though the curtain in front of which is a mask, of which *D* is the section. *B*, is an elevation of the face of the pier; *C*, the relieving arch; and *A*, the scarp wall.

107...This mode of construction offers the advantages of a more stable structure, and rendering it more difficult for the assailant to make a practicable breach in the wall, whilst, by a suitable arrangement of the relieving arches and their piers with the earth of the rampart, a sufficient space can be secured behind the scarp wall to form a gallery for defensive purposes.

108....The arches and piers form the top and sides of the gallery, the scarp wall forming the front, and the back or rear being either partly or wholly closed by a wall which retains the earth behind it. The gallery is thus divided up into chambers, the communication between which is effected by door-ways made through the piers.

109....The width and height of the gallery should in all cases be sufficient to allow the men ample room for handling their fire-arms, and to admit of a circulation through the gallery, when the troops for the defence are posted in it.

110....From three to four loop-holes are made in the portion of the scarp wall that forms the front of each chamber. The dimensions and forms of the loop-holes are the same as already described, and they are otherwise arranged for defence as in detached scarp walls.

111...In Pl. 4, Fig. 16, a section of a scarp gallery constructed in one of our forts is shown. *A*, is the scarp wall; *B*, the pier of the relieving arch, *C; D*, the rear wall which closes the gallery and sustains the earth behind it. The section also shows the parts of the rampart and parapet, and the breast-height wall, *E*.

112...In Figs. 17, 18, 19, the plan, section and rear elevation of a gallery is shown as given in French authorities. The peculiarity of this example, Fig. 19, consists in the arrangement of the rear of the gallery, which instead of being entirely closed by a wall is only partly so; a small wall, *a*, which rests upon an arch, *b*, built between the two piers, is placed parallel to the back of the scarp wall, and at a distance from it equal to the width of the gallery, the top of the wall being raised to the level of the surface of the earthen slope, which falls in behind from the top of the arch. The section, Fig. 18, through *r s*, and elevation, Fig. 19, show the position of the loop-holes, and the vent for the escape of the smoke, which is pierced in the scarp wall just below the crown of the arch. *B*, are the piers; *A*, the arches with their capping; *D*, the door-ways through the piers.

113...Figs. 20, 21, represent the plan and section of a scarp gallery in two tiers, as given in an Austrian work. The rear of the gallery is closed by a simple wall. Besides the vent-holes for the escape of smoke, drains are made in the scarp wall, at the level of the gallery floor, to convey off any water that may collect in it.

114...Figs. 22, 23, are a plan and section, from the same authority, of a gallery behind the lower portion of the scarp wall, the upper portion being connected with relieving arches, so arranged that, being open to the rear, the foot of the slope of earth will just touch the back of the wall at its foot within. In this example, the pressure of the earth being supposed to be great, the gallery is closed in the rear by arched walls; the arches being built into the vertical piers, *B*, of the relieving arches, *C*. This example also shows the manner of barricading the door-ways through the piers by vertical grooves, made in the opposite faces of the piers, to receive the scantling forming the barricade.

115...In Fig. 28 is shown the section of a gallery behind the lower portion of the scarp, with the upper portion arranged with recesses for loop-holes.

116...Counterscarp Galleries. Pl. 4, Fig. 35. The most simple method of arranging a gallery behind a counterscarp wall, for the defence of a ditch, is to build another wall parallel to that of the counterscarp, and to throw an arch over between the two to cover the top of the gallery. The counterscarp wall is pierced with loop-holes arranged in the same way as in scarp galleries.

117...The example selected is from one of our works, and shows a section of the gallery through a loop-hole. *A*, counterscarp wall; *D*, parallel wall; *C*, arch and capping; *E*, glacis mask covering the scarp wall.

118...In Figs. 29, 30, 31, are shown a plan, section on *r s*, and a section and interior elevation on *o p*, of a counterscarp gallery taken from a French authority In this case counterforts, square in plan, are built along the back of the counterscarp wall, leaving 8 feet between them. Parallel to the counterscarp wall, and 4 feet in rear of the counterforts, another wall is built, which, with the counterforts, serves as the support of a series of arches perpendicular to the counterscarp wall, sprung between the counterforts, and another parallel to it and resting on the counterforts and parallel wall. The arches between the counterforts form, with them, recesses, *A*, for the men serving the loopholes, pierced in the counterscarp wall; whilst the covered space, *B*, in rear, serves for circulation, without disturbing the men engaged in firing.

119...Counterscarp galleries may also be arranged for a ditch defence with artillery—short guns, like carronades, being used for this purpose. A plan, Fig. 32, a vertical section and side elevation on *D C*, Fig. 33, and a section and back elevation on *A B*, Fig. 34, taken from one of our works, shows a disposition of this kind in the re-entering angle of the counterscarp.

120...BASTIONNETS. In small works, where a flanking disposition cannot be obtained from the enceinte, as in lunettes and redoubts, the ditches may be swept by covered chambers, Pl. 5, Fig. 39, attached to the scarp wall either at the centre of the sides of the work or at the angles.

These chambers, Pl. 5, Fig. 39, are usually of a pentagonal form—the sides which join the scarp wall serving to flank it, and the two exterior sides, forming a salient angle, delivering their fire on the opposite counterscarp and its crest. From their form and purposes, they have received the name of bastionnets.

The dimensions of these constructions will depend upon the amount and kind of fire to be delivered. Their scarps should be as high as that of the main work. They communicate with the interior of the main work, either directly by gallery or postern, or from a scarp gallery

Fig. 39 shows a plan of a bastionnet, *D*, at an angle communicating with a scarp gallery, *E*. In rear of the scarp gallery, and opposite to the bastionnet, is placed a small powder magazine for its service. The example is from Austrian authority, and is arranged for one small gun on each flank besides the loop-holes for small arms.

121...As a general rule, it may be laid down that the salient angles of the redoubt are the most suitable positions for the bastionnets, as they will thus form small bastioned fronts, in which both the sides of the main work and those of the bastionnet will be swept by the flanks of the latter. The only danger in this arrangement is, that the loop-holes in one flank may be fired into from the opposite one. This, however, may be guarded against by a suitable position given to the loop-holes.

122...As the main object of covered defences is protection against shells, it is essential that the arches of the galleries and bastionnets should be bomb-proof. As the span of these arches is usually small, a thickness of 2 feet given to the masonry, and a covering from 4 to 6 feet of earth above it, is ordinarily considered sufficient for the object in view.

123...With regard to the front walls of these constructions, as they are too thin to withstand the direct action of artillery, they must either be covered by earthen masks, as a glacis raised beyond the counterscarp for example, or be used only in positions where they are not exposed to this fire.

124...It should be observed that whatever advantages covered defences afford as shelter from the assailant's fire, they present the inconveniences of a comparatively narrow and obstructed field of view to the assailed, which is further obscured by the smoke which may gather within the gallery, and in front of the loop-holes. From these causes the assailed having to aim at a venture, his fire is likely to be less effective than in open defences where the smoke disperses rapidly and leaves a clear field of view. The same may be said of loop-holed walls covering exterior corridors where the space to the rear is confined.

Owing to these considerations, loop-holed and covered defences of the kind in question should be restricted to special defensive purposes, where an object within the field of fire can be attained with some certainty, whether seen or not by the assailed; as, for example, the protection of a ditch, or a scarp wall which cannot be flanked from within the work for sweeping a covered-way, or the interior of any outwork which cannot be brought well under the fire of the parapet of the main work.

125...CAPONNIERE DEFENCES FOR THE ENCEINTE DITCH. These works are classed under the head of what are termed *defensive casemates*, which are bomb-proof arched structures for receiving cannon, which fire through embrasures pierced in the front or mask wall of the casemates. Defences of this class, when used to flank the main ditch, are usually termed *casemated caponnières.*

126...These defences are usually placed in the main ditch at the middle point of the side or front to be flanked. The outline of their plan is mostly that of a lunette, Pl. 5, Fig. 36—the flanks being perpendicular to the line of the scarp, and the two faces making a salient angle of 60° The caponnière is either built in juxtaposition with the enceinte, or else detached from it. In the latter case, an enclosure is formed between the two by a loop-holed wall which connects the flanks with the scarp wall. Each flank consists of one or two tiers of arched chambers—the piers of the arches being perpendicular to the back of the walls of the flank. Each chamber is of sufficient dimensions for the service of a single gun with a contracted field of fire, Pl. 5, Figs. 36, 37 In some cases, loop-holes are pierced for small arms on each side of the embrasure; in others, the casemates of one story are pierced for cannon and the other for small arms.

127...The casemates are closed in rear by a thin wall, which is provided with windows for light and ventilation; and the piers are pierced with door-ways, to form a communication between the chambers and to assist the ventilation. Flues or vents, Fig. 37, are made in the front wall, just under the arches, for a like purpose. Where it may be necessary, the lower floor is drained by a conduit through the front wall.

128...An open court is left between the flanks, and each flank is covered at top with from 4 to 6 feet of earth. The flanks are separated from the faces by a closed corridor, which serves as a communication.

129...In front of the corridor and on each side of the axis of the caponnière, a casemated chamber, which is open in front, is arranged for one mortar, Figs. 36, 38. The arches of these chambers rise toward the front, the better to subserve the object in view.

130...On one side of the chambers the powder magazine is placed, with a store-room. On the other side a stair-way between the stories is built.

131...The space within the salient angle, enclosed by the walls of the faces and the front of the mortar casemates, is open at top. It has an open corridor for communication, and the front walls are arranged with loop-holed recesses for small arms, Figs. 36, 38.

132...The enceinte, in rear of the flanks of the caponnière, is arranged with a scarp gallery, to flank the caponnière flanks and the court between them. A break is, in some cases, made in the line of the scarp wall, perpendicular to the caponnière faces, and casemates for cannon and small arms arranged behind the scarp wall to flank these faces. In some cases these flanking dispositions are placed in front of the scarp wall, the casemates being open to the rear, looking on a narrow court between them and the scarp which is closed on the sides by a loop-holed wall.

133.. The example here given of a casemated caponnière is from an Austrian authority. Fig. 36 is the plan; Fig. 37 a section and elevation on *A B* of one flank and the end wall of the corridor looking toward the court between the flanks; Fig. 38 a section and elevation along *C′D′* of the corridor, mortar casemate and triangular court; Figs. 37, 38, are on an enlarged scale.

134...CASEMATES ON LAND FRONTS. Various modes have, from time to time, been proposed for arranging defensive casemates for the exterior defence on land fronts. The difficulty in covering the masonry from the batteries of the assailant has been the chief objection to these structures, and is the more prominent as the fire of artillery becomes more accurate, as such casemates would soon be ruined or rendered untenable by embrasure shots.

135...The structure for this purpose which has been most applied within late years, is what is termed the *Haxo casemate;* the details having been first proposed by General Haxo, one of the first authorities of the French school of engineers. These casemates consist, Figs. 45, 46, 47, of a series of arched bomb-proof chambers, closed in front by a thin mask wall, which, except around the embrasures through it, is covered from the assailant's artillery by the parapet. To present but a small surface of masonry to fire, the arches, which are horizontal and perpendicular to the mask wall for the greater portion of their length, descend toward the front, leaving, where they join the mask wall, just sufficient height within for the service of the gun. To effect this, the anterior portion of the arch must be conoidal in shape.

136...The piers of the arches are pierced with wide arched openings, which serve the double purpose of a communication between the casemates and to give the gun a wider traverse for firing.

137...Embrasures are pierced in the parapet in prolongation of those of the mask wall, and it is proposed to cover the small portion of the masonry necessarily exposed by this arrangement, by placing several thicknesses of heavy timber in front of it to receive the shot.

138...When the casemates serve simply for the cover of the cannon, the arches are covered with from 4 to 6 feet thickness of earth, and are left open to the rear for the more prompt escape of the smoke, and a ditch is sometimes made just in rear of the casemates to catch bombs and limit the effects of their explosion. When the arches are made longer than for the service of the guns alone, the earthen covering is sometimes arranged with a parapet to cover cannon in barbette, or for small arms.

139...The examples shown by the Figures is from a French

authority. Fig. 45 is a plan on *m n*, Fig. 47; Fig. 46 a section and interior elevation toward the mask wall on *o p*, Fig. 47; and Fig. 47 a section and side elevation on *r s*, Figs. 45, 46.

140...In Figs. 48, 49, is shown an arrangement of two casemates of the Haxo kind, from an Austrian authority. In this case, the masonry is covered on the flanks from enfilading fire by earth. Fig. 48 is an interior elevation of the arches, and the back wall that retains the earth on the sides. Fig. 49 is a longitudinal section, and shows the manner of covering the masonry in front and securing the earthen embrasure by a timber facing.

141...MORTAR CASEMATES. In Fig. 50, Pl. 6, is shown a longitudinal section of a mortar casemate placed in rear of a parapet, by which it is covered from direct fire. The arch is covered, as in the preceding case, by earth, to break the shock of shells. It rises toward the front, to give ample room for the shell in its flight. The casemates are covered on their flanks from enfilading fire by an embankment, and are partly closed by a wall in rear. A small ditch is made in front of the chamber, and a slight wall built within it, to give cover from the splinters of shells falling between the parapet and casemate. Arched chambers are, in some cases, made beneath the mortar chamber, which serve as store-rooms and temporary magazines.

142...When these casemates are placed in rear of a portion of the parapet, but little exposed to direct fire, the thickness of the parapet in front of them may be reduced, and the interior slope be replaced by a breast-height wall along the front of the casemates, in order to give better cover in flank and from slant fire, by throwing forward the casemates more under cover of the parapet.

143...The example given is from the same authority as in the preceding example of casemated caponnières.

144...CASEMATES FOR WATER FRONTS. In the casemated batteries for sea-coast and harbor defence, the scarp or mask wall of the chambers for the guns, being exposed to the fire of ships alone, are not covered, as on land fronts, by an earthen mask; these walls being built of sufficient thickness and strength to withstand the fire of the heaviest guns within the range that ships can venture to attack, and being far less vulnerable than the wooden or iron sides of vessels thus far brought into general use.

145...These batteries, in our own and European works, consist of a series of arched bomb-proof chambers, which serve for the service of the guns alone; or else they receive such dimensions that the portions of the chambers immediately in rear of the mask wall are appropriated to the service of the battery, and the rear portions are converted into quarters, store-rooms, and other necessary purposes for the garrison.

146...In the earlier sea-coast casemated defences constructed in our service, the gun chambers have received dimensions to admit of two guns in each chamber, Pl. 5, Figs. 40, 41. The chambers are usually formed of segmental brick arches of 120°, which rest upon stone piers built back perpendicular to the mask wall. In the example given, the arches, *C*, have a uniform thickness of 3 feet, exclusive of the roof-shaped capping, which is generally of rubble and beton, and which is covered on top by the earth of the parapet and rampart. The stone piers, *B*, are 6½ feet thick, and are pierced with arched communications, *F*, a few feet in rear of the mask wall, so placed as to give the gun-carriage a wider traverse by allowing it to run under this opening. Arched recesses, *E*, are made in the mask wall to admit the muzzle of the gun being well run out, so as to clear the casemate of smoke. An embrasure, *e*, is pierced at the centre of each recess, the sole being at the proper height above the floor of the casemate, to accommodate the casemate chassis and top carriage. In Fig. 40, is shown the plan and dimensions of the embrasures usually adopted in our works, until a very recent date; and in Fig. 41, which is a vertical section of the casemate through the axis of an embrasure, is shown the elevation and dimensions of the cheeks, *c*, of the embrasure. In the casemates of some of our works, flues for ventilation and carrying off rapidly the powder smoke, run from the top of the carriage recesses, *E*, through the masonry of the scarp wall, and have their outlet in the top of the wall. In others, the flues run from the casemate arch to the top of the parapet. Beneath the embrasure a recess, termed the *tongue-hole*, which in plan is triangular, is made to receive the tongue of the chassis. The tongue is confined in its place, and the chassis traverses around a pintle which is received into the *pintle-hole*, made at the centre point of the throat of the embrasure, and extending into the masonry below the tongue-hole.

147...When the casemates serve also as quarters for the garrison, the rear, toward the parade, is closed by a brick or stone parade wall, which forms the front wall of the quarters. A brick partition wall separates the quarters from the gun gallery. Arched recesses and flues are made in the piers for chimneys; and the parade wall, the sides of the piers, and soffit of the arch, are suitably finished to give a dry and well-ventilated dwelling.

148...In the example here given, as in most of our earlier casemated works, there is but one tier of casemated guns: this tier being surmounted by a barbette battery, covered either by an earthen or stone parapet on the water fronts.

149...Casemates adapted to two guns in each room, present a more vulnerable mark in the portion of the mask wall between the piers; expose more men to danger from embrasure shots; present a greater opening, in rear, to the assailant's fire, when not closed by a parade wall; offer less resistance to the shock of shells, and are more difficult to construct, without settling, than rooms for single guns. These advantages in favor of casemates for single guns are the more marked where, for the purpose of obtaining a heavy fire in some fixed direction, it is desirable to resort to a castellated structure, consisting of several tiers of casemates.

150...In Pl. 6, Figs. 42, 43, 44, is shown a plan, Fig. 42, on *E F*, of the first tier of casemates; a vertical section and side elevation, Fig. 43, on *A B*, of the three tiers of casemates and the top barbette battery; and, in Fig. 44, an interior elevation on $C D$, of one of the most recent of these structures for the defence of the channel leading to one of our harbors. Besides the wide arched openings, F, through the piers, for communication and the traverse of the guns, smaller door-ways, a, are made for communications in rear of the battery. The casemates are open in the rear. The arches of the top tier are alone made bomb-proof; those of the lower tiers receiving sufficient strength to receive the armament and admit of the service of the guns with safety.

151...EMBRASURES. The form, dimensions and construction of embrasures in mask walls, present a problem which has offered no little difficulty, in a satisfactory solution, to engineers, by which the best cover could be given to the guns and men, by exposing the least surface to embrasure shots, whilst the guns should receive a suitable traverse to command a wide field of fire.

152...In the embrasures of our works, the general form is the same as those usually found in Europe, but they present a very considerable less amount of exterior and throat-opening than European embrasures. See Pl. 7, Fig. 59, which is the plan of a French carriage recess and embrasure for a single gun, and Fig. 60, which is one of the same parts of an English fort for sea-coast defence. In some of our earlier works, the sole, cheeks and top of the embrasures are constructed of brick, as being a material that would be less destructive through the splinters driven in by embrasure shots. This view, however, has been abandoned in our more recent works, the embrasures being constructed, on the contrary, of heavy stone blocks, carefully and strongly bonded; a brick arch being thrown above the embrasure, within the mass of the mask wall, to secure the upper portion from yielding should the block forming the ceiling of the embrasure be damaged.

153...A further and most important step has been more recently taken, in the application to embrasures of wrought-iron casings and throat-pieces, with shutters of the same material, as a security against heavy shot and grape. The first application of this means has been made to the embrasures of one of our works now in the course of construction; and the forms, dimensions and construction of the embrasures are the results of experiments carefully made with the heaviest solid shot and grape, upon walls and embrasures of various forms and dimensions, under the directions of General Totten, chief engineer.

154...The form adopted is shown in plan in Pl. 8, Fig. 61—the interior portion being trapezoidal, and the exterior, beyond the throat, rectangular. This form was adopted with the double view of limiting the effects of embrasure shot which, in the old forms, striking the oblique surfaces of the cheeks of the exterior portion and glancing inward, occasioned considerable casualties, and to form a suitable recess for strong iron shutters to protect from grape entering through the throat whilst the gun was out of battery. The two principal wrought-iron throat-pieces are trapezoidal in plan, being 8 inches thick and 17 inches base, the oblique side having the same slant as the inner cheek of the embrasure. Exterior to these two pieces are two plate-pieces, each two inches thick, against which the shutters, which are also two inches thick, rest when open or closed, as shown in Fig. 61. There is also a wrought-iron plate casing around the exterior opening of the embrasure, as shown in Fig. 61, and in the exterior elevation, Fig. 64. In Fig. 62 is shown an interior elevation of the carriage recess, the embrasure, and the tongue-hole; and, in Fig. 63, a vertical section and side elevation on *A B*, Fig. 64, of the embrasure, carriage recess, and the pintle and tongue-holes.

155...The exterior width of the embrasure, the obliquity given to the cheeks of the interior portion, and the depth and slant given to the carriage recess and its sides, are arranged with a view to the traverse of the gun, which is fixed at 60°, or 30° on each side of the axis of the embrasure.

156...All the parts of the wall adjacent to the embrasure are constructed of the largest sized blocks of the toughest stone, the blocks being carefully fitted and bonded, and having the additional strength afforded by a very ingenious arrangement of hollow bolts, and a concrete of lead and chippings of stone run together. A brick arch, as shown in the elevations and sections, is turned over the embrasure and within the mass of the scarp wall.

157...BOMB-PROOF BUILDINGS. Casemated bomb proof quarters are indispensable to the safety and comfort of the garrison during siege, or any prolonged attack for the annoyance or reduction of the work by a bombardment. In small works like the most of our forts. which are chiefly designed for sea-coast defence, casemated quarters are arranged as has been seen in the rear of the batteries, a portion of each casemate toward the parade being partitioned off and suitably disposed for the object in view. In some cases advantage is taken of a scarp wall, on a land front, which is well covered by a glacis or other face cover, to form in its rear quarters of this character. In all cases, care should be taken to place such quarters on those fronts which are best covered from a direct fire, and the parade walls of which are not exposed to reverse fire. Whenever the plan of the work admits of it, quarters of this kind should be arranged for defence, by being pierced with loop-holes, and even with embrasures for cannon. Defensive casemated quarters form a prominent and distinctive feature in what is now known as the German school of permanent fortification. They consist of bomb-proof buildings of a curvilinear or polygonal plan, arranged for one or more stories of covered defences, with an ordinary open defence surmounting the casemates. The casemates of the upper story are covered by bomb-proof arches, whilst those of the lower stories receive flat segment arches of only sufficient thickness and strength to bear the weight of the guns and to subserve the other objects of the structure. When employed as caponnières, as gorge defences, or as interior retrenchments, the front walls of these structures are masked from direct views, either by the glacis or by the parapet of the work in which they are placed, and they receive a thickness of at least 5 feet. But as a mask wall even of this thickness, when pierced with loop-holes and embrasures, is liable to damage from shot which plunge over the parapet in front of it, Pl. 7, Fig. 53, the portions of the casemate piers, *B*, where they join the mask wall, *A*, are made thicker, in some cases for a distance of a few feet back, than their general thickness, in order to receive two vertical grooves in the face of this thicker portion, into which scantling being inserted horizontally, and the space between the two partitions thus formed filled in with sand-bags or other shot-proof materials, a temporary shelter can be formed when the ruin of the mask wall exposes the interior of the casemate to view.

In our service, Pl. 7, Figs. 51, 52, when casemated quarters are constructed of two stories, the upper one alone is covered with a bomb-proof arch, the floor between the two being of timber, and constructed in the ordinary way.

158...In Fig. 51 is shown a plan on *A D*, Fig. 52, of bomb-proof casemated quarters in rear of a scarp wall and of a counterscarp gallery, both arranged with loop-holed defences. Fig. 52 is a section and side elevation on *CD*, Fig. 51, showing the rampart and parapet over the arch and the fireplaces and chimneys in the piers of the arches. The floor of the second story is of timber. The rear or parade wall is pierced with doors and windows.

159...In Fig. 53 is shown the plan of the end of a casemated defensive barrack, from an Austrian authority. The front wall, *A*, is arranged and pierced for cannon, each arched chamber for one gun. The end wall is loop-holed for musketry, and the rear wall, *C*, has windows and doors.

160...Powder Magazine. The structures for this purpose are built with strong, full centre, bomb-proof brick arches, supported on heavy stone piers, which form the outward walls and to which interior buttresses are sometimes added. The capping of the arches is covered with from 4 to 6 feet of solidly packed earth. The interior of the magazine, the floors, and the doors and windows, are built with a view to security from fire; and to preserve the powder from dampness, by a good system of drainage around the foundations, and of ventilation by means of air-holes made through the piers, and panels of copper pierced with small holes placed in the doors. No iron or steel fastening or sheeting is allowed in any part of the structure; and in arranging the air-holes through the piers, they receive a broken direction and have a copper mesh-work placed across them, to prevent any combustible material, or rats, or mice, penetrating to the interior of the magazine.

In large works the magazines are isolated, as far as practicable, from the enceinte, so as not to endanger it should an accidental explosion take place. The magazine is enclosed by a strong high wall for security, and is provided with lightning-rods. In small works some one or more of the casemates, in the least exposed position to the assailant's fire, is built for the purposes of a magazine.

COMMUNICATIONS.

161...The communications form a very important element in the defence of permanent works. They consist of *ramps*, *stairs*, *posterns*, *gate-ways* and *bridges*.

162...RAMPS. Ramps are inclined planes, or paths, leading from one level to another, as from that of the parade to the terreplein of the enceinte. Their width at top, for the service of the artillery and other vehicles, may be from 10 to 15 feet, and their inclination from $\frac{1}{6}$ to $\frac{1}{15}$, or less, depending on the difference of level to be overcome. They are usually placed in positions where they will occupy the least room of the parade—as along the rampart-slope of the enceinte. As a general rule, their side-slopes are of earth; but where it is desirable to economise room on the parade, the side-slopes are replaced on one or both sides by a wall which sustains the earth of the ramp. When ramps serve for infantry alone, their width may be reduced to 6 feet, and in some cases to 4 feet.

163...STAIRS. Stairs, except for temporary purposes, are constructed of stone; each step being a solid block which is 6 feet long in the clear; its breadth at top or the tread 12 inches, and its height or rise 8 inches. Stairs are usually placed along the counterscarp and gorge walls of the outworks, forming a communication, for infantry only, between the ditch and the terreplein of the work to which they lead. They are also used within the enceinte in positions where there is not sufficient room for ramps; or where, for greater security from surprise, it is desirable to present a narrower and more difficult defile to the assailant. In cases where room is wanting and the communication not in habitual use, the width of the stairway may be reduced to 4 feet.

164...POSTERNS. Posterns are arched passageways constructed under the terrepleins and ramparts, forming subterranean communications between the parade and the enceinte ditch, or between the ditches and the interior of the outworks. The width and height of the interior of posterns depend upon the use to which the communication is to be applied. For artillery, the width is usually taken at 10 feet, and the height under the crown or key of the arch at least 8 feet. Posterns for infantry may be only from 6 to 4 feet wide, and from 6 feet 6 inches to 8 feet high under the crown of the arch. The thickness of the piers of the arches is generally taken at about half the width of the postern. The arches are from 18 inches to 2 feet thick. As any injury to the arch from the bursting of a shell over it might obstruct the communication, the arch should be covered with a thickness of at least 3 feet of earth, and, when convenient, with 5 or 6 feet for greater security. A strong wooden door is placed at each outlet of the postern to secure it against surprise. The door-way in posterns for the service of artillery should be of just sufficient height for the convenient passage of a gun— about 7 feet for each dimension is usually allowed for this purpose.

165...The most important postern is the one leading from

the parade to the enceinte ditch. This generally receives a width of 12 feet, and the same height under the crown. For greater security from surprise, its outlet at the enceinte ditch is at least 6 feet above the bottom of the ditch—this difference of level being overcome by means of a temporary wooden ramp, which receives an inclination of at least $\frac{1}{6}$. With a like object, besides two strong doors at the two ends of the postern, there is a partition of masonry about midway between the two ends, which is pierced with a door-way of the same size as the door-ways of the ends, and closed by a strong door which, as well as the partition wall, is loop-holed for musketry.

166...In cases where the postern forms the main entrance to the work, an arched chamber is placed on one side of it, at the outlet, which serves as a *guard-room* for a few men, to secure the outlet from surprise. The wall between this chamber and the postern is loop-holed, so that a fire can be brought to bear on the door-way of the postern; and, as a farther precaution against surprise, a machicoulis defence is sometimes arranged at the top of the scarp wall just above the door-way of the postern.

167...GATE-WAY. In works with large garrisons, where the means of frequent communication with the exterior are requisite, posterns of the ordinary dimensions are found not to afford a sufficient convenience for the daily wants. In such cases a passageway of sufficient width to admit of at least a single carriage road, with narrow foot-paths on each side, has to be opened through the rampart, which, whenever it is practicable to do so, should be arched, and covered with earth to render it bomb-proof. This passage-way should, for security, have the bottom of its outlet at least 12 feet above the bottom of the enceinte ditch: and when this difference of level cannot be obtained, the main ditch should be deepened sufficiently for the purpose below the outlet. A gate-way of sufficient height and width for the passage of the ordinary vehicles for the service of the garrison is made through the scarp wall. This gate-way is arched at top, where a machicoulis defence may also be arranged to guard the outlet on the exterior.

168...The communication across the enceinte ditch, leading from the gate-way, is usually an ordinary wooden bridge built on piles. The bay of this bridge at the gate-way is spanned by a drawbridge of timber, which, when drawn up, closes and secures the gate-way. This drawbridge is manœuvred by some of the usual mechanisms employed for this purpose.

169...PORTCULLIS. When the gate-way is not preceded by a ditch, and is, therefore, without a drawbridge, a barrier, termed a *portcullis*, which can be lowered or raised vertically by machinery, is sometimes added to secure the passageway from surprise. The ancient portcullis was a framework of heavy beams, placed vertically, leaving a few inches only between each pair of beams. These vertical beams were either solidly confined between horizontal beams, or clamping-pieces in pairs; or else they were so arranged that they could slide upward between the clamping-pieces. Each of the vertical beams was shod at the bottom with a strong pointed iron shoe. The horizontal pieces were framed securely with two heavy vertical beams that formed the sides of the frame, and were fitted into vertical grooves made in the side walls of the passageway, in which the frame could slide when raised or lowered. By arranging the vertical beams to slide upward between the clamping-pieces, it will enable the passageway to be closed in places where an obstruction might be designedly placed below the portcullis to prevent this being done; as the beams which meet the obstruction would be pushed upward, whilst the others would fall to their ordinary level and close the passageway on each side of the obstruction.

170...In the works recently constructed with us, the portcullis, and even the doors preceding them, have been constructed of a strong open lattice-work of wrought-iron bars bolted strongly to the wrought-iron uprights and cross pieces forming the framework of the lattice. This is a great improvement for these purposes, both as to durability and defence.

171...Passageways of this description should be secured

by all the means at an engineer's disposal. A large guard-room, with loop-holes bearing on the passage, should be erected on one side, near the gate-way; and if the enceinte is a simple one, without outworks beyond its ditch, a small lunette, or a loop-holed tambour of masonry or timber, should be constructed beyond the counterscarp, forming a *tête-de-pont*, for the security of the bridge from surprise.

172...The drawbridge, which for convenience of manœuvring should not be longer than 12 feet, is constructed in the usual mode. Care should be taken that it shall fit the recess in the face of the wall so closely that there will not be room enough between it and the jambs of the gate-way to insert an iron lever to force back the bridge.

Elements of the Plan of Enceintes and Outworks.

ENCEINTES.

173...The most simple mode of fortifying a position in a permanent manner, consists in enclosing it with a rampart, surmounted by a parapet with a ditch, the scarp of which, when dry, is revetted with masonry, and so covered by an earthen mask that it cannot be breached except by batteries placed on the border of the counterscarp.

174...An enclosed line of fortification of this simple character is termed the *enceinte*, the *body of the place*, or the *main enclosure*.

175...The general outline of the enceinte may be curvilinear, or a polygonal figure of any character.

176...SYSTEM OF FORTIFICATION. Although an infinite diversity of figures may thus be presented in the outline or plan of the enceinte, they may be all classed under four heads, to each of which engineers generally have applied the term, *system of fortification.* These four classes are: 1, the *circular* or *curvilinear system;* 2, the *polygonal* or *caponnière system;* 3, the *tenailled system;* 4, the *bastioned system.*

177...The term *method of fortification,* instead of system, is now usually applied to the manner of fortifying, which is generally prevalent in any country; or to the mode adopted by any individual, as the *German method, Vauban's method,* etc.

178....CIRCULAR SYSTEM. The circular system consists of an enceinte, the plan of which is circular, or curvilinear.

179...POLYGONAL SYSTEM. In the polygonal system, the plan is either a polygon, with salient angles alone, Pl. 8, Fig. 72, each side of which, *A A,* is flanked by a casemated caponnière, *C,* placed in the ditch, *D,* and midway between the two salients, *A;* or else each side of the polygon is broken inward at the centre, so as to form a slight re-entering, Pl. 8, Figs. 73, 74, 75, 76, 77, to procure a casemated flanking arrangement, *F F,* for the caponnières, *C,* which occupy these re-enterings, and also, in some cases, to flank works in advance of the enceinte.

180...TENAILLED SYSTEM. The tenailled system, Pl. 8, Fig. 78, consists of a tenailled line, the re-entering angles of which are between 90° and 100°, and the salient angles not less than 60°

181...BASTIONED SYSTEM. The bastioned system, Fig. 79, consists of lunettes or bastions connected by curtains, *D D,* between the extremities of their flanks, *B D.* The bastions usually consist of two faces and two flanks, the scarps of each of which are plane surfaces. In most of the older fortifications, and in a few of the more recent works in Europe, the flank is broken; the portion of it at the shoulder angle forming a projecting mass, which is termed an *orillon,* whilst the portion between the orillon and the enceinte curtain is retired, or brought in toward the interior of the bastion, and is thus partially covered by the orillon from fire, except in the prolongation of the enceinte ditch. In some cases the plan of the orillon, as well as that of the retired flank, is curvilinear; in others they are both rectilinear.

182...Front of Fortification. The term *front of fortification* is applied either to the portion of the enceinte comprised between the capitals of two adjacent salient angles of the polygon, or to this portion and any other works within or beyond it which are comprised between two adjacent capitals, and are connected with this portion by relations of defence.

Outworks and Detached Works.

183...A work consisting of an enceinte alone is more or less exposed to surprise, as it must have outlets of some description to keep up a communication with the exterior and a bridge, or other means for crossing the ditch. But this is not the only defect of a fortification of this simple character; for, having no covers beyond the ditch for its garrison, their action must be restricted to what may be termed a passive resistance alone; as, in any attempt to operate on the exterior, they are exposed to fire so soon as they emerge from the ditch; and in a retreat toward the work, if closely pursued by the assailant, they will not only run the risk of being cut off, but a retreat under such circumstances may lead to the capture of the work itself, by the assailant being enabled to enter with the retreating force.

184...To provide against dangers of so grave a character, engineers have devised other defences beyond the ditch, and which they have placed in immediate defensive relations with the enceinte, being under its fire and in positions where, if assaulted, they can be readily succored by the garrison. To this class of exterior defences the term *outworks* has been applied. The works which come under this head are the *covered-way*, the *tenaille*, the *demilune*, the *counterguard*, the *redoubt* or *réduit*, the *tenaillon*, the *hornwork* and the *crown-work*.

185...Covered-way. The covered-way, as its name imports, is an open corridor or passage, masked from the assailant's view by an embankment, which borders the ditch of the enceinte alone when there are no other outworks; but, in the contrary case, also envelops the ditches of these, forming thus a continuous covered line of communication around the fortification.

186...The covering embankment itself is arranged toward the covered-way like an ordinary parapet, and it receives on the exterior a gentle slope or glacis. By this arrangement the garrison have a covered position beyond the ditch where they can assemble with safety, either for the purpose of making a sortie or to guard the ditches and the communications across them; and which affords them also a secure point of retreat if repulsed in a sortie, as a reserve left in the covered-way will be at hand to check the pursuit by their fire, and enable the retreating party to gain the enceinte.

187...Places of Arms. The covered-way, from the direction given to the counterscarps of the enceinte and outworks, forms a line of communication with salient and re-entering parts, Pls. 8, 9, Figs. 80 to 85. The salient portions, *S*, are termed *salient places of arms;* and the re-entering parts the *re-entering places of arms.*

188...The salient places of arms, it will be seen, result from the general plan of the covered-way; but the re-entering places of arms are formed by changing the directions of the two branches where they form the re-enterings, *R*, so as to make a salient within the re-enterings; thus enlarging the covered-way at these points, and procuring a flanking arrangement, by which the glacis can be swept, and a cross-fire be brought to bear on the ground in advance of the salients.

189...Traverses. The covered-way, from its position and the usually slight command given to the crest of its glacis, is very much exposed to the effects of an enfilading fire. With a view to remedy this defect, and also to enable the garrison to dispute, foot by foot, the possession of this outwork by the assailant, earthen masks, formed like an ordinary parapet, and termed *traverses*, are thrown up across it. The traverses usually extend to the counterscarp, the wall of which is built up to sustain them. At the end toward the glacis a passage, or defile, is left between them and the covering embankment, to admit of a free communication throughout the covered-way.

190...TENAILLE. The tenaille is a low work, placed in the re-entering formed in the enceinte ditch by the curtain and flanks of the bastioned system, being isolated by a ditch between it and these parts of the enceinte. Its chief purpose is to serve as a mask, covering the scarp walls of this re-entering from fire as well as the outlets to the enceinte ditch, which are usually placed in the centre of the curtains.

191...The tenaille has received various forms from engineers. In some cases it has been made with two faces or wings, making a re-entering angle opposite the centre of the enceinte curtain. In others the two wings, instead of being prolonged until they meet, are connected by a short curtain parallel to that of the enceinte. In some examples, it has the form of a small bastioned front. In others, it consists of two flanks connected by a curtain. The flanks in some cases have been casemated for guns and mortars. The tenaille is usually revetted with masonry, both in front and rear. In some cases the ends alone, toward the flanks of the enceinte, are revetted, the intermediate portions consisting of an ordinary earthen parapet, without either scarp or gorge wall.

192...DEMILUNE. The demilune, Pl. 9, Figs. 81, 82, 83, 84, is a work in the form of a redan, *D*, placed in front of the enceinte curtain, which it masks from fire, as well as a portion of each face of the enceinte, at the shoulder angles of the bastions. It is isolated from the enceinte by the main ditch, and from its own covered-way by its ditch. From its importance the scarp and gorge of the demilune are generally revetted, though in some cases the revetement has been omitted.

193...COUNTERGUARD. The counterguard is an isolated

work, *C*, Fig. 83, in the form of a redan, which envelops the faces of a bastion. In some cases it consists simply of an earthen mask having the profile of an ordinary parapet; but it is usually revetted both in front and rear.

194...REDOUBTS. The term redoubt, or réduit, is applied to outworks placed within other outworks; their object being to strengthen the defence of the principal work.

195...A work of this class is usually placed within the demilune, and is termed the *demilune redoubt.* Small works of this kind are also placed in the salient and re-entering places of arms of the covered-way, and are termed the *redoubt of the salient*, or *re-entering place of arms.* These redoubts are, in some cases, simple earthen works; in others, they are revetted; and in others, casemated, both for the service of artillery and small arms.

196...TENAILLON. The term tenaillon, Pl. 9, Fig. 81, is applied to a kind of face cover, or counterguard, *T*, of the demilune. It is only to be met with in some of the old fortified places of Europe, and was added to give more strength to the fronts where the demilune was too small.

197...HORNWORK. The hornwork, Pl. 9, Fig. 82, usually consists of a bastioned front, *H*, with the ordinary outworks, having two long branches, *F F*, or wings, which rest upon two adjacent bastions, or two adjacent demilunes, *D D*, of the enceinte—its covered-way forming, with that of the enceinte, a continuous line of communication. The object of this outwork is to strengthen a salient or other weak portion of the enceinte.

198...CROWN-WORK. The crown-work, Pl. 9, Fig. 83, consists of two or more bastioned fronts, *C*, with their outworks, placed in front of some portion of the enceinte, to give it additional strength. It is terminated, like the hornwork, by two wings, *F F*, which rest either upon the enceinte, or upon the demilunes, *D D*. Its covered-way, like that of the hornwork, forms a continuous communication with that of the enceinte.

199...DETACHED WORKS. There are two other classes of exterior defences besides the outworks, termed *detached works* and *advanced works*, the object of which is either to strengthen some weak portion of the enceinte or to occupy positions which would be of advantage to an assailant in his attacks on the enceinte.

200...Detached works are such as are placed beyond the covered-way of the enceinte, but within the range and support of its fire. Advanced works are such as, from their advanced position, receiving but little or no support from the fire of the enceinte, must rely upon their own resources for defence. The former class are usually open in the rear, so that their interior may be exposed to the fire of the enceinte; whilst the latter should be closed throughout and of sufficient strength of profile to secure them from an open assault.

201...In Pl. 9, Fig. 84, is a detached work, *L*, flanked by the demilunes, *D*, of the enceinte. The plan of this work is a lunette, with its covered-way and places of arms, *R* and *S*.

Interior Retrenchments.

202...Besides the works exterior to the enceinte, the object of which is to retard the assailant in his attempts to enter it by breaching, engineers have placed within it other works which, in some cases, are designed simply to enable the garrison to make an effectual defence of the breach, when the assault upon it is made, and give them a secure point of retreat and safety when driven from it; and in others, these interior works are chiefly designed to bring a plunging fire to bear on the assailant's siege works exterior to the enceinte. The former class, intended for the defence of the breach alone, are termed *interior retrenchments;* and the latter, *cavaliers.*

203...Interior retrenchments are either placed within the

bastions, which are the parts of the enceinte usually breached, or in rear of their gorges. Those which are placed within the bastions extend across them, either between the faces or between the flanks. When placed at the gorge, they connect the two adjacent curtains.

204...The plan of these works varies with their position, the size of the bastions, or the more or less of openness of their salient angles.

205...In small bastions with acute salients, when the retrenchment rests upon the faces, it usually receives the form of a tenaille or inverted redan, the angle of the tenaille being about 100° When the bastions are large and the salient angle quite open or obtuse, the retrenchment may receive the form of a small bastioned front, Pl. 9, Fig. 85, resting upon the faces.

206...Either of these forms may, in like manner, be used, when the retrenchment rests upon the flanks of the bastion. But as this position enables a retrenchment of the form of an ordinary redan to have its ditches swept by the fire of the flanks of the adjacent bastions, this form is in some cases used in preference.

207...When placed between two curtains at the gorge of a bastion, the plan of the entrenchment is always a bastioned front.

208...Cavaliers are placed either upon the curtains or within the bastions. The latter is the more usual position selected for them. Their plan in this position is usually that of a lunette, the faces and flanks of which are parallel to those of the enveloping bastion. Cavaliers receive a considerable command over the parapet of the enceinte, and, in some cases, they are arranged with a tier of casemated fire, above which is an open battery.

209...Interior retrenchments are usually constructed with a revetted scarp and counterscarp, to secure them from an open assault; and, in some cases, a covered-way, with a small re-entering place of arms, *R*, Pl. 9, Fig. 85, closed by traverses, is arranged in advance of the ditch, to insure the safe retreat of the garrison when driven from the breach.

Bastioned System.

210...A bastioned enceinte consists of a series of bastions which occupy the salient angles of the polygon, within which the enceinte is enclosed; the flanks of the bastions being usually connected by straight curtains.

211...The sides of the polygon which connect the salient angles of the bastions, are termed the *exterior sides*, in contradistinction to the sides of an interior polygon, which, being parallel to the first and occupying the positions of the curtains, are termed the *interior sides.*

212...The bastioned enceinte, when its relief and plan are suitably arranged, possesses the advantage of having its ditches thoroughly swept from within the enceinte itself, thus securing the flanking arrangement of the scarp, whilst the garrison also is kept within the enceinte under the immediate eye and orders of their commander, up to the moment of the fall of the work; of bringing a cross and flank fire to bear upon the approaches on the salients of the enceinte in the directions of the capitals of the bastions; and furnishing a strong direct and cross fire upon the site in advance of the curtains and the faces of the bastions.

213...The principal objections urged against the bastioned system are, that its chief characteristic—a perfect flanking disposition for the entire line of the scarp—is attainable only under certain relations between the requisite relief for a permanent work and the length of the exterior side and curtain, which, therefore, restricts it in its application to fortification of a permanent character; that, in order to secure sufficient length of flank for an effective flanking disposition, the angle between the face of the bastion and the exterior side, termed the *diminished angle* of the polygon, has to be made so great as to decrease considerably the space enclosed within the polygon, whilst the development of the line of the enceinte is greatly increased by it; that this direction, necessarily given to the faces from this cause, throws their prolongations in positions very favorable to the erection of enfilading batteries against them; that the flanks, upon which the whole system is based, lie in positions in which, like the faces, they can be not only easily enfiladed, but are further exposed to a reverse fire from shot which may pass over the parapet of the faces as well as the opposite flank; and that these objections are the stronger as the salient angles of the polygon are smaller, or as the number of sides is decreased.

214...Besides these objections, which, to a certain extent, are well founded, where the defensive arrangements are chiefly open, as is the case in most land fronts, others have been urged against this system, which, being rather of a comparative character, as showing the advantages of other systems over this, will best be examined elsewhere.

215...As the plan and relief of the bastioned enceinte, employed among engineers of the present day, differ in no very material points from those adopted about the period of Vauban, when the art of fortification assumed somewhat less of mere mechanical routine, it has become the practice in military schools in Europe to deduce, from the description of the bastioned method of Vauban and his immediate successors, the principles upon which the forms and dimensions, both of the enceinte and its outworks, as well as their defensive relations, are based. As this course has the further advantage of exhibiting the views of men who are still looked to as the safest authorities in the art, whilst it gives, at the same time, a history of its progress and changes from the period when it may be said to have first broken loose from the trammels of mere routine up to the present day, it has been also adopted as the basis of the instruction given on this subject in this institution.

Vauban's First Method.

216...Vauban has left examples of three different methods in the places planned by him. The Fortress of New Brisac is fortified after his third method; those of Landau and Befort after his second; but the greater part of the places fortified by him are planned according to his first, or earliest method.

217...NOTE. In the following description of the methods of Vauban, Cormontaingne and some other French authors, the English yard has been substituted for the French *half toise* and the *metre*, each of which is so nearly the equivalent of the yard as not to affect in any sensible manner the principles or the defensive relations of the parts. In like manner the English foot has been substituted for the French foot.

218...PROFILE OF ENCEINTE. In the profile of this method, Fig. 1, Pl. 1, the scarp wall is 36 feet high, its slope being five perpendicular to one of base; surmounting this is another wall from 4 to 6 feet high, the object of which is to sustain the exterior of the parapet. The parapet is 18 feet thick, the superior slope being $\frac{1}{9}$; the interior crest is 8 feet above the terreplein, which is 42 feet in width. The mean command of the interior crest above the site is about 26 feet. The bottom of the ditch is about 17½ feet below the site.

219...PLAN OF ENCEINTE. Vauban adopted no arbitrary or invariable combination of parts in his methods. His great excellence as an engineer is shown in the acknowledged skill with which he adapted the fortifications he planned to the defensive requirements of the sites. Selecting long, medium, or short exterior sides, and varying the lengths and directions of the faces and flanks so as to procure the best command over the exterior ground, and to withdraw these parts from the enfilading views of the assailant. In his works, however, he has generally taken 360 yards as the greatest limit of the exterior side; the perpendicular of the front $\frac{1}{8}$ when the polygon is a square; $\frac{1}{7}$ for the pentagon; and $\frac{1}{6}$ for all higher polygons. With these starting points he procured diminished angles which gave more than 60° to the salient angles of the bastions in all cases, and flanks of suitable length both to flank the main ditch and to encounter with advantage the counter-batteries which could be erected against them. The following constructions, both for the enceinte and outworks, are taken from the best French authorities as adopted by him for polygons higher than the pentagon.

220...In the plan or *traçé*, Fig. 2, Pl. 1, the magistral is taken as the directing line; the exterior side is 360 yards; on the perpendicular of the front a distance of $\frac{1}{6}$ the exterior side is set off; lines drawn through this point and the extremities of the exterior side, determine the directions of the faces and the lines of defence; from the salients a distance equal to $\frac{2}{7}$ of the exterior side is set off, which gives the lengths of the faces and the positions of the shoulder angles; the flank is drawn by taking the opposite shoulder angle as a centre; and with a radius equal to the distance between the shoulder angles, describing an arc to intersect the line of defence, the chord of this arc is the flank; the curtain is drawn by joining the extremities of the flanks. By this construction the flanks will be about 54 yards; the curtain, 146; and the lines of defence, 267—the length of these being determined so that the salients of the bastions can be defended with the *rampart gun*, or *wall-piece*.

221...TENAILLE. In many of the places constructed before Vauban's time there was a low work, enveloping the enceinte and connected with it, called a *fausse-braie*. This work, which had many defects, was suppressed by Vauban, who was the first to use the tenaille in its place. The tenaille has many valuable properties: it covers the arched communication, or *postern*, under the curtain; masks the masonry of the curtain and flanks, so that a breach cannot be made in them, and in this way prevents retrenchments, resting against those parts, from being turned; a place of arms is formed between it and the curtain, where troops can be assembled for sorties in the ditches; finally, its fire sweeps the ditch and counterscarp, and helps to cover the retreat of troops from the other outworks. The tenaille is separated from the curtain by a ditch 10 yards wide, and from the flanks by ditches of 6 yards. The form of the tenaille, as used by Vauban, was variable: in some cases he made it with a curtain and two small flanks parallel to those of the enceinte; in others, it consisted simply of two wings placed on the prolongations of the faces; and, finally, he gave it the form in Fig. 2, with a small curtain and two wings, which is the one at present most generally adopted. The relief of the tenaille is so arranged as not to mask the fire of the flanks on the ditch of the enceinte along the faces; for this purpose Vauban places its interior crest on a level with the site, or a little below it.

222...Main Ditch. Vauban followed no invariable rule in regulating the dimensions of the enceinte ditch; its most usual width at the salients of the bastions, where the counterscarp is an arc of a circle, is about 36 yards; the rest of the counterscarp is tangent to this arc, and directed upon the opposite shoulder angles.

223...Demilune and Reduit. Vauban increased the dimensions of the demilune which had been used previous to his time. The object of this work is to secure the gates of the place from a surprise; to mask from the enemy's batteries the flanks and curtain of the enceinte; and give cross fires on the salients of the bastions. The plan and dimensions of the demilune vary also in Vauban's works. Its magistral is generally laid out by taking a point on the bastion face at 10 yards from the shoulder angle, and drawing a line from this point to the perpendicular of the front, so as to make the face of the demilune equal to $\frac{2}{7}$ of the exterior side. The parapet of the demilune is the same as that of the enceinte; its command is 3 feet less than that of the enceinte. All the outworks in this system are commanded by the enceinte; the outworks most advanced being also commanded by those in rear.

224...To strengthen the demilune, and secure for the troops entrusted with its defence a safe retreat when it is carried, Vauban placed in it a small redoubt. This work, in some instances, was only a simple *crenated wall*, with a ditch in front; sometimes it was made of earth, and after the commencement of the siege.

225...The ditch of the demilune is generally about 24 yards wide, and of the same depth as that of the enceinte; its counterscarp and that of the enceinte forming a continuous wall.

226...COVERED-WAY. The covered-way envelops the entire counterscarp. Vauban placed a high value on this work, which, to use his own words, "Costs less to the defence and more to the assailant than any other work." The covered-way prevents all access to the ditch, by a strong fire of musketry, which sweeps all the exterior ground; it is a secure position, where troops can be assembled in safety for sorties; it covers the retreat of troops from the exterior into the other works. The general width of the covered-way is 12 yards. To set out the re-entering place of arms, two points are taken at 20 yards from the re-entering angle, made by the interior crests of the covered-ways of the demilune and bastion, and upon these crests, and from these points as centres, with radii of 24 yards, arcs are described; the point of their intersections being joined with their centres, gives the crests of the re-entering place of arms. The parapet of the covered-way is terminated in a glacis, the foot of which is from 40 to 50 yards from the interior crest.

227...TRAVERSES. To close the place of arms, and enable the troops to defend the covered-way foot by foot, *traverses* of earth formed into parapets are placed at the places of arms. *Defiles* or *passages* of 4 feet are left between the traverses and the crest of the covered-way, for the circulation of the troops.

The covered-way is palisaded to prevent surprise.

228...COMMUNICATIONS. The *communications* constitute an important part of every system. In Vauban's front, ramps are made to ascend from the plane of sight to the terreplein. A postern is made under the curtain, to communicate from the interior with the ditch; another postern is made under the tenaille, to lead to the demilune; a *double caponnière*, which is a passage covered on each side by a parapet terminated in a glacis toward the ditch, covers the communication through the ditch to the gorge of the demilune; single caponnières are placed in the ditch of the demilune, and cover the troops from the enemy's fire through its ditch; *stairs* are placed at the gorges of the tenaille and demilune, and along the counterscarp at the places of arms, to ascend from the ditch to the terrepleins of those works. To communicate with the exterior, narrow openings are made in the faces of the re-entering place of arms, to lead from the terrepleins to the glacis; they are termed *sortie passages*, or *sally-ports*, and are closed by barriers.

REMARKS.

229...ENCEINTE. In the *traçé* adopted by Vauban for the enceinte, it may be observed that the length and positions of the lines of the front resulting from it are in good defensive relations, both for cannon and small arms.

230...In the first place, the foot of the scarp, throughout the length of the curtain and the bastions, is thoroughly exposed to the fire of the flanks, which, from the diminished angle assumed in the hexigon and higher polygons, which is about $18\frac{1}{2}°$, and the curtain angle, which is nearly 100°—can sweep both the curtain scarp and that of the bastion face from an embrasure placed at the curtain angle.

231...In the second place, the length of the flank is sufficient to contain as many cannon, at least, as the assailant can place to counter-batter the flank from the glacis crest opposite the flank; and the flank can also bring an efficient fire of small arms to bear on this battery of the assailant.

232...The bastions are of good size, and would admit of

efficient interior retrenchments being thrown up in them, although Vauban does not indicate this auxiliary means in his 1*st Method.*

233...TENAILLE. Vauban substituted the tenaille for the fausse-braie, as this latter work facilitated an escalade, and, moreover, exposed the troops in it to the annoyance of the splinters from the walls behind, when exposed to the assailant's fire. The tenaille was devised mainly to mash the scarp wall of the curtain and flanks, whilst its relief was so regulated as not to intercept the fire of the flanks on the enceinte ditch before the bastion faces. The plan of the earlier tenailles consisted of two flanks connected by a curtain, which were parallel to the same lines of the enceinte. This form was subsequently abandoned, as the flanks were found to be exposed to both an enfilading and reverse fire from the assailant's positions in front of the enceinte; and the one now in most general use, consisting either of two wings simply, or of two wings connected by a short curtain, adopted in its place.

The tenaille, however, only partially subserves its object, as it does not cover the entire height of the scarp of the enceinte curtain and flanks; and, what is a more serious defect, it leaves the entire height of scarp of that portion of the curtain opposite to the ditch, between the tenaille and the bastion flank, entirely exposed from the same position, and liable to be breached.

234...DEMILUNE. From the small size of this work, it gives but little cover to any portion of the enceinte except the curtain. It is not sufficiently thrown to the front to give a good volume of cross fire on the glacis in advance of the bastion salients; and the re-entering formed at this point, by the two adjacent demilunes, is, from the same cause, shallow, and of but little strength. Owing to this last defect, the assailant can easily breach and storm the enceinte at the same time as the demilune.

Besides these defects, the demilune is not provided with a permanent rèduit—a work necessary to enable the demilune to make a vigorous defence, by the support it affords the assailed.

235...COVERED-WAY. From the width given to the demilune ditch, the covered-ways are exposed to a slant reverse fire, from which they are but badly screened by the traverses. Their command over the site is rather too little. Their main defect, however, is the small size given to the re-entering place of arms, and the failure to secure this important position for assembling troops for sorties by a permanent rèduit, by which any open attack of the covered-way could be prevented.

236...DITCHES. The dimensions given both the enceinte and demilune ditches present a formidable obstacle to an open assault, and render the assailant's passage of the ditch by the sap more difficult. The demilune ditch, however, offers a wide opening, through which the scarp of the bastion face can be seen down to its foot from the assailant's batteries on the glacis crest in the prolongation of the demilune ditch.

237...COMMUNICATIONS. The communications within the enceinte, and from it to the main ditch, are sufficient and convenient for the character of the defence designed. Those of the outworks are for the most part narrow, inconvenient, and badly screened from the assailant's fire, and, therefore, do not furnish a good provision for an active defence beyond the enceinte.

238...PROFILES. The great command over the site, and the high relief given to the enceinte, are very much in favor of the defence, both as to the effect of the fire on the assailant's approaches, and for security against an escalade. But, in attaining these objects, Vauban has left exposed to the assailant's distant fire a considerable portion of the scarp wall, which, being destroyed, would lay the enceinte open to a surprise.

Vauban's Third Method.

239...In his 3d Method, Pl. 14, which differs from his 2d only in some minor modifications, Vauban adopted what may be termed a double enceinte, the interior one being continuous, and consisting of small casemated bastioned towers, *L*, *R*, *O*, placed at the angles of the polygon, which are connected by curtains, *P*, *Z*, *W*, *U'*, in the form of bastioned fronts, the flanks of which are also casemated, and intended, with those of the towers, to sweep the ditch of this enceinte.

240...The second, or exterior enceinte, is not continuous, but consists of large bastions, *A*, *H*, *K*, or counterguards with flanks, which cover the towers and the faces of the bastioned curtain between them, and of a tenaille, which lies between the flanks of the counterguards and covers the curtain of the interior enceinte.

241...In advance of this exterior enceinte is placed a demilune, arranged with flanks, which contains a small revetted redoubt, and a covered-way similar to the one in his 1st Method.

242...PLAN. The lines joining the salients of the counterguards form the exterior sides, and are taken at 360 yards. The perpendicular, *C D*, is one-sixth of the exterior side, or 60 yards. The face, *A H*, one-third the exterior side, or 120 yards. The flank, *H K*, is constructed as in the 1st Method.

243...The tenaille consists simply of two wings in the prolongation of the faces of the counterguards; a ditch 10 yards wide is left between the tenaille and the flanks of the counterguard. The gorge line of the tenaille and the flanks of the counterguards lie on the line *L M*, joining the salients of the towers.

244...To set out the towers and connecting curtain, a

line, $N T$, is drawn parallel to $L M$, and at 16 yards. The flanks, R, Q, of the towers are drawn through points P, at 14 yards from N. The portion of the flanks, P, R, exterior to the curtain, being 12 yards, and the interior portion, $P Q$, 8 yards. The faces are found by joining the points L, R.

245...The perpendicular, $T V$, of the bastioned curtain is 10 yards. The flanks, Z, W, are on the prolongations of the counterguard flanks. The curtain, $W U'$, is parallel to $L M$.

246...The gorge of the counterguard is constructed by describing an arc from L, as a centre, with a radius of 14 yards, and drawing a tangent to this arc from the point corresponding to Z, on the opposite flank, to $Z W$

247...The salient, C'', of the demilune is at 110 yards from the point O, where a line parallel to the counterguard face, and 30 yards from it, cuts the perpendicular of the front. The demilune face, $C'' F'$, is 96 yards, and ranges on a point D', at 30 yards from the point H. The flank, $F' E'$, ranges on a point at 2 yards from the point H, and is terminated on the counterscarp of the exterior enceinte, which is drawn from a point B, at 6 yards from O, tangent to an arc described from A, with a radius of 30 yards.

248...The salient of the demilune redoubt is at 46 yards from the point O. The face of the redoubt is 36 yards, and parallel to that of the demilune; its flank, $G' H'$, is also parallel to that of the demilune.

249...The demilune ditch is 20 yards, and that of the redoubt is 12 yards. The general arrangement of the covered-way is the same as in the 1st Method.

250...PROFILES. The profiles of the interior enceinte and of the demilune redoubt are alike, as shown on $C'' D''$; and those of the counterguard and demilune are the same as shown on $E'' F''$

251...The parapets of the towers are of stone, the flanks being pierced with two embrasures. The flanks of the casemates are also pierced for two guns. The centre of the tower is occupied by a stone traverse. The casemated flank, $Z W$, is pierced for only one gun—all the other defences are open.

252...Remark. The plan and profiles are referred to a plane of comparison taken 24 feet below the horizontal plane of site. The references are in feet and fractional parts of feet. The horizontal distances in yards and feet.

253...The leading idea which seems to have governed Vauban in the dispositions of his 2d and 3d Methods, was to make the interior enceinte serve as a general retrenchment with covered defences, which could be brought into play at the moment when an attempt was made to pass the interior ditch either by sap or openly. Besides this prominent feature of the 2d and 3d Methods, they are both great improvements on the 1st Method, in the greater dimensions given to the counterguards and demilunes; in the organization of the latter work with a permanent though small redoubt, and in the better cover afforded to the masonry of the two enceintes and the outworks, both from the relative position and relief of these elements. This last purpose, however, is but partially effected, for the interior enceinte, which, owing to the small flanks given to the demilune (which last have but a slight bearing on the defence, and, therefore, might have been omitted), and the opening between the tenaille and counterguard flanks can be breached from a position near the re-entering place of arms, and thus be exposed to assault at the same time that the breach of the counterguard is attacked. Besides this defect, a great part of the scarp wall of this enceinte in rear of the tenaille is exposed to the enemy's view over the tenaille, as the relief of this work has to be so far reduced that the fire of the counterguard flank can be brought to bear on the breach that may be made in the face of the opposite counterguard.

254...The stone towers are badly contrived, both for strength and defence. The upper platform, surrounded as it is with a stone parapet, and having a traverse of the same material in the centre, would be a perfect slaughter-house under a heavy fire of artillery directed against it.

The arches of the casemates are inconveniently placed for the service of the guns, and, having the exterior walls for one of their abutments, would give way with the destruction of these walls, and bring down all the superstructure by their fall.

255...Besides these defects, it may be observed that the interior enceinte and the counterguards have the same command, which would be found greatly to the disadvantage of the former as soon as the enemy has succeeded in gaining possession of the latter.

256...The low revetements of the counterguard and the wide berm at top, would subject this work to be assaulted by escalade at points along its face and flanks at the same time that an assault is made on its breach; thus paralyzing the action of temporary retrenchments thrown up within this work to protect the breach.

257...It was owing, probably, to these obvious defects, and the great cost of the bastioned towers, that Cormontaingne, who, in his writings, professes to follow out the leading ideas of Vauban, selected the main features of his 1st Method rather than those of his 2d and 3d, in the bastioned front which has received his name. Although imperfectly devised, both as to plan and construction, the 3d Method of Vauban presents more elements of resistance than Cormontaingne's front; and, with suitable modifications of the interior enceinte and the demilune to remedy the defects which have been pointed out, and by increasing the dimensions of the interior enceinte so as to afford good-sized bastions, with strong flanking dispositions, it would offer far superior defensive means than it now possesses.

Cormontaingne's Method.

258...Cormontaingne, the immediate successor of Vauban, holds a place only second to this master of the art in the estimation of the engineers of the French school. Cormontaingne, who to superior abilities united a wide range of experience, both in the construction and in the attack of permanent works, studied with great care the results of Vauban's immense labors. In working out the front which has received his name, Cormontaingne seems to have applied himself rather to remedy the defects noticeable in the methods of Vauban, than to produce any radical change in the combinations which had thus far received the sanction of engineers generally. He was thus led to reject the 1st and 2d Methods of Vauban from the defects which have been noticed, and also from the increased cost of constructing the bastioned towers, and to take the 1st Method as the basis of his own changes.

259...Cormontaingne was the first to develop clearly the influence of large demilunes on the progress of the attack, by their forming deep re-enterings between them in front of the bastion salients, and also the increased strength gained by fortifying on a right line, or on polygons with a great number of sides, as in both of these cases the fronts assailed cannot be enveloped by the assailant's works, and the demilunes from their salient position intercept the prolongations of the bastion faces, and thus mask them from the positions from which alone an enfilading fire could be brought upon them. Besides this, Cormontaingne lays down as a principle, that *no masonry* shall be exposed *to the distant batteries of the assailant;* and to obtain this point he has so arranged the height of his principal scarps, and the command given to the glacis crest in front of them, that the top of the scarp shall not lie above the level of this crest, thus masking the entire scarp, by the earth forming the glacis, from all positions in advance of the glacis crest.

His modifications of the plan and profile of Vauban's 1st Method, chiefly result from the above as a basis.

260...ENCEINTE. The modifications of Vauban's traçé, Fig. 4, Pl. 1, are different in the various works of Cormontaingne; but the following he indicates in his memoirs as the most perfect. The exterior side is 360 yards; the perpendicular $\frac{1}{6}$; the faces of the bastions $\frac{1}{3}$ of the exterior side; the flanks are 40 yards, and are so placed that the curtain shall be 120 yards; this combination makes the lines of defence somewhat less, and the bastions somewhat smaller, than in Vauban's method.

261...The dimensions of the enceinte ditch are so regulated by Cormontaingne as to furnish earth sufficient for the embankments. It is 28 yards wide at the salient, and from 2 to 4 yards wider opposite the tenaille; this admits the entire fire of the flanks to sweep the ditch.

262...TENAILLE. The tenaille is made with a curtain and wings; a ditch 10 yards wide being left between it, the curtain and the flanks.

263...DEMILUNE. Cormontaingne placed little value on small demilunes, as they form but slight and, therefore, weak re-enterings before the bastions, and, consequently, retard but little the enemy's attack upon the bastions; besides this, a small demilune covers but very imperfectly the shoulder angles of the bastions. To remedy these defects, his demilune is so laid out that the prolongations of the magistrals of its faces will intersect the bastion faces at 30 yards from the shoulder angles; the lengths of its faces being 120 yards.

264...By thus enlarging the demilune, sufficient space is gained to place a strong redoubt in its interior. The defence of the demilune may be made with more obstinacy, from the support it receives from the redoubt; and the enemy will be obliged to carry the redoubt before he can assault the breach he may have made in the bastion face, as this breach is seen in reverse by the fire of the flanks of the redoubt.

265...DEMILUNE REDUIT. To circumscribe as much as practicable the space in the demilune which the enemy, after he gains it, requires for his works, the extremity of the demilune terreplein, which is also the top of the counterscarp of the redoubt, is drawn at 20 yards from the magistral of the face; the ditch of the redoubt is 10 yards wide, and the magistral of its face is parallel with the counterscarp. By this arrangement the ditch of the redoubt is well flanked by the face of the bastion near the shoulder angle. To lay out the flanks of the redoubt, the counterscarps of the enceinte are prolonged to intersect the perpendicular of the front; from this point of intersection a distance of 20 yards is set off along each counterscarp, the two points thus obtained are joined by a right line, which is the gorge of the redoubt; from the extremities of the gorge two lines are drawn parallel to the capital of the demilune, these lines limit the terreplein of the flanks; the magistrals of the flanks are drawn parallel to and at 16 yards from the last lines. The ditch of the demilune is 20 yards wide; its depth is the same as that of the enceinte.

266...COVERED-WAY, ETC. The general width of the covered-way is 10 yards. Cormontaingne enlarged considerably the re-entering place of arms, to which he added a redoubt with a revetted scarp and counterscarp. The addition of this redoubt is a great improvement upon the covered-way of Vauban, who indicates in his works small redoubts of earth, or tambours of wood, for the same purpose. Cormontaingne's redoubt increases the strength of the covered-way; the troops assembled in the covered-way, for sorties, are secure under its fires; it sees in reverse, and protects any breach made in the face of the demilune; finally, it serves, in connection with the extremity of the demilune, to cover the opening left between the flanks of the bastion and the wings of the tenaille, through which, if a breach was made in the curtain, the interior retrenchments, resting upon either the flanks or faces of the bastion, could be turned.

267...To lay out the interior crests of the re-entering

place of arms, two points are taken on the counterscarps of the bastion and demilune, at 54 yards from their point of intersection; from these points as centres, with radii of 60 yards, arcs are described, whose intersection, joined with the centres, gives the direction of the faces. The magistral of its redoubt is found by a similar construction; distances of 40 yards being set off along the counterscarps, and the faces being drawn from these points so as to be 36 yards long. The ditch of the redoubt is 5 yards wide and 2½ yards deep.

268...Traverses are placed along the covered-way, to close the places of arms, defend the covered-way, and intercept projectiles fired in ricochet.

269...The crest of the glacis is broken into a cremaillére line, to allow room for the defiles of the traverses. The short branches of the cremaillére throw a fire on the salients of the covered-way; the positions of the long branches are so taken that the defiles may be seen and swept by the fire of the works in their rear.

270...PROFILES. Cormontaingne, after a series of trials, whose object was to give the ditches such dimensions that they should furnish the earth required for the embankments, regulated the command of the different works as follows. The lowest work, which is the demilune covered-way, he lays down as a rule, shall command the exterior ground by not less than 7½ feet; and the works most advanced shall be commanded by those in their rear.

271...It was found that, for the purpose of equalizing the excavations and embankments of the front, the crest of the demilune covered-way should have a command of 10½ feet above the natural ground. The crest of the bastion covered-way, and of the re-entering place of arms, command the crest of the demilune covered-way by 2 feet. The magistral of the enceinte is horizontal, its elevation being the same as the mean elevation of the crest of the bastion covered-way. The salient of the bastion commands its covered-way by 8 feet. The total height of the scarp is 30 feet. This dimension has since been generally adopted by engineers—

a wall of this height opposing a sufficient obstacle to an attempt at escalade. The absolute relief of the flanks is thus made $37\frac{1}{2}$ feet; with this relief a piece, firing under a depression of $\frac{1}{6}$ through an embrasure in the flank, and in the direction of the curtain, will strike the bottom of the ditch at the middle point of the curtain; so that were the relief increased, the length of curtain remaining the same, the ditch would no longer be thoroughly flanked.

272...The relief of the tenaille is determined as in Vauban's Method, so as not to mask the fire of the flanks upon the ditch opposite the extremity of the demilune, as it is here that a breach may be made in the bastion face through the ditch of the demilune.

273...The demilune is commanded by the enceinte, 3 feet, and by its own redoubt, $1\frac{1}{2}$ feet; the demilune, therefore, commands its covered-way, 7 feet, which is more than is indispensably requisite; for an enemy, standing on the crest of the covered-way, cannot have a plunging fire into a work in the rear of it if the latter commands the crest by 5 feet.

274...The redoubt of the re-entering place of arms commands the crest of the glacis only $4\frac{1}{2}$ feet; its interior crest is so placed as not to mask the fire of the bastion faces on the glacis in advance of it.

275...The interior crests of all the works are $7\frac{1}{2}$ feet above their terreplein, except that of the tenaille, which is $6\frac{1}{2}$ feet, and of the redoubt of the re-entering place of arms, which is 9 feet. The interior crests of the faces of all the works exposed to enfilading fires are one foot higher at the salients than at the extremities.

276...The profile of the parapet of the principal outworks is the same as that of the enceinte.

277...Communications. The communications are generally of the same nature, and placed about in the same positions, as in Vauban's Method.

278...Glacis. The planes of the glacis are so determined that they may be swept by the fire of the works in the rear; their inclination is usually about twenty-four base to one altitude.

279...INTERIOR RETRENCHMENTS. Cormontaingne indicates the gorge and shoulders of the bastion as the position for an interior retrenchment, when this addition to the front is made solely with a view of disputing the breach in the bastion and its interior with the assailant. In this case he gives the retrenchment the form of a tenaille, or a bastioned front, resting it either upon the shoulder angles of the bastion, or upon the two adjacent curtains, on points beyond the prolongation of the ditch between the tenailles and the flanks, and in this position he gives it the form of a bastioned front.

In the former case, the portion of the interior of the bastions between the flanks is preserved for the defence, but the retrenchment is liable to be turned, by a breach made in the flank, or in the portion of the curtain where it joins the flank. In the latter case, a breach in the bastion places the whole of the interior within view of the assailant, but the retrenchment itself is secure from its position from being turned, as a breach in the curtain cannot be made in rear of it.

280...CAVALIER. When a greater command of the site than that afforded by the enceinte is requisite on any front, Cormontaingne places a cavalier within the bastion. To this work he gives the same form as that of the bastion, placing the faces and flanks of the two parallel to each other. The faces of the cavalier are alone revetted, as well as the counterscarp of their ditch which is cut within the bastion. This ditch is broken off at the shoulder angles of the cavalier and directed upon the faces, these portions also having a revetted scarp and counterscarp. A parapet is thrown up behind the scarp and between the flank of the cavalier and the bastion faces, thus isolating the anterior portion of the bastion, and furnishing an interior retrenchment which, when the shoulders and flanks of the bastions are masked from the assailant's view, can only be carried by a breach made either in the cavalier face or in the portions resting on the cavalier and bastion faces.

281...REMARKS. From the preceding description, it appears that the most important modification made by Cormontaingne, in Vauban's 1st Method, consists in the means taken to cover the *masonry* from distant batteries; capacious bastions, susceptible of receiving efficient permanent interior retrenchments; an enlarged *demilune,* which places the bastions in strong re-enterings, covers the shoulder angles, and admits of a *redoubt* in its interior, which work strengthens the demilune, and sees in reverse the breach made in the bastion face; an enlarged re-entering place of arms, containing a redoubt, which strengthens the entire covered-way, and covers the movement of the troops in sorties.

282...These modifications, although of great value, and constituting an important step in the art, still leave much to be desired; and engineers, since Cormontaingne's time, have sought to remedy the defects of his method, of which the following are the principal. The enceinte has rather too slight a command, and is without any bomb-proof shelters: the inclination of the superior slope of its parapet, which is $\frac{1}{9}$, is too small to have the ditches well flanked; a breach can be made in the bastion face through the ditch of the demilune; there are dead spaces in the ditch of the demilune near the extremities of its faces; the redoubt of the re-entering place of arms is not tenable after the demilune is taken; the traverses of the covered-way do not afford the requisite protection to that work; finally, communications are mostly inconvenient, and not well covered from the assailant's fires.

Methods of the Schools of Mezieres and Metz.

283...The School of Application for engineer and artillery officers, first established at Mèzières and subsequently at Metz, has given to France, from about the period of the French Revolution down to the present day, the far greater portion of the many able officers who have gained such universal and deserved celebrity for these two corps.

284...In these schools the precepts of Vauban and Cormontaingne have been jealously guarded as the highest authority, and their manuscripts and published works have formed the basis of the instruction given in them.

285...Some slight modifications were proposed in the front of Cormontaingne by two engineers, *Chatillon* and *Duvigneau*, and taught by them in the course of permanent fortification given in the school. These changes chiefly consisted in enlarging the demilune and making it more salient; and in placing in the flanks of its redoubt casemates for cannon, with reverse views on the breaches that might be made in the bastion faces.

286...The teaching of the school of Metz has received its principal impress from General Noizet, himself a pupil of General Haxo, regarded as the first among the successors of Vauban and Cormontaingne, who, for several years, whilst a captain of engineers, performed the functions of professor of fortification, and who has recently given to the public the results of his lectures delivered in the school.

287...The front, which for some years back and up to the present time, has been taught in this school, goes by the appellation of *Noizet's Method.* In it there is no sensible departure from the views and methods of Vauban and Cormontaingne; the object being to introduce such modifications into the front of the latter as would remedy some of its acknowledged defects. In doing this, another object was kept in view, which was to present in the combinations of this front a problem, in the solution of which the pupil would be called upon to apply both the elementary principles of fortification and the geometrical methods that the engineer has to use as his principal tool in such problems to a special case, that of a front adopted to a *horizontal site.* It is in this point of view that the analysis and construction of this front have been adopted as the basis for the elementary instruction given in permanent fortification in this institution.

Noizet's Method.

288...General Requirements. Noizet, in his front, takes as the basis of the construction of the enceinte, the length of the exterior side and the command; assuming these within the limits laid down by Vauban and Cormontaingne; and in the combinations of outworks with the enceinte, following the latter engineer; introducing only such modifications as seem to best fulfil the general conditions of the problem, which are as follows:

1st. The enceinte must be secure from a surprise by escalade; present an unbroken line on every side by which it can be approached by the assailant; and have its scarp thoroughly swept by fire from within the enceinte.

2d. The parapets of the enceinte and outworks must be proof against projectiles of the heaviest calibre.

3d. The scarp walls of the enceinte and outworks must be masked from all positions that can be taken up by the assailant for his breaching batteries beyond the crest of the glacis.

4th. The flanking dispositions, both of the enceinte and

outworks, must be adapted to the range of small arms within accurate limits.

5th. The command of the enceinte must be so regulated as to overlook all the outworks and bring their interior, their ditches, the glacis and the site beyond it thoroughly under fire of both artillery and small arms.

6th. The command of the outworks must be so combined that the more advanced shall be commanded by the more retired; and, when this cannot be effected, the retired one, which is commanded by an advanced one, must have its interior defiled from the latter.

7th. The outworks must be so combined that they shall fall into the possession of the assailant in succession, from the more advanced to the more retired; and the more important ones should receive a sufficient height of scarp wall to secure them from being entered by a sudden rush of the enemy.

8th. There must be a sufficiency of the various kinds of communications to admit of a prompt circulation, both within the enceinte and to the exterior, for the ordinary service of the garrison and for sorties against the assailant.

289...General Data of the Enceinte. In the following description and analysis of the front of Noizet, the plane of comparison is assumed at 60 feet below the horizontal plane of site, the reference of which will be, therefore, (60,0). The yard is taken as the unit for the horizontal dimensions of the plan; and the foot as the unit for the references and vertical dimensions.

Converting the French measures into their equivalent English units, the exterior side of the front is 380 yards; the height of the scarp wall, 33 feet; the command of the interior crest of the curtain over the plane of site, 21 feet; and its height above the magistral, 13 feet.

290...Profile of Enceinte. Pl. 2, Fig. 4. The profile of the enceinte here given is similar to that of Cormontaingne, and was adopted by subsequent engineers until the more recently modified one already described. Its slopes and dimensions are as follows: The scarp and counterscarp slopes, $\frac{20}{1}$, or one base to twenty altitude. Exterior slope, $\frac{1}{1}$, or 45° Superior slope, $\frac{1}{6}$. Interior slope, $\frac{3}{1}$. Banquette-slope, $\frac{1}{2}$. Rampart-slope, $\frac{2}{3}$. Terrepleins 8 feet below the interior crests. Berm, 2 feet. Distance between the magistral and foot of the exterior slope, 1.5 feet. Thickness of parapet, 20 feet. Height of interior crest above the banquette-tread, 4.5 feet. Banquette-tread, 4.5 feet. General width of terreplein, estimated from the vertical through the interior crest, 48 feet.

291...MAGISTRAL OF THE CURTAIN. The length of this is determined by the condition that the artillery fire from the flanks, under the depression of $\frac{1}{6}$, shall attain a point at 1.5 feet above the bottom of the ditch, at the centre of the curtain; the bottom of the ditch itself, at the centre, being, for the purposes of drainage, 1.5 feet higher than at the extremities of the curtain, thus giving to the scarp a height of 31.50 feet at the centre, instead of 33 feet, the general height throughout the enceinte.

Supposing, now, a section, Pl. 2, Figs. 2, 4, to be made through the flanks by a vertical plane passed through the foot of the curtain scarp, and that a line be drawn in it, parallel to the superior slope and at 3 feet below it, to represent the direction of the artillery fire, this line must attain the point at 1.5 feet above the bottom of the ditch, at the centre of the curtain, to fulfil the required condition of a thorough flanking disposition throughout the entire extent of the enceinte. If, then, a horizontal line be drawn from the point to be attained to intersect the vertical through the interior crest, it will be the horizontal distance between the interior crest and the centre of the curtain, and, from the construction, will be equal to six times the perpendicular distance intercepted between it and the line of artillery fire.

Now, from the above there is given to calculate this base the entire height of the interior crest, above the bottom of the ditch, 44.50 feet; the height of the same point above the line of artillery fire, 3 feet; and the height of the point to be attained above the bottom of the ditch, 1.5 feet. The distance sought, therefore, will be 6(44.50 ft.—4.50 ft.)= 240 ft.

To obtain the length of the magistral corresponding to this distance, it will only be requisite to subtract from it the horizontal distance between the interior crest and the point of the section corresponding to the magistral of the flank. This last distance is composed of the thickness of the parapet, the base of the exterior slope, and the berm. The first is 20 feet. The second is found by taking from the height of the interior crest, above the magistral, which is 13 feet, one-sixth the thickness of the parapet, or 3.33 feet, which gives 13 ft.—3.33 ft.=9.66 feet. The third is 1.50 feet. The required distance, therefore, is 240 ft.—(20 ft.+9.66 ft.+1.50 ft.)=208.84 feet, or 69.61 yards.

292...MAGISTRAL OF ENCEINTE. Pl. 2, Fig. 5. Having found the length of the magistral of the curtain, the projection of the magistral of the enceinte on the plane of reference is determined as follows: Draw a line for the exterior side, and set off on it *A B*=380 yards; bisect this distance by a perpendicular, on which set off $CD=\frac{1}{6}$ *A B*= 63.33 yards; from *A* and *B* draw lines through *D*, these are the directions of the faces and lines of defence; draw a parallel to *CD*, on each side of it, and at 69.61 yards, the length of the half curtain, from it, join the points *G* and *H* where these parallels intersect the lines *A D* and *B D* prolonged; *G H* is the position of the curtain; *G B* and *H A* the lines of defence; from *G* and *H* draw a line, making an angle $\frac{1}{6}$ with the perpendicular, to the curtain at each of these points, the parts *G E* and *F H* of these last lines are the flanks; and *A E* and *B F* the faces.

293...The position of the magistral with respect to the plane of reference is determined as follows: The magistral of the curtain is horizontal. As it is 13 feet below the interior crest, and this line is placed at 21 feet above the plane of site, the magistral is 8 feet above this plane, and, therefore, from the position given the plane of comparison, 68 feet above this last plane; its reference, therefore, is (68.0) The flank is 1.5 feet lower at the shoulder than at the curtain angle, the reference of the shoulder is, then, (66.50). The face is horizontal, and its reference also (66.50.)

294...MANNER OF DETERMINING THE POSITION OF A POINT OF THE INTERIOR CREST. To determine the projection of a point of the interior crest contained in a profile plane, the height of the point above the magistral being known, we first subtract from this height $\frac{1}{6}$ the thickness of the parapet, the remainder will be the height of the exterior crest above the magistral, and, when the exterior slope is $\frac{1}{1}$, will also be the base of the slope; adding together the thickness of the parapet, the base of the exterior slope as just determined, and the distance from the foot of the exterior slope to the magistral, the sum will be the horizontal distance between the magistral and interior crest, or the distance to be set off, along the trace of the profile plane, from the magistral, to obtain the projection of the required point of the interior crest.

295...INTERIOR CREST OF THE ENCEINTE. Pl. 2, Fig. 6. The position of the interior crest above the magistral is fixed as follows: That of the curtain is parallel to the magistral, and 13 feet above it. Those of the flanks and faces of the bastion are contained in the same plane, the scale of declivity of which is taken parallel to the bastion capital. The position of this plane is determined by placing its horizontal, which coincides with a pancoupé 4.30 yards in length at the bastion salient, at 4.50 feet above the horizontal drawn through the points where the flanks join the curtain.

The reference of the interior crest of the curtain from the above data will, therefore, be (81.0); and the horizontal distance of any point of it from the magistral 31.16 feet, or 10.38 yards, as these two lines are parallel.

Having drawn the projection of the interior crest of the curtain, the point where it joins the flank may be determined approximately, and with sufficient accuracy, by bisecting the curtain angle of the magistrals, and taking the point, where the bisecting line cuts the interior crest, as the extremity of the flank. From this point, of which the reference is (81.0), if a line be drawn perpendicular to the bastion capital it will be horizontal (81.0) of the plane of the interior crests of the bastion; that at the pancoupé is 4.50 feet higher, and its reference will, therefore, be (85.50). To find the position of this last horizontal, which is also that of the pancoupé, draw two lines parallel to the bastion capital, and 2.15 yards from it, they will limit the pancoupé. Now, as the extremity of the pancoupé is a point of the interior crest of the bastion face, and its reference is (85.50), the height of this point above the magistral is 19 feet, as the reference of this last line is (66.50). The horizontal distance, therefore, from this point to the magistral is (20 ft.+15.66 ft.+1.50 ft.)=37.16 ft.=12.38 yds. Drawing a parallel, therefore, to the magistral of the face, and at 12.38 yards from it, the point where it cuts the parallel to the capital, at 2.15 yards from it, will be the required point, through which the horizontal (85.50) is drawn.

Having two horizontals of the plane, its scale of declivity can be constructed, and other horizontals be determined. The projection of the point of the interior crest of the face on any given horizontal, can be found by the same process as the one just described. For example, take the horizontal, (84.0); the perpendicular distance of the point on it from the magistral is (20 ft.+14.16 ft.+1.50 ft.)=35.66 ft. or 11.88 yds. The two points thus determined being joined, will give the projection of the interior crest of the face.

To find that of the flank, of which one point, (81.0), has been found, bisect the shoulder angle of the magistral, the point where the bisecting line cuts the interior crest of the face will give, approximately, the other extremity of the line required.

The constructions for the interior crests, just given, are only approximations to a true result; as the horizontal distances calculated, being those contained in profile planes, ought to have been set off perpendicular to the projection of the interior crest; but the difference between the results of this approximate method and one rigorously accurate will, in the present case, be so small, owing to the slight divergence between the projections of the magistral and interior crest of the face, as not to affect, in any appreciable degree, the real positions of the required points. The same remarks are applicable to the constructions for finding the extremities of the flank.

296...PARAPET OF ENCEINTE. Having drawn the interior crest of the enceinte, all the other lines of the parapet—except the foot of the exterior slope—and the inward line of the terreplein are drawn parallel to it. The foot of the exterior slope is drawn parallel to the magistral.

TERREPLEIN OF ENCEINTE. Pl. 2, Fig. 6. The terrepleins of the faces and flanks are in a plane parallel to that of their interior crest and 8 feet below it, estimated vertically. To find the reference of any horizontal of the terreplein, it will be only necessary to subtract 8 feet from the corresponding one of the interior crests. Thus, (85.50) being a reference of a horizontal of the interior crest, that of the terreplein corresponding is (77.50.)

The terreplein of the curtain slopes 1 foot from the foot of the banquette-slope to its inward line, which places this last line 9 feet below the interior crest.

297...RAMPART-SLOPE AND RAMPS. Pl. 2, Fig. 6. The rampart-slopes are planes of $\frac{4}{3}$, passed through the inward lines of the terrepleins. The lines of intersection of the rampart-slopes and plane of site are found in the usual way.

The ramps leading from the plane of site to the terreplein receive an inclination of $\frac{1}{6}$, and they are 4.30 yards wide. Two of them are placed on the curtain, one on the flank, and one on the face.

298...ANALYSIS OF CONSTRUCTIONS ADOPTED FOR THE ENCEINTE. Noizet, in the plan of his enceinte, has adopted dimensions and constructions which give results, for the most part, the same as those of Vauban and Cormontaingne, making the defensive properties of these different methods about equal. The extent of the exterior side, the length of the curtain, the diminished angle, and the direction assumed for the flanks, produce a combination by which an efficient flanking, both as to direction and amount of fire, for the entire scarp, and a powerful cross-fire upon the covered-way and its glacis in advance of the bastion salient. The lines of defence, by this combination, being within the effective range of small arms, and the flanks capable of receiving a battery superior to the counter-battery that can be brought against them from the glacis crest of the opposite covered-way.

299...The dimensions and form of the profile are those usually adopted for permanent works, where the embankments are formed of ordinary earth, and the revetement walls of good masonry.

They are such as experience has shown will give durability and stability to the masonry, from the pressure of the embankments and the ordinary causes of destructibility to which it is liable when exposed to the weather; and to the rampart and parapet the strength to resist the action of the heaviest artillery; whilst they offer to the assailed every convenience for their prompt action and the use of their arms.

300...The width and slopes of the ramps are regulated for the passage of artillery. Where the height to be overcome is slight, as that between the terreplein and barbette, the slope of the ramp may be as great as $\frac{1}{6}$, and its width be 3.30 yards. Where the height is greater, the declivity of the ramp should be proportionally less steep, and its width be 4.30 yards at least.

301...The position of the terreplein with respect to the interior crests, is that usually considered necessary to give shelter to the troops and materiel on it. By inclining that of the bastion, the *materiel* and *personnel* on the faces and flanks are better covered from the enfilading and richochet fire than they would be if the terreplein was horizontal: as a ball passing over the salient will reach an inclined terreplein at a point farther from the salient than one which is horizontal. The height, 4.50 feet, at which the salient is placed above the curtain, is as great as can be admitted in a hexagon, the least polygon to which the traçé adopted is applicable; because, if placed higher, the plane of the interior crest of the bastion, prolonged back, would intersect the plane of site in a line which would fall without the salients of the two adjacent bastions of the polygon, and these bastions would, therefore, not cover the one between them from reverse fire.

The slopes, moreover, of the terrepleins keep them in a serviceable state, by not allowing the rain-water to collect and remain upon them.

302...PARTICULAR CONDITIONS OF THE OUTWORKS. The outworks, besides satisfying the general conditions already laid down, are connected with each other by several minor relations of defence and suitableness, growing out of their relative positions, which give rise to many seemingly arbitrary constructions and details for each one, the bearing of which cannot be clearly explained until a description of the whole as a system has been gone into.

303...The scarp walls of outworks, as well as their gorges where they are exposed to be turned, should not be less than 12 feet high, to secure them from a sudden open assault.

304...Their parapets are of the same form as that of the enceinte; and for the more important ones, which are much exposed to the artillery of the assailant, of the same dimensions. In those less exposed, the thickness of the parapet may be reduced to 12 feet, or 4 yards.

305...The terrepleins of the smaller outworks, which are not habitually armed with artillery, should not be less than 8 yards; those of the larger should not be less than 10 yards.

306...The banquette-treads of outworks, which, like the caponnières and covered-ways, require a palisading for their greater security from assault, should be 6 feet wide.

307...TENAILLE. Pl. 3, Figs. 1, 2. The form of the tenaille is that of Cormontaingne's front; the magistral of its curtain being parallel to that of the curtain of the enceinte, and the scarp of its wings on the prolongation of the scarp of the bastion faces.

308...A ditch of 13 yards is left between the gorge of the tenaille and the enceinte curtain, and one of 11 yards between each of its wings and the flanks. The magistral of its curtain is horizontal, and 13 feet above the crests of the double caponnière. The magistral of each wing is a broken line, the lowest point of it being 13 feet above the bottom of the enceinte ditch. Its gorge and the extremities of its wings are revetted. Its interior crest is horizontal throughout, and 4.50 feet below the magistral of the enceinte curtain. The thickness of its parapet, 12 feet. The width of the terreplein at its curtain, 8.66 yards. The parapet is terminated at the wings by traverses 12 feet thick, which extend from the interior crest to the scarp wall of the wings; the top of each traverse is on the same level as the interior crest. The traverses are terminated toward the parapet by planes of $\frac{1}{1}$.

309...To construct the principal lines of the tenaille from the preceding data, first draw a line parallel to the enceinte curtain, and 13 yards from it, for the gorge of the tenaille curtain; another line parallel to this, and at 8.66 yards, is the interior crest, of which the reference is (63.50), as it is 4.50 feet below the enceinte magistral at the curtain.

310...A level passage at 31.50 feet below the magistral of the enceinte curtain and at the reference (36.50), leads from the main ditch, between the enceinte and tenaille, under this last work, and through a double caponnière in the main ditch in advance of it. The crests of the caponniere are 9 feet above the level of the passage and at the reference (45.50); and the magistral of the tenaille curtain 13 feet above these crests, and at the reference (58.50). The interior crest of the tenaille having the reference (63.50), is, therefore, 5 feet above its magistral. The horizontal distance, then, between the magistral and interior crest, Art. 65, is $12 + 3 + 1.5 = 16.5$ ft., or 5.50 yds.; and as these lines are horizontal, their projections will be parallel and at this distance apart.

311...The interior crest and magistral of the wing will result from the following data: The scarp wall of the wing extends to the top of the traverse reference (63.50); its magistral then descends from this level in the plane of $\frac{1}{1}$, which terminates this traverse, to a level of 13 feet above the bottom of the enceinte ditch, which, being at this part 3 feet lower than the passage of the double caponnière, and at reference (33.50), will give (46.50) for the reference of the lowest point of the magistral of the wing; the reference of the point where it joins that of the curtain being, as already determined (58.50).

312...To find, then, the lowest point of this magistral, draw a line 12 feet, or 4 yards, from the extremity of the wing, for the exterior line of the traverse; parallel to this line draw another at 17 ft. = 5.66 yds., which is the base of the slope of $\frac{1}{1}$ that terminates the traverse, where this line cuts the line of defence is the required point. The horizontal distance between this point and the interior crest, calculated in the usual manner, is 12+15+1.50=28.50 ft.= 9.50 yds.

313...Describing, from the point just found, an arc, with a radius 9.50 yards, and from the other extremity of the magistral another arc, with a radius 5.50 yards, and drawing a tangent to these arcs, it will be the interior crest of the wings.

314...The gorge line of the wing is not drawn parallel to the interior crest, but determined as follows: From the point of intersection of the interior crests of the curtain and wings, describe an arc with a radius 8.66 yards; from the point where the enceinte curtain magistral prolonged cuts the interior crest of the opposite flank, draw a line tangent to this arc, which will be the direction of the required line.

315...The gorge wall rises to the level of the terreplein. That which terminates the wing is limited by the planes of the parapet, terreplein, and top of the traverse, and is termed a *profile wall*, from the form of its outline.

316...ANALYSIS OF CONSTRUCTIONS, ETC., OF THE TENAILLE. The tenaille is more important as a mask than as a defensive work. It covers the postern in the curtain, and also the masonry of the flanks and curtain from the enemy's batteries; which last is an essential point, if there are interior retrenchments resting either on the flanks or curtain of the enceinte, as it will then be impracticable for an enemy to turn them, as he cannot make a breach in the enceinte behind the tenaille. As a defensive work its fire bears upon the ditches and their counterscarps, and it thus serves to cover the retreat of the troops from the other outworks. When the ditches are dry it is an indispensable part of the front, as the space in its rear forms a large place of arms, where troops can be assembled to manœuvre against the enemy when in the ditches.

317...Vauban and Cormontaingne, we have seen, so fixed the relief of the tenaille as not to mask the fire of the flanks on the breach in the bastion. It is on this principle that Noizet has determined the position of its interior crest, and placed it at 4.50 feet below the magistral of the curtain.

318...In regulating its scarp wall, it is supposed that an enemy would attempt an assault from some point in the dead space in front of it; and its height is, therefore, arranged so that no part of it shall be less than 13 feet above any point that the enemy might there occupy

319...The position given to its interior crest still leaves some portion of the masonry behind it exposed; but, were the exposed part battered away, there would be still a formidable height of scarp left to the enceinte, the parapet of which, also, would be but slightly diminished in thickness by it. The portion of the enceinte flank exposed, near the shoulder angle, would be very considerable were the exterior slope of the tenaille parapet extended to the extremity of the wing; it is to prevent this that a traverse is here placed.

320...The tenaille is seldom armed with cannon, although mortars are frequently placed in it; on this account *its terreplein is reduced to* 8.66 *yards.*

321...Every part of the ditch between the tenaille and curtain should be swept by the flanks. It is to satisfy this condition that the gorge line of the wing is so drawn as to be seen by the piece that flanks the curtain of the enceinte.

322...The tenaille, although procuring decided advantages to the bastioned form, deprives it of one of its characteristic points—that of flanking every part of the ditch. For, in front of the tenaille, there is a dead space, where an assailant could assemble in safety to assault it. This defect, however, is of trifling magnitude, since, were the tenaille taken, he could not establish himself in it; and the width given to the ditch, between it and the enceinte flank, is such as to preclude any attempt to escalade the enceinte from the top of the tenaille.

323...The terreplein of the tenaille is inclined, for the purpose of defiling it from the enemy's establishment on the terreplein of the demilune redoubt. The inclination of the plane of defilement depends on the arrangement of this redoubt.

324...Double Caponniere. Pl. 3, Figs. 1, 2. The passage of the double caponnière is 3.30 yards wide at the bottom, and on the same level as the bottom of the ditch at the middle of the curtain reference (36.50). The interior crests of this work are at 9 feet above the bottom of the passage; they are horizontal, and their reference (45.50). In the profile of the caponnière, the base of the interior slope is 0.50 yards; the banquette is 2.0 yards wide; and the base of the banquette-slope, 3.0 yards; the horizontal distance, then, between the interior crest and the foot of the banquette-slope is, 5.50 yards, which, being doubled and added to 3.30 yards, the width of the passage, gives 14.30 yards for the distance between the interior crests. The crests are drawn parallel to the perpendicular of the front, and limited by the curtain of the tenaille on one side and a line drawn parallel to and 3.30 yards within the exterior side on the other.

325...The embankment of the caponnière is terminated on the exterior by a glacis, which is prolonged to the bottom of the ditch. This glacis is determined by passing a plane through the interior crest of the caponnière, and through the shoulder angle of the interior crest of the opposite bastion lowered three feet.

326...The caponnière is terminated toward the exterior side by a profile wall along the line, at 3.30 yards within the exterior side; this wall is prolonged from the exterior line of the banquette-tread to a point at 2.0 yards beyond the interior crest; at this point the direction of the wall is changed, so that, being prolonged, it may cut the interior crest of the enceinte flank, at a point 4.0 yards from the shoulder angle. The remaining part of the embankment on this side is terminated in a glacis, the plane of which is passed through the interior crest of the enceinte curtain, and through a line on the bottom of the main ditch, at 4.0 yards within the exterior side. This plane intersects the first glacis in a line, *ab*, Pl. 3, Fig. 2, which is prolonged to its intersection, *b*, with a line, *bc*, on the first glacis, at 6.66 yards from the interior crest. A part of the first glacis is terminated at this line, by a plane of $\frac{1}{1}$; the line of intersection of this plane of $\frac{1}{1}$ with the second glacis, is prolonged to intersect the line of the wall directed on the flank, which gives the point where this wall terminates.

As the bottom of the enceinte ditch has not yet been fixed throughout, its intersection with the first glacis still remains to be determined.

327...Analysis of the Double Caponniere. The caponnière serves both as a communication and as a defensive work for the ditch. As the former, the passage should admit of a convenient circulation, without being too wide, which has determined its width at 3.30 yards. The interior crests should cover the troops within the caponnière from the enemy's establishments on the crest of the bastion covered-way; a relief of 9 feet has been found sufficient for this purpose.

328...As a defensive work, its fire should sweep the ditch. It is for this purpose that its embankments are arranged on the interior as an ordinary parapet and on the exterior in the form of a glacis. Its banquette-tread is made 2.0 yards wide, as it should be palisaded.

329...In order that the embankment of the caponnière may not, by its relief, form dead spaces in the ditch, the plane of the first glacis is arranged so as to be swept by the artillery fire of the opposite flank. The plane of the second glacis and the return wall are so arranged as to be swept by the fire of the curtain and of a part of the flank.

The portion of the first glacis, near the extremity, is made into a *glacis coupè*, leaving a sufficient thickness of parapet to cover the passage.

330....MAGISTRALS OF DEMILUNE SCARP AND COUNTERSCARP. Pl. 3, Fig. 3. To construct the magistral of the demilune, two points are taken on the exterior side at 103 yards from the perpendicular; through these points perpendiculars are drawn to the exterior side; the points where they cut the magistral of the bastion faces are joined, and on this line an equilateral triangle is constructed, its sides will give the directions of the magistral of the demilune. The extremity, *b*, of the demilune face, is found by drawing a line at 11 yards without the exterior side.

The counterscarp of the demilune is parallel to the scarp and at 18 yards.

331....COUNTERSCARP OF THE ENCEINTE. Pl. 3, Fig. 3. To construct the counterscarp of the enceinte, an arc is described from the salient of the bastion, with a radius of 26 yards; a perpendicular, *b f*, of 6.60 yards, is drawn to the demilune face; if a tangent be now drawn to the arc, and a perpendicular be demitted from the point *f*, on the tangent, their point of intersection, *f'*, should fall on the line drawn through the extremity of the double caponnière, parallel to the exterior side. The point, *f'*, is found by constructing the curve, which is the locus of the above conditions. The arc, with the tangent drawn through *f'*, is the magistral of the counterscarp.

332...REDOUBT OF THE RE-ENTERING PLACE OF ARMS. Pl. 3, Fig. 3. To determine the magistral of the redoubt of the re-entering place of arms, a line is drawn through the point, *b*, of the demilune face, and the extremity of the curtain, and prolonged beyond the demilune counterscarp.

A point, *a*, is next taken on the perpendicular, at 5.0 yards from the demilune salient; and through this point and a point, *c*, assumed on the demilune counterscarp, an indefinite line is drawn. A line, *c d*, is next drawn, making an angle of 60° with the line *a c*. Two lines, *c′ d′* and *c′ c″*, are drawn, the first parallel to *c d*, and 4.30 yards from it; the second parallel to *a c*, and at 2.0 yards from it. If the point of intersection, *c′*, of these two lines falls on the line drawn through *b*, it will be the angular point of the redoubt; and the line *c′ d′*, the magistral of one of its faces. If the point *c′*, does not fall on the line drawn through *b*, then a second point, *c′*, must be chosen, and the same construction be again made. The different intersections, *c′*, will be points of a curve, which is the locus of the above conditions; and the intersection of this curve with the line drawn through *b*, will give the required point. Having the face *c′ d′*, the other face is determined as follows: a line is drawn parallel to the demilune counterscarp, and at 27.0 yards from it; a point is found on this line, at 7.83 yards from *c′ d′*; from this point, with a radius of 7.83 yards, an arc is described; a tangent drawn to this arc, from a point on the interior crest of the bastion face, at 13 yards from the pancoupé, is the direction of the required face, *d′ d″*, which is terminated at the bastion counterscarp.

333...Pl. 3, Fig. 3, and Pl. 4, Fig. 1. The ditch of the redoubt is horizontal; and the reference of its bottom is determined by supposing the plane of the superior slope of the bastion face to be prolonged to the enceinte counterscarp, finding the reference of the point, *d″*, in this plane, and taking a point 4.50 feet below this; the reference thus found is (57.90). The scarp wall of the redoubt is 13 feet high, the reference of its magistral will, therefore, be (70.90).

334...The salient of the interior crest is 5.33 feet above the magistral—its reference is, therefore, (76.23); and its projection is evidently the point which we have already determined, at 7.83 yards from the magistral. The interior crest of the face, *d′ d″*, has a slope of two feet from the salient to the extremity of this face, which condition fixes the extreme point of the interior crest at 7.16 yards from the magistral.

Having the interior crest of one face, that of the other, $c' d'$, is found from the scale of declivity of the plane of the interior crest. This scale is drawn parallel to the bastion capital, and since we have already found two points of the interior crest, by referring them to this scale we can, as in the case of the bastion, Art. 294, determine any required point of the other face.

335...A small flank of 6.0 yards is made perpendicular to the line $c' c''$, the line of the profile wall of the face, $c' d'$

336...The terreplein of the redoubt is 8.66 yards wide; its gorge is revetted with a wall 13 feet high.

337...ANALYSIS OF THE REDOUBT, ETC. Having given the construction of the principal lines of the redoubt, we will now give the reasons in support of them.

338...We first observe that, on account of the ditch between the tenaille and the enceinte flank, a breach might be opened in the curtain, by means of a battery established on the glacis of the re-entering place of arms, if there was no mask between the ditch referred to and this glacis. By placing the angle, c, of the redoubt on the line drawn through the extremity of the curtain, and the extremity, b, of the demilune, it is readily seen that these two works, so combined, cover the opening left by the ditch; since it will be necessary to battle down either the angle c', or the angle b, to unmask the curtain. The means here resorted to is of frequent use in fortification; and the problem may be thus stated: *a line being given, which is partially covered by an existing mass from fires in a given direction, to interpose another mass which, combined with the first, shall entirely mask the given line.*

We have thus established that the point, c', shall be found on the line drawn through b and the extremity of the enceinte curtain.

The communication along the gorge of the redoubt to its ditch, is by means of stairs placed along the profile wall, $c' c''$ The width of the stairs is 2.0 yards. The stairs, like all other communications, to be safe, must be covered from the enemy's fire. The point where the enemy can establish himself, to fire on the stairs, is along the crest of the demilune covered-way, around the salient place of arms. It is readily seen, from the position of the stairs and the demilune, that this work will partially cover the stairs; and, therefore, we shall only have to interpose some other mask, combined with it, to attain the object in view. The mask used is the point c, which is the angle of masonry formed by the counterscarp walls of the demilune and redoubt; the ditch of the redoubt being here 4.30 yards wide. The position of the point a, through which the line $a c$ is drawn, is so taken on the exterior slope of the demilune parapet, that the line of fire drawn through it will pass over a man's head at the top of the stairs.

339...The angle, c', between the profile wall and face wall, is made 60°, as this is the minimum angle for masonry, to give it sufficient strength. The minimum is here taken to bring the face, $c' d'$, as far in as possible, and thereby make the re-entering as deep as the case will admit of.

340...The object of the redoubt is to strengthen the covered-way, and sweep with its fire the enemy's establishments on the glacis of the demilune. The principal works on this glacis are the breach and counter-batteries, which occupy a space of about 17.0 yards, estimated from the crest of the glacis; if to this we add 10 yards, for the mean width of the covered-way, we obtain the distance 27.0 yards, which is the least distance that the salient of the redoubt can be from the counterscarp of the demilune, to sweep the entire flank of the batteries.

341...The direction given to the face, $d' d''$, is such as to allow of its being flanked by the bastion face. The face is thrown out as far toward the salient of the bastion covered-way as possible, for the purpose of crowding the space along the crest of this covered-way, which the enemy requires for his batteries.

342...The redoubt being directly in front of the bastion

face, its relief should be so reduced that the fire of this face may not be too much masked. To effect this, we commence by establishing the bottom of its ditch, so that the point of it nearest the bastion may just be seen by the musketry fire of the face; we then adopt nearly a minimum relief of scarp wall; finally, we arrange the interior crest of one face, so as to allow no exterior slope at one extremity, and make the other at the salient 2 feet higher. This slope of 2 feet and the direction given to the scale of declivity of the interior crest, determine a plane of defilement for the redoubt, the prolongation of which will pass at about 3 feet above the salients of the two demilunes, which are symmetrically situated with respect to the bastion capital. This is done in accordance with a principle generally adopted, that when one work is less advanced than another, and commanded by it, the plane of its interior crest prolonged should pass 3 feet above the points which the enemy can occupy on the advanced work—which, from the nature of the attack, must fall first into his possession—so that he may not have a plunging fire into the retired work, from his establishments, which are generally about 3 feet above the parapet of the work occupied.

343...The small flank of 6.0 yards perpendicular to the profile wall, is to obtain a reverse fire on the breach made in the demilune. The gorge of the redoubt is revetted to secure it from an assault.

344...Demilune Redoubt. Pl. 3, Fig. 3, and Pl. 4, Figs. 1, 2. The salient of the redoubt is 33.0 yards from the magistral of the demilune; finding a point on the perpendicular, at this distance from the magistral, we obtain the salient. The magistral of the face is found, by drawing a line from this point to the interior shoulder angle of the bastion.

345...To find the position of the interior crests of the face, the reference of the magistral must be given, and the scale of declivity of the plane of the interior crest. To determine the first, the salient of the demilune interior crest is placed at 3 feet below that of the enceinte curtain;

this gives (78.0) for the reference of this point. The salient of the magistral of the redoubt is fixed at 8 feet below the salient of the demilune, which gives its reference (70.0). The magistral slopes from the salient toward the exterior side, and this slope is arranged so that the point where the magistral cuts the exterior side shall be 5.70 feet, or 1.90 yards lower than the salient; the reference, then, of this point will be (64.30). Having thus two points of the magistral, its position is fixed.

346...To determine now the interior crest, a pancoupé of 4.30 yards is made in the salient of the redoubt, and this commands the salient of the demilune by 1.5 feet. The reference, then, of the pancoupé, is (79.50). From the pancoupé to the gorge of the redoubt, which is on the exterior side, the plane of the interior crest has a slope of 1.5 feet, and its scale of declivity is parallel to the perpendicular. To find the crest from the above data, it may be observed that the problem is similar to the one already solved, Art. 294, in the case of the bastion; except here, the magistral being an inclined line, the distance of any one of its points, to the point on the interior crest, contained in a profile, is not known, since only one of the points is given. The following is the method, which applies to all similar cases for doing this: It will be observed that, if the foot of the exterior slope be drawn, it will have the same slope as the magistral. Through the foot of the exterior slope, then, which is known, the plane of the exterior slope whose inclination is $\frac{1}{1}$, is passed. If any horizontal line be now drawn in this plane, the horizontal distance, Art. 294, between this line and a known point of the interior crest, contained in a profile, can be readily found.

To apply this to the case in point, first draw the foot of the exterior slope, which is 0.50 yard from the magistral; the reference of this line at the salient is (70.0), and at the gorge (64.30). To obtain the horizontal of the plane of the exterior slope whose reference is (70.0), describe from the point (64.30) an arc, with a radius 5.70 feet, or 1.90

yards; the tangent drawn to this arc from the point (70.0), is the required line. The reference of the pancoupé being (79.50), its distance from this horizontal line—the thickness of the parapet being 20.0 feet—is 26.17 feet, or 8.72 yards; and the reference of the interior crest at the gorge being (78.0), its distance from the same line is 8.22 yards; the two points thus found fix the position of the interior crest of the face.

347...The redoubt is made with flanks, the interior crests of which are parallel to the perpendicular, 22.0 yards in length. To find the flanks, draw a line parallel to the exterior side, and at 22.0 yards; where this cuts the interior crests of the faces will be the interior shoulder angles of the redoubt, from which the flanks are drawn parallel to the perpendicular.

The magistral of the flank is horizontal, its position is, therefore, easily found.

348...Joining the point, *b*, of the demilune, with the extremity of the interior crest of the flank; the direction of the wall which terminates the flank, the ditch of the redoubt and the extremity of the demilune is found.

349...The terreplein of the redoubt along the face is 8.66 yards wide; along the flank the width is 11.0 yards. This terreplein, which is 8 feet below the plane of the interior crest, is called the *upper*, to distinguish it from the remaining interior space, called the *lower terreplein*, and which is 13 feet below the upper. A portion of the upper terreplein, for a length of about 14.0 yards from the extremity of the flank, is sustained by a wall of masonry. A portion of the interior space between the terrepleins of the two flanks, for about 6.0 yards from the exterior side, is excavated to the bottom of the ditch.

350...The upper terreplein, along the face, is connected with the lower by a slope of $\frac{2}{3}$. Two ramps 3.30 yards wide, with a slope of $\frac{1}{6}$, connect the two terrepleins. The details of these constructions are best studied from Pl. 4, Fig. 1. The scarp wall of the redoubt is 16.50 feet high.

351...Analysis, etc., of the Demilune Redoubt. As the

object of the demilune redoubt has been already explained, the reasons for the constructions employed in determining its dimensions, etc., only remain to be stated.

352...The redoubt should be as advanced as possible, to see in reverse the lodgments of the enemy on the glacis of the collateral works. To effect this, its salient is taken at 33.0 yards from the demilune magistral; this distance is sufficient to allow their proper dimensions to the parts of the demilune.

353...The face of the redoubt is directed on the interior shoulder angle of the bastion, to have its ditch flanked by the bastion face.

354...In placing the salient of the magistral at 8 feet below the salient of the demilune, the top of the scarp wall will be nearly on the level with the demilune terreplein. This arrangement will force an enemy, lodged on the demilune terreplein, either to lower his battery, to effect a breach in the redoubt, or else to employ a mine for this purpose; either of which operations will cost him much labor and loss of time.

355...The least command has been given to the redoubt over the demilune, to enable the fire of the redoubt to sweep the demilune terreplein. This command of 1.50 feet, with the slope given to the plane of the interior crest, will prevent an enemy from having a plunging fire into the redoubt from his lodgments in the demilune.

356...The flanks of the redoubt are principally to procure a reverse fire on the breach in the bastion face; their length estimated for 3 guns.

The piece nearest the extremity of one flank should be covered by the extremity of the opposite flank, from the reverse fire which might come through the redoubt from the enemy's lodgment on the bastion covered-way

The terreplein of the flank is made 11.0 yards, as it is habitually armed.

357...In the outworks, wherever it can conveniently be done, bomb-proof arches should be made, to serve as magazines, shelters, etc. This point has been effected in the redoubt, by the position given to the lower terreplein; by this means, sufficient space is gained under the flank for a bomb-proof shelter. The terreplein of the flank is sustained by a wall, which is the interior facing of the shelter.

358. The scarp wall of the redoubt might have been reduced to the minimum dimension of 12 feet. But, on account of its importance, and, also, not to diminish too much the interior space, it has been found that the dimensions adopted, 16.50 feet, best satisfy the requisite conditions. The top of the wall slopes toward the gorge, so that at the shoulder angle it may be about 4 feet lower than at the salient; the object of this is, to expose as small a portion of the wall as possible to the enemy's fire through the demilune cut, which, from its width, might admit of a breach being made in the redoubt, through it, from the enemy's lodgment on the re-entering place of arms. It will be seen further on, how the scarp of the redoubt is covered by the bottom of the cut.

359...DEMILUNE AND ITS CUT. Pl. 3, Fig. 3, and Pl. 4, Fig. 1. To return now to the demilune, and finish what relates to it and the cut in its face.

360...To construct the scarp of the cut, the face, *c′ d′*, of the redoubt of the re-entering place of arms, is produced to intersect the magistral of the demilune; joining this point with the interior shoulder angle of the demilune redoubt, the magistral of the scarp is obtained.

361...The exterior width of the cut is found by setting off 6.60 yards on the demilune magistral, from the point where it is intersected by the face, *c′ d′* To obtain the interior width, an arc, with the radius of 10 yards, is described from the exterior shoulder angle of the demilune redoubt; a tangent is drawn to this arc, parallel to the face of the redoubt; this tangent gives the direction of a wall which limits the cut on the interior, and also the portion of the demilune, from the cut to the extremity of the face. From the point where the magistral of the cut intersects the tangent, set off 11.0 yards, which is the width of the cut on the interior. This point joined with the point on the exterior, gives the counterscarp of the cut.

362...A parapet 20 feet thick is made behind the scarp of the cut. The relief of this parapet is so determined that, at the highest point of the magistral, which is the point on the interior, there shall be no exterior slope; which places the interior crest 3.33 feet above the magistral at this point. The scarp wall itself, at this point, is 13 feet above the bottom of the cut on the interior; and the interior line of the bottom is 13 feet nearly above the bottom of the ditch of the redoubt. These conditions fix the reference of this point of the magistral at (76.17). The interior crest, which is horizontal, is, therefore, at the reference (79.50).

363...The bottom of the cut has a slope of 4.80 feet from the interior to the demilune scarp; and the magistral of the cut is parallel to the bottom, and at 13 feet above it. This gives the reference of the exterior point of the magistral (71.37). The magistral of the demilune, from this exterior point to the point *b*, is held horizontal and at the same reference (71.37). The parapet of this portion of the demilune face is 12 feet thick; its interior crest is determined by passing a plane through the interior crest of the parapet behind the cut, and allowing the prolongation of this plane to pass 3 feet above the demilune salient. The preceding data are sufficient to determine the lines in question.

364...Analysis of the Cut. The cut isolates the part of the demilune, near the extremity of the face, from the salient portion; this part being arranged with a parapet behind the cut, can be defended after the enemy has effected a lodgment on the demilune salient. The cut thus prevents the enemy from driving the besieged from the redoubt of the re-entering place of arms; which he might do, were the whole demilune to fall at once into his possession.

365...The position of the cut is so determined as to allow the face of the demilune redoubt to flank the face, *c' d'*. Widening the cut on the interior facilitates this object.

By making the interior line of the bottom of the cut 13

feet above the bottom of the ditch, the scarp of the demilune redoubt is partly covered; and, at the same time, an obstacle is placed in the way of an enemy, who might attempt to carry the work behind the cut by first getting into the cut.

366...It will be seen, in examining the demilune ditch, that the slope, 4.80 feet, given to the bottom of the cut, still leaves a height of 15 to 18 feet between the exterior line and the bottom of the demilune ditch, which will secure the cut from an assault on that side. The object of this slope is chiefly so to diminish the height of that part of the demilune scarp, from the cut to the point *b*, that it may not be exposed to a battery, which can be placed on the glacis of the re-entering place of arms.

367...As to the interior crest, it is placed as low as possible, and is arranged to cover the interior from the plunging fire of the enemy when established on the demilune salient.

368...DEMILUNE. Pl. 4, Fig. 2. To return to the demilune, of which only the magistral and the relief of the interior crest at the salient have been determined.

The magistral at the salient is placed 11.40 feet below the interior crest; and as the reference of the latter is (78.0), the reference of the former will be (66.60). The magistral has a slope of 1.50 feet from the salient to the cut; and the interior crest is parallel to the magistral; this condition will determine the interior crest when the salient is known; and this is arranged so as to have a pancoupé of 4.30 yards.

The scarp wall of the demilune is 22.50 feet high.

369...The terreplein is 11.0 yards wide. A ramp, 3.30 yards wide, having a slope of $\frac{1}{6}$, leads from the ditch of the demilune redoubt to the demilune terreplein. The position and arrangement of the ramp are shown in Pl. 4, Fig. 2.

370...The terreplein is finished by a slope of earth, instead of being sustained by a wall. This slope is thus arranged: the part terminating the ramp is a plane of $\frac{1}{1}$;

the position in the angle is formed by an inclined cylindrical surface, which touches the two interior lines of the terreplein; the width of the ditch at the salient of the redoubt, terminated by the base of the cylinder, is 4.30 yards. The remaining portion of the slope is formed of a warped surface, the elements of which are horizontal, connecting the cylinder and the plane of $\frac{1}{1}$. This construction is purely arbitrary; the object being to have the portion of the slope in the salient as gentle as practicable, so that this part may serve as a ramp for infantry.

371...ANALYSIS OF THE DEMILUNE, ETC. The principal properties of the demilune were mentioned in describing Cormontaingne's method; and it was there observed that he improved upon Vauban's, by augmenting the dimensions of the demilune. Engineers, since Cormontaingne, finding that the demilune still admitted of being enlarged with advantage, have accordingly so determined its dimensions, that it may be thrown so far to the front as will still place the breach, which an enemy may make in its face, within the range of the musketry of the bastion face. In large fronts, like this under consideration, the demilune may be thus made to cover about 30 yards of the bastion faces from the shoulder angle, and thus secure retrenchments resting against this part from being turned by a breach made near the shoulder angle.

372...These considerations limit the salient angle of the demilune to 60°, and place the salient at not more than 210 yards from the bastion face, as this distance will bring the breach at about 180 yards from this face, or within the effective range of musketry.

373...The demilune thus arranged places the bastions, in all cases, in strong re-enterings; but when the angles of the polygon are very obtuse, the faces of the bastions, prolonged, also fall within the salients of the demilunes, and are, therefore, not easily enfiladed. The fire from the demilune is very effective on the enemy's works along the bastion capitals. Finally, it is a work of which the enemy can only obtain possession after great labor and loss of time;

and when carried, it is with great difficulty that he can render it tenable, as it is exposed to the fire of the enceinte, within a short range.

374...The demilune, with these advantages, is not without defects. Its faces, from their position, are exposed to an enfilading fire; it deprives the curtain of all action on the exterior ground; and it is only when the angles of the bastion are very open, that the re-enterings formed by the demilunes become of a formidable character. The glacis of the demilune covered-way forms a ridge, which is serviceable to the enemy by masking his works on one side of the ridge from the fire of the collateral works on the other.

Having noticed these general properties of the demilune, the further particular constructions may be examined.

375...In terminating the face at 11.0 yards from the exterior side, a passage made along the extremity of this face, and a face cover for the bastion, of which mention will be made farther on, are allowed for; moreover, the flank of the demilune redoubt, intended to defend the breach in the bastion face by a reverse fire, is unmasked by it.

376...The command of the curtain over the demilune is reduced to the minimum; and to obtain as much interior space for the demilune redoubt as practicable, the height of the interior crest above the magistral is fixed at 11.40 feet, the interior space evidently depending on this height. The terreplein is reduced to 11.0 yards, partly for the same reason, and partly to give an enemy great trouble in establishing a battery on it; as, to do this, he will be obliged to cut away a part of the parapet, and will thus expose the rear of the battery to the fire from collateral works.

377...The terreplein is terminated by a slope of earth, for economy, and, also, because this slope is favorable to offensive movements made to drive the enemy from the breach.

378...It is not probable that an enemy would attempt to carry the demilune by escalade; it is well, however, to provide against such an attempt in so important a work; it is chiefly on this account that the scarp wall is made 22.50 feet high. This dimension also allows the bottom of the cut to be so placed that it can be swept by the fire of the demilune redoubt.

379...FACE-COVER OF THE BASTION. Pl. 3, Fig. 3, and Pl. 4, Fig. 1. By prolonging the bastion counterscarp to the point f', it serves as a face-cover to the bastion scarp, masking it from the fire of the breach battery erected around the salient place of arms of the demilune covered-way. The angle, f', of the face-cover is placed on the same line as the extremity of the double caponnière, for the purpose of covering the troops, as they debouch from the caponnière, from the enemy's establishment along the glacis of the bastion covered-way. The height of the wall, at the point f', is so determined as to intercept the enemy's fire, coming from a point 3 feet above the crest of the bastion covered-way, and passing at 7.50 feet above the bottom of the ditch, at the extremity of the caponnière. From the point f', to the gorge of the redoubt of the re-entering place of arms, the top of the wall ascends, so as to cover the ramp leading from the ditch to the top of the counterscarp at $f f'$, and also the passage leading from this point to the gorge of the redoubt.

380...SINGLE CAPONNIERE AND TRAVERSE IN THE DEMILUNE DITCH. This last passage is also covered from the enemy's works on the glacis of the demilune salient place of arms, by the crest of a single caponnière, in the ditch of the demilune. The glacis of this work is determined by passing a plane through the point, (83.40), of the interior crest of the bastion face, found by producing back the demilune magistral, and through two other points in the demilune ditch: one taken at 13 feet below the ditch of the redoubt of the re-entering place of arms; the other, at about 16.50 feet below the cut in the demilune. The crest of the caponnière is held in this plane; and in projection, is drawn parallel to the magistral of the face-cover, so as to allow space enough between it and the foot of the wall, which terminates the demilune face, for a banquette-tread of 2 yards, and its slope of $\frac{1}{1}$; all of which will require about 4.30 yards. The passage referred to is 4.30 yards wide. In order that it shall be covered by the crest of the caponnière, the bottom of it must be at least 8 feet below the crest.

381...The preceding construction subserves two purposes: 1st, from the position of the glacis it is swept by the fire of the bastion face; so that the dead space, which was noticed at this point of the demilune ditch, in Cormontaingne's method, is here removed; 2d, it covers the troops crossing the demilune ditch from the fire coming from the demilune salient place of arms.

382...As it is important to keep this passage open, even after the enemy obtains possession of the demilune, a traverse is placed at the extremity of the caponnière, so as to cover the postern which communicates with the terreplein of the redoubt of the re-entering place of arms. A portion of this traverse has to be sustained by a wall, which is so arranged as to afford the least possible shelter to an enemy, who, from behind it, might attempt to carry the redoubt by the gorge.

383...The face-cover is terraced, the embankment being 2.50 yards thick at top, and sloped inward toward the passage.

REMARK. The details of this part of the construction being rather complicated, will be better understood by referring to Pl. 4, Fig. 1, than by any written explanation.

384...MASK IN THE DEMILUNE REDOUBT DITCH. Pl. 4, Fig. 1. To cover the curtain wall from a fire through the opening between the flank and the tenaille, coming from a battery established on the demilune terreplein, an embankment is formed in the ditch of the demilune redoubt, the wall, which separates this ditch from that of the enceinte, being built high enough to support the embankment. The embankment is sloped on top, and terminates in a point near the demilune cut, being terminated on the side toward the redoubt by a slope, the foot of which is 4.30 yards from the foot of the redoubt scarp. The crest of the embankment is on the line drawn through the shoulder angle of the redoubt and the angle of the tenaille.

385...The bottom of the ditch between the embankment and redoubt, is about 12 feet above that of the enceinte ditch, which secures the demilune from being turned through this ditch.

386...By separating the embankment from the demilune redoubt, this work is secured from an attempt to carry it from the embankment. For the same reason, the gorge wall behind the cut is raised 13 feet above the top of the embankment. A like expedient is resorted to in all similar cases, as in the gorge wall of the redoubt of the re-entering place of arms, and the counterscarp of the demilune cut, as shown in the details on Pl. 4, Fig. 1.

387...Covered-ways. Pl. 5, Figs. 1, 2. The bastioned covered-way is 11.0 yards wide—the interior crest being drawn parallel to the counterscarp.

388...The crests of the re-entering place of arms are drawn parallel to the magistral of the redoubt, and 20 yards from it.

389...The crest of the demilune covered-way is a broken cremaillére, or crochet line. The short branches of the cremaillére are 6.60 yards long, and are perpendicular to the direction of the demilune capital.

390...Remarks on the Traverses and the Defiles. The objects of the short branches of the crochets are to cover the *defiles*, or passages, between the ends of the traverses and the crest of the covered-way; and to give a column of fire in the direction of the demilune capital. To fulfil this last object, the short branches are provided with a banquette, with a slope of only $\frac{1}{1}$, to bring the crest of this branch as near as practicable to the traverse. A passage of 2.0 yards is left between the foot of the banquette-slope and the wall, which terminates the end of the traverse; the direction of this wall is parallel both to the long and short branches of the crotchets, leaving a passage between it and the long branch, 2.0 yards wide.

391...To find the position of the short branch, the base of the interior slope being 1.5 feet, the banquette-tread 6 feet, the base of the banquette-slope 3.50 feet, and the width of the defile 6 feet—17 feet, or 5.66 yards, is the entire distance sought between the crest of the short branch and the wall that terminates the traverse parallel to this branch.

392...The portion of the long branch, opposite the traverse, is without a banquette, etc., for the purpose of leaving the least distance between the crest of the crotchet and the traverse, so that the defile may be covered in the best manner. To effect this, a vertical wall is placed parallel to the end of the traverse, and at 2.0 yards from it, to leave space for the defile; this wall sustains the earth, but is not built up higher than within 1.50 feet of the crest. The earth of the glacis has the natural slope of $\frac{1}{1}$ from the crest to the top of the wall; the base of this slope, consequently, will be 1.50 feet, and a berm of 0.50 feet being left on the top of the wall. These distances, together, give 2.66 yards for the distance between the crest of the long branch and the wall parallel to it, which terminates the traverse.

393...TRAVERSES ON THE DEMILUNE COVERED-WAY. There are four traverses on the demilune covered-way; which, to avoid repetitions, will be designated as No. 1, No. 2, No. 3, and No. 4—No. 1 being nearest the re-entering place of arms.

394.. To construct the crotchets of traverses Nos. 1 and 2, a line, *l m*, is drawn parallel to, and at 13.0 yards from, the demilune counterscarp; parallel to this line, and at a distance of 6.60 yards, measured on a perpendicular to the demilune capital, a second line, *l′ m′*, is drawn. The salient and re-entering angles of the crotchets, between Nos. 1 and 2, rest on these two lines.

395...To construct traverse No. 1, a line, *n n′*, is drawn parallel to *l′ m′*, and at 2.66 yards; from the point of intersection, *n*, of this line with the crest of the re-entering place of arms, a line, *n o*, is drawn, so that its intersection, *o*, with the demilune counterscarp, shall be perpendicular to a line drawn from *o*, to the point *a*, on the demilune. The line *n o*, is the interior crest of No. 1. The exterior crest, *n′ o′*, is parallel to it, and at 6.66 yards.

396...From the point n', as a centre, with a radius of 5.66 yards, an arc is described; a tangent drawn to this arc, perpendicular to the demilune capital, gives the short branch of the crotchet.

397...To construct traverse No. 2: from the extremity of the short crotchet, just found, with a radius of 6.60 yards, an arc is described; a tangent, drawn from the point a to this arc, will give, by its intersection, o, with the counterscarp, a point of the interior crest of No. 2; the interior crest is drawn from this point, perpendicular to the tangent. The exterior crest, $n' o'$, is drawn at 4.33 yards from $n o$.

398...To obtain the crotchets from any assumed point, n', of this exterior crest, with radii of 2.66 and 5.66 yards, two arcs are described; tangents are drawn to these arcs—one from the inner extremity of the short branch of No. 1 to the arc of 2.66 yards, the other to the arc of 5.66 yards, and perpendicular to the demilune capital. If these two tangents intersect on the line $l' m'$, then the point n' is one point of the end No. 2, and the line $n n'$ is drawn parallel to the long branch; if the tangents do not intersect on $l' m'$, then some other point, n', must be chosen, and a similar construction made, until the intersection is found on the line $l' m'$, which will be the salient angle of the crotchets.

399...To construct No. 3 and its crotchets, a point is taken on the short branch of the crotchet last found, at 4.30 yards from its salient angle; from this point an arc is described, with a radius of 4.50 yards; a tangent drawn to this arc from the point a, will give the point, o, on the counterscarp, where the interior crest of No. 3 is to be drawn, perpendicular to the tangent. The exterior crest of this traverse is at 4.33 yards from the interior crest.

400...The short branches of the crotchets of No. 3 and No. 4, have the same direction as the others; but they are limited by two lines, one drawn parallel to the counterscarp, and at 11.0 yards from it, the other at 6.60 yards from this, measured on a perpendicular to the demilune capital. These two lines being drawn, the position of the salient and re-entering angles of the crotchets that rest upon them will be found by a construction, similar to the one just described.

401...The re-entering angle of the crotchet of No. 2 is cut off, by drawing a line through the centre of the arc, and parallel to the tangent drawn to it from *a*.

402...To construct No. 4, commence by finding the foot of its exterior slope. This is done by describing an arc from the angular point, *c′*, of the redoubt of the re-entering place of arms, with a radius of 4.30 yards; a tangent drawn to this arc, through the demilune salient, being produced to the covered-way, gives the foot of the exterior slope. The interior crest of No. 4 is parallel to this line; its position is found by allowing 4.66 feet, or 1.55 yards, for the base of the exterior slope, and 20 feet, or 6.66 yards, for the thickness of parapet. Having the exterior and interior crests, the point *n′*, and the crotchets, are found as in the preceding cases.

403...The interior crest of the salient place of arms is on the line, *l m*, produced; which is at 11.0 yards from the counterscarp. A pancoupé of 4.30 yards is made in the salient.

404...Traverse on the Bastion Covered-way. Pl. 5, Fig. 1. To construct the traverse and its crotchets on the bastion covered-way, a line, *t r*, is drawn at 5.50 yards, parallel to the crest of the bastion covered-way; the extremity of the traverse, *n n′*, is drawn parallel to *t r*, and 2.60 yards from it. From the point *n*, on the crest of the re-entering place of arms, the interior crest of the traverse is drawn perpendicular to the bastion counterscarp. The exterior crest is 20 feet, or 6.66 yards, from the interior crest.

To find the other branch of the crotchet, *n n′* is taken, equal to 5.0 yards; a line is drawn through *r* and *n′*, and produced to *s*, on the crest of the bastion covered-way; an arc, with a radius of 2.66 yards, is now described from *n′*, and the tangent, *s t*, drawn to this arc, is the branch required.

405...COMMAND OF THE COVERED-WAY AND TRAVERSES. Pl. 5, Fig. 2. To arrange the relief of the covered-way and traverses, the following method is pursued: The salient of the demilune covered-way is 7.50 feet lower than the salient of the demilune; the reference of this point then is (70.50). The interior crests of the salient place of arms of traverse No. 4, and the long branch between Nos. 3 and 4, are held in the same plane; the scale of declivity of which is parallel to the demilune capital; its inclination being determined by placing the extremity of the long branch, just referred to, 0.75 feet lower than the salient of the demilune covered-way.

406...The short branch of the crotchet of No. 3 has the same reference as the salient of the covered-way, (70.50). This line, the interior crest of No. 3, and the long branch, are held in the same plane, whose scale of declivity is parallel to the demilune capital, and whose inclination is such that, being produced, it will pass 3 feet above the salient of the covered-way

407...The relief of No. 2 and its crotchets is determined in the same manner as in the preceding case. The reference of the short branch being fixed at (70.20).

408...The salients of the bastion covered-way, and the re-entering place of arms, command the salient of the demilune covered-way by 1.50 feet. Their reference, therefore, is (72.0).

409...REMARKS ON THE COVERED-WAYS AND TRAVERSES. The demilune covered-way is made wider toward the re-entering, to cover the traverse defiles with more ease. The width, 11.0 yards, of the portion near the salient, makes the covered-way so narrow that, should an enemy find it necessary to lower his breach battery into it to effect a practicable breach, he will be obliged to cut away a part of the glacis to obtain sufficient room for his works.

410...The counterscarp of the redoubt of the re-entering place of arms is a slope of earth, so as to make the re-entering place of arms more spacious, by joining the ditch of its terreplein.

411...The interior crests of the re-entering place of arms and its two traverses are held in the same plane, whose scale of declivity is parallel to the bastion capital. This plane produced, passes 3 feet above the salients of the two collateral demilunes, from which this place of arms is thus defiled.

412...The crests of the bastion covered-way are in the same plane, whose scale of declivity is parallel to the bastion capital. This plane, prolonged, also passes 3 feet above the same points as the last mentioned, and for the same object.

413...The traverses serve as masks to cover the terreplein of the covered-way from ricochet shots; for this purpose, Nos. 2 and 3 may be only 4.33 yards, or 13 feet thick. But the other traverses, which close the re-entering and salient places of arms, being more important, have a thickness of 6.66 yards. As the general height of the traverses is 2.66 yards, it is readily seen that, supposing the extreme limit of ricochet firing to be an angle of $\frac{1}{10}$, the traverses should not be more than 26.6 yards apart, in order that a shot striking the crest of one may imbed itself in that immediately in rear of it.

414...The traverses also serve as a defence; and for this purpose are made like an ordinary parapet. To enable the besieged to defend the covered-way, they are palisaded, and barriers are placed at the defiles. As the means of protracting the defence are only effective when the defiles are perfectly secured from the fire of the enemy, established along the crest of the salient place of arms, the reason for the particular construction given for each traverse will now be apparent. The interior crests of Nos. 1, 2 and 3 are so arranged that they can concentrate their fire on the salient place of arms; and each traverse is so combined with the demilune, as effectually to mask the defile of the one in rear of it. The defile of No. 1 is masked by No. 2, and a passage of about 2.0 yards at the foot of the banquette-slope of No. 1 is covered, so that the troops can pass through this defile in perfect safety.

415...The defile No. 2 is less easily covered by No. 3. To effect it, the inner angle of the crotchets has to be cut off and the banquette-slope suppressed, substituting in its place steps; by these means, a passage of 1.0 yard is covered, and No. 3 placed not too far from No. 2.

416...As it is not practicable to cover the defile of No. 3, the position of No. 4 is determined, so as to make the salient place of arms as spacious as possible. This is done by placing No. 4 in a position, to allow its exterior slope to be swept by the fire of the bastion face, penetrating between the salient of the demilune and the angle of the redoubt of the re-entering place of arms.

417...The defile of the traverse on the bastion covered-way, is arranged to prevent any line of fire penetrating through it into the re-entering place of arms.

418...The precautions which are here taken would be still insufficient, could the enemy, in possession of the crest of the salient place of arms, have a plunging fire upon the covered-way behind the traverses. It is to prevent this that the interior crests of the different traverses and their respective crotchets are held in the same plane; which is so arranged that the terreplein shall be defiled from the enemy's lodgment on the crest of the salient place of arms. This arrangement necessarily places the terreplein between the traverses on different levels; small ramps will, therefore, be necessary to pass from one level to the other. They are placed at the defiles.

419...The salient place of arms is inclined for the purpose of partially defiling it from the trench cavalier.

420...Finally, the traverses are sustained on the side of the counterscarp by a profile wall, which is the prolongation of the counterscarp wall; and they are terminated at the other extremity by a wall, so as to make the defile convenient as a communication.

421...Counterscarps of the Bastion and Demilune. Having determined the relief of the covered-way crests, which, it may be observed, is such that they mask all the masonry of the scarps, and, at the same time, are so low that an enemy cannot, by the ordinary methods in use, obtain a plunging fire from them upon the terrepleins of the works in their rear, the position of the counterscarp crests can now be fixed.

422...The top of the counterscarp wall should be at least 8 feet below the planes of the interior crest of the covered-way, and the height of the wall for the body of the place should not exceed 24 feet, and for the demilune it may be reduced to 18 feet. These dimensions will, therefore, be assumed, as the greatest that can be allowed with a proper regard to economy. And a continuous wall of these heights may be regarded as a powerful auxiliary obstacle, in securing the works from all attempts at surprise.

423...Adopting the limit of 24 feet for the counterscarp of the bastion, it will be seen that the bottom of the ditch at the foot of this wall is higher than at the foot of the scarp wall of the bastion face; and, as the bottom of the ditch, at the extremity of the double caponnière, has already been determined, these different levels must be connected by planes, combined in the most simple manner.

424...CUNETTES AND BOTTOMS OF THE DITCHES. Pls. 4 and 5. A cunette, 4.0 yards wide at top, and 3 feet deep, is made in the main ditch to serve as a drain. A *culvert*, or small arch of masonry, is made under the double caponnière, connecting the cunette on the opposing sides of it. The cunette is placed parallel to the bastion face; the bottom of the ditch having a slope of 1.50 feet from the foot of the scarp wall to the edge of the cunette, and a slope from the opposite edge up to the foot of the counterscarp wall. These details will be best understood by referring to Pls. 4, 5, Figs. 1. The slopes here given serve to keep the bottom of the ditch dry; they assist in rendering the breach, made in the bastion face, rather steeper than if the bottom were horizontal; and, in the passage of the ditch, the enemy's work is thus more exposed than if the bottom were not sloped from the foot of the counterscarp wall to the cunette.

The demilune ditch is arranged upon similar principles.

A cunette and culvert are placed in it, to convey the rain-water from it into the main ditch.

425...PLANES OF THE GLACIS. The glacis of the covered-way may now be considered. One principle is chiefly to be attended to in disposing the different planes of the glacis. They should all be swept by the artillery fire of the works immediately in their rear, and by the musketry fire, at least, of the bastion face.

426...The glacis of the bastion covered-way should be swept by the artillery of the bastion face.

427...The glacis of the re-entering place of arms should be swept by the fire from its redoubt.

428...The glacis of the demilune offers more difficulty in its arrangement, owing to the cremaillére form of the interior crests. The best method seems the following: planes are passed through each long branch, so as to be swept by the artillery fire of a portion of the face of the demilune; these are connected by another series of planes, which are passed through the salient point of each crotchet, below the plane of musketry fire, of at least one-half of the bastion face; and below that of artillery fire, of a part of the demilune face.

429...It will be readily seen, from the nature of this problem, that it admits of many solutions. In selecting amongst them, the following considerations may serve as guides. When the planes of the glacis have a very gentle slope, they are better seen by the works in their rear; but the construction is more expensive, on account of the greater quantity of embankment.

430...When the slope is more steep, the enemy's works on the glacis are better exposed to the reverse views of the collateral works, although not so well seen by those directly in rear of the glacis; but the quantity of embankment is smaller.

431...OUTLETS, OR SORTIE PASSAGES. To communicate from the covered-way with the glacis, an *outlet* or *sortie passage* is cut in the least exposed face of the re-entering place of arms; and one, also, on the long branch, between the 3d and 4th traverses. They are from 3.30 to 4.0 yards wide. The cut is about 6 feet in depth, the earth being sustained on each side by a profile wall. The bottom of it is a ramp leading from the terreplein of the covered-way to the top of the glacis. As the outlet is closed by a barrier, it should be arranged at the bottom, to allow the barrier free play in opening and shutting.

432...COMMUNICATIONS. There is no part of a fortification where more care and judgment are required than in the dispositions made to communicate from the interior with the outworks. The safety of the besieged essentially depends on a proper disposition of the communications, which should afford every facility for offensive movements, and, at the same time, a secure and easy means of retreat. This subject has been treated with peculiar care by Noizet.

433...Besides the ramps, which have already been explained, posterns and stairs form a part of the system of communication.

434...Posterns, as already has been stated, are arched communications of masonry, made under the rampart or terreplein. When these communications are required for the passage of artillery, they should be at least 10 feet wide, and 8 feet high under *the crown* or *key of the arch*. When for infantry, they may be reduced to 4 feet in width, and 6 feet in height, under the key. The arch of the postern is generally a semi-circle, or what is called a *full centre arch*. To be *bomb-proof*, it should be at least 3 feet thick through the masonry of the arch, and be covered by at least from 3 to 4.50 feet of earth.

435...Stairs are only used in situations where ramps cannot be placed; as for example, to communicate with the interior of works, the gorges of which are revetted.

Each step is generally formed of a single block of stone, which is 2.0 yards long *in the clear*, 0.30 yard in width, and 0.20 yard high. From these dimensions of the height, or *rise*, and width, or *tread*, of each step, we obtain the following formula for the base of a *flight of steps*, when the height between the two *landings* is given, $\frac{3}{2}h—0.30=$base.

Stairs are not so convenient as ramps; and they are, moreover, liable to be easily put out of order by the effects of shot and shells.

436...COMMUNICATION OF THE ENCEINTE WITH THE DITCH. The postern of the enceinte leads through the middle of the curtain, descending from the plane of sight to the ditch. The inclination of the bottom should never exceed $\frac{1}{8}$. The bottom should not come out upon a level with the bottom of the ditch, but about 6 feet above it—a wooden ramp being used to descend from the postern to the bottom of the ditch.

The width of this postern should be 12 feet, both on account of the greater circulation through it, and because it may be used as a bomb-proof shelter for the troops on duty.

The entrance to this postern, both toward the ditch and the interior, is by door-ways; one through the scarp wall, which closes the postern toward the ditch, and one through a vertical wall of masonry, at the extremity of the enceinte terreplein, which closes the mouth of the postern toward the interior. The earth of the rampart-slope is cut away, to leave the passage to the postern free. The sides of the cut are sustained by wing walls, which make a small angle with the vertical wall of the postern mouth. The door-way may be 7.0 feet wide, and 7.50 feet high. The postern itself being 10 feet under the key.

For more security, a partition wall, with a door-way, is sometimes made across the postern, about the middle point. The leaves of the folding-doors here have loop-holes to fire upon an enemy, should he, by a surprise, gain possession of the exterior door-way.

437...COMMUNICATION WITH THE TENAILLE. A postern, for the passage of artillery, is made under the tenaille, and leads to the double caponnière. Two stairs are placed at the gorge of the tenaille, to communicate with its terreplein.

438...COMMUNICATION WITH THE TERREPLEIN AND DITCH OF THE DEMILUNE REDOUBT. Two stairs are placed at the gorge of the demilune redoubt, to communicate with its terreplein. A postern for artillery leads from the main ditch to the ditch of the redoubt, under its flank, for the communication between the main ditch and the demilune.

439...Communication from the Enceinte Ditch with the Exterior. To communicate with the covered-ways, a ramp of earth sustained by walls is placed along the wall that terminates the demilune and its redoubt. This ramp is separated from the extremity of the face-cover by a cut 4.30 yards wide.

440...Communication with the Demilune Cut. The communication with the work behind the demilune cut is by a postern and stairs for infantry, which lead from a point on the ramp just described to the terreplein of the work—passing in a winding direction under the terreplein and parapet of the work.

441...Communications of the Redoubt of the Re-entering Place of Arms, etc. The passage behind the single caponnière, in the demilune ditch, has already been described. The passage leads to a postern for artillery, made through the face of the redoubt, to its ditch. From the ditch, a ramp for artillery leads to the terreplein of the re-entering place of arms. At the angle of the redoubt on the demilune ditch, stairs are placed to ascend to its ditch; a ramp for infantry leads from the ditch on this side to the terreplein.

442...To ascend to the terreplein of the redoubt, a small postern for infantry is made through the face to the ditch, being placed alongside the postern just described; from this, a winding postern and stairs lead to the terreplein of the redoubt.

The foregoing, with what has been said respecting the caponnières, traverse defiles, etc., completes the description of the communications of the front. This subject may be closed with a recapitulation of the principal conditions which should regulate every system of communications.

443...Remarks on the Communications. 1st. *The communications should never, from their position, compromise the safety of the enceinte.*

Frequent instances could be cited of works which have been surprised by an enemy obtaining possession of the gates. Therefore, too many precautions cannot be taken to secure the principal outlet from the body of the place from similar attempts. It is on this account that the postern in the body of the place is arranged as has been described, to frustrate any sudden attack that might be made upon it.

444...2d. *The communications should admit of a convenient circulation of the besieged.*

To subserve this purpose, the dimensions, slopes, etc., of the posterns, ramps, and other similar works, should be convenient for the service to which they are applied; and they should be placed in such positions as lead directly to the point to be arrived at. In examining the form, dimensions and position of the ramps, etc., of the front, it will be found that these conditions are well satisfied.

445...3d. *The position chosen for any communication should be such, that when an enemy gets possession of it, he may obtain no advantage by it.*

To be useless to an enemy, the communication, when in his possession, should not offer a shelter for his works; nor enable him to carry them on with more ease. This end will be obtained by placing the communications in a position to be enfiladed by the fire of the works in their rear; and so arranging them as to preserve the counterscarp wall unbroken, by which means any facility for attempts at surprise will be avoided.

4th. *The communications should be covered from every point where an enemy might establish himself, during the whole period that they can be of service to the besiegers; and they should be swept by the fire of the enceinte.*

Without these precautions, an enemy might cut off all communication from the enceinte with the outworks; and in cases of retreat, the troops could not derive any assistance from the enceinte, if he attempted to press upon them.

446...In covering the communications, existing masses should, when convenient, be used, which form a part of the general arrangement of the works. Examples of this are shown in the manner in which the *débouché* from the double caponnière, and also those from the traverse defiles, are covered. In the first case, by the angle of the counterscarp wall and the salient of the bastion; and in the second, by the angle of the profile walls of the traverses and the demilune salient. Sometimes a special mask has to be raised, an example of which is seen in the traverse at the gorge of the redoubt of the re-entering place of arms, which covers the door of the postern of the redoubt.

447...5th. *The communications should be so placed as not to compromise the retreat of the troops.*

This is effected by placing the communication in the re-enterings, which are the most secure points, as an enemy to arrive at them will have to brave a powerful column of flank fire. Barriers, gates, and movable bridges of timber should be placed at suitable points, to cut off one communication from another; and thus arrest the progress of a pursuing enemy.

448...6th. *Finally, each work should be independent of every communication, except the one destined for its particular use.*

This is an important object, as it prevents an enemy, should he succeed in gaining possession of a communication leading through it, from seizing upon the work itself. Examples of this arrangement are shown in the postern, through the face of the redoubt of the re-entering place of arms, which leads to the exterior, and which is not connected with the small postern destined for the service of the redoubt itself; also, in the postern leading from the main ditch to that of the demilune redoubt, for the service of the demilune. This postern does not interfere with the safety of the redoubt.

449...By examining the communications of the front, generally, according to these conditions, it will be found that their arrangement is as judicious as the nature of the problem seems to admit.

450...Interior Retrenchments. The front, as it has now been described, appears to be of a character to protract the siege to the longest duration. When, however, a breach is made in the enceinte, although military usage and a point of honor require of the garrison to sustain, at least, one assault, the consequences of defeat are of too serious a character to expect such an effort, unless a place of safety is provided, into which the garrison may retreat, after defending the breach, and obtain an honorable capitulation. On this account, and also to lengthen the defence, interior retrenchments are made in the bastions. These works may be either of a temporary or permanent character; but it is, generally, conceded that the latter class alone offers a serious obstacle to the enemy. The former, moreover, requires that the bastion should be full, and that the retrenchment should be thrown up during the siege—an undertaking of great difficulty, both from the annoyance of the enemy's fire and the fatigued state of the garrison occasioned by its ordinary duties.

451...Therefore, only the permanent interior retrenchments with a revetted scarp and counterscarp will be given; and which may be regarded as an element of a regularly fortified front.

452...Noizet, like Cormontaingne, proposes four classes of interior retrenchments. 1st. Those that rest against the faces of the bastions. 2d. Those that rest against the flanks. 3d. Those that rest against two adjacent curtains. 4th. Those that comprehend several bastions.

453...First class resting on the Faces. Pl. 6, Figs. 1, 2, and *A*, *B*, Fig. 3. The first class may be either the form of a cavalier, shut in by cuts across the bastion faces, or an inverted redan; or, finally, if the bastion is very open, a small bastion front. Of this class, the cavalier has been generally employed. The cavalier receiving a relief so great as to give it a plunging fire upon the enemy's works on the glacis of the bastioned covered-way; whilst the interior of the bastion, in advance of the cavalier ditch and of the cuts or ditches across the bastion terreplein, between the scarps of the bastion and cavalier, is swept, and the breach that might be made in the bastion salient can be defended from the parapets behind the cuts. These parapets, with the portions of the cavalier faces in advance of them, forming the interior retrenchment.

454...This class presents the advantages of defending the breach within a short distance, and by enclosing the flanks of the bastion within them, they preserve the flanking arrangements of the body of the place until the retrenchment is carried. The principal objection to them is that, by a breach made at the shoulder angle, the enemy can turn them.

455...SECOND CLASS RESTING AGAINST THE FLANKS. Pl, 6. Figs. 4 and *C*. The second class may be of an inverted redan, or a small bastion front; or, finally, of a redan resting against the middle of the flanks, its faces having such a direction that its ditch may be swept by the fire of the flanks of the adjacent bastions.

The last form admits of defending the breach within a short distance; it preserves also the flanking arrangements of the enceinte, and can only be turned by a breach made in the curtain. To sweep its ditch from the opposite flank, it will be necessary to cut down a part of the scarp wall of the flank on which the ditch rests, which will make the height of the wall less than 11.0 yards, and somewhat expose the enceinte to escalade.

456...THIRD CLASS RESTING ON TWO ADJACENT CURTAINS. Pl. 6, Fig. 4, *D*. The third class is usually of the form of a bastioned front; but as the fire of its faces would be masked by the curtain of the enceinte, it is generally best to construct the front simply with a curtain and two flanks.

This class being thrown farther from the salient of the bastion, does not defend the breach so directly as the two preceding; but its position is stronger, and will force an enemy to employ more means to carry it. From its dimensions, it will require more space on the interior, and will be also more expensive than either of the preceding forms.

457...FOURTH CLASS ENCLOSING SEVERAL FRONTS. The fourth class, which is placed in the rear of several bastions of the enceinte, or properly, several fronts, is a kind of second enceinte within the first. An arrangement of this character would, of course, require a peculiar locality, and would seldom find an application.

458...CAVALIER WITH CUTS IN THE BASTION FACES. Pl. 6, Figs. 1, 2. The faces of this work are parallel to those of the bastion in which it is placed; its ditch should be about 18 feet below the bastion terreplein; its scarp wall about 24 feet high. And it may be here observed that all interior retrenchments, to oppose a serious obstacle to an enemy, should have revetements of about these dimensions.

459...The interior crest of the face should be so high that the line of fire, from the salient of the cavalier to the salient of the bastion covered-way, shall pass above the bastion salient. By placing the counterscarp of the cavalier at 14.0 yards from the interior crest of the bastion—allowing 11.0 yards for the width of the ditch, and making the bottom of the ditch 18 feet below the bastion terreplein—it will be found that the reference of the bottom of the ditch will be (58.50); the scarp wall being 24 feet high, the reference of its magistral will be (82.50). Now, if the reference of the interior crest be taken at (97.50), or 15 feet above the magistral, its projection will be at 33.16 feet, or 11.06 yards from the magistral; and as both the lines are horizontal, parallel to it. Drawing, then, three lines parallel to the bastion interior crest, at the distance above mentioned, the projections of the counterscarp, scarp and interior crest of the cavalier are obtained. The position here given to the interior crest of the face will satisfy the condition first laid down.

460...The interior crest of the flank is also horizontal; its reference, therefore, is (97.50); the direction of the flank is perpendicular to the line of defence of the bastion; the flank, moreover, is not revetted like the face, but is terminated by prolonging its exterior slope to the bastion terreplein; the lowest point of the foot of this exterior slope will, therefore, be about (73.00), the reference of the bastion terreplein at the extremity of its flank; the least width of the bastion terreplein, between its flank and that of the cavalier, should be 14.0 yards. If, then, from the interior angle of the curtain, with a radius of 14.0 yards, an arc be described, and a tangent be drawn to this arc, perpendicular to the line of defence, this tangent may be taken as the horizontal of the exterior slope of the cavalier flank, whose reference is (73.0); the interior crest of the flank is drawn parallel to this horizontal, and at 41.16 feet, or 13.72 yards from it; which will be the distance found by calculation, the thickness of the parapet being 20 feet, the superior slope $\frac{1}{6}$, and the exterior slope $\frac{1}{1}$.

461...The length of the flank is found by drawing, through the angle of the curtain, a line parallel to the line of defence; and where it cuts the interior crest of the flank, will be the extremity of the flank.

462...To terminate the gorge of the cavalier, a plane of $\frac{1}{1}$ is passed through the extreme points of the interior crest of its flanks. A passage of 4.30 yards is left on the bastion terreplein, at the gorge of the cavalier, to communicate with it; and also to preserve an uninterrupted communication between the two adjacent curtains. A ramp, 3.30 yards wide, with a slope of $\frac{1}{6}$, leads from the gorge of the cavalier to its terreplein. This ramp is generally placed along the capital of the bastion.

463...CUTS IN THE BASTION FACES. Pl. 6, Figs. 1, 2. To determine the cut across the bastion face, a distance of 13.0 yards is set off from the shoulder angle of the bastion, along its interior crest; from this point a line is drawn, making an angle of 100° with the interior crest; this line being produced to intersect the magistral of the cavalier face, is the interior crest of the parapet behind the cut. The reference of this line where it intersects the magistral is (82.50), the reference of the other extremity being (84.0): it is held in the same plane with the portion of the interior crest of the bastion, between the shoulder angle and the point at 13.0 yards from it; the reference of the shoulder angle remaining as already found; it will be seen that the plane of these two lines produced, passes 3 feet above the bastion salient. The thickness of parapet is only 12 feet.

464...The magistral of the scarp of the cut is horizontal,

its reference being (76.50). From the preceding data, its position is easily determined. A line drawn parallel to the magistral, and at 6.60 yards from it, will be the counterscarp of the cut. The counterscarp wall of the cut is carried up to the top of the bastion face, and forms a profile wall to sustain the earth. The scarp wall of the cut is of the same height as that of the cavalier; the bottom of the cut will, therefore, be referenced (52.50), a portion of the ditch of the cavalier face has the same reference: this portion is found by holding at the level (58.50), that part of the bottom of the ditch toward the salient which can be swept by the fire of the parapet behind the cut; placing the bottom of the remaining portion toward the cut, on the same level as the bottom of the cut, or at the reference (52.50); the two levels being separated by a vertical wall 6 feet high, which retains the earth of the upper level.

465...This arrangement of the ditch of the cavalier subjects only a part of it to the fire of the parapet behind the cut. By placing the door of the postern that leads into the cavalier ditch, at the point where the vertical wall separates the two levels, it will be partially covered from the enemy's lodgment on the bastion terreplein.

466...The object of the cut is similar to the one in the demilune face; it confines the enemy to the salient part of the bastion, preventing him from extending his works along the bastion terreplein, to turn the cavalier by its gorge; so that to obtain possession of this work, he must make a breach in its face.

467...There is a dead space in the cavalier ditch throughout the lower level, which might offer some advantages were the enemy to attempt to carry the parapet of the cut by escalade. To remedy this defect, it has been proposed to place a crenated gallery behind the scarp wall of the cut, to flank the entire ditch.

468...The disposition of the cavalier and cuts within the bastion do not leave sufficient space upon the terreplein of the latter to organize a covered-way But in the retrenchments of open bastions, resting on the flanks or curtains, to which the form of a tenaille, or a small bastioned front is given, a covered-way, with a re-entering place of arms, closed by traverses, can be organized, which will give considerable additional confidence and security in the defence of the breach in the bastion with the bayonet — as this covered-way will cover the retreat of the troops, guarding the breach, into the ditch of the enceinte—whereas, when the counterscarp is not secured in this way, the retreating body run the risk either of being cut off or of having the enemy follow so closely on their heels as to force their way into the retrenchment, and deprive the defence of this last resort for making favorable terms of surrender.

469...The organization of these covered-ways presents no peculiarity. They should, as far as practicable, be defiled from the besieger's lodgments with the bastion assailed.

Chasseloup's Method.

470...Chasseloup was one of the most distinguished engineers under Napoleon, and had the principal charge of the fortifications constructed by the French in the north of Italy, whilst it was a part of the French empire. His views are to be gathered chiefly from some short memoirs published without his name, in which are to be found many of the leading ideas of several later engineers of the French school, and what is now termed the German school.

471...Chasseloup adheres to the bastioned system as the basis of his enceinte, in which, however, he proposes the following modifications of the combinations usually admitted by his predecessors, viz: 1st, in giving a greater length to the exterior side, which he proposes to vary, if necessary, between 440 and 660 yards; 2d, in so arranging the plan of his enceinte that the portion of the bastion faces toward the salients shall be covered by the demilunes from enfilading views; 3d, in throwing back the parapets of certain portions of his front, which are exposed to be breached, so far to the rear that when the scarp wall is battered down the breach will still be closed by the parapet; 4th, in arranging the tenaille with casemated flanks solely for ditch defence, which are covered by a mask from the counter-batteries at the salient of the bastioned covered-way; whilst by openings pierced in the mask, the fire of the flanks can be directed on the point to be attained; 5th, in placing in the main ditch a casemated caponnière to obtain a reverse fire on the breaches in the bastion faces; 6th, in isolating the main ditch from the ditches of the outworks, covering it and the caponnière by a covered-way, organized with casemated traverses and redoubts for defence; 7th, in detaching the demilune from the enceinte, throwing it so far forward as to cover the bastion faces from enfilade, and in placing in the demilune a casemated redoubt to procure reverse views on the approaches on the bastion salients; 8th, in organizing the demilune covered-way in the same manner as that of the enceinte; 9th, in placing within his bastions strong interior retrenchments, with casemated shelters for the artillery in reserve, and defensive casemated quarters for the garrison.

472...PLAN. The exterior side, Pl. 17, *XY*, is taken at 580 metres (French); the perpendicular, *ZU*, is $\frac{1}{8}$ of *XY*; a portion of each face, *Xm*, *Ym'*, equal to 60m. lies on *XY*; from *m* and *m'* lines of defence are drawn through *U*, on which the interior portions of the faces, each 160m., are set off; the flanks are drawn perpendicular to the lines of defence, and are about 48 m.

473...The tenaille is separated from the curtain by a ditch of 10 m., and from the flanks by ditches of 15 m. The rear portion, *e*, Figs. 1, 2, of the flank, is casemated for three guns, each casemate being open to the rear; an open court, *c*, of a rectangular shape, is left opposite the casemates, in front of which is the mask, *d*, pierced with arched openings, through which the shot from the casemated guns are directed. The gorge of the tenaille has a counterscarp gallery.

474...The salient, *S*, of the caponnière in the main ditch is at 55 m. from *Z*, on the exterior side; its faces, *S*, *F*, are 65 m., and directed on points *Q*, *Q′*, at 50 m. from the bastion shoulder angles; the flanks are parallel to the perpendicular of the front, and 60 m. The parapets of this caponnière are thrown back from the scarp wall to increase the difficulty of the breach; the parapets of the faces being higher than those of the flanks, to cover them from enfilade views. The masonry of the flanks of this work is covered by a glacis, *y z f*, which is revetted, leaving ditches of 5 m. between it and the scarp and counterscarp of the enceinte, and of 10 m. between it and the caponnière flanks.

475...The counterscarp of the main ditch is 20 m. wide at the salients, and directed on the flanks of the caponnière at points 5 m. from the shoulder angles. The ditch of the caponnière at the faces is 10 m. wide.

476...The covered-way has a re-entering place of arms at the re-entering between the counterscarps of the enceinte and caponnière faces, which extends to within 50 m. of the front *S′* A salient place of arms, of a polygonal form, like that of the demilune covered-way, but not represented on Fig. 1, is arranged in front of each bastioned salient. Each of these places of arms, Fig. 4, is occupied with a polygonal casemated redoubt. The branches of the covered-way, between the places of arms, are broken into a cremaillère line, the longer branches of which, prolonged, fall within the bastion salients. Traverses, either casemated for reverse fires or of the ordinary construction, are placed in the enlarged portions of the covered-way formed by the long and short branches of the cremaillère. The directions of the crests of the covered-way, and their lengths, are given by the dimensions on the plan.

477...The salient, *T*, of the demilune, is at 170 m. from the point *S′*, on the caponnière counterscarp; its faces are directed on points *p*, *p′*, at 100 m. from the bastion shoulder angles. A cut of 5 m. is made in each face of this work at 70 m. from the salient. The faces are prolonged 50 m. beyond the cut, and are terminated by arcs described from the shoulder angles of the demilune redoubt and lines drawn from these centres to points on the bastion capitals, at 40 m. in advance of the salient place of arms. Within the salient of the demilune a curved traverse is arranged, with countersloping embrasures for howitzer firing along the capitals, in rear of which is a small casemated redoubt, *R*. The demilune ditch is 20 m. wide.

478...The ditches of the demilune redoubt, *O*, are 18 m. wide; the faces of this work are 32 m.; its flanks, 20 m. The flanks, Fig. 3, are casemated for 2 guns. The gorge of the redoubt is a small bastioned front. The faces and flanks have an open defence covered by a parapet.

479...The demilune covered-way is organized like that of the enceinte, with casemated redoubts, *A′*, *B′*, in the salient and re-entering places of arms. Between these redoubts are two traverses, *a b*, *a b′*; the latter covers the masonry of the redoubt, *A′*, and closes the re-entering places of arms.

480...The glacis of the enceinte slopes off toward the gorge of the demilune and its redoubt, so that all the rear of these works is exposed to the face of the enceinte.

481...Besides the ordinary open communications, Chasseloup's front is organized with a very extensive combination of posterns and galleries for scarp and counterscarp defences and mines, both for the service of the defences of the enceinte and of the outworks.

482...The principal features of Chasseloup's combinations consist in his mode of closing the opening for breaching the bastion faces, as seen in Vauban's fronts, through the demilune ditches, by throwing forward the demilune as a detached work; in his organization of his covered-ways with casemated redoubts, and of his demilune redoubt with casemated flanks having reverse views on the bastion glacis. It has been objected to the position he gives the demilune that both this work and its covered-way are exposed to be carried by an open assault at the gorge, in which case its redoubt would readily fall, and the advantages proposed be lost; also, that the casemated redoubts in the covered-ways will be so damaged by the ricochet fire of the enfilading batteries as to be useless when the covered-way is attacked.

Haxo's Method.

483...General Haxo holds the first rank among the more recent engineers of the French school. Having served under Chasseloup in the construction of the fortifications of Northern Italy, he subsequently acquired a distinguished reputation by his services in the Peninsular war, where he was engaged in several of the remarkable sieges of that epoch, and he finally became President of the Board of Engineers, and in that capacity directed several of the most important fortifications of recent date in France.

Nothing of General Haxo's views on the subject of fortification came before the public during his life. The front which accompanies this description he had engraved, and copies of it distributed among the officers of his corps, but under an injunction of secrecy.

484...PLAN. The exterior side, CD, of the enceinte, Pl. 18, is 393.48 yards; the lines of defence, CH, DG, are directed on the point D', at 43.72 yards from C', or one-ninth of the exterior side; the faces CE and DF, are 74.32 yards; the flanks EG, FH, are perpendicular to the lines of defence.

485...The tenaille consists of a curtain and flanks; it is revetted only on the exterior of the two flanks; it is separated from the curtain of the enceinte by a ditch 13.11 yards wide, and from the flanks by one of 6.50 yards: the flanks of the tenaille are about 3 feet higher than its curtain, and are arranged for three guns. The foot of the exterior slope of the tenaille curtain extends 76.5 yards on each side of C', to the point where the exterior revetement wall of the flank commences.

486...Counterguards are placed in front of the bastions; the ditches between them and the bastions being 16.39 yards wide at the salient, and their counterscarps being directed on a point D'', 38.25 yards from C'; the salients of the counterguards are on the line $A B$, parallel to CD, and 49 yards from it; the faces $A K$, $B M$, are 138.81 yards, and parallel to the counterscarps directed on D'', which form the gorge walls of the counterguards; the flanks $K L$, $M N$, are perpendicular to the exterior side, and are terminated on a line parallel to it through the shoulder angles of the bastions.

487...An elbow cut, 5.46 yards wide, is made across the counterguards at 84.16 yards from the salient; the portion of the counterguard behind the cut is arranged for cannon. The ditches of the counterguards are 21.86 yards wide at the salients; the counterscarps are directed upon a point, O'', at 18.53 yards from C'.

488...A casemated caponnière is placed in advance of the counterguards, the middle of its gorge being on the line, $A B$, joining the salients of the counterguards, and its salient, P, at 103.83 yards from C'; its faces, P, U', are 29.51 yards long, and directed on points at 5.46 yards from the shoulder angles, K, M, of the counterguards; its flanks, U', V, are 36.07 yards long and perpendicular to the exterior side.

489...To construct the demilune, points M'', M''' are taken on the bastion faces at 18.58 yards from the shoulder angle, and on the line joining them an equilateral triangle is formed, the vertex of which, H, is the salient of the demilune, and the two sides the directions of the faces, $H S$, $H T$, which are 164 yards long. An elbow cut, 5.46 yards wide, is made on each face at 109.3 yards from the salient H, and separates the portion J from the salient.

490...The salient, Q, of the demilune redoubt is 55 yards from the salient, P, of the caponnière; its faces, Q, U, are parallel to those of the demilune, and 65.58 yards long.

The flanks, $U V$, $X Y$, are parallel to the capital, and terminated on lines, $x x'$, drawn from x on the counterscarp of the redoubt to x' on the line $A B$, at 6.56 yards from the flanks of the caponnière.

491...The counterscarps of the counterguards, from the points e'', e''', on the prolonged faces of the demilune, are directed on points on the flanks of the caponnière, at 10.93 yards from their extremities, to points f, at 13.11 yards from these flanks; and from f they are broken parallel to the flanks, and continued to g on the line $x x'$

492...A casemated redoubt is placed in each re-entering place of arms; its face, $b c$, is directed on a point, e', at 36.07 yards from e'', and is 39.35 yards long; the other face, $b d$, is perpendicular to $b c$, and 21.86 yards long.

493...A casemated redoubt is also placed in the salient place of arms of the demilune covered-way. The covered-way and the re-entering places of arms are arranged in the usual manner for sorties, and with traverses.

494...Interior retrenchments are arranged in the bastions. In the one on the right, the parapet of the flank is broken to increase the amount of flank fire. In the one on the left, a high cavalier is placed, having one tier of casemated fire, with earthen embrasures like those already described, and which, from their having been introduced by Haxo, are known as the Haxo casemate, with an upper tier of uncovered fire.

The ditches of these retrenchments are swept from the opposite flanks.

495...Haxo casemates are placed in the salients of the counterguards and the salient of the demilune.

496...The portions of the curtain parapet of the enceinte, near the curtain angle, are retired to give a more effective direction to the guns on these portions, and to lengthen the parapets of the flanks.

497...The communication from the enceinte to the main ditch is by a postern under the curtain. The communications with the counterguards and other outworks are through the ditch, between the flanks of the enceinte and the tenaille; the communication in front of the tenaille being covered by the crest *l*, *l* of the glacis in front of it, and by the traverse *R*, and that across the main ditch to the main caponnière by the double caponnière *K′*.

498...The ramps, stairs and other passages leading to the terrepleins of the different works are indicated on the plan, and are so placed as to satisfy the conditions laid down for these important elements of a front.

499...The plane of comparison to which the plan is referred is taken at 60 feet below the plane of site. The relative command and the relief of the enceinte and other component parts are thus easily deduced; and it will be seen that every advanced part is well swept by the fire of the more retired parts.

500...From an examination of the plan, it will be further apparent that, by the position and length given to the faces and flanks of the bastions, the former are less exposed to enfilading views, and the fire of the latter is considerably increased, as compared with Cormontaingne's method and the subsequent modifications of it; this increase in the number of guns that may be brought to bear on the positions of the besieger is further increased by the flanks of the tenaille, those of the counterguards, and the flanks of the cavalier.

501...The counterguards, with the tenaille, mask completely the scarp of the enceinte from any position that the besieger's batteries can occupy beyond the main ditch. All the outworks exterior to the counterguards are well swept and flanked by the fire of the latter.

502...The batteries of the flanks of the casemated caponnière sweep effectively every point in advance of them, and see in reverse the breaches that can be made in the counterguards. The scarp of this work, as well as that of the counterguards, is masked by the plan and relief given to the counterscarp of the main ditch and the covering masses of earth behind it, from the besieger's batteries on the crests of the bastion and demilune salient places of arms.

503...The demilune, from its salient position, has strong

reverse views, upon the glacis in advance of the salients of the enceinte, from the casemated battery in its salient; whilst the mass of this battery serves as a traverse to cover the portions of the faces in rear of it from enfilading fire. The demilune redoubt serves the usual purpose of this work; its flank is casemated.

504...Although not clearly indicated on the plan, the parapets of those portions of the works exposed to be breached are thrown back from the scarp wall, and a *chemin de ronde* is formed at the foot of the parapet. By this disposition, a breach, when made, will be more difficult of assault; the retired position of the parapet will be less exposed to ricochet fire, and the *chemin de ronde* will afford both greater security from surprise and a good position for sharp-shooters against the trenches.

505...It is estimated that, by allowing the usual progress of the besieger's approaches, Haxo's front will require about 50 days for its reduction. The besiegers, besides the ordinary trenches, batteries and descents, will have to resort to at least five epochs of breaching batteries: 1st, for opening the demilune and the redoubt of the salient place of arms; 2d, against the demilune redoubt, the portion of the demilune in rear of the cut, and the redoubt of the re-entering place of arms; 3d, against the counterguards and the casemated caponnière; 4th, against the bastion faces; and, 5th, against the interior retrenchments.

Choumara's Method.

506...Choumara, a French officer of engineers, of distinguished abilities, is the author of several remarkable memoirs on the defects of the bastioned system, and the means by which they may be removed, and very great additional strength be thereby given to the defences. His propositions for this purpose may be briefly stated as follows:

507...1st. That part of a permanent work which can undergo no modification during the progress of a siege is the masonry, and it may, therefore, be regarded as the really permanent feature; all the parts of earth, as the parapets, etc., being susceptible of such modifications as circumstances may demand.

This Choumara terms the independence of the parapets as respects the scarps. This latter, upon which the security of the work against an open assault or a surprise depends, must necessarily receive a direction, such that it can be swept by the flanking arrangements, a necessity that does not exist for the parapets, which may receive any direction compatible with the interior space.

The parapets may, therefore, be thrown back from the salients, as in the bastion, Pl. 19, Fig. 1, and receive a curvilinear form to throw a greater volume of fire in the direction of the capital; or they can be retired from the faces, as in the bastion, Fig. *A*, for the purpose of giving them such directions that their prolongations shall cut the adjacent demilunes, and thus be masked from enfilading views; or they may be prolonged so as to afford a greater column of flank fire, as in the flanks *I*, Fig 1; or they may be broken into any direction for the same purpose, or to give a more effective direction to their fire; or, finally, they may be thrown back from the scarp walls instead of resting immediately upon them, and thus render a breach less practicable, since the whole, or a portion of the parapet, will still retain its place after the breach has been made in the scarp—depending on the distance at which the parapet has been moved back. In all of these cases of the application of the independence of the parapets, Choumara proposes to convert the space left between the foot of the parapet and the scarp wall into a *chemin de ronde*, or corridor, which is covered in front by a slight parapet, and from enfilading fire, by a *bonnet* of suitable height at the salients, as in Figs. 1, *A*, *B*, etc. This corridor is occupied by sharp-shooters, to annoy the besieger's trenches. Furthermore, Choumara regards the corridor as an additional security against surprise and escalade.

508...2d. Choumara proposes to place high traverses in the bastion salients, to cover the faces from enfilade, and the flanks from reverse views; and similar traverses at the shoulder angles, with the same object. These he also proposes to casemate, or else construct with blindages for artillery to obtain a fire in the directions of the capitals, and reverse views on the demilune glacis and the breach in the bastion face. As these traverses, from their height, might give the besiegers in possession of them a plunging fire on the bastion retrenchments, Choumara proposes so to arrange them that they can be readily destroyed at any moment by mines, or, if of timber, be burned.

509...3d. To mask the masonry of the enceinte and demilune from breaching batteries, erected in their usual positions along the crests of the glacis, Choumara proposes to form what he terms an *interior glacis*, or covering mass of earth, in the ditches, the crests of which shall mask the masonry of the scarps from the positions in question; and the upper surface of which, forming a glacis, shall be swept by the fire of the works in its rear. In this manner, Choumara proposes to force the besiegers to the difficult operation of making lodgments in this glacis, to obtain suitable positions for their breaching batteries.

510...4th. Choumara proposes, by a judicious selection of positions for some of the outworks, to occupy those positions on the exterior which are most favorable to the sharp-shooters of the besiegers, and thus cripple this important arm of the attack.

511...5th. By giving greater extent to the exterior side, and a more retired position to the curtain, which is also to be made as short as possible, Choumara proposes to obtain bastions of ample size, not only to admit of the modifications he proposes for the parapets, traverses and *chemins de ronde*, but for strong interior retrenchments, so organized with bomb-proof shelters, and arranged defensively toward the interior, that each bastion will admit of a defence to the rear at its gorge, after the besiegers may have effected a breach at other points, and penetrated within the enceinte.

512...PLAN. In adapting these propositions to a bastioned front, Choumara proposes, in order to obtain the requisite room in the interior of the bastions and a large increase of flank fire, to take the exterior side from 400 to 600 metres, French. In the front, Fig. 1, Pl. 19, for example, the exterior side is 440 metres; the lines of defence are drawn through a point on the perpendicular of the front at 74 m., or $\frac{1}{6}$ of 440 m. within the exterior side; the faces are 150 m., and the flanks, drawn perpendicular to the lines of defence, are 85 m.—a length which prolongs them 35 m. within their intersections with the lines of defence. By this construction, the curtain, which will be 115 m. long, will be well swept, and the gun at the curtain angle can be brought to bear on the one of the besieger's counter-battery against the flanks which are furthest out, thus giving a very great preponderance in fire to the flank over the counter-battery.

513...The deep re-entering thus formed between the flanks and curtains, gives ample room for a tenaille with flanks for four guns; these guns are covered in flank by a traverse. The tenaille is not revetted in front of its curtain and flanks, or at its gorge. It masks sufficiently the scarp of the flanks and curtain of the enceinte, to prevent any danger to the latter from the destruction of the portion of the scarp wall that can be seen over the tenaille.

514...The salient of the demilune is the vertex of an equilateral triangle, the base of which is drawn between two points on the bastion faces, at 18 m. from the shoulder angles. The faces of the demilune, *D*, are 144 metres, and revetted. The parapet of the demilune is thrown back from the revetement, leaving a corridor covered by a parapet at the foot of its exterior slope. The parapet is broken near the gorge, so as to give two short flanks of 13 m. perpendicular to the exterior side. The salient is occupied by a casemated traverse with flanks for three guns. This traverse masks the interior of the demilune and the corridor from enfilading views. A disposition is shown for cuts across the demilune faces, the parapets of which are to be thrown up after the siege commences. The demilune ditch is 17 m. wide. The portion of this ditch toward the gorge slopes upward as a glacis, and is swept by the fire of the enceinte.

515...The interior glacis of the demilune commences at the counterscarp of this work, and has a glacis-slope outward, its width being 45 m. Here commences the revetted gorge of the covered-way. The width of the covered-way is 10 m. Its interior crest is an indented line. There are no traverses in this work, unless required for its defilement.

516...A spacious and strong redoubt is placed in the demilune salient place of arms. Its faces are 132 m. long, and revetted. Its parapet is thrown back, leaving a corridor in front of it, and is curved at the salient for five guns, sweeping along the capital. A bonnet is placed in its salient to cover the corridor from enfilade, and two traverses for the same object on its terreplein. This redoubt forms a mask for the portion of the demilune occupied by the traverse.

517...Choumara places strong redoubts, *M*, with revetted scarps and gorges in the re-entering place of arms. The parapets of these works are curved at the salients for batteries to sweep the approaches on the bastion capitals and the demilune glacis, and they are thrown back from the scarp walls to give a corridor for sharp-shooters. As these redoubts are necessarily contracted, Choumara prefers to them a strong redoubt of larger dimensions, placed in the bastion salient place of arms, and organized like the preceding.

518...One of the most striking features of Choumara's modifications, is the mode in which he proposes to organize the large bastions, with defences which shall serve as an interior retrenchment in case the bastion is one of the points of attack; or convert the bastion into an isolated fort, or citadel, for the garrison, in case the besieger gains possession of the interior of the enceinte through an assault. This he proposes to accomplish by increasing the lengths of the exterior side, and also of the bastion flanks.

519...With this object, Choumara places a row of casemates within the bastions, on a line perpendicular to their capitals. Each casemate is from 60 to 80 feet long, from 12 to 20 feet wide, and 12 feet high. This row of casemates serves as a curtain both for the retrenchment of the bastion and for the defence of the gorge against an interior attack. For the defence of the salient portion of the bastion, a cut is made across each face and extended to the capital. The scarp of this cut is made into the form of a bastion front with orillons at the shoulder angles; the casemates forming the curtain of this front. The counterscarp of the cut may be either revetted or have a simple slope of earth. In the latter case, the bottom of the ditch of the front at the foot of the scarp wall is at a suitable level to admit of a suitable height of scarp wall to secure it from escalade. A broad ramp leads from the centre casemate, along the capital toward the bastion salient, to the counterscarp of the cut, and there branches into two other ramps, leading up to the bastion terreplein on the right and left. Until the besiegers are about to breach the bastion faces, their parapets are left intact, and the portions of the cut along which the parapets run are filled up, as in the bastion on the right, thus leaving a free communication throughout the interior of the bastion. So soon as it is thought necessary to cut off this communication, and to get the retrenched portion in a state of defence, that portion of the parapet across the cuts is demolished, the cut excavated and suitably arranged, and the parapet of the retrenchment formed in part of the earth arising from these changes. The parapet of the front of the retrenchment is thrown back, leaving a corridor for sharp-shooters covered by a slight parapet; that portion of this corridor along the retired flank being covered by the earthern mask of the orillon. Choumara further proposes, where there is a probability of the scarp of the bastion face, which closes the cut on the exterior, being opened, so that a breach might be made, by firing through it, on the flank of the retrenchment, to run the scarp wall of the retrenchment at right angles across the cut, as shown on the right face of the left bastion, and to arrange the bastionnet, which this modification would give at the shoulder angle, for sharpshooters.

520...To expose the interior of the retrenchment to the fire of the flanks of the adjacent bastions, and to the parapet of a second retired interior retrenchment, resting on the two curtains adjacent to the bastion of attack, a portion of the parapet of the bastion flanks, near the curtain, is demolished, and a slope is given to the portion of the terreplein on which it rested. The retired interior retrenchment Choumara proposes to make an earthen-work in the form of a bastioned front, breaking the faces in the most suitable manner to sweep the rear of the retrenchment in its front.

521...The dispositions to convert the bastion into a citadel are similar to the preceding, consisting of a small front, the faces of which are nearly in the prolongations of the adjacent curtains, with orillons to cover the corridor of the retired flank. This front has a covered-way and glacis in advance of it, the crest of which masks the scarp.

522...Choumara has made an ample provision for an easy communication between all points of the enceinte and the outworks, so placing them as to be well covered from the besieger's fire and well swept by that of the garrison—preferring wide ramps for this purpose. The communication from the enceinte with the main ditch is through gateways in the scarp wall of the curtain, at its extremities. The rampart at these points is removed to the level of the main ditch; the portion of it between them, along the centre of the curtain, being sustained at the ends by revetement walls run back perpendicularly to the scarp wall of the curtain. Ramps lead from the gorges of the bastions down to these outlets into the main ditch. From these outlets the communications to the outworks are around the flanks of the tenaille, and through the enceinte ditch, to ramps placed along the enceinte counterscarp leading into the demilune, the demilune ditch, the enceinte covered-way, and its redoubts in the places of arms; and from the demilune ditch to the redoubt of the demilune salient place of arms. Posterns on the faces and flanks of the bastions, near the shoulder angles, lead to the corridors of the enceinte. Passages are left at the ends of the faces of the outworks, leading from their corridors to the interior of the works. To keep open the communication between the bastions, a gallery between their gorges is made along the curtain wall.

523...For the security of the casemates, barricades can be made in their doors and windows, by means of timber let in grooves made in the walls; the space between the exterior and interior timber facing being filled with sand-bags.

524...REMARKS. The memoirs in which Choumara brought his propositions before the public naturally attracted attention, as much, perhaps, from their polemical character and piquancy of style as their professional interest. They contain but few things, the germs of which are not to be found in writers who preceded him. His modifications respecting the parapets, throwing them back from the scarps and breaking them into directions best suited for defence, are to be met with in *Chasseloup's* propositions. His proposals for lengthening the bastion flanks, and occupying the salient places of arms by redoubts with considerable command, are to be found in the method of *de la Chiche.* To *Virgin* he seems to be indebted for his organization of interior retrenchments, which are to convert each bastion into an independent work, equally provided for defence against approaches, both from the interior and exterior of the enceinte. Like disputants, usually of an ardent temperament, he over estimates the value of many of his propositions, and loses sight of their countervailing defects. By laying down as a principle what may be exceptionably good in practice, he has rather weakened his own positions. This is the case, particularly, with his rule of the independence of the parapets on the scarps, which, if adopted in all cases, might demand a greatly increased and hurtful command, and cut up to great disadvantage the interior spaces of the bastions. His introduction of the *chemins de ronde* on the faces of the bastion and demilune, add really very little, if at all, to the exterior defence; whilst they contract the interior space of these works, break in upon the unity of the defence, and place the troops in them in a very exposed position to the means of annoyance possessed by the besieger. His expectations with respect to the effect of his fire in the direction of the capitals, in delaying the besieger's approaches up to the third parallel, were hardly warranted by the experience gained in artillery and small arms, even at the time the last edition of his memoirs appeared. It is hardly to be questioned, now that these weapons have been so greatly improved, both in range and accuracy of fire, that, considering the increased development of the besieger's parallels, which gives him a choice of positions for his batteries on so extended a line, the concentrated fire he could bring to bear on the batteries in question would not only soon ruin their casemates, but would greatly damage the adjacent faces, and also the flanks of the bastions, although covered from enfilading views, either by the direction of the parapets of the faces or the high traverses raised with the same object. These advantages in the position of the besieger, it is thought, would prevent any delay in pushing forward his approaches up to the third parallel. After this, the approaches would probably be retarded beyond the usual time allowed in the attack on Cormontaingne's front, owing chiefly to the redoubts in the bastion and demilune salient places of arms and the arrangement of the face-cover in the enceinte ditch.

525...Supposing an enceinte organized according to his method, and containing interior retrenchments to oppose the besieger's approaches, both from without and within the enceinte, Choumara estimates at least six separate epochs of breaching batteries, as follows: 1st, against the redoubt of the demilune salient place of arms; 2d, against the demilune and the redoubt of the bastion salient places of arms; 3d, against the bastions; 4th, against the bastion retrenchment; 5th, against the retired retrenchment; 6th, and finally, against the bastions converted into citadels by the fronts with which their gorges are closed. According to the estimate of time made by Choumara, it would require 112 days from the opening of the trenches to the final assault and reduction of the last defences.

Coehorn's Method.

526...Coehorn, a Dutch engineer of great eminence, was the contemporary and rival of Vauban, both in actual warfare and in the engineer's art. Like Vauban, he is the author of several methods, in which he has shown the same pre-eminent skill as Vauban, in the adaptation of his art to local features, and, perhaps, more originality in his combinations; for Vauban rather made use of, and improved upon, the defensive branch of his art, as he found it, than originated; whereas, many of Coehorn's devices are his own.

527...Coehorn's fronts are arranged with a view to aquatic sites, like those of Holland, where water is found by excavating to the depth of a few feet below the natural surface, by means of which, wet ditches can be combined with those which are dry, so as to procure not only security against a surprise, but, as will be seen further on, to afford facilities for an active defence against the enemy when in possession of the dry ditches.

528...PLAN. Coehorn has adopted the mode of laying out the lines of his front, used by some of the earlier engineers; fixing, in the first place, the *interior sides* of the space to be enclosed, taking these lines as the magistrals or exterior lines of the curtains in the bastioned system.

529...Assuming *A B*, Pl. 15, as the position of the interior side, Coehorn makes its half length, *A B*, 75 toises, French measure. From *A*, the same distance, 75 toises, being set off to *C*, on the capital, or bisecting line of the angle of the polygon, gives the salient of the exterior side; this side in the hexagon being 224 toises. Bisecting *A B*, the half, *B D*, is taken for half the curtain.

The lines of defence are drawn from the extremities of the curtain, thus determined, to the opposite salients of the exterior side. From the salients of the exterior side, as centres, with the lines of defence as radii, arcs, *D G*, being described, give the faces, *C G*, of the bastions measured along the lines of defence.

The portions of the faces thus determined are not revetted toward the ditch; the exterior slopes of their parapets descending below the water level to the bottom of the ditch, as shown on the cross section *G′ H′*

530...At the shoulder angle of the bastion, Coehorn has placed a stone tower, of which *G I L K H* is the plan.

An interior elevation of this tower is shown on the section *Q R*. This tower is arranged on top with a parapet for an open defence. It is arranged with bomb-proof arches, and is casemated on the interior side, *G H*, to sweep the dry ditch between the bastion and the cavalier within it.

To set out the tower, *G H* is drawn perpendicular to *G C*, and 18 toises in length; a distance, *G I*, of 8½ toises is taken on the prolongation of *C G; H K* is drawn parallel to *G I*, and 4 toises in length; *K L* is found by joining *K* with the opposite salient, making *K L* equal to 14 toises taken along this line; the points, *I* and *L*, thus determined, are joined by an arc of 60°

The curved projecting portion of the tower forms an orillon, which covers the concave flank *P D*, which is also an arc of 60°

531...The faces and flanks of the cavalier have a revetted

scarp, as well as the portion *D S* of the curtain, which is thrown back on the prolongation of the line of defence, and closes the gorge of the bastion. The magistral of the face of the cavalier is parallel to *C' G'*, and $22\frac{1}{2}$ toises from it. The magistral, *O S*, of the flank is concentric with the one, *P D*, of the bastion, a ditch 16 toises wide being left between the two flanks.

532...The interior of bastion face *C G*, which forms the counterscarp of the cavalier, is arranged with a loop-holed gallery for sweeping the cavalier ditch.

533...The space between the orillons and curtain is occupied by a tenaille, of which *I U T V* is the exterior line at the water level. The point *T* is on the line of defence, and at 140 toises from the salient; the portion *T U* is perpendicular to this line of defence, and the portions *I U* and *T V* are on the lines of defence.

534...The enceinte ditch is 24 toises wide at the water level. An earthen counterguard, *D' C'*, for musketry defence is placed in front of the bastion.

535...The salient, *Z*, of the demilune is at 93 toises from the point *W*, where the enceinte counterscarp cuts the capital of the front; its demigorge, *W X'*, is $53\frac{1}{2}$ toises. The demilune ditch is 18 toises wide, and that of the counterguard is 14 toises.

536...The demilune contains a small redoubt, the faces of which are revetted, and parallel to those of the demilune. The ditch of the redoubt is dry, and 16 toises wide. A curvilinear space is formed at the gorge of the redoubt, to afford a covered harbor for boats used for communication. A small caponnière, in the form of a lunette, is placed at the gorge of the redoubt to secure the retreat of the troops from it to the boats. The walls of this caponnière are pierced with two tiers of loop-holes; the work being divided into two stories, the lower being covered with heavy beams and earth to resist shells, the upper being uncovered.

537...A similarly covered caponnière, of a rectangular shape, for one tier of fire, is placed across the ditch of the redoubt, near its extremity. A small wet ditch is placed in front of this work, and is flanked by a counterscarp gallery under the portion of the demilune face opposite to it.

538...A like construction, of a pentagonal form, is placed within the salient angle of the demilune, the faces of which, toward the interior of this work, are loop-holed to sweep the ditch of the redoubt and the interior of the demilune.

539...The covered-ways of the counterguard and demilune are 13 toises wide; a re-entering place of arms is formed at the junction of the two, the faces of which are 30 toises.

540...A redoubt of a quadrangular shape, the faces of which are respectively 12 and 15 toises, and which is a simple loop-holed wall, closes, in connection with two traverses, the gorge of the re-entering place of arms.

541...A gallery, covered with heavy timber and earth, is placed 6 toises in advance of the re-entering place of arms, to furnish a fire of musketry to sweep the glacis in front.

One of the most prominent features in Coehorn's method is the combination of wet and dry ditches, with a view to security from surprise, and for protracting the defence and disputing the possession of every point foot by foot. For these purposes the wet ditches are made very wide and contain water, at least six feet in depth, thus forcing the enemy to the construction of long dikes to effect their passage; whilst the bottom of the dry ditches are kept slightly above the general water level, so as to compel the enemy to bring the earth, as well as the other materials requisite for their passage, from other points. In addition to these purely passive means, the dry ditches are organized for an active defence by sorties, and are well swept by direct and reverse fires from casemates, counterscarp galleries and caponnières. The portion of the dry ditch between the faces of the cavalier and bastion is swept by artillery in the casemates under the orillon, and by two pieces behind a wall pierced with embrasures, which closes the space between the shoulder angle, *O*, of the cavalier, and the extremity, *H K*, of the orillon. In like manner, the ditch between the flanks is swept from casemates under the portion $S D$ of the curtain. A reverse fire of musketry sweeps the ditch along the face, from counterscarp galleries under the bastion faces, and from a gallery along the capital, which serves as a communication between these galleries and the interior.

To cut off the communication between the ditch of the face and flank, a wet ditch is made in front of the orillon and the connecting wall. This ditch is flanked by the counterscarp gallery Two drawbridges over this ditch form a means for sorties on the enemy whilst effecting the passage of the ditch of the face. A drawbridge for a like purpose is thrown over the wet ditch, in front of the caponnière in the ditch of the demilune redoubt. Besides these provisions for carrying on what the French well express by *une guerre de chicane*, Coehorn makes a profuse use of palisadings in all parts of his front where an obstinate stand is to be made, besides employing countermines to destroy such parts as, being in the enemy's possession, would be prejudicial to the defence.

542...The question may very naturally be here asked, to what extent such means of defence may be depended upon? The answer is, only so far as they can be kept in a good condition for the moment when they can be brought into play With the present improved practice of artillery there is little doubt but that all of these means for the ditch defences, as provided by Coehorn, except the counterscarp galleries, would be destroyed by the ricochet fire of the enemy's enfilading batteries at an early period of the siege, the masonry of the loop-holed redoubts and caponnières being altogether too slight to withstand the effects of this fire. Could these means be kept in a good condition, we have the warrant of numerous sieges in favor of their efficacy in the hands of an intelligent and resolute garrison.

543...PROFILES. In the plan and profiles the horizontal plane of site is assumed at 24 feet above the plane of comparison. From an examination of the references on the figures of the plate, the relief and relative command of all the works are readily deduced. It will be seen, on examining the plan, that a portion of the bastion face, adjoining the salient, is raised 3 feet higher than the portion toward the orillon, thus forming a *bonnette*, which not only gives a greater command to this portion, but masks more effectually the ditch and masonry of the cavalier. A like arrangement is seen in the demilune face, both at the salient and toward the gorge, and with a like view to mask the caponnière and the loop-holed redoubt in the salient of the demilune.

544...REMARKS. It will be seen, on reference to the plan and sections, that Coehorn has given but a slight command to all his works—his object in this being economy, and to depend rather upon the near than the distant defence, his dispositions having been made almost exclusively for the former. The command of the crest of the covered-way is only $4\frac{1}{2}$ feet over the natural site, the terreplein of this work, which is $7\frac{1}{2}$ feet below the crest, being thus placed a little above the water level, with a view to compel the besiegers to bring the earth and *materiel* from a distance to form a cover for his approaches in the covered-way.

545...The only dispositions for the distant defence by artillery are in the cavalier and demilune redoubt, except in the dry ditches, where guns and mortars might be placed to fire over the low parapets of the exterior works.

546...Besides the exposure to ricochet caused by this slight command, the directions given to all the faces of the works are very favorable to the enemy's enfilading batteries.

547...The dimensions of the parapet of the counterguard, which serves as a mask for the triple flank fire of the cavalier, bastion and tenaille, and those of the parapets of the bastion and demilune, which serve as face covers for the cavalier and demilune redoubt, are insufficient for these purposes, as they could readily be opened by shells fired horizontally into them, or by small mines, and expose the scarp of the interior works to the enemy's breach batteries on the glacis. The scarp walls, moreover, of the works in question, are not of sufficient height to secure them from an open assault. The only feature, then, of the ingenious combinations of this celebrated engineer, which would find an application in the present state of the art, is the combination of wet and dry ditches for sites similar to those for which his dispositions were designed.

Tenailled System.

548...Several engineers, of professional eminence, have proposed tenailled enceintes, as offering defensive properties superior to bastioned enceintes. This system has found but few advocates; and, except in particular localities, where the natural features of the site demanded it, and for small works, it has met with no practical applications.

549...Requiring that the salient angles shall not be less than 60°, and the re-entering angles between 90° and 100°, the tenailled system is only adapted to regular polygons of a sufficient number of sides to admit of these conditions being satisfied. If the exterior sides are kept within the limits usually admitted by engineers for bastioned enceintes, the faces of the tenailles become very long and the re-enterings very deep; thus presenting two serious defects: long lines which are very much exposed to enfilade, and a great diminution of the interior space as compared with the bastioned enceinte. The ditches when dry can only be swept by casemated defences in the re-entering angles; and even then but partially, unless the casemate embrasures are placed very near the level of the bottom of the ditch, in which case the enceinte would be exposed to a surprise through the embrasures; and, in the contrary case, liable to a like attempt from the dead space at the re-enterings below the embrasures. In wet ditches this exposure to surprise would be much less if the ditches could not be forded. In either case the defect arising from embrasure casemates placed in a re-entering angle, would be a serious objection to using the guns of each side simultaneously. When the salient angles of the tenailles are acute, the effect of the enfilading fire would not be felt alone on the face enfiladed, but upon the adjacent face in front, and shot passing over would damage the adjacent tenailles.

The foregoing are the chief objections to this system. It presents no advantage but the very illusory one, considering the consequences arising from it, of long faces presenting a mutual flanking and cross fire of considerable extent.

Carnot's Tenailled Method.

550...The great reputation acquired by Carnot during the French revolution, in which he played so conspicuous a part as a soldier, statesman and executive officer, connected with his professional education as an engineer officer, gave for a time a certain *prestige* to his views on fortification, which caused them to be adopted in Germany, where they have been applied in some of the works constructed since 1815.

551...Struck with the exposed state of the artillery, on ramparts without bomb-proof shelters, to ricochet fires, and the feeble resistance offered by garrisons in some of the sieges of his day, particularly in an active defence by sorties, Carnot seems to have considered the weakness attributed to existing fortifications to the want of such shelters, and also of such means of communication with the exterior which would enable the garrison to sally out in force and assail the trenches of the besiegers.

552...The systems of defence which he has proposed are devised to remedy these two prominent defects, and consist in providing a number of casemates, on suitable points of the defences, from which a constant shower of small projectiles and hollow shot can be brought upon the besieger's works; and, instead of the revetted counterscarp, which constitutes one of the main securities against a surprise—but as ordinarily arranged is an obstacle in the way of throwing rapidly forward a considerable body of troops from the interior to operate on the exterior—he proposes to form an earthen one with so slight a slope that troops can ascend it with ease to make sorties; the ordinary covered-way and glacis being also done away with to facilitate these operations.

553...Carnot, in his published works, has given his views upon the ameliorations of which the fortifications of his time were susceptible, besides some new combinations for a bastioned system and two tenailled systems for aquatic and irregular sites, in which the defects of this latter system are less objectionable, and to which they can be more easily applied.

554...PLAN. This consists of a continuous enceinte, Pl. 16, Fig. 2, formed of tenailles, the re-entering angles of which are 90°, and the salient angles not less than 60°. The interior of the place is enclosed by a wall, *A*, of sufficient height to be secure from escalade; the plan of it is a tenailled line, with re-entering angles of 90° and salients of 60°; it is arranged with two tiers of loop-holes for musketry, which are within arched recesses in the wall, of sufficient depth to screen the men serving them from vertical fire. Casemated batteries, *Q*, for artillery, are placed at the re-enterings, to flank the ditch between the wall and the earthen rampart of the enceinte. This wall serves the same end as the one in Montalembert's method. The salients, *A A*, are about 250 yards apart.

555...The rampart and parapet of the body of the place, *C*, are detached from the scarp wall in front, a narrow corridor being left between the foot of the exterior slope and the back of the wall. The wall is arranged like the interior one, with one tier only of loop-holes for musketry fire. At its re-entering it is broken forward and is pierced with embrasures, to form a position, *W*, for cannon to flank the ditch between it and the tenaille.

556...The tenaille, *G*, masks the greater portion of the scarp of the body of the place, its wings being about 120 yards in length; it is closed by a detached wall with loop-holes.

557...From the re-entering of the tenaille a double caponnière of earth leads by a ramp to an earthen redoubt, *K*, placed at the re-entering formed by the counterscarps. This redoubt is intended to hold troops in readiness for sorties, and is without a ditch, so that they can move out over its parapet.

558...Earthen counterguards, the salients of which, *B B*, are about 390 yards apart, mask the walls of the body of the place and the tenaille; sufficient space only being left between their extremities, *F*, *F*, and the caponnière for the circulation through the ditches. This work, like the tenaille, has a narrow terreplein, and is intended only for a defence of musketry, except at the salient portions, which, like the salients of the enceinte, are arranged for artillery to fire in the direction of their capitals from behind blindages or casemated traverses.

The foot of the parapet, *M M*, of the redoubt is placed 40 yards within the line joining *B B*.

559...PROFILE. The positions of the different lines on the plan are readily ascertained from the section on *J K*, Fig. 2, as the lines are all parallel. The relief and the relative command of the different parts are also given on the same section.

560...REMARKS. The expectations of Carnot with respect to the efficacy of the proposed shower of small projectiles upon the trenches of the besiegers, from the casemates for mortars and howitzers, have been shown from experiments as not likely to be realized. From similar experiments, the detached scarp walls proposed by him would soon be overthrown by a heavy curvated fire, which might be brought to bear upon them over their earthen masks. The ditches and terrepleins of all the parts of his tenailled method are peculiarly exposed to ricochet fire, whilst the long wings of the tenaille and the double caponnière mask, to a great degree, the fire of the enceinte along the ditches. The provision made for sorties from the redoubt at the re-entering of the earthen inclined counterscarps is exceedingly feeble, and it is not easy to see what would prevent an active enemy, on the repulse of a sortie, from following the retreating troops into the works themselves, or, having driven them into the ditches, from regaining their trenches with comparatively little loss.

Polygonal System.

561...The polygonal system has been proposed by several engineers of distinction, but its most ardent advocate has been the celebrated Montalembert, whose views have been, more or less, carried out in many of the more recent constructions of the engineers of Germany.

Consisting of either a simple polygonal enceinte without re-enterings, the sides of which are flanked by casemated caponnières, placed at the middle point of the fronts; or of fronts either slightly tenailled, or of a bastioned form, with short casemated flanks to flank the faces of the central caponnières, this system affords more interior space, and, from the mode adopted for flanking the enceinte, will admit of much larger fronts than either the bastioned or the tenailled systems. The salient angles, moreover, will be more open in this than in the other two systems. From these peculiarities of this system, the positions suitable for the erection of batteries to enfilade the faces of the enceinte are less advantageous, from their being thrown in nearer to the adjacent fronts, than in either of the other systems; whilst a greater development of trenches will also be requisite to envelop the fronts of attack. These obvious advantages, however, are more than counterbalanced by the want of the concentrated cross fires which are afforded, in both the bastioned and tenailled systems, in advance of the salients of the enceinte, and upon the ground generally in advance of the fronts. Each front of the polygonal system offers, moreover, a long and vulnerable line to enfilading and slant fire, which will also, to some extent, take effect on the reverse of the adjacent fronts. But the chief objection to this system lies in the mode adopted for flanking the enceinte. The casemated caponnières for this purpose being exterior to the enceinte, it will be exposed to escalade as soon as the fire of the caponnières is silenced, which, considering the structure of the caponnière, and the exposure of its embrasures to the enfilading batteries, will, in all probability, take place at an early period after this fire is opened.

Montalembert's Polygonal Method.

562...Among the writers on permanent fortification whose works have had an important bearing on the progress of the art, Montalembert holds a conspicuous place, although not educated as an engineer. Struck by the evident defects of the methods of his predecessors, particularly the want of casemates, both for defensive dispositions for artillery and musketry and the shelter of the garrison and munitions, Montalembert devoted his time, talents and fortune, to bringing about a change in the direction in which it seemed to him called for. His efforts, however, led to no modifications of consequence during his life (which was principally spent in angry controversies with his opponents), except the extension of casemated defences for sea-coast works; and it is only within a comparatively recent period, since the termination of the great wars in Europe, in the present century, that a new school of engineers has grown up in Germany, based upon the views put forth mainly by Montalembert; and that these views have met with favor in other parts, although still opposed by many able engineers, in all countries, who contest their soundness.

563...The principal propositions of Montalembert consist in the entire rejection of the bastioned system as, according to his views, unsuitable to a good defensive disposition; and in its stead he proposed to use either the *tenailled system* or the *polygonal system;* in basing the strength of these last systems upon an overwhelming force of artillery fire in defensive casemates, and in organizing strong permanent works within and independent of the body of the place, which are to serve as a secure retreat for the garrison when forced to give up its defence.

564...Most of the objections urged against the bastioned system and its outworks having already been adverted to in the analysis of the front, it will be unnecessary to recapitulate them here; and as the tenailled system, composed of faces of equal lengths, with re-entering angles of 90° and salient angles of 60°, and termed by Montalembert *perpendicular fortification*, from the position of the faces at the re-enterings, has many obvious and more serious defects than either of the other two; it is proposed to give here a description of the polygonal system alone, and that in its most simple form: the one in which Montalembert presented it for the fortifications at Cherbourg, one of the most important naval stations in France.

565...Montalembert first gave the name polygonal system to a traçé of the enceinte in which all of the angles are either salient, or where the re-enterings are very slight. The distinctive features of his method are shown in the works which he projected for the defence of the harbor of Cherbourg.

566...PLAN. In the traçé proposed for this place, *A Y*, Fig. 1, Pl. 16, is the exterior side, or direction of the scarp.

The body of the place consists of the scarp wall, *D*, Fig. 1, and section on *P Q*, arranged with casemates for artillery and musketry; of a corridor, *C*, between these casemates and the earthen rampart and parapet, *B*. In rear of the rampart is a high wall, *A*, arranged with loop-holes, within which the garrison retires when driven from the defence of the rampart.

567...Casemated caponnières, *M*, which are secure from a *coup de main*, are placed along the rampart, and so arranged that a fire can be thrown from them over the parapet, and also along the terreplein. The corridor, *C*, is also swept by a casemated caponnière, *G*, for musketry, and the front of the wall, *A*, by a like arrangement.

568...The principal caponnière for flanking the main ditch is in the form of a lunette, and placed at the middle of the exterior side, its flanks joining the casemated gallery, *D*, of the enceinte. The flanks, *H*, and the faces, *K*, of this work, are arranged with two tiers of artillery and musketry fire, each flank carrying ten guns, and each face twelve guns. A wet ditch, *I*, separates the faces and flanks; a loop-holed wall encloses the portion between the flanks, from which the opposite portion between the faces is swept by musketry.

569...The caponnière is covered in front by a face cover, *N*, of earth in the shape of a redan. The scarp of the enceinte is covered in like manner, by the continuous face cover, *O*, of earth, in the re-entering angles of which, casemated batteries of two stories, for artillery and musketry, are placed to flank the ditches, and sweep the positions for counter-batteries around the salients of the covered-way. These batteries are masked in front by the earthen works, *S* and *Q*. The whole is covered by the covered-way, arranged in the usual manner.

The better to flank the main caponnière, the portion of the casemated gallery joining it is arranged with two tiers of artillery fire, the remaining portion having but one tier of guns.

570...PROFILES. The sections along *P Q*, *R S*, and *T U*,

show the relative command of the different works, and the width of the ditches and earthen ramparts.

The communications between the different works are by bridges across the wet ditches.

571...It is now admitted on all hands that, although Montalembert has rendered important services to the progress of fortification, particularly as regards the more extensive employment of casemated defences, still, many of his projects were visionary How far the recent works constructed in Europe, which are based on his views, will answer their ends, remains to be seen by the test of actual siege operations against them.

The partisans for and against these views are equally confidant in their arguments; but with the rapid improvement in artillery which has taken place within the last few years, and the heavier calibre which will doubtless be hereafter used in siege operation, it is very doubtful whether, from what experience has already shown as to the effects of artillery on casemate defences, they will be found to withstand these powerful means, in which case the systems based upon Montalembert's view must fall to the ground.

Recent German Fortifications.

572...In the large additions made to the fortifications of the German states since the general peace in Europe in 1815, the German engineers have, for the most part. of these new structures, embraced the ideas put forth in the works of Montalembert and Carnot, adopting for the plan of their enceintes the polygonal system with flanking caponnières, combining with these numerous casemates for defence, for bomb-proof shelters, for quartering the troops, and preserving the munitions and other stores.

573...From what has been published on this subject by the German engineers themselves and other European writers, the following appear to be the leading features upon which these works are based:

1st. To occupy the principal assailable points of the position to be fortified, by works which shall contain within themselves all the resources for a vigorous defence by their garrisons; these works being placed in reciprocal defensive relations with each other, but so arranged that the falling of one of them into the besieger's hands, will neither compel the loss of the others nor the surrender of the position.

2d. To cover the space to the rear of these independent works, either by a continuous enceinte, usually of the polygonal system, with a revetted scarp of sufficient height to secure it from escalade; the parts of this eneeinte being so combined with the independent works, that all the approaches of the besiegers upon each, both during the near and distant defence, shall be swept in the most effective manner by their fire; or else to connect these works by long curtains; or, finally, to employ these works, as in a system of detached works, either to occupy important points in advance of the main work or for forming capacious entrenched camps with a view to the eventualities of a war.

3d. To provide the most ample means for an active defence by covered-ways strongly organized with casemated redoubts, and with spacious communications between them and the interior for sorties in large bodies.

4th. So to organize the artillery for the near defence that it shall be superior to that of the besiegers at the same epoch, and be placed in positions where it will be sheltered from the besieger's guns up to the time that it is to be brought into play.

574...PLAN. The plan of the independent works may be of any polygonal figure which is best adapted to the part assigned them in the defence of the position; but they are generally in the form of lunettes, Pl. 23, Fig. 2, having a revetted scarp and counterscarp to secure them from escalade. In the gorge of the work a casemated defensive barrack is placed, which serves as a réduit or keep; a simple loop-holed wall, which is flanked by the barrack, closing the space between it and flanks of the work, and securing the latter from an assault in the rear. The ditches of the work are either flanked from the enceinte in their rear, or, when the work is a detached one, by caponnières, or counterscarp galleries. The work is usually organized with a covered-way, having one or more casemated redoubts, and a system of mines both for the exterior and interior defence.

575...The barrack is usually arranged for two or three tiers of covered fire, and an upper one, with an ordinary parapet and terreplein, on which the guns are uncovered and destined for the distant defence. The two upper tiers of covered fire are for artillery, to sweep the interior of the work, and to reach, by curvated fires, the approaches on the exterior. The lower tier is loop-holed for musketry to sweep the interior. The barrack is surrounded by a narrow ditch on the interior, and this, when necessary, is flanked by small caponnières placed in it, which are entered from the lowest story The barrack communicates with the interior by a door at some suitable point; and the communication between the interior of the work and the exterior is through doors in the wall enclosing the gorge.

576...Considerable diversity is shown in the profiles of these works. They usually consist of a parapet and rampart, of ordinary dimensions, for the uncovered defence; of scarps either partly detached and loop-holed, with a corridor between them and the parapet; or of scarps with relieving arches arranged with loop-holes for musketry; or of a combination of these two. The height of the barrack, and the command of the parapet of the exterior work are so determined that the masonry of the former shall be perfectly covered from the direct fire of artillery, and the exterior be perfectly swept by the artillery of the work. The portions of the counterscarps at the salients are also arranged with defensive galleries to sweep the ditches—usually with musketry, but in some cases with artillery.

577...In the salient angles of the work casemates are arranged for mortars, to fire in the direction of the capitals; and one or more casemated traverses are placed on the terreplein, to obtain a fire on the exterior and to cover the terreplein from ricochet. The masonry of these traverses is masked by the parapet.

578...Posterns lead from the interior of the work to the scarp galleries, the corridors, the ditch caponnières and the casemated mortar battery in the salient.

579...The system of mines for the exterior defence consist simply of listening galleries leading outward from the counterscarp galleries. That for interior defence is similarly arranged; the communications with it being either from the barrack caponnières or from the counterscarp of its ditch.

580...The work is provided with powder magazines, which are placed at the points of the interior least exposed to the enemy's fire; and covered guard-rooms, store-rooms for mining tools, etc., are made in connection with the posterns.

581...PROFILES. In the profiles of their works, the German engineers follow nearly the same rules for the forms and dimensions of their parapets as those in general use in other services. They employ three kinds of scarp revetements: 1st, the ordinary full revetement, Pl. 20, Fig. 1, or sustaining wall, with counter-forts; 2d, revetements with relieving arches, Pl. 21, Figs. 1, 2, either with or without defensive dispositions, as circumstances may demand; 3d, scarp walls, either partly or wholly detached from the rampart and parapet. In all of these cases, they give to their scarp walls a height from 27 to 30 feet for important works, and about 15 feet for those less so. The batter of these walls is usually one base to twelve perpendicular. For the full revetement with counter-forts, they regulate the dimensions of both so as to afford the same stability as in the revetements of Vauban.

582...In their revetements with simple relieving arches, they use either one or two tiers of arches; placing the single tier either near the top or toward the middle of the wall, according to the nature of the soil and the pressure to be sustained.

583...Revetements with relieving arches for defence, or scarp galleries, are arranged for one or two tiers of fire. The back of the gallery is sometimes left open, the earth falling in the natural slope in the rear; or it is enclosed either with a plane or a cylindrical wall, according to the pressure to be sustained.

584...When the upper part of the wall is detached, Pl. 20, Fig. 7, to form a corridor between it and the parapet in its rear, the top portion alone is, in some cases, arranged with loop-holes and arcades, or with recesses to their rear, to cover the men from shells; in others, a scarp gallery is made below the floor of the corridor to give two tiers of fire. The corridors are from 8 to 20 feet in width, and when deemed requisite they are divided, from distance to distance, by transverse loop-holed traverse walls for defence.

585...When the scarp walls are entirely detached, Pl. 20, Figs. 4, 5, 6. they are arranged for either one or two tiers of fire, with arcades to cover the men; the banquette-tread of the upper tier of loop-holes resting on the arches of the lower tier of arcades.

586...The counterscarps are revetted, either with the ordinary wall, or arranged with a defensive gallery, with a full centre arch, parallel to the face of the counterscarp wall.

587...The German engineers make a liberal use of bomb-proof casemates for mortar and gun batteries. The former are either placed in the rear of the parapet, or of the rampart, and along the faces, or else in a salient angle. In the former case they are covered in front by the parapet, in the latter either by the scarp wall alone or by a casemated defensive mask placed in front of the battery. When placed along a face, Pl. 20, Fig. 9, they are arranged for one or several mortars, and frequently with two tiers of arches, the upper one for the service of the mortar and the lower one for a bomb-proof shelter for troops or munitions. The chamber occupied by each mortar is a rectangle, 12 feet wide, and about 20 feet in depth; this is covered by a full centre rampart arch, the height of the piers at the back of the chamber being 4 feet, and in front from 6 to 9 feet above the level of the mortar platform. This enables the shell to clear the top of the parapet in front, which is about 12 feet above the level of the platform, and 21 feet in front of the battery. The chamber is, in some cases, left open both in front and rear, to allow the smoke to escape readily and to diminish the effect of the concussion of the discharge on the masonry; in other cases it is closed by a wall in the rear—an opening being left in this wall, immediately under the arch, for the same purpose. A small ditch is placed in front of the battery; and the wall in front is extended about 3 feet above the platform, to shelter the men from the explosion of shells that may fall into the ditch. The abutments of the arches are 7 feet thick, and the piers 4 feet. The arches are 2 feet 6 inches thick; they are covered on top by from 4 to 6 feet in thickness of earth; and, in like manner, the arch and abutment are secured on the side exposed to an enfilading fire. An ordinary traverse is placed on the same side, to cover the masonry and communication between the front of the battery and the parapet; the chambers of the mortars are entered from the front, or from the sheltered side, by a door in the abutment.

588...When placed in an obtuse salient, Pl. 21, Figs. 3, 4, behind a scarp with a corridor, a space of 10 or 12 feet is left between the back of the scarp wall and the front of the battery. The platforms of the mortars are about the same distance below the top of the scarp. The arches are covered by the earth of the parapet, to the depth of 5 or 6 feet. The dimensions and arrangement of the chambers and arches are the same in this as in the preceding case. The communication from the interior of the work to the battery is by a postern, 6 feet in width. A casemated guard-room is made in connection with the postern; and when the scarp is arranged with relieving arches, either for defence, or for other purposes, an arched stairway is in some cases made as a communication from the postern to the casemates. A transverse wall with a door-way, serves to cut off the court in front of the battery from the corridor to the rear of the wall.

589...In the less obtuse salients, the front of the battery is made circular; the chambers being so placed that the fire of the mortars can be thrown in the direction of the capital. A casemated defensive traverse, placed in the salient, masks the battery in front, and it is covered on the flanks by the earth on the top of the arches. The details, otherwise, are the same as in the preceding case.

590...In the arrangement of casemated traverses for guns, Pl. 20, Figs. 10, 11, 12, the chamber for each gun is a rectangle, 24 feet in depth, estimated from the interior crest of the parapet, and 12 feet wide. The chamber is covered by a full centre arch, the height from the level of the platform to the crown of the arch being 8½ feet. The arch is 2 feet thick, the piers between the arches 3 feet, and the abutments 3½ feet. The mask wall in front of the chamber is 3 feet thick. This wall is covered in front by the parapet, and by several layers of fascines or of heavy timber, laid across the embrasure in the parapet and above the one through the mask wall. The cheeks of the embrasure in the parapet are likewise revetted with heavy timber, to some distance in front of the mask wall. The masonry is covered on top and on the sides with 5 or 6 feet thickness of earth, to secure it from shells and enfilading shot. The casemates are left open to the rear.

591...In some cases, a blinded battery for a single gun, Pl. 20, Fig. 12, is arranged by enclosing the sides and front of the chamber with walls, and covering it with a layer of heavy timber, supporting two thicknesses of large fascines, covered with a thickness of 5 or 6 feet of earth. The dimensions of the chamber are the same as in the preceding case.

592...The caponnières, Pl. 21, Figs. 8, 9, 10, for flanking the main ditch, usually consist of two faces and two casemated flank batteries of two stories each; the lower story being loop-holed for musketry and the upper pierced for artillery. Each battery consists of several rectangular chambers, each chamber for a single gun being 12 feet wide and 24 feet deep, or of smaller dimensions, according to the calibre of the gun and the kind of carriage on which it is mounted. The upper chambers are covered with bomb-proof arches, the lower one by arches of sufficient strength for the weight thrown upon them. The front mask wall of the casemates is 6 feet thick; the wall in rear is 3 feet thick, and is pierced with windows for light and ventilation. Openings for the escape of the smoke are also made in the front mask wall, immediately below the crowns of the arches. An interior court 30 feet in width is left between the two flank batteries, and when the batteries are detached from the scarp wall, the space between is enclosed by a loop-holed wall built on each side in the prolongation of the front mask wall.

593...The faces of the caponnière form a salient of 60° They are separated from the flanks by two stories of arched corridors, in front of which are two arched chambers of two stories, the upper chamber being arranged for mortars. An open triangular court is left between the front walls of these chambers and the faces of the caponnière. The upper part of the walls of the faces, along this court, are arranged with arcades and loop-holed for musketry, and have an open corridor in their rear on the same level as the chambers of the second story.

594...The caponnière is provided with a powder magazine and other necessary conveniences for the defence.

595...The flanks of the caponnière and its interior are swept by the musketry of the scarp galleries in its rear. The faces in like manner are swept by artillery and musketry in casemates behind the scarp.

The arched chambers of the upper story are covered by a thickness of 5 or 6 feet of earth.

596...Caponnières of smaller dimensions, termed *bastionnets*, Pl. 22, Fig. 1, placed at the angles of redoubts to flank the ditches, are usually arranged for musketry, but sometimes receive artillery. Those for flanking the ditches of the independent works in advance of the enceinte are sometimes placed in the ditches of these works, sometimes behind the scarp wall of the enceinte, and sometimes in casemates in the main ditch, detached from the scarp wall.

597...The communications from the interior with the caponnières are by posterns.

598...The defensive barracks, Pl. 21, Figs. 6, 7, forms one of the most distinctive features in the organization of the German fortifications. The plan of these works may be of any figure to suit the object to be subserved by them. When placed in the gorge of an independent work and serving as a keep to it, their plan is usually semicircular.

599...The barrack consists of one or two stories of arched chambers for covered fire and an open battery on top, with an earthen parapet and terreplein.

600...The arched chambers are formed by connecting the front and rear walls of the barrack by transversal walls, which serve as piers for the arches of the ceiling, the soffits of which are either cylindrical or conoidal, according as the piers are parallel or otherwise. The chambers are about 18 to 20 feet wide and 60 feet in depth; their height, under the crown of the arch, from 9 to 11 feet. The arch of the highest chamber is 2½ feet thick, and, being covered with a capping and the earth of the open battery on top, is bomb-proof; the arches of the lower stories are 1½ feet thick. The front wall of the barrack is usually 6 feet, and is pierced in each chamber with one embrasure and two loopholes. The rear wall is 3 feet thick, and has a window in each chamber for light and ventilation. Openings for ventilation are also made in the front wall, just beneath the crowns of the arches. Door-ways are made through the transversal walls to form a communication between all the chambers. These are sometimes placed along the centre of the piers, at others near their extremities, so that the chambers being divided by slight partitions into two compartments, for the quartering of the troops, there will be a continuous hall either along the centre or near the rear wall, upon which all the apartments open. The barracks are, otherwise, arranged with all the requisites for lodging the troops comfortably and healthfully. The lower story of the barrack is surrounded by a narrow ditch. A drawbridge across this ditch secures the entrance to the barrack at the gorge.

601...In some cases, Pl. 21, Fig. 5, where the front wall of the barrack is much exposed to the besieger's fire, the piers are made thicker near the front wall; and they each have two vertical grooves to receive timber, laid horizontally, between which sand-bags can be packed in to afford shelter when the front wall has become much damaged by the besieger's artillery.

602...The foregoing summary description, with the plates, will give a good general idea of the principal defensive arrangements, constructed of masonry, which enter so largely into the recent German fortifications, and upon the details of which the German engineers have bestowed great attention.

603...The adoption of the polygonal system, with caponnière defences for the main ditch, has enabled the German engineers to give, in their fortifications, a greater exterior side than in the bastioned system generally, and still admit of lines of defence in which grape, canister and small arms, particularly the later improved musket, will tell with efficacy upon the besieger's works on the glacis around the salients of the enceinte. With a few exceptions, nothing of a very reliable character has been published as to the traçé of these works, further than the general defensive dispositions. From these it appears that, keeping in view the cardinal point in all fortification, the adaptation of the various fronts to the site of the work, so that all the approaches upon them shall be commanded and swept by their fires, whilst the principal lines of the enceinte receive the best direction to place them as little as possible within the range of enfilading positions, the exterior side is usually kept somewhere between 400 and 600 French metres, or between 450 and 700 yards.

Fronts of Posen.

604...The following is an outline of the traçé and defensive dispositions of a front of the fortifications of Posen, one of the most noted of these recent structures. The exterior side, *A B*, Pl. 22, Fig. 2, is 580 yards; a distance, $CD = \frac{1}{15}$ *A B*, is set off on the perpendicular of the front and within it; and on the line joining the salients *A*, *B* with *D*, distances, *A H*, *B M*, equal $\frac{1}{6}$ *A B*, being set off give the faces of the front. The salient, *E*, of the independent work is on the perpendicular of the front, and at a distance from *C* equal to $\frac{1}{3}$ *A B*. Describing from *E* an arc with a radius of 20 yards, and drawing tangents to it from the points *H* and *M*, gives the counterscarps of the independent work; the faces, *E F*, *E F′*, are parallel to the counterscarp, and equal to $\frac{1}{4}$ *A B*. The ditches of this work are flanked by casemated caponnières, *H I*, *M N*, which are 35 yards in length, or sufficient for four guns. The directions of these flanking casemates being nearly perpendicular to the direction of the faces *E F*, *E F′* The flanks, *F G*, *F G′*, receive the most suitable directions for sweeping the approaches in advance of the salients of the front. The main ditch is about 30 yards wide, its counterscarp being parallel to the faces of the enceinte, and the gorge of the independent work is on the prolongation of this counterscarp. The curtains of the enceinte are directed from the points *I*, *N*, on the point *C*, and are thus nearly parallel to the exterior side. The main ditch is flanked by a large, casemated, defensive barrack, having three stories of covered fire, the lower for musketry and the upper for artillery, and an open battery on top. The plan of this work is that of the letter *U:* the circular part projects within the independent work, and serves as its keep; the sides are nearly perpendicular to the faces of the enceinte and are prolonged within the enceinte, serving as a defensive caponnière to flank the main ditch, to sweep the terrepleins of the enceinte curtains, and also the interior, within the range of the guns of two round towers with which the sides are terminated. The sides of the barrack are separated from the rampart of the curtain by lateral ditches 10 yards wide, which give access to the main ditch from the interior for troops in large bodies for sorties. The parapet of the enceinte, Pl. 20, Fig. 4, is thrown back from the scarp, leaving a corridor between the foot of its exterior slope and the scarp wall, the floor of which is 12 feet above the bottom of the main ditch. The scarp wall rises 16 feet above the level of the floor, thus giving it a total height of 28 feet above the bottom of the main ditch. This wall is loop-holed for small arms. The counterscarp wall of the main ditch is 24 feet in height. The faces and flanks of the enceinte have a relief of 44 feet; the relief of the curtain being only 40 feet. The corridors of the curtain terminate at the court or open space behind the flanking casemates, *H I*, *M N*. Posterns lead from the interior to the corridors of the faces and flanks, and from the lateral ditches to the corridors of the curtain. The interior open space between the sides of the defensive barrack is closed by a loop-holed wall between the end towers. A ditch surrounds the towers and the gorge between them, across which a bridge, terminated at the wall by a draw, gives access to the interior open space and the barracks.

605...The scarp, rampart and parapet, Pl. 22, Fig. 5, of the independent work, are arranged with a profile similar to that of the enceinte. The circular portion of the defensive barrack which serves as the keep, is surrounded by a ditch, which is swept by small caponnières attached to the keep. A circular mortar battery, covered in front by a casemated traverse, is placed in the angle of this work, and behind this a casemated battery for howitzers is placed on its terreplein, in the direction of its capital, to give reverse views on the glacis of the collateral independent works. The gorge of this work is closed by a loop-holed wall which extends between the keep and the scarp wall of the flanks. The communication between the main ditch and the interior is through a gate-way in this wall. Posterns lead from the interior to the corridors of the faces and flanks, and to the mortar battery in the salient.

606...The counterscarp of the independent work is arranged with a defensive gallery, with which a system of mines for the exterior defence is connected. A system of mines for the interior defence is connected with the small caponnières in the ditch of the keep.

607...The covered-way is without the usual traverses, its interior crest being broken into a cremaillère line. Its salient and re-entering places of arms are occupied by casemated redoubts. The communications from the main ditch to the covered-way are by wide ramps, which are at the gorges of the re-entering places of arms, and under the fire of their redoubts.

Fort Alexander.

608...Among the most reliable of the traçés published of German fortification, is that of the main front of Fort Alexander, a detached quadrilateral work of the fortifications of Coblentz, given in the description of these fortifications by Col. Humphrey.

609...PLAN. The exterior sides of the enceinte of this fort, Pl. 22, Fig. 6, form a parallelogram, the acute angles of which are 85° The main and rear fronts are each 500 yards, and the other two 420 yards each. The main front is of the polygonal system, with a strong defensive caponnière to flank the main ditch. The caponnière is covered by a demilune, and the salients of the enceinte by counterguards; the ditches of these works being flanked by casemated batteries at the re-entering formed between them. There is no covered-way in front of these outworks, their counterscarps being of earth, with a gentle slope. A small earthen work, containing a casemated redoubt, is thrown up at the salients of the counterguard counterscarp.

610...To construct the traçé, take $a\,b=500$ yards, for the exterior side of the enceinte, which divide into three equal parts, $a\,d=d\,e=e\,b$. Bisect $a\,b$ by a perpendicular, on which set off $h\,H=h\,d=h\,e=\frac{1}{6}\,a\,b$. Through H, drawing a parallel to $a\,b$, and setting off along it the distances $H\,A=H\,B=320$ yards, the points A and B will be the salients of the counterguards.

611...From H as a centre, with the radii $H\,d$, $H\,e$, describe two arcs, on which set off from d and e the chords, $d\,i=e\,k=33$ yards, these will be the lengths of the casemated flanks; $i\,k$ being joined, gives the enceinte curtain. The salient angle of the main caponnière is constructed by drawing, from a point, m, on the capital, at a distance of 20 yards from the lines, $H\,d$, $H\,e$, lines to the extremities, i and k, of the casemated flanks. The flanks of the caponnière, $t\,n=v\,o$, extend back to the exterior side, and are 33 yards in length and 33 yards apart, or each $16\frac{1}{2}$ yards on each side of the capital. The faces of the counterguards are directed on a point, $C=\frac{1}{2}\,A\,B=53\frac{1}{2}$ yards on the capital from H. The salient, F, of the demilune is $\frac{1}{6}\,A\,B=106$ yards from the point C; its faces, $F\,D$, $F\,E$, are parallel to the lines $H\,d$, $H\,e$, which last, joined by an arc of a circle, described from m as a centre, with a radius of 20 yards, and terminated at the counterscarp of the enceinte ditch, which is 28 yards from $a\,b$, will give the demilune gorge. A casemated battery for three guns, behind the demilune scarp wall, flanks the counterguard ditch, and one for three guns flanks the demilune ditch, and closes the opening between the demilune and counterguard at this point. A narrow ditch, 10 feet wide, is left between the flank of this battery and the extremity of the counterguard, as a communication between the main ditch and the ditches of the outworks. This opening is masked by an overlap of the counterguard.

612...Casemated, or blinded batteries, are made in the salients of the enceinte and of the demilune.

613...PROFILES. The main caponnière, Fig. 8, has two tiers of covered artillery fire on the flanks, of five guns each; the lower to sweep the main ditch, the upper the terrepleins of the counterguards; its faces have two tiers of loop-holes. It has no uncovered fire, but a simple covering of earth as a bomb-proof.

614...Casemates, for five mortars each, are placed in the salients of the enceinte, at the foot of the rampart slope.

615...A narrow corridor, Fig. 6, the floor of which is 20 feet above the bottom of the main ditch, is left behind the scarp wall of the enceinte, the faces and curtains of this wall are loop-holed, and arranged with arcades to shelter the men, like the detached scarp walls of Carnot. These scarps are 30 feet high. The command of the enceinte over the parade is 26 feet.

616...The scarp walls of the demilune and counterguards, Fig. 7, are arranged like those of the enceinte. The command of these works is 16 feet. Their counterscarps are arranged with loop-holed galleries, from which communications lead to a system of mines for exterior and interior defence.

617...The rear side of this fort, not being exposed to artillery, is simply closed by a loop-hoped wall and ditch. A large, circular, defensive barrack occupies the centre ot this rear front, serving as a keep to the fort, and to sweep by its fire the ground on the rear and flanks of the front.

618...It will be seen that, in the arrangement of the plan of this work, the polygonal system, with caponnière defences, of Montalembert, has been adopted as the basis, with such modifications as the features of the site afforded, to withdraw the principal lines from the range of the enfilading views from without.

Work at Germersheim.

619...In the organization of works with wet ditches, the German engineers adopt the same general disposition of the elements of a front as they do in dry ditches; occupying the most important points of the polygon to be enclosed by independent works, and composing the enceinte of fronts of the polygonal system; taking their exterior sides between the limits of 350 and 650 yards, and sweeping the main ditch, and the positions for the besieger's breaching batteries around the salients of the enceinte, by the flanks of a defensive caponnière. The following concise description of a front of the *tête de pont* opposite Germersheim, will give a good idea of the general defensive arrangements in such cases.

620...PLAN. The front, *X Y*, Pl. 33, Fig. 1, is a tenailled line with a slight re-entering at the centre of the exterior side. The salients of the front are occupied by small bastions, with a scarp gallery on the faces and flanks, and having its gorge closed by a loop-holed wall, with a defensive, casemated réduit at its centre.

621...The centre of the front is occupied by a capacious, casemated edifice, which extends from the interior of the gorge of the independent work, across the main ditch, to within the enceinte. The circular portion of this edifice, within the independent work, has two tiers of covered fire, with an open battery on top, and serves as the réduit of this work. The central portion has two tiers of covered fire, and serves as a caponnière for sweeping the main ditch, etc. Underneath this portion are arched passages, to communicate by water between the ditch on each side of the caponnière. The part of the edifice within the enceinte is a defensive barrack, with three tiers of covered fire, and an open battery on top, from which the terreplein of the enceinte curtain, the gorges of the bastions and the glacis of the enceinte can be swept.

622...The enceinte curtain is not revetted with masonry. The exterior slope of its parapet descends to a wide berm several feet above the water level of the wet ditch, and which, in many places, is planted with a thorn thickset hedge as an obstacle to an assault. The rampart of the curtain is sustained within by a high wall, which joins the loop-holed walls of the bastion gorges, and is flanked by the bastion réduits.

623...The independent work is in the form of a lunette; its faces being divided into three parts, each with a greater command than the one in its rear. The profile of this work is like that of the enceinte curtain; its ditches are dry, their bottoms being slightly above the water level of the main ditch. The ditches are flanked by casemated caponnières which extend across them to the gorges of the re-entering places of arms, for which works they also serve as réduits. They are connected with the central réduit by loop-holed walls.

624...The covered-ways are without traverses. A casemated réduit or traverse separates the re-entering places of arms, on each side, from the covered-ways of the enceinte and independent work, and sweeps them both. These are connected by loop-holed walls in front, which join those in their rear.

625...The counterscarps of the enceinte and independent work are of earth.

626...A passage leads from the interior across the main ditch on each side of the central casemated edifice, and extends along the counterscarp of the enceinte. This passage is a few feet above the water level, the two ends being connected by bridges across that portion of the main ditch where the arched communication under the main caponnière is placed. This passage is swept by two small, casemated caponnières, which project from the sides of the main caponnière.

627...Ramps lead from the level of this passage to the interior of the independent work at its gorge, and to that of the re-entering places of arms.

628...An interior and exterior system of mines is connected with the independent work and the réduits of the re-entering place of arms.

629...In the application of this system to wet ditches, the means of communication between the enceinte and the various outworks, by the passages and small bridges, across the main ditch and along the sides of the central caponnière, are principally noticeable, as the other features do not differ in any great degree from its application to dry ditches. Here one of the main objections to wet ditches, the difficulty of keeping open a communication by means of rafts or boats, for sorties and other purposes, is obviated by the arrangement of the passage in question. The bridges, connecting the break in this passage, may be so arranged as to be readily removed or destroyed when the besieger has gained such a footing beyond the main ditch as, by a rapid assault, to endanger the safety of the enceinte. This mode, however, of establishing a foot communication between the enceinte and the outworks of a front, is not peculiar to this system; as like means are used in the bastioned system, by placing the bottom of the double caponnière slightly above the water level of the main ditch, connecting the two parts of this ditch, on each side of the caponnière, by a narrow ditch, between this and the gorge of the demilune redoubt, over which a slight temporary bridge is thrown, so long as it is found necessary to keep open this communication.

630...The German engineers apply the preceding dispositions to every class of detached works, whether within reach of the artillery of the main work or beyond it. In the former case, the work is either in the form of a lunette or a redan, according to the requirements of the site, the gorge of the work being secured by a slight, loop-holed wall that can be readily destroyed by the artillery of the place, and thus open its interior to view when occupied by the besieger. In the latter, the plan is that of a polygonal redoubt enclosed on all sides by a parapet. The ditches in all such cases are flanked by small caponnières, placed at the angles of the work, and arranged both for musketry and artillery, besides a counterscarp gallery, which serves as the point of departure for the galleries of the exterior system of mines.

631...REMARKS. The apparently wide divergence between the German fortification of the present day and the bastioned system, which last had been adopted as the normal one throughout the world until these innovations were practically introduced, has given rise to active discussions among engineers in Europe, in which, as in all such cases, very ultra ground has been taken by both parties to the dispute. In each system the points admitted as essential in all fortification of a permanent character are sought for, viz: 1st, an enceinte secure from escalade and thoroughly flanked by artillery and small arms; 2d, such an adaptation of the plan of the enceinte to the site as shall secure, as far as practicable, the principal lines from enfilading views; 3d, outworks of sufficient strength in themselves, and of such defensive relations to the enceinte, as to force the besieger to carry them by regular approaches before being able to assault the enceinte; 4th, interior defensive works, or keeps within the assailable points of the enceinte, and in the outworks first subject to an attack, to give confidence to their garrisons in holding out to the last extremity; 5th, the means necessary for an active defence; 6th, the use of mines as an auxiliary; 7th, the protection of all masonry by earthen masks from the distant batteries of the besieger.

632...The only question then is, by which of these two systems the object in view is best attained. In the solution of this question, we are met at the outset by the absence of any reliable tests as to the real value of the defensive means adopted in the German system. No place fortified by this mode has yet been subjected to a siege, and nothing can, therefore, be with certainty stated as to the degree of resistance the peculiar defensive means adopted may be expected to afford, except some experiments made at Woolwich, England, some years ago, to test the practicability of breaching detached scarps, like those of Carnot, when covered by an earthen mask, with heavy guns throwing their projectiles, within the usual range of ricochet fire, over the earthen mask to reach the wall covered by it; and others made at Bapaume, France, on the effects of shot on defensive casemates. These experiments, together with some facts drawn from the sieges in Italy and Spain, during the period between the first French revolution and the peace of 1815, and the more recent attacks on fortifications during the struggle between Russia and the Allies, go to show that all structures of masonry, whenever they can be reached by heavy projectiles within the range of 800 to 1,000 yards, whether in view or not, may be greatly damaged if not entirely ruined; and that troops within defensive casemates exposed to such a fire, would be soon driven out of them by the embrasure shots, and the cannon destroyed. That the flanking caponnières of the enceinte and of the independent works in the German systems are thus exposed and liable to these objections, does not admit of a question. Like assertions may be made of the scarps, which are either wholly or partly detached, and of the traverse walls by which the corridors of the enceinte are divided for defence. The defensive barracks in the gorges of the independent works, and which serve as their réduits, as well as the loop-holed wall by which the gorges of these works are closed, being thrown back from the cover of their parapets, are also similarly exposed. The German engineers, it is said, have, by the dispositions made in some of their more recent structures, by abandoning the countersloping glacis of Carnot and his detached scarps, employing in their stead, on fronts of attack, scarps with relieving arches, and covering, to some extent, their ditch caponnière defences by earthen masks, shown some distrust of the methods mostly used in their first structures, planned upon the views of Montalembert and Carnot.

633...The polyognal traçé, which obtains in most of the recent German works, has certain prominent advantages and defects which may be seen by a slight comparison with the bastioned system. As the exterior sides are longer, and the re-enterings of the enceinte less deep than in the bastioned systems, it follows: 1st, that the interior space enclosed by the enceinte is greater in the polygonal traçé; 2d, that the faces of the enceinte are less exposed to ricochet from the greater obtuseness of the salient angles; 3d, that the fire of the faces have thus a better bearing on the distant defence; 4th, that, requiring fewer fronts on a given extent of line to be fortified, there will be fewer flanks and more artillery, therefore, disposable for the faces and curtains; 5th, that, in the usual mode of attack, the besiegers will be forced into a greater development of trenches for the same number of fronts. Such are the advantages inherent in this traçé.

634...Its defects are: 1st, that the enceinte having no other flanking defence than the main caponnière, it will be exposed to an escalade so soon as the fire of this defence is silenced; 2d, that the progress of the besiegers, during the last and most important period of the siege, is but little delayed, owing to the slighter re-enterings formed by the independent works in front of the enceinte salients.

635...The defects in the bastioned traçé, and the modes proposed by different engineers to remedy them, particularly those of Haxo and Choumara, have been sufficiently dwelt upon to show that, with the advantages inherent in this traçé of preserving the means of flanking the enceinte ditch to the last, of throwing the bastion salients into deep re-enterings, and giving a better direction to the enceinte faces for sweeping the ground in advance of the demilune salients, it is susceptible of receiving all the means of casemated defences, of a great development of flank fire, of defensive arrangements of mines, of ample communications for an active defence, and an extension of the exterior side, fortified commensurate with the improvements of late years in artillery and small arms.

636...In the discussions which have taken place upon the merits of these two traçés between engineers of the two rival schools, each has seemed disposed to exaggerate the defects and to depreciate the advantages of the system analyzed, and has conducted his mode of attack accordingly. The true point, however, as to the inherent merits of the question, does not lie in a comparison of the means of resistance of a bastioned traçé, with defective communications and without casemated defences and mines, and that of the German system, but between the former, with these additions, now regarded by engineers of every school as indispensable to a vigorous defence against the greatly improved means of attack of the present day, and the latter.

637...The fragility of masonry, and the ease with which it can be ruined by distant batteries of heavy calibre, particularly when pierced with embrasures and loop-holes, like the casemated caponnières and defensive barracks of the German system, must naturally incline engineers to limit its employment as much as possible, reserving its use for positions where it will not be subject to this exposure, or where it can be so covered with an earthen mask that nothing may be apprehended from the besieger's heavy guns.

German Forts.

638...In their detached works, or isolated forts, the German engineers follow the same defensive measures as in the independent works belonging to a continuous enceinte. A strong, casemated barrack, Pl. 33, Fig. 2, the plan of which is either curvilinear or polygonal, with several tiers of fire, serves as the réduit or keep of the work, and is placed either within it or at its gorge, according to the position to be occupied. The interior is provided with casemates for guns and mortars, placed at the salients and along the terreplein—frequently under traverses, when these are used to cover a face from enfilading views. The scarp walls are usually built with relieving arches, defensive scarp galleries, and open corridors behind the upper part of the scarp wall, which is also loop-holed. The ditches are flanked by small caponnières, placed at the angles of the work, or along its faces, and by loop-holed counterscarp galleries; and mines for exterior and interior defence are connected with these galleries and with the ditch which usually surrounds the keep.

639...TOWER FORTS. The favor with which the views of Montalembert have been received in Germany, has led to the adoption of his circular casemated towers, both as isolated forts and combined in a system of detached works for covering a space to their rear for an entrenched camp, as at Lintz. These towers, in their interior arrangements, are the same as the defensive barrack already described, with the exception of those differences in the details of the construction which the difference in their plans would call for. They have several tiers of covered fire for artillery and musketry, and an open battery on top, the parapet of which is either of earth or of masonry, according to the dimensions of the tower. In the towers at Lintz they are surrounded by a ditch, and the whole of the masonry which would be exposed to the besieger's batteries is covered by a glacis, leaving only the guns on top to have direct views on these batteries, the second tier firing under an elevation over the crest of the glacis mask. The ditch toward the interior is crossed by a temporary fixed and a drawbridge leading to the second story of the tower. The guns of the top battery are placed on a revolving platform, their carriages being of a peculiar construction, to admit of the axes of the guns remaining parallel, so as not to have their shot diverge from the object to be reached, and, at the same time, to occupy as little space, laterally, as will just suffice for the service of the guns. An earthen parapet covers the guns on the side exposed to the besieger's fire, and one of masonry toward the interior. These towers, with the exception of the open battery, have the defects of divergent fires, common to all works with a circular plan; and the open battery is liable to be rendered useless, or be ruined by a well-aimed shot or two, or a heavy shell falling on its platform. The tower without earthen masks can only be used with advantage in positions where it will not be exposed to being breached from a distance, and is a very good auxiliary in sea-coast defence, for points where the object is solely to prevent an enemy's vessels from making use of a safe anchorage on the coast.

The Adaptation of Permanent Fortification to the Topographical Features of Frontiers.

640...No state, in the present condition of civilization, can be regarded as secure from foreign military aggression, the accessible points of whose frontiers are not occupied by permanent fortifications of such strength as shall prevent an enemy from obtaining possession of them by a sudden assault, and thus procuring the means of penetrating into the interior. Guided by the experience of centuries of wars, and the daily increasing facilities which the improvements in the *materiel* of armies and their transportation afford for rapid and powerful offensive operations, the ruling states of continental Europe have, within the last quarter of a century, not only made every effort to place their frontiers in an unassailable condition, but also their great centres of population and wealth in the interior, beyond the chances of a sudden attack from an enemy who might force his way through the frontier defences, and march rapidly upon them, thus making these positions the rallying-points where a defeated army can find a safe resting-place, until it can be reorganized and sufficiently strengthened to resume the offensive. Such seems to be the result at which the generals and statesmen of Europe have arrived, after the most mature and careful consideration of the important problem of national defence, during which the utility of permanent fortifications was seriously called in question by some who pointed, in support of their views, to the very inefficient part the great number of fortified places had played in the wars waged by Napoleon, when, by means of overwhelming numbers, he was enabled to disregard such places, the garrisons of which were too feeble to make any efficient offensive movements, until the defeat of his adversary, in one or more great pitched battles, necessarily also threw them into his possession.

641...In view of the arguments based on these events, the opinions of Napoleon himself should carry great weight. In speaking of the bearing of permanent fortifications in a defensive war, he says: "If fortresses can neither secure a victory nor arrest the progress of a conquering enemy, they can at least retard it, and thus give to the defensive the means of gaining time, a most important advantage in all warfare." In like manner, the Archduke Charles, of Austria, who showed himself one of the ablest adversaries with whom Napoleon had to cope, takes the ground: "That a defensive warfare cannot be systematically and successfully carried on in a country which is not provided with fortresses that have been planned and distributed according to strategical requirements." Like views were held by the Duke of Wellington, and it is probable that no great general, from the earliest period of military operations down to the present moment, has ever entertained the contrary. Without going further back than the two great contests which have taken place in Europe within the last few years, we gather the strongest testimony to the soundness of these views. We find, on the one side, the efforts of powerful Russian forces paralyzed by the obstinate defence of a few weak fortresses, and, in some cases, of simple field-works by the Turks; on the other, the gigantic armaments, by sea and land, of France and England combined, held at bay in the East, and in the Black sea; and, more lately, the career of France arrested in the very flush of victory, by the time which it must necessarily have cost her to break down the barriers which Austria had placed in her way in the strongholds of Northern Italy. The only question, then, on this subject that remains for solution by a state is in what way such a means of security from aggression can be best adapted to its own geographical, political and military status.

642...In a country like our own, with so vast an extent of sea-coast and inland frontier, and with political and social institutions which are so antagonistic to every approach to the maintenance of a large standing army as a measure of national safety, this question is one of peculiar importance, both from the open character of this extensive frontier, and from the almost incredible facility with which, as in the late struggles in Europe, and in the contests of China and India, considerable armies, with all their *materiel*, can be concentrated on distant points by the aid of steam.

643...The want of military means of some of our immediate neighbors, and the daily increasing mutual commercial interests between us and the greatest naval power of the world, from whom alone we have any serious danger to apprehend along our inland frontier, would seem to favor the hope that the day may never arrive in which our country will have to provide against invasion except along the sea-coast; and we may, therefore, dismiss from our consideration any further provision against this eventuality than the security of our principal harbors, naval stations and commercial marts from a naval attack, or from one combined with the descent of a land force, which last, from the great resources of our country in men and means, would hardly attempt to penetrate inland beyond one or two marches.

644...In the organization of the frontier fortifications of a state, the points to be chiefly regarded are the principal avenues of access to the interior, and the topographical features of the frontiers, as they lend themselves, more or less, to strengthen artificial defences. In conducting an invasion across an inland frontier, the march of the enemy must necessarily be along the roads that intersect it, as these afford the only good avenues for transporting the *materiel*, etc., of the army The points, therefore, or places in their neighborhood, where the principal roads or other avenues of communication cross the frontier, particularly those which lead to the great centres of population and wealth, are the ones which necessarily require permanent defences. No absolute rule can be laid down for the distribution or the strength of such works. Everything must depend upon the more or less of facility presented to an enemy for penetrating at one point rather than another, and of the ulterior advantages which the possession of one may present to him over another.

645...Rivers and mountain ranges are the natural fortifications of states, and, where they form the frontiers, they greatly facilitate the application of artificial defensive means, as they present but few, and those, in general, important points of access. When the points of communication on a river are fortified, an invading force, however powerful, cannot, without great risk, cross the river before first gaining possession of them ; for, even should a sufficient detachment be left to observe and blockade the fortresses, the main army, in case of retreat or any disaster, might be placed in an extremely critical position, in its movements to recross the river, with the garrisons of the fortresses threatening its flanks and rear. In offensive operations, fortresses upon a river frontier form one of the strongest bases of operations for an army If a river intersects the frontier, the point where it crosses it, or some one in its vicinity, should be occupied by a permanent work. Among such points, those are more peculiarly necessary to be held where a river, forming the frontier, is intersected by another navigable one which lies wholly within the frontier.

646...With respect to mountain passes, the main roads alone will require permanent works. If the passes are independent of each other, a work will be necessary for each one separately; but where several unite at the same point, upon or within the frontier, a single work, placed upon this point, will suffice. Local circumstances will determine the point in each pass which, occupied, will offer the greatest advantage of obstructing the march of an invading force. The only rule that can be given is that, whilst the position selected shall satisfy this condition, there shall be every facility of communication between the fortress and the interior for receiving supplies and reinforcements. This rule would lead generally to the selection of some point of the outlet lying within the frontier as the proper one.

647...The number of fine natural harbors and roadsteads on our seaboard, where the largest fleets can find a secure anchorage at all seasons; the proximity to the ocean of many of our most important cities, towns and populous villages, by which they are not only exposed to the usual dangers of naval attacks, but to incursions from an enemy's land forces; together with the large rivers which, having their outlets on this seaboard frontier, are navigable for long distances within it by vessels of the greatest burthen, have given to the subject of sea-coast defences a particular prominence among ourselves. The means of defence disposable for the security of these points, consist in permanent works arranged to meet an attack both by sea and land, and of such strength as the presumed nature of the attack will demand; of such temporary fortifications as the exigency of the moment may point out; of movable land forces; and of floating defences to act in aid of the others.

648...The character of the permanent defences will depend upon the object in view. Where this is simply to exclude an enemy's fleet from the use of a harbor, or roadstead, which offers to him no other inducement for its occupation than that afforded by a secure anchorage, one or more small works of sufficient strength to prevent the success of an open assault upon them, armed with heavy mortars and guns with long ranges, that can reach by their fire every point where an enemy's ship could safely anchor, will be sufficient.

649...The points to be occupied by these works, as well as their plan, will depend upon the natural features of the harbor or roadstead. They will usually consist either of open works, armed with guns in barbette and mortars that can sweep all points of approach to and within the harbor, or of a combination of casemated and open works. The gorge of the works in all cases being occupied by a casemated tower, of sufficient strength and capacity to hold a garrison of sufficient force to beat off an open assault on the battery by land, and be itself secure from a *coup de main.* Like defences will also be sufficient for the security of the smaller classes of towns and villages, which would probably offer a temptation only to a small naval force.

650...In the case of important commercial cities and large naval depôts lying within harbors more or less accessible both to sea and land attacks, the character of the defences called for should be commensurate with the magnitude of the interests to be guarded, and the consequent temptation to an enemy to put forth great efforts for their occupation and destruction.

651...The avenues of approach to these objects by sea, which can be brought within range of cannon and mortars, in fortifications on the shore, or in works erected on natural or artificial islands, should be occupied to a distance that will prevent a fleet from approaching near enough to open a bombardment; and, if practicable, should also force the enemy, if he ventures a land attack, to disembark his troops either at so great a distance from the object to be reached that he will not be able, by a sudden descent, to effect a surprise, or to limit his landing to such points on the coast as, from their exposed position, may render the co-operation of the naval and land forces very uncertain, and, in case of a storm, place the latter in a very perilous condition if attacked.

652...The exterior chain of the defences will consist of works of the above character. Within these, batteries, either open or casemated, as the locality may seem to demand, should occupy all the most suitable positions both for sweeping the path that a fleet must follow by powerful cross, direct and enfilading fires, and for reaching every point of anchorage within the harbor. On the land approaches, points should be occupied by forts of a permanent character, which will prevent a sufficiently near approach to bombard the city or *depôt*, and, in combination with temporary works, afford an intrenched field of battle for the troops on the defensive. These will form the exterior line of the land defences; the interior line being either a continuous enceinte of permanent fortification which will require a regular siege for its reduction, or else a suitable combination of either continuous or detached field-works of such strength and armament that the enemy, in any attempt to carry them by an open assault, will be made to suffer heavily, even if he is not repulsed. The security of objects of this character will be greatly increased when they lie at some distance within the sea-coast frontier, and can only be approached either by water, through such comparatively narrow defiles as even our largest rivers present, or by land only after one or more marches. These defiles will, for the most part, not only present admirable positions on their banks from which they can be enfiladed within the range of the heaviest guns, but frequently others, at points where the river narrows, or changes its course, where works, occupying the opposite banks, will give the means of rendering the river impassable by booms, rafts or other floating or sunken obstructions, which cannot be removed except by getting possession of the defences, by which they are guarded, by a land attack.

653...Wherever harbors or bays are of that extent that their entrance cannot be interdicted to an enemy's fleet, nor secure anchorage within them be prevented, of which we have examples on our coast, the case falls beyond the province of fortification and must be left to floating defences for a solution. Here even some fortified harbors on the shores of such extensive estuaries may give secure places of refuge for ships of war, from which they may at any moment sally when they can take the enemy at disadvantage, or into which they can retreat if attacked by a superior force.

654...The necessity of fortifications for the security of frontiers being admitted, there is seldom any doubt as to the points to be occupied, as these are usually unmistakably marked out by nature herself. Of the character of the defences for these points, the features of the locality and the importance of the points themselves to military operations, either defensive or offensive, beyond the immediate range of their guns, must decide. Here the question comes exclusively within the domain of the engineer, and its solution will be more or less perfect as he has the ability to adapt, in the best manner, all the resources of his art to the peculiar circumstances of the case before him.

655...In the powerful military states of continental Europe, the question, as to what extent the great centres of population and wealth in the interior should be covered by fortifications, has been submitted to the investigation of the ablest engineers and statesmen, from the time of Vauban down to the present day, but more particularly since the fall of Napoleon, a catastrophe which might not have taken place had Paris been secured by fortifications, which would have prevented a *coup de main* when the armies of the Allies gained possession of it as the result of a pitched battle. Whatever differences of opinion have been called forth, as to the mode of accomplishing this object, as shown in the published views on the proposition to fortify Paris, there seems to have been none, among those best qualified to decide upon it, as to the great importance of so fortifying this capital, and other large places in the interior, as Lyons, etc., which, from their position, must be of the highest strategical value, in the case of a successful invasion by a large army, as not only to prevent their wealth and resources from falling into the possession of the invading force, but to make them safe rallying-points for beaten and dispersed forces, and depôts for organizing new armies. The plan that has been adopted for this end both in France and in most of the other parts of Europe, which have been either newly fortified or had their old works strengthened within this period, is to surround the city by a continuous enceinte of greater or less strength, but one secure from a *coup de main;* and to occupy, with forts of a permanent character, the most suitable points in advance of the enceinte, to prevent an enemy from bombarding the city, or penetrating between the forts without first gaining possession of them. By this plan, it is proposed to gain all the advantages offered by the passive resistance of fortifications, and the activity of a disposable, movable force occupying the zone between the enceinte and the forts as an intrenched camp, upon which the forts with temporary works thrown up between them would render an open assault too perilous to be attempted.

656...The enceinte of Paris consists of continuous bastioned fronts without outworks, having a revetted scarp of the usual height to secure it from escalade, and a ditch with a counterscarp of earth. The advanced forts are either quadrangular or pentagonal bastioned works, enclosing all the means of security for their garrisons, as bomb-proofs, etc., their plan being skilfully adapted to the site, and to their mutual bearing on the defence. The fortifications of Lyons present more diversity, both in the plan and details of the enceinte and forts, although the general system is the same as that of Paris. In the last is seen a more extensive application of casemated and gallery defences, both for exterior flanking and for the defence of the interior of the forts: growing out of the more broken features of the site generally, and frequently from the more confined space occupied by them.

657...In Germany, the same general system of a continuous enceinte, with strong advanced isolated works, has been followed, the whole being planned and combined according to the distinctive features of what is known as the German system of fortification.

658...In our own country, where our largest centres of population and wealth lie almost immediately upon the seaboard, it would seem impracticable, in view of the rapid spread of population around them, and the consequent changes in local features, to resort to any defences of a permanent character, to secure them from a land attack, even were the nation willing to assume the burthen of the great outlay for such an object, as in a few years the works of to-day might be rendered useless by the changes referred to. Even in Europe, the strongest despotic governments have been obliged to cede, what seemed military exigencies, to the demands of the social condition, and either to raze the fortifications of cities, to give room to a crowded population, or else to suffer such encroachments on the ground necessary for the functions of the works as to render them nearly useless. The only defensive resource that seems left to ourselves, in like cases, is in the use of field-works, one which our military experience shows may be relied upon with confidence, so long as the military aptitude of our population remains unchanged, from what it has thus far been.

Summary of the Progress of Fortification.

659...The records of history and the vestiges of remote civilization show that the art of fortification, in some guise or another, has been in practice throughout all nations, even in the lowest stages of social progress, and that, wherever it has been cultivated, its character has been more or less influenced, not only by the natural features of the country, but by the political and social conditions of its inhabitants. In its earliest applications, we find men resorting to one or more simple enclosures of earthen walls; or of these surmounted by stakes placed in juxtaposition; or of stakes alone firmly planted in the ground with a strong wattling between them; or of timber in its natural state, having its branches and the undergrowth strongly interlaced to form an impervious obstruction, with tortuous paths through it, known only to the defenders.

660...A resort to such feeble means shows not only a very low state of this branch of the military art, but also of that of the attack, as defences of this kind would present but a slight obstacle, except against an enemy whose habitual mode of warfare was as cavalry, or of one not yet conversant with the ordinary plans for scaling. This class of fortifications for the defenee of entire frontiers has been mostly met with in the east of Europe, and was, doubtless, at the time, found to be a sufficient protection against those nomadic tribes that for ages have roamed over its vast plains, and who are only formidable as a mounted force.

661...The next obvious, and, in humid countries, necessary step was to form walls either of rough bloeks of stone alone, or of these interlaced with the trunks of heavy trees. Obstructions of this kind eould only be used to a limited extent, and were confined to the defences of places forming the early centres of population. As human invention was developed, these, in their turn, were found to present no serious obstacle to an assault by escalade—giving to the assailed only the temporary advantage of a more commanding position—and they gave place to walls of dressed stone, or brick, whose height and perpendicular faee alike bade defiance to individual attempts to climb them, or the combined efforts of an escalade. From the tops of these inaccessible heights, sheltered in front by a parapet of stone, and, in some cases, by a covered corridor behind it, the assailed could readily keep at bay any enemy, so long as he could be attained by their missiles; but having reached the foot of the wall, he here found shelter from these, and, by procuring any cover that would protect him from objects thrown from above, could securely work at effecting a breach by mining. It was probably to remedy this defect of simple walls that towers, which, at first, were nothing more than square or semicircular projections built, from distance to distance, in the wall itself, were first devised. These, subsequently, were not only enclosed throughout, but divided into stories, each of which was provided with loop-holes, to flank the adjacent towers and the straight portions of the wall between them, and was isolated at top from the straight portion of the walls adjacent to it by a break or ditch, on the interior, between the tower and the wall, across which a communication between the two could be established by a temporary bridge.

662...These formidable defences were, in their turn, found to be insufficient against the ingenuity and skill of the assailant, who, by means of covered galleries of timber, sometimes above ground and sometimes below, gradually won his way to the foot of the wall, where, by breaking his way through it, or by undermining and supporting it on timber props, to be subsequently destroyed by fire, he removed the sole obstruction to a bodily collision with the assailed. In addition to these means the besiegers, in some cases, resorted to the use of lofty wooden towers, which were covered by raw hides to protect them from fire, from within which an incessant shower of arrows and other missiles was directed against the assailed. These ponderous engines were gradually moved toward the walls, on inclined planes of earth, erected with incredible toil, to give the assailants a commanding position, and to enable them, when the tower was brought sufficiently near to the wall to lower a drawbridge from it, to bridge the chasm, and bring on a hand-to-hand contest with the assailed.

663...These methods of attack led to new modifications in the defence, which consisted in surrounding the place by wide and deep ditches, of which the walls formed the scarp—the counterscarp being either of earth or revetted with stone. This placed a formidable obstacle to the mode of attack by mining, as well as to the use of earthen mounds, as these last had to be erected across the ditch before sufficient proximity to the wall could be gained, either to form a communication with its top, or to plant the battering ram—a heavy beam, with an iron or brass head, which, swung horizontally within a wooden tower, could be driven by men with sufficient force to breach the heaviest walls. The ditches, also, were filled with water whenever this obstruction could be procured. When dry, they formed a defile through which the assailed often sallied upon the assailant with success.

664...The gigantic proportions often given to the fortifications of antiquity, as well as their extent, seem almost incredible in the present day In many cases a double wall of stone or brick was filled in between with earth, forming a wide rampart upon which several vehicles could go abreast. Not only was the space enclosed within the walls sufficient for the habitations, but ground enough was said to be taken in, also, for agriculture, so as to add considerably to the food of the inhabitants and cattle, for the long periods to which blockades were in many cases extended, when the besiegers had failed in all other means of reducing the place.

665...The wall built by the Romans in Britain, between Carlisle and Newcastle, to restrain the incursions of the Picts into the southern portions of the island, was sixteen miles in extent, about twelve feet in height, and nine feet in thickness. The extent and dimensions of this work sink almost into insignificance when compared with those of the celebrated wall of China, built to restrain the incursions of the Tartars. This structure is about 1,500 English miles in length, has a height of 27 feet, its thickness at top being 14 feet. The lower portion of it is built of dressed stone, the upper of well burned brick. It is flanked at distances of about 80 yards apart by towers, in which iron cannon are found. In the great extent it embraces, it necessarily crosses hills and valleys, and in many places important defiles. An examination of its parts has shown that in its plan there was an evident design to adapt it to those features of its site, as it is well thrown back to the rear, of difficult passes; and, at points where there is most danger to be apprehended from invasion, there are several walls in succession.

666...The mode of attack of fortified places resorted to by the ancients, was reduced to settled rules and brought to the highest state of perfection by the Greeks, about the epoch of Alexander the Great, and the immediate successors to his vast conquests. An essential feature in it, whether in the sieges of inland fortresses or of those on the seaboard, was to cut off all communication between the place and the exterior, by hemming it in by sea and land; with stationary forces, covered, themselves, by lines of intrenchments strengthened by towers, and, in the case of sea-coast places, also by fleets. The besiegers were thus prepared to repel all assaults, both from without and from the invested place. Having selected the portions of the place on which the main attack was to be directed, a second line was formed parallel to the first, which was covered, and constructed of timber and wicker work, and secured with raw hides to prevent its being set on fire. From this sheltered position, which served also the purposes of a lodging for the besiegers, the besieged were annoyed with missiles thrown from all the artillery known in that day, consisting of the ordinary bow, the cross-bow, and the various machines for projecting heavy stones and other projectiles. Under the diversion thus made, the besiegers pushed forward from this line several covered approaches directly upon the place, for the purpose of gaining the counterscarp, and from that position filling up the ditch with stones, earth, heavy bags, etc., to prepare the way for placing the battering-ram in position to breach the wall. The tower in which this machine was placed usually consisted of several stories, and was occupied by troops, who cleared the top of the wall of the besieged. This operation was frequently aided by other high towers, which were advanced either on the natural level of the ground, or upon artificial mounds, forming inclined planes, so that any desirable command over the interior could be obtained.

667...The defence was mostly of a passive character: the besieged trusting mainly to the strength of their defences, under cover of which they resorted to all the means used by the besiegers, for attaining the latter when they came within reach of their missiles; using, for the near defence, cranes and other devices to seize upon the implements planted at the foot of the wall; and constructing galleries of countermines to overwhelm the artificial mounds and their towers.

668...The Romans evinced their decided military aptitude, not only in the employment of the ordinary systematic methods of the attack and defence of fortified places, but in their application of the cardinal principle of mutual defensive relations between the parts of a fortified position, obtained by advanced and retired portions of the enceinte; and also in the adaptation of intrenchments to the natural features of the site, as shown in the fortifications of some of the permanent frontier camps of their military colonies. The application of these principles have also been noticed in some of the fortified positions of India, which consist of a mural enceinte with earthen ramparts, flanked by round towers, and of round towers in advance of the enceinte and connected with it by caponnières.

669...With the decadence of the Roman empire, the art of fortification, like the other branches of the military art, was brought to so low a stage that strongholds which, defended with skill and energy, would have baffled the efforts of a well-trained assailant in the art of attack, fell, almost without resistance, into the possession of the fierce Northern hordes by which the whole of civilized Europe was overrun. The remains of the structures raised for defensive purposes, during the prosperous days of the empire, were probably the sole means of protection afforded to the inhabitants of the towns that still maintained a nucleus of population, until the rise of the Western empire under Charlemagne; and it was the necessity felt by this conqueror, not only of securing his conquests, but of checking the irruptions of the barbarous tribes along his extended frontier, which led him to erect *têtes de pont* on the frontier rivers, and a line of strong towers, for garrisons of a few men, upon the most inaccessible and prominent points of this frontier; the latter being a means which was subsequently resorted to for a like purpose in the Spanish peninsula. Henry I, of Germany, introduced a more important and more systematic addition to these permanent frontier defences, by surrounding the frontier towns and villages, occupied by military colonists, with walls and ditches, to secure them from such attacks as they might be exposed to, and, subsequently, by adding a second line of strongholds within the frontier, by which an irruption through the frontier line might still be checked.

670...During the general disorganization of states under the feudal system, the free cities, which depended for their defence on the burghers composing the different crafts, every individual who could maintain a few retainers in his pay, and the clergy even resorted to such means of defence as would best secure them from the attacks of others in a like condition, or which would enable them to carry out that system of pillage that had become general amongst the nobles and other military chieftains.

671...From this state of society sprung up those castles, placed in the most inaccessible positions on the lines of communication which the little inland commerce that was still carried on was obliged to traverse. These castles were provided with every possible device for an obstinate passive defence, being surrounded by a wide and deep ditch, or moat, over which a drawbridge was the only communication to the main entrance, which, itself, was flanked by towers on the exterior and closed with massive doors; the tortuous passage, which led from the towers to the interior of the castle, being further secured by a grated portcullis which could be dropped, at a moment's notice, to arrest a sudden assault. Besides the ordinary measures of loop-holes and machicoulis in the walls and towers for annoying the assailant, a high interior tower, termed a keep, or donjon was often added, which, commanding the exterior defences, served also as a watch-tower over the adjacent country.

672...The keep, being the last defensible point, was in some cases provided with a secret subterranean passage, having its outlet in a distant concealed spot, through which succor could be introduced into the beleaguered castle and, in the last extremity, the garrison find safety in a stealthy flight.

673...The fortifications of towns partook of the same characteristics as those of castles. From the custom of assigning to the different burgher crafts, each of which had an independent military organization, the exclusive guardianship of portions of the enceinte, as well as their erection and repairs, great diversity, and, frequently, a whimsicality, in the defensive arrangements, was the natural result; the evidence of which still exists in the remains of the walls of some of the old continental cities. The art, for the most part, was practised by ambulatory engineers, who, like the secret orders by whom the bridges and churches of the same period were built, offered their services wherever they were wanted. Many new ideas were also introduced from the East by the Crusaders, as exhibited in the fortifications of castles and cities belonging to the templars and other religious military orders.

674...With the invention of gunpowder and its application to military purposes, a gradual revolution took place in the general forms and details of fortification. It was soon seen that naked walls alone did not afford space enough for the new military machines, nor sufficient protection against the projectiles thrown from them. This led to the introduction of earthen ramparts and parapets, which were placed against the walls and suitably arranged to meet the exigencies arising from this change. The art began to receive something like a scientific basis about this time in Italy, from which the names and forms of most of the elements of fortification now in use are derived. The Italian engineers, like their predecessors, went from state to state to offer their services wherever they were needed, and, in this way, disseminated the principles of their school throughout Europe. It was at this epoch that the bastioned form of fortification first appeared, but the precise date and the author of the invention are both unknown. With its introduction, the importance of separating the parts of a line of fortification into advanced and retired parts, the latter flanking and defending the former, seems to have been recognized as an essential principle of the art. With these changes in the form of the enceinte the art was gradually improved, by the addition of outworks to increase the amount of cross and flank fire; the introduction of bomb-proof shelters for the troops and other purposes; the substitution of earthen for stone parapets; and the attempt to conceal the scarp walls from the enemy's batteries, by decreasing the command and deepening the ditches of the enceinte.

675...By these gradual changes, stone walls, which in the old fortifications were the essential defensive features, came at length to be regarded in their true character, simply as passive obstacles to an open assault by escalade. The property of earthen parapets of resisting, without material loss of strength, the long continued fire of the assailant's heaviest guns, showed that the same defensive means were applicable both to works of a permanent and of a temporary character, and were equally available for the purposes of the assailant and the assailed. The measures for the attack and for the defence of positions were thus reduced to the same general principles, differing only in the forms and dimensions of the elementary parts, as circumstances seemed to demand.

676...ITALIAN SCHOOL. As above stated, the first employment of bastions, as they now exist, was made by the Italian engineers; and, as far as has been ascertained, toward the close of the fifteenth, or the commencement of the sixteenth century. To whom the credit of their invention is due, is not known. In the earlier fronts of the Italian school the bastions are very small, and they are connected by curtains varying from 250 to 500 yards in length. The bastion flanks, which were usually perpendicular to the curtains, were divided into two portions: that next to the curtain, which was one-third of the entire flank, was thrown back, and covered by the portion in advance; the advanced portion, thus formed, received the name of the *orillon*. The lower part of the retired portion was casemated for cannon; and behind this, and separated from it by a dry ditch, rose a second flank, having the same command as the other parts of the enceinte parapet. In some cases, a small and very obtuse bastion was erected at the middle of long curtains. The ditches of the enceinte were usually about 100 feet wide, and 24 feet deep, the counterscarps being parallel to the bastion faces. A scarp gallery, for the purpose of mining, ran throughout the enceinte scarp, and communicated with galleries leading to other points. The parapets, at first of masonry, were afterward of earth, and made from 18 to 24 feet thick. The earth of the rampart was sustained on the interior by a wall. Ramps established a communication between the interior and the rampart.

677...The defects of these early fronts were soon felt, and a more complicated but improved traçé adopted, in which the bastions were enlarged, and the curtains diminished. The retired flanks were still retained, but the orillon, instead of being angular, was rounded. To these improvements cavaliers were sometimes added to the bastions, which, in those cases, were made without retired flanks, or they were placed on the curtains, when, from the configuration of the site, some portion of the ground within cannon range could not be swept from the enceinte parapet. The covered-way was introduced, and became an integral part of the front; and a small demilune, or ravelin was placed in advance of the enceinte ditch, forming a tête de pont to cover the communication, at the middle of the curtain across the main ditch, between the enceinte and the exterior. The covered-way, which at first was of uniform width, and bordered the main and demilune ditches, was subsequently provided with salient and re-entering places of arms. These various essential parts of a fortified front were gradually ameliorated by the Italian engineers, but not before the Italian school had left its impress upon the fortification of all the other states of Europe, as the Italian engineers, from their superior acquirements, were in demand throughout these states.

678...SPANISH SCHOOL. This school, as seen in the existing fortifications of Spain, shows the influence of the Italian school, though modified by national characteristics. These are observed in the greater dimensions given to their profiles, an augmentation of the means of annoying the besiegers by artillery and musketry, the construction of complex interior retrenchments, and, frequently, the omission of a covered-way; the entire organization of the works pointing toward an obstinate passive defence, rather than to one in which sorties may play an essential part—a mode of defence in which the Spaniards, at all periods of their history, have exhibited consummate skill and perseverance.

From the broken character of many of the sites of their fortifications, the Spanish engineers have resorted to detached works to occupy commanding positions in advance of the main work. These detached works are also organized for a purely passive defence; being left to their own resources rather than to any support from the main work.

679...DUTCH SCHOOL. This school took its rise in the political necessities of the times, in which the national spirit was aroused to throw off an onerous foreign yoke. The aquatic character of Holland, and the want of time and pecuniary means, suggested those expedients of defence which are never wanting under like circumstances. The deficiency of earth led to the formation of low parapets for the main enceinte, and wide ditches filled with water. The main enceinte was usually preceded by a second one with a very low parapet, to sweep the surface of the wet ditch; and this second enceinte was separated from the first by a dry ditch, which favored sorties, and which was provided with all the means, as palisades, tambours and block-houses, for offensive returns and surprises. The second enceinte was covered by a glacis in advance of the main ditch. The covered-way left between the glacis and the ditches was, to a great extent, frequently deprived of its essential offensive feature, by the introduction of an exterior wet ditch, placed at the foot of the glacis and enclosing it; over which communication with the exterior was kept open by temporary bridges. The works were usually greatly multiplied and their combination complicated. The whole of the defensive measures of this school seem to have had for their object a strictly passive resistance. With this view, long lines of intrenchments, supported, from distance to distance, by forts, connected their frontier towns and villages, affording a sufficient obstacle to marauding expeditions, by requiring the efforts of a strong force to break through them. At a later period, taught by the experience of their earlier efforts against the most military state of that epoch, covers that would afford security against incendiary môdes of attack were provided; and revetements of masonry substituted for the earthen slopes of the ramparts, particularly where the ditches were dry. These successive changes, partly induced by the Italian and Spanish schools, with whose methods the Dutch engineers became acquainted through their connection with Spain, were the natural precursors of the methods of Coehorn, the most distinguished engineer of the Dutch school, whose works are characterized by many of its essential features.

680...GERMAN SCHOOL. The Germans reckon a number of original writers on fortification, among the most noted of whom are the celebrated painter Albert Durer, Daniel Speckles, and Rimpler. In the propositions of these writers are to be found the influence which the Italian school naturally exercised throughout civilized Europe, and the germs of many of the views held by the German school of the present day, which last seem, however, to have been taken more immediately from the propositions of Montalembert and Carnot.

681...SWEDISH SCHOOL. The part played by Sweden upon the theatre of Europe, under her two celebrated monarchs, Gustavus Adolphus and Charles XII, served to develop in this nation every branch of the military art. A number of distinguished generals and engineers arose under these monarchs, who combined, with the practice of their profession, a study of its theory Among the engineers of this school Virgin holds the first place. The climate and the nautical habits of a large portion of the inhabitants seem to have led to the construction of land defences analogous to those of ships: as shown in the use of casemated batteries in several tiers, both for sea-coast and inland fortifications. In this school the bastioned system seems to have been generally adopted for the enceinte, great attention being paid to covering the faces of the works from enfilading fire, to providing casemates having reverse views on the besieger's works, and particularly in so arranging the interior defences that each part should not only contribute to the support of the others but be capable of an independent resistance. These dispositions necessarily led to a great complication and multiplicity of works, as shown in the writings of Virgin.

682...FRENCH SCHOOL. What may be termed the characteristics of this school are to be seen rather in the method of Cormontaingne, and the teachings of the two celebrated schools, Mèzières and Metz, for the education of engineers, than in the practice of Vauban, although his authority has exercised a preponderating influence throughout Europe; and is still appealed to, in all great problems of the art, by each side in polemical disputes. The French have evinced in this, as in all the other arts, that spirit of systematic combination which forms one of their most striking national traits. Without excluding an active defence, the most noted authors of this school have based their methods more upon a combination of elements by which the besieger's progress can be checked, step by step, by the fire of the works than by sorties. Until within the last thirty or forty years, the French school was, perhaps, open to the reproach of a too exclusive method, and a subjection to mere authority. This accusation, however, was true rather of the polemical writings of the day, growing out of the propositions of Montalembert, than of the practice of the French engineers; and it was, in a measure, strengthened by a misconception on the part of foreign engineers, of the real purposes of the instruction given in their schools of professional training. Still, recognizing in Vauban and Cormontaingne the chief founders and authorities of their school, the French engineers of the present day discard no defensive element that has stood the test of experience, or is consonant with sound professional views. Basing their art upon incontrovertible principles, its practice is made by them to conform to the exigencies of each case as presented by its own data.

Progress of the Attack since the Invention of Firearms.

683...The introduction of cannon, although it led to important changes in the measures both of the attack and defence, still did not, for a considerable period, bring about any very decisive results in the length of sieges. The means which it afforded the defence of reaching the besiegers at a distance, and destroying all the methods of approaching and annoying the place which had been hitherto used, led to the substitution of the ordinary trenches of the present day for the wooden galleries and other similar expedients for approaching under cover; and to the erection of batteries at distant points to open breaches in the walls. Lines of circumvallation and countervallation, which formed so prominent a feature previously to this epoch, was the only one which still kept its place, as it has done to a greater or less extent to the present day For the purpose of effecting an entrance into the place, breaching batteries were erected opposite the points deemed most favorable. They were placed either on natural elevations of the ground or upon artificial mounds, with the object of attaining the wall to be opened near its foot and thus form a breach of easy ascent. These batteries were enclosed in works of sufficient size and strength to hold garrisons to secure them from sorties. The approaches were made as at present by zig-zags, along the capitals of the salients, to the counterscarp, where a covered descent was made into the ditch, opposite the breach, preparatory to its assault. When the wall was not exposed to a distant fire, the besiegers were obliged to carry the covered-way by assault and establish their breaching batteries on the crest of the glacis. In carrying forward these works, the besiegers were subjected to great losses and delays, owing to the magnitude and multiplicity of the works they were obliged to complete; to the imperfect character of their artillery and the faulty position of their batteries, by which they were unable to keep under the fire of the place; the want of connection between the separate approaches; and the exposure of the workmen in the trenches to sorties, the troops for their support in the enclosed works in the rear being too distant to give timely succor; besides this, as these enclosed works naturally became the chief objects for the fire of the besieged, the agglomeration of troops in them added materially to the losses of the besiegers. Owing to these imperfections in the measures of attack, the besieged were able to make a vigorous and prolonged defence; sieges became the most important military operations of this period, in which captains of the greatest celebrity sought for opportunities of distinction.

684...But little deviation was made in the methods just

described, until Vauban appeared upon the scene. Previously to him, Montluc, a distinguished French general and engineer of his day, had introduced short branches of trenches, which were run out from the angles of the zigzags, to post a few troops for the immediate protection of the workmen, but these were found to be very insufficient in repelling sorties of any strength. The event which seems to have had the greatest influence on the subsequent progress of both the attack and defence was the memorable siege of Candia, in which volunteers from all parts of Europe were engaged, who, after its close, disseminated throughout their respective countries the results of the experience they had there acquired. Whether the idea of the parallels, now in use in the attack, originated there, or with Vauban, this eminent man was the first to establish them in a systematic manner, and to demonstrate by experience their controlling importance in repressing sorties. The introduction of this important element in the attack; the concentration of the fire of batteries, by giving them enfilading positions; the invention of the ricochet, as the most powerful destructive means against the defences; the avoidance of open assaults, which, even when successful, are made at a great sacrifice of life, preferring to them the less brilliant but slower method of skill and industry, by which the blood of the soldier is spared, and the end more surely attained, such are the important services which the attack owes to Vauban; which has given it its present marked superiority over the means of defence; and to which the science and experience of engineers since his day have added nothing of marked importance.

685...CONCLUSION. Whilst the attack has thus been brought to such a state of perfection, and its destructive means are still on the increase, from the rapid improvement daily making in the range and certainty of aim of cannon, as well as in the ease with which the most gigantic armaments can be now transported to distant points, both on sea and land, the means of defence, so far as relates to fortification alone, are but little, if at all, in advance of what they were in the time of Vauban. Upon the chief defects and wants of the art, there exists but slight divergence of opinion among engineers generally; not so with respect to the remedy; opposite opinions being frequently drawn from the same class of facts, and the same authority frequently cited to sustain opposite views. Whilst each new disputant denounces systematizing and the systems of others, his remedy for the abuse complained of is usually a system of his own, which not unfrequently offers but the *disjecta membra* of those of others. The sum of the whole matter is, that fortification is an art the component elements and principles of which are few and simple. Its efficiency consists neither in short lines of defence nor long lines of defence; nor in large or small bastions; nor in the adoption of this or that system; but in the judicious adaptation of these principles and elements to the locality to be defended, and the purposes of the defence. In this resides the excellence of the engineer's art. He who should combine his elements in the arrangement of a small work, with a weak garrison, as in one intended for the occupation of an extensive position by a large force, or should blindly adopt the same methods for an irregular site that he would for a horizontal one, whatever his acquisitions or pretensions may be, has but a small claim on the title of military engineer.

686...From the preceding brief summary, it will be seen that the art of fortification, in its progress, has kept pace with the measures of the attack; its successive changes having been brought about by changes either in the arms used by the assailant, or by the introduction of some new mode of assault. The same causes must continue to produce the same effects. At no past period has mechanical invention, in its bearing on the military art, been more active than at the present day The improvement that has already been made in the range and accuracy of aim of both small arms and cannon, the partial adoption of wrought-iron and steel for floating batteries and sea-coast defences, point to the commencement of another important epoch in the engineer's art. The great improvement in cannon will give to the assailant a still wider range in the selection of positions for his batteries, and will thus increase the difficulties of the engineer in adapting his works to the site, and in giving adequate shelter to the garrison and armament. Whilst the defence will be to this extent weakened, the approaches of the besieger will be rendered more perilous and more difficult, from the greater range and accuracy of small arms. The great destruction of life, in open assaults, by columns exposed within so long a range, must give an additional value to intrenched fields of battle; and we may again see field-works play the part they did in the defence of Sebastopol; and positions so chosen and fortified that not only will the assailant be forced to intrench himself to assail them, but will find the varying phases of his attack met by corresponding changes in the defensive dispositions.

687...The engineers of our own country, without servilely copying any of the systems in vogue in Europe, have, in most of their enclosed works of any size, adopted the bastioned system. As the works erected by them are chiefly for sea-coast defence, their water fronts usually consist of one or more tiers of casemates surmounted by a barbette battery; whilst the land fronts present a rampart arranged for open defences. In small works, where the properties of the bastioned system could not be developed, owing to the limited size of the fronts, flanking dispositions have been made, either by casemated caponnières or by counterscarp galleries; and, in cases where a large amount of fire was requisite to sweep a given approach by sea, they have resorted to the castellated form of casemated batteries; combining several tiers of casemates with a barbette battery on top.

Whilst thus adhering to well settled principles and the practice of the best European authorities, our engineers have contributed their share to the improvement of the details of the art. The works erected by them, within the last thirty or forty years, are remarkable for the excellence of the materials employed by them, the superior skill shown in the workmanship, and the care with which every detail is worked out to subserve the object in view In these respects and in the general adaptation of the plan to the site, it is not claiming too much to say that the works erected by them are not surpassed and, in some points, not equalled by any similar works in Europe.

Influence of Irregularities of Site on the Forms and Combinations of the Elements of Permanent Works.

688...In treating the subject of permanent fortification, the same order is usually followed as in the discussion of temporary fortification, viz: 1st. An exposition of the general principles with their applications to a horizontal site. 2d. The various modifications of detail occasioned by irregularities of site as presented in nature. 3d. The various accessory means of strengthening weak points, called for by peculiar circumstances of locality, which either preclude the application of the ordinary means or require others in addition to them.

689...Whether the site is perfectly level within the range of the fire of the work or is irregular, the same general conditions are to be satisfied in each case, in order that the work shall have all the efficiency of which it is capable. These are: 1st. That every point exterior to the defences over which the enemy must approach them, or from which he can annoy them by his fire, should be brought under the fire of the defences. 2d. That no point of the defences shall be left unguarded by their own fire, or present any position where the enemy, obtaining temporary shelter from fire, may gain time to renew an onset. 3d. That the troops and *materiel* within the defences shall be sheltered from the enemy's fire in any position he may take exterior to them.

690....The problem presented for solution to the engineer in irregular sites is, frequently, one of no ordinary complexity; demanding a minute and laborious study of the natural features of the position in their relations to the defence; connected with a tentative process, of which the object is so to modify the plan, relief and details ordinarily adopted, as to adapt them in the best manner to the given position. No rules, but of a very general character, can be laid down for the guidance of the engineer in such cases. Of this class the following are the most obvious and essential, and, when practicable, should be adhered to.

691...1st. It has already been observed that, from the means used in the attack of permanent works, the more plunging the fire of the work the more efficacious will it prove in retarding the enemy's progress. The efficiency of this fire will depend upon two causes, the command of the work over the point to be attained, and the direction of the ground with respect to the lines by which it is swept.

692...As to the command of the work over the exterior ground, it has already been shown that motives of economy restrict it, in most cases, within very narrow limits, where to obtain it artificial embankments have to be employed. To augment, therefore, in the greatest degree this element of the defence, advantage should be taken of the natural features of the locality, by placing the principal lines, from which the exterior ground can be seen, on the most commanding or highest points of the site. If, with this position given to the principal lines, the ground swept falls, or slopes toward them, the most favorable combination for an efficacious plunging fire will be obtained; for, with this direction of the ground, the enemy will meet with far greater difficulty, to put himself under shelter by his works, than where the ground falls, or slopes from the line by which it is swept; as the surface, in the latter case, descending in the rear of the cover thrown up by the enemy, will be screened to a greater extent than in the former, where it rises in the rear of the cover.

693...The general rule, therefore, which the engineer is to take as a guide, in order to satisfy the condition of bringing the exterior ground under an efficacious fire from the work, is *to place the principal lines of his work on the most commanding points of the site, and in such directions as to bring the exterior ground to be swept in a position sloping toward these lines;* and this will generally be best effected by placing the salient points of the work on the most commanding and salient points of the site; as, in this position of the salients, the faces, which are usually the principal lines bearing on the exterior ground, will occupy the salient and commanding portions of the site, whilst the re-enterings, being thrown on the re-entering and lower portions of the site, will be in the best position for sweeping the ground immediately in advance of the faces; and, at the same time, they will be masked by the faces from the enemy's view, and thus preserved from serious injury up to the moment when their action may be rendered most effective; that is when the enemy, despite the fire from the faces, has succeeded in planting himself upon points on which this fire cannot longer be brought to bear.

694...2d. The condition of leaving no point of the defences unguarded by their fire, will depend, in a great degree, for its fulfilment on the same rule as the preceding. But where both conditions cannot be satisfied, the distant defence should be sacrificed to the near, as upon the latter the more or less of obstinacy of resistance depends, since the fire of the work and the action of the garrison are the more effective as the point to be guarded is the nearer to the defences.

695...3d. The condition that the troops and *matériel* within the defences shall be sheltered from the enemy's fire, from all commanding points without, will depend upon the relative positions of the principal lines and the exterior commanding points; and as far, therefore, as it can be done, without sacrificing either of the preceding and more important conditions, the plan of the work should be so arranged that the principal lines shall present themselves in the most favorable direction to the exterior ground to avoid plunging, enfilading or reverse views upon their terrepleins from any point of it.

696...To effect these objects, when the work is in the vicinity of commanding heights within cannon range, and the crests of these heights, as seen from the work, present a nearly horizontal outline, the principal lines of the work, fronting the heights, should receive a direction as nearly parallel as practicable to that of the commanding crests; when the outline of the crests presents a nearly continuous line, but one which declines or slopes toward the site of the work, the principal lines toward the height should receive a direction converging toward the point where the line of the crests, as seen, if prolonged would join the site.

The reasons for the positions assigned to the principal lines, in these cases respectively, may not, at a first glance, be obvious; but, by examining the relative positions of the crests of the heights and of the principal lines, as here laid down, it will, without difficulty, be seen that they can be brought in the same plane, and the latter be so placed as to give a nearly uniform command to the parapets of the principal lines over the site; and that by keeping the terrepleins of these lines in planes parallel to the one in which the crests of the heights and those of the parapets are held and at suitable levels below it, the parapets will be made to cover the terrepleins from the fire of the heights in the simplest manner.

697...The foregoing general methods, for determining the direction of the principal lines fronting commanding heights, so as to cover from direct fire, in the easiest manner, by their parapets, the space to the rear occupied by the troops and *materiel*, present, at the same time, the simplest cases of the adaptation of the plan of a work to the features of the locality, to subserve the object in view. In most cases, all that can be done is to avoid giving such directions to any of the principal lines as shall be favorable to enfilading or reverse views of the enemy; which may be effected by so placing them that their prolongations shall fall on points where the enemy cannot establish his works; or, on those which, if occupied by him, will afford disadvantageous positions for his batteries, either for enfilading or reverse fires.

698...DEFILÈMENT OF PERMANENT WORKS. The greater importance of so adapting the plan and command of permanent works to the features of irregular sites as to satisfy the conditions of sweeping, thoroughly, by their fire all approaches exterior to the defences, and completely flanking the latter, seldom places it in the power of the engineer to fulfil the condition of withdrawing the interior of the defences from either enfilading or reverse views by a modification of either the plan or the command. To shelter the terrepleins which would be exposed to these fires, as well as such as would be attained by a plunging fire in front, resort must be had to the usual expedients of defilement; that is, giving to the terrepleins such positions with respect to their parapets that the troops and *materiel* upon them will be screened from a plunging fire in front, by the parapets; and, when the terrepleins are exposed to either enfilading or reverse views, so placing earthen traverses or other masks, as to intercept these views, and cover the troops, etc., from the enemy's projectiles.

699...The defilement of permanent works, like that of field-works, proposes the same end, and employs nearly the same means. They differ mainly in their practical details; the latter being reduced to a simple practical operation on the field, whilst the former, from the usually greater complexity of the arrangements of permanent defences, requires the aid of mathematical science, and demands results of extreme accuracy

700...For the solution of all problems of the defilement of permanent works, the engineer requires: 1st. The limit exterior to the defences beyond which the effect of the enemy's fire may be regarded as so uncertain as to be neglected. 2d. The presumed positions within this limit that the enemy may take up to bring his artillery to bear upon the works. 3d. An accurate topographical map of all the ground within the above limits, as given by its horizontal curves referred to a plane of comparison. 4th. The magistrals and interior crests of the works, as either definitively or approximately arranged, referred to the same plane.

701....The limits beyond which the enemy's fire, from the usual siege guns, may be disregarded, owing to the uncertainty of long ranges, are 1,500 yards, where the work is exposed only to a direct, or front fire; and 2,000 yards, when open to a reverse fire. When the terrepleins, therefore, are covered, either by their parapets or other means, from batteries at these distances, they may be considered as offering shelters sufficiently secure for the troops, etc., upon them.

702...It may happen that there are points beyond these limits, but within the extreme range of siege guns, which, from their positions, it would not be safe to disregard; but these will form exceptional cases, and, when they occur, will be treated in the same manner as those within the limits.

703...The surface embraced within the limits and the line of defences, may be divided into three zones: one lying between the limits and the position of the first parallel of the attack, which is usually 600 yards from the salients of the line of defences; the second between the positions of the first and second parallels, or to a line within about 300 yards of the salients just mentioned; the third between the positions of the second and third parallels, or up to within 60 yards of the salients. In any position that the enemy can take up for his batteries, within the first zone, it is usually estimated that he will not throw up any parapet with a greater command than 10 feet over the ground on which it is placed. Granting this, the muzzles of his guns, behind the parapets, will not be raised higher than 6 feet above the natural surface; so that, assuming the surface of this first zone to be raised 6 feet above its true position, this may be regarded as the limit, vertically, within which the enemy's lines of fire will be restricted; and, therefore, if the interior of the defences is covered from the fire within this limit, the troops, etc., will be secure. That the enemy will not, in all likelihood, elevate his guns above this limit will seem probable, when it is taken into consideration that any advantage he might derive from doing so would not be commensurate to the labor it would cost him. For, suppose the enemy to have taken up a position for an enfilading battery at 1,000 yards from any salient, to enfilade one of its faces of the length of 100 yards; and that he should decide upon raising his guns 3 feet, or one yard above the limit just laid down; a simple proportion will show that, by this increase in the height of his battery, he will be able to attain a point at the farther end of the face only 3.6 inches lower than he would have done in the position of the assigned limit; an advantage which, considering the uncertainty of the fire at the assumed ranges, would hardly compensate the additional labor of giving to his works the additional command.

704...In the zone between the first and second parallels, the limit may be reduced to 4.5 feet, for at this distance from the defences their fire is so destructive and certain that the enemy cannot, without great loss of life and time, raise the parapet of his batteries higher than 8 feet above the natural surface.

705...From the third zone, the musketry of the enemy may be brought to bear upon the defences; and, from this position, during sorties from the defences, or at any other opportune moment when their fire is not active, the enemy might mount on the parapet of his trenches, and from there deliver his fire. This would bring his line of fire about 10 feet above the natural surface. The limit, vertically, of this zone may, therefore, be assumed at 10 feet above the natural surface.

706...The limits of the dangerous ground exterior to the line of defences may be marked off on the topographical map of the site, Pl. 7, Fig. 1, by drawing lines concentric with the line connecting the most advanced salients of the defences, and at the respective distances from it of 1,500 or 2,000 yards (as the fire may be brought to bear on the front or rear); 600 yards; 300 yards; and 60 yards; and then, considering the references of the horizontal curves of the ground, within the zones thus marked off, to be increased 6 feet in the first; 4.5 feet in the second; and 10 feet in the third.

707...In the defilement of each part, separately, of the line of defences, those portions alone of these zones should be regarded as dangerous which are embraced within arcs, or other lines drawn at the foregoing distances from the salients, or the faces of the part to be defiled. It may also happen that, within the limits of dangerous ground for one portion of the line of defences, there may be other portions which, from their position, may mask the portion to be defiled from all the dangerous points beyond them; in which case the points thus shut off need not be regarded, in effecting the operations of defilement. If, for example, Pl. 7, Fig. 1, the limits of dangerous ground for the demilune *A* being marked off, it is found that the demilune *B* masks the demilune *A* from all fire that might come from the ground beyond *B;* then this portion of the zones of danger need not be regarded in defiling *A*. To ascertain this point, it will be only necessary to conceive a right line to be so moved as to rest in each of its positions upon a point of the interior crest of *A* and on one of *B;* and if this line, in all its positions, passes above the surface of the dangerous zones beyond *B*, then will *B* serve as a mask for *A*.

708...In covering masonry from the enemy's artillery, 800 yards is usually regarded as the longest range at which destructive effects can be produced; and, also, that within this distance the angle of incidence of the ball on the surface must be greater than 45°, to do serious injury to it.

709...In the defilement of works of limited interior capacity, as, for example, the redoubt of the re-entering place of arms, the double caponnière, and the like, which are, moreover, not habitually occupied by troops, the extreme limits may be reduced to 1,000 or 1,200 yards.

710...Within the limits of the zones of danger, positions may be found for direct or front, for reverse, and for enfilading fire. If the two faces, for example, of a work be prolonged to intersect the extreme limit of dangerous ground, the sector which they embrace may be termed *the limits of direct* or *front fire;* since, from every position that can be taken up within this sector, a direct fire alone can be brought to bear upon the two faces. The two sectors which lie adjacent to this may be termed *the limits of lateral*, or *reverse fire*, since they afford positions from which a reverse fire can be obtained against one of the faces, and a front fire upon the other. It is also only within these last limits that positions for enfilading the terrepleins of the faces can be obtained.

711...The problems of defilement which present themselves for solution may embrace one or more of these cases in any example; depending upon the relative positions of the interior crest of the work to be defiled, and of the dangerous ground embraced within the foregoing limits. In the case of only direct fire, the terrepleins can be screened by their parapets alone; in that of a reverse fire on one face alone, its terreplein, in some cases, may be screened by a suitable position given to the parapet of the other; where both are exposed to this fire, one or more traverses must be resorted to as a screen; against an enfilading fire on one face alone, a portion of the parapet of the other, near the salient, may be a sufficient protection in some cases; but, for the most part, traverses, placed across the terreplein, will be the only remedy.

712...It does not come within the scope of this summary to examine the many cases of defilement which may arise from irregularities in the site; those alone will be discussed which are of most ordinary occurrence, and which require for their solution the usual geometrical constructions involved in tangent and secant planes and other surfaces, to a surface defined by the projection of its horizontal curves. The cases which will here find their application may be arranged under two heads: 1st, the plan and command of a work being definitely decided upon, to ascertain the exact portions of the zones of danger from which any description of fire can be brought to bear upon its terrepleins, and to defile them from it; 2d, the plan of a work being definitely fixed, but its command only approximately within certain limits, to ascertain the easiest method of defiling the terrepleins of the work by varying the command, or position of the interior crest, within the assigned limits.

713...PROB. 1, PL. 7, FIG. 2. *The command or position of the interior crests of the faces of a work being fixed, to ascertain the dangerous points on the exterior, and to defile its terreplein from these points.*

Let *ab*, *ac*, be the projections of the given crest; and the curves (28.0), (29.0), etc., those of the natural surface.

Prolong outward to *c* and *d*, the faces; construct the scales of declivity of the two lines *ae*, *ad;* and, from them, the scale of declivity, *ef*, of their plane. From the salient *a*, supposing an arc to be described with a radius of 1,500 yards, the dangerous ground will be included between it and the two faces of the work. Now, if the plane of the interior crests, of which *ef* is the scale of declivity, be indefinitely extended, and its intersection with the surface parallel to the natural surface and 6 feet above it be found, it is evident that the portion of this raised surface which lies below the plane may be disregarded, as no fire from it can have a plunge upon the interior of the work. But, from every point of the surface above the plane, a plunging fire can be brought to bear on the terreplein. Having drawn the horizontals of the plane *ef*, and found their intersections with the corresponding horizontals of the raised surface (which last will be given by adding 6 feet, or 2 yards, to the references of the curves of the ground), of which *xyz* is the projection. That portion of the surface which lies above this curve will alone have a plunging fire upon the work, and will be the only portion for which defilement will be necessary.

Now, as this intersection falls entirely within the angle *d a e* of the faces prolonged, or within the limits of front fire, it is evident that the terrepleins will require to be defiled only from direct fire.

To effect this, let a plane be passed through the face, *b a d*, of the work, and tangent to the raised surface above *x y z*. This plane will pass above all the dangerous ground, except at its point of contact with it; and, being extended back from the face within the work, it is clear, if the terreplein of this face be so taken with respect to this plane that no point of it shall be less than 8 feet below the plane, that then every point of the terreplein will be screened from a plunging fire by the parapet of the face *a b*. Now, if the same series of operations be gone through with for the face *c a e*, then will its terreplein be defiled in like manner; and thus the defilement of the whole work be completed for this case.

The tangent planes which satisfy the above condition are termed *Planes of Direct Defilement*, and they may be defined as *planes which, passed through the interior crest of a parapet, leave at least* 6 *feet below them all the dangerous ground of front fire, and pass at least* 8 *feet above every point of the terreplein behind the parapet.*

The terrepleins are usually parallel to their respective planes of direct defilement, and 8 feet below them. But when the declivity of the plane of defilement exceeds $\frac{1}{25}$, then the terreplein, if it is to receive cannon, must be kept within this limit.

In the Fig. 2, the references are put down in yards. The tangent plane through *b a d* is determined in the usual manner, by finding the horizontal (in this case 30.0), among all those drawn to the curves of the raised surface, which makes the minimum angle with *b d*. The line *h i*, perpendicular to this horizontal, is the scale of declivity of this plane; and the point *p*, that of contact. The line *k l* is, in like manner, the scale of declivity of the other plane, and *o* its point of contact.

714...It might happen, from the steepness of the terre-pleins, that the re-entering, or gutter, formed at their intersection, would be inconvenient, and it would, therefore, be desirable to have this portion raised, when it can be done without exposure to a plunging fire. This, in most cases, may be effected in this way. It will be seen, from an inspection of the Fig. 2, that the points *o* and *p* are the only ones from which the enemy's fire passes exactly at 8 feet above all the points of the respective terrepleins determined by the tangent planes; and that if, from these points, lines of fire, *o a r* and *p a s*, be drawn, every other line of fire through *a*, from the ground in the angle *p a o*, will pass more than 8 feet above the portion of the terrepleins embraced in the angle *s a r*, since the ground within the exterior angle lies below the tangent planes. If, then, *a* be taken as the vertex of a cone, the elements of which are tangent to the raised surface within the angle *p a o*, and if these elements be prolonged within the work, their prolongation will form a cone of lines of fire, which will pass more than 8 feet above the terrepleins. If these last, therefore, be connected by a surface parallel to this cone, and 8 feet below it, this surface may be taken as the portion of the terreplein which, connecting the two plane portions, will remedy the inconvenience pointed out.

715...Prob. 2, Fig. 3. *The data being the same as in the preceding case, and the work being exposed to both direct and reverse views, to cover its interior from these views.*

Suppose the plane of the interior crest of the faces extended within the limits, and its intersection with the dangerous ground determined, as in the preceding case; and let *x y z*, *m n o* and *p q r* be the curves of this intersection.

The face *a b* will be exposed to direct fire alone from the ground above the two curves, *x y z* and *m n o*, and to reverse fire from that above the curve *p q r*. In like manner, the face *a c* will be exposed to direct fire from *x y z* and *p q r*, and to reverse fire from *m n o*.

The defilement of each face, from the direct fire, will be effected precisely in the same way as in the preceding problem. The lines *h i* and *k l* are the scales of declivity of the planes of direct defilement of the faces respectively

For the reverse defilement, a plane is passed through *a b*, tangent to the surface above *p q r;* and one through *a c*, tangent to the surface above *m n o*, and their line of intersection *a a'* found. The line *u v* is the scale of declivity of one of these planes, termed a *Plane of Reverse Defilement*, and *s t* that of the other.

Now, if a traverse is so placed that its crest shall occupy the position of the line *a a'*, it will cover all between it and the two faces, as high as the interior crests, from the reverse fire on each side. But as it is desirable to have the troops, when on the banquettes, screened from this fire, the crest of the traverse should be raised from 18 inches to 2 feet above the line *a a'*, to effect this.

The traverse should extend so far toward the gorge of the work that the entire line of each face shall be covered by it. To determine its length with this condition, lines are drawn from the extreme point, *b* and *c*, of the faces, tangent to the curves *m n o* and *p q r*, and their points of intersection with *a a'* marked; the one that falls farthest from the salient, will evidently give the required length.

If the line *a a'* should fall so near either of the faces that the traverse, if placed along it, would incommode the service of that part of the work, it will be best to place its crest in the vertical plane *a a''* of the capital of the work. When so placed, the intersection of this vertical plane with each of the planes of reverse defilement must be found, and the crest of the traverse be taken 18 inches above the one that lies highest.

716...The position of the crest of the traverse, as determined by either of the preceding methods, will be in a vertical plane passing through the salient *a* of the work. From the thickness and slopes which traverses usually receive, they would ordinarily, if placed in this position, take up all the interior space within the salient, and leave no room there for dispositions either for artillery or musketry. To prevent this, a break is made in the direction of the crest, at some point on the vertical plane through the salient, from which it is directed on a point of either of the faces, so far from the salient that sufficient room will be left for the object in view. In the Fig. 4, which illustrates this arrangement, the traverse is withdrawn far enough from the salient to leave room for a barbette battery for several guns.

The face upon which the traverse is directed, will be determined by the condition of covering both faces in the most effective manner, by the position taken for the traverse.

717...The cross section of traverses for permanent works is similar to those used in field-works. The top of the traverse receives a slight slope each way from the crest to the sides. The thickness at top is from 12 to 20 feet, to render it shot-proof. The sides take the natural slope from the top, either to their intersections with the planes of direct defilement or to the terreplein. If, to gain interior space, these slopes are terminated at the planes of direct defilement, then the portions of the traverse below these planes are made more steep, and the earth supported by retaining walls. The top of the traverse, where it joins the parapet, being higher than the superior slope, is run out above this slope, upon which the side slopes fall; its extremity terminates in the plane of the exterior slope, extended above the exterior crest.

718...Traverses may be arranged for bomb-proof shelters and musketry defence, by throwing a bomb-proof arch between the side retaining walls, and piercing the wall bearing on the portion of the terreplein which will first fall into the enemy's power with loop-holes.

719...When, from any circumstance, a single traverse cannot be used for reverse defilement, resort must be had to several, which should be so combined that no line of fire can penetrate between their extremities to attain any point which they should cover. The examples of like combinations given in the Front, will readily suggest the manner of making others; of which farther illustrations will be found in the following case.

720...Where a demilune is arranged with a redoubt, a traverse placed in its salient cannot be extended farther back than the counterscarp of the redoubt, and an open space, therefore, will be left at the ditch, through which a reverse fire would attain that portion of either face which is not covered either by the traverse in the salient or by the parapet of the redoubt. To cover the part thus exposed, it will be necessary to place one or more traverses which, in combination with the one in the salient and the parapet of the redoubt, shall subserve this end.

To simplify the case, let the face $a\,c$, Pl. 7, Fig. 5, be the one exposed, and let the point x be one the fire of which is most dangerous. Having, in the first place, arranged the traverse t, as in the last example, and drawn the two lines of fire, $x\,b$ and $x\,d$, from the point x, through the extremity of the traverse and the top of the parapet of the redoubt at the salient, the length, $b\,d$, of the face intercepted between these lines will be the part to be covered. If a second traverse, t', be placed across the terreplein of the other face of the demilune, and in a position such that one of its ends shall rest on $x\,b$, and the other on $x\,d$, it will evidently cover the portion $b\,d$.

721...In selecting the positions of several combined traverses, attention must be given to avoid those where, if one be placed, the enemy would find shelter behind it from the fire in the rear. In the example just taken, the slope of t, toward the salient, should be swept by the fire from the rear, through the redoubt ditch; the like slope of t' should be swept by a portion of the redoubt face near its salient; and neither so fall as to have the space behind it masked from fire by the one to its rear.

722...Traverses usually present not only the easiest solution of all problems of reverse and enfilading defilement, but, affording the means of rendering the command independent of the fire from without, they enable the engineer to regulate this element solely with a view to the effect which he desires to attain by his own fire. From the space required for their erection, traverses may, as in the cases of narrow terrepleins, like those of the covered-ways, and of the demilune with a redoubt, be inconvenient, both from embarrassing the communications and from taking up ground that may be wanted for batteries.

723...PROB. 3. *The plan of a bastion being definitively fixed, and one point of its command approximately, to defile the work in the most advantageous manner, by shifting the position of its interior crest within certain limits.*

Let Fig. 6 be the plan of the work, and *a* the salient, the command of which can be varied within certain limits, without impairing any of the other conditions; and let the dangerous ground be embraced within the arc *m n*, at 1,500 yards from *a*, and the lines *a u* and *a v* supposed drawn from *a*, through covering masses on the right and left of the work.

The front limits of defilement in this case are embraced within the sector *m a n;* and the lateral limits within the other two, *m a u* and *n a v*. Now, the most favorable case of defilement here will be that, where a plane, containing *a* taken within its extreme positions, shall pass above all the exterior ground, and give such a command to the interior crest throughout, when held in it, as shall satisfy the other conditions of defence. To ascertain the existence of such a plane, let *a* be taken as the vertex of a cone which envelops all the dangerous ground, any plane tangent to this cone will satisfy the condition of defilement, and it will, therefore, only be necessary to find whether any one of these planes of defilement will satisfy the other, of giving the points *b*, *c*, *d* and *e* a suitable command. If no such plane can be obtained, the next most favorable case will be to find one that shall satisfy all the requisite conditions of command, and intersect the ground only within the front limits. In this case it is clear, from the position of this plane, if the interior crests are held in it, that the interior of the work will be exposed only to the direct fire from that portion of the ground which lies above the plane.

Let *xyz* be the curve of intersection of the plane with the ground, found in the usual way Through the faces *ab* and *ad*, let planes of direct defilement be passed; the terrepleins of the faces being held parallel to them will be covered by their respective parapets from all plunging fire. But, in order that the planes of defilement of the faces shall also defile the flanks, it is necessary that each flank be placed in the plane of defilement of the adjacent face, and its terreplein in that of the terreplein of the face. Now, in giving the interior crests of the flanks these new positions, they will lie below the plane that contains the curve *xyz*, and in which the interior crests of the faces lie. This being the case, it may happen that the parapet of one of the flanks will not cover the opposite face from reverse fire, coming from the lateral limits opposite the flank. In this contingency it will be necessary, in order to cover the face, to place the flank in the plane of the curve *xyz*, as this plane defiles from the lateral limits; but, in doing this, the flank *de*, for example, will be exposed, in its turn, to the ground above *xyz;* and to cover it, the only remedy is to erect a traverse, at some suitable point, which shall intercept all this dangerous fire. The least inconvenient position for the traverse will usually be at the shoulder angle. From this point, it must extend so far back as to intercept all fire from above *xyz*, both on the terrepleins of the flank and curtain, where they unite, and be high enough to screen the troops on the banquette.

If the defilement cannot be effected by either of these processes, there remains no other means than, having first definitely fixed the command, to divide the bastion by a traverse, either along its capital or some other convenient direction, and, having given it a suitable height, to cover each portion from direct fire by the usual method.

724...The foregoing problems embrace in their solution all of the more ordinary cases of defilement. and suggest the route to be followed in treating others. In all cases of the defilement of combined works, like the enceinte and its outworks, etc., it must be borne in mind that the advanced works, which, from their position, must first fall into the enemy's power, become thus a portion of the dangerous ground for the works more retired, and which must also be held after the fall of the others. The retired works, under such circumstances, must be defiled from the advanced; their planes of defilement being made to pass from 3 feet to 4.5 feet above the portion of the advanced work on which it is presumed the enemy may make a lodgment, and which, from its position, may be regarded as the most dangerous to the retired work. It is according to this rule that the redoubt of the re-entering place of arms is defiled from the parapets of the two adjacent demilunes; its plane of defilement extended outward, passing at 3 feet above the salients of these works. The tenaille, in like manner, is defiled from the upper terreplein of the demilune redoubt, as the tenaille must be held after the enemy has established himself on this terreplein. For like reasons, the more retired portions of the covered-ways are defiled from the enemy's lodgments on the glacis of the demilune salient place of arms.

725...Where a work has considerable command, and is open at the gorge, like the cavalier retrenchments, for example, and the works in its rear do not mask its interior from reverse fire, it may be necessary to place the traverse, termed a *parados*, across its terreplein at the gorge, giving it sufficient height to subserve the end in view.

726...The methods of defilement here laid down are those now followed by engineers. They unite mathematical accuracy in results, with great simplicity of detail; and render the defilement altogether secondary to the other conditions of defence, upon which the plan and command are made essentially to depend. Before they were adopted, the results of the method then followed were, in most respects, like those obtained in the practical operations for defiling field-works. A line, the position of which was determined by a series of trials, having for their object to obtain the most satisfactory results, both as to the economy of the requisite embankments and the best disposition of command of the various parts at or in rear of the gorge of the work to be defiled; this position coinciding with the natural surface, or being above or beneath it, as the case required. Through this line a plane was passed tangent to the dangerous ground. This plane, termed, as in field defilement, *a Rampant Plane*, was taken as the artificial site of the work, in reference to which the relative command of all the parts was arranged as upon a horizontal site. Or, in other words, the result was nearly the same as if the works had been arranged on a horizontal site, and then the whole combination turned around some fixed line of this site, until it was brought into the position of the required rampant plane. The defects of this method are evident at a glance. It preserves the relations of defence of the various works the same as in a horizontal site; but it, to a great extent, leaves out of consideration the bearing of the command on the exterior ground, and, in many cases, may lead to excessive excavations and embankments which the methods now followed enable the engineer, for the most part, to avoid.

727...REMARKS. In the preceding discussions it will be observed that the limits of defilement, *horizontally*, have been based upon the range and presumed accuracy of fire of artillery and small arms before the changes which, within a few years back, have taken place in both these particulars, and which—from the zeal and intelligence with which experiments are now being carried on, in every part of the civilized world, on the forms of cannon and projectiles and the quality of powder—will, in all probability, be extended and lead to still more remarkable results. These improvements, however, will have no other effect upon the rules and modes of defilement now in use than to change the limits, *horizontally*, to correspond with the increased ranges of projectiles. So far as an improvement in the accuracy of fire is concerned, it will render a strict defilement of all parts of the interior of a work more imperative, and will lead engineers to resort to every means by which the troops and *materiel* can be hidden from an enemy's view within the extreme range of projectiles. As to the *vertical* limits, there would seem to be no good reason for changing those now established. When it is, also, taken into consideration that the relative command and plunge of heights decrease with their distance from the work defiled, and, also, that the accuracy of aim is greatly affected by the same cause, it is questionable whether any considerable extension of the limits hitherto laid down will be neeessary, except in marked cases of locality.

Mines.

728...The subject of mines admits of a division into five parts:

1st. The nomenclature.

2d. The results of experiments, and the theory founded on them.

3d. The manner of using mines in the attack and defence.

4th. The conditions to which mines should be subjected in their arrangement and uses.

5th. The construction or details of the practical operations.

To these may be added a sixth part, comprising the uses of mines in temporary works.

729...NOMENCLATURE. The term *mine* is applied both to the underground excavations charged with powder for the purpose of producing an external explosion, and to the communications which lead to these excavations.

The excavation in which the charge of powder is lodged is termed the *chamber.* The pit formed by the explosion is termed the *crater.*

The form of the crater in ordinary soils has not been exactly ascertained. The only use of the exact determination of this form would be to calculate precisely the quantity of earth thrown from the crater, and by that means to proportion the charge to the effect to be produced. Different figures have been assigned by engineers to this solid; some assuming it to be a cone, of which the centre of the powder was taken as the vertex; others, a paraboloid, of which the centre of the powder was the focus. To afford a uniform and simple rule for calculating the volume of the crater, the solid, Fig. A, is assumed to be a truncated cone, the radius, *o d*, of the lower circle being one-half the radius, *p b*, of the upper circle. The radius, *p b*, of the upper circle is termed the *crater radius.* The line, *o p*, drawn from the centre of the powder perpendicular to the surface where the explosion takes place, the *line of least resistance.* The line, *o b*, drawn from the same centre to any point in the circumference of the upper circle, the *radius of explosion.*

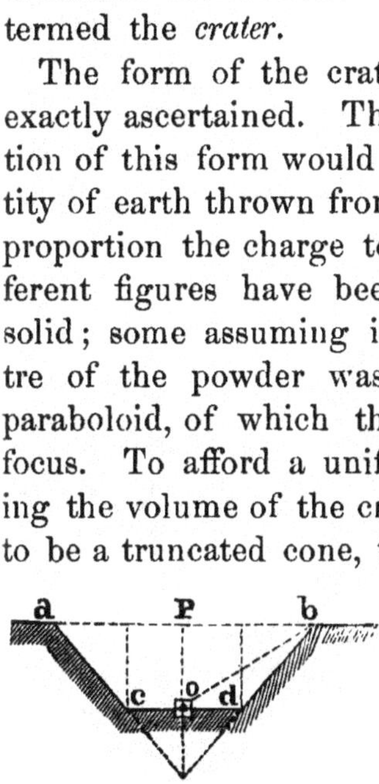

Fig. A.

The term *common mine* is applied to a crater when its radius is equal to the line of least resistance When the crater radius is greater than the line of least resistance, the terms *overcharged mine* and *globe of compression* are used. When the crater radius is less than the line of least resistance, the mine is termed *undercharged.* A small mine with a line of least resistance not greater than 9 feet, which is formed by sinking a shaft from the surface of the ground, is termed a *fougasse.* The term *camouflet* is applied to small mines used to suffocate the enemy's miner without producing an external explosion.

The underground communications required for the service of mines are termed *galleries.* The galleries are either arched communications of masonry, or else a framework and sheeting of timber. The principal gallery immediately behind the counterscarp wall, is termed the *counterscarp* or *magistral gallery.* An *enveloping gallery* is one parallel to the counterscarp gallery, and at some 30 or 40 yards in advance of it. The galleries leading outward from the counterscarp gallery are termed *listening galleries.* The galleries which connect several listening galleries are termed *transversal* or *cross galleries.* Galleries receive, also, particular names from their size, as the

Great or *grand galleries*,	which are	6	feet high and	6	feet wide.
Common galleries,	"	6	" "	3	"
Half galleries,	"	4½	" "	3	"
Branches,	"	3½	" "	2½	"
Small branches,	"	2½	" "	2	"

730...EXPERIMENTS. But little advance by experiment has been made in the subject of mines, owing to the time, labor and expense, which a prosecution of the subject demands; and the practice has, therefore, undergone but slight changes since the earliest introduction of this means of attack and defence. The following facts, drawn from observation, comprise almost all that is at present known on the subject:

1st. In solid rock, an explosion causes the rock to split in various directions, and if the charge is heavy, will break it into small fragments, which are frequently thrown to a great distance.

2d. In sand, the gazes seem to penetrate between the grains, producing a crater of a regular form, the radius of the upper circle of which is generally small in comparison with the depth.

3d. In ordinary tenacious soils, the first effect of the explosion is to produce a rumbling noise, and a sensible trembling of the earth around the mine to a considerable distance; the ground directly over the mine is next observed to rise in the form of a spherical segment, which increases perceptibly until the smoke commences to issue forth around its base; the explosion outward follows immediately on this last change, the earth, mingled with smoke and flame, being thrown upward and outward, so as to assume a form something like a water-spout; part of the earth falling back into the crater and a part without, forming a ridge around its mouth.

The two most remarkable features of the explosion are its internal and external effects; the first producing the crater, the second so disturbing the earth for a considerable distance around the crater as to fill up cavities, destroy galleries, etc., within the sphere of its action; these effects extending farther in a lateral than in a downward direction.

The charges and their effects do not follow the same ratio, the last increasing less rapidly than the first. Experiment has shown that the charges may even be increased one or two pounds per 4 cubic yards, without increasing the crater radius; the only effect of this increase of charge being to throw more of the earth clear of the crater.

From experiments made on common mines, with a line of least resistance not exceeding 15 feet, it has been ascertained that the tenacity of the earth is completely destroyed around the crater, to a distance equal to the line of least resistance, and that empty galleries are broken in at a distance of one and a half the same line.

In homogeneous soils, the resistance due to the tenacity of the soil is nearly proportional to the mass.

It was for a long time supposed by miners that a crater could not be formed with a diameter greater than twice the line of least resistance, with any charge; but the experiments of Belidor have shown that, by successive augmentations of the charge, the crater radius may be increased to six times this line, but not much beyond; that within this limit the ratio of the diameters of the craters is nearly that of the square root of the charges; and that galleries can be destroyed by such mines at distances of four times their line of least resistance.

731...THEORY. The physico-mathematical theory of mines is still very imperfect, owing to the impracticability of ascertaining the exact effects of the explosion of powder in a medium which is seldom homogeneous, and the resistance of which, arising from its tenacity, compressibility, etc., to the expansion of the gazes, can only be arrived at by a wide range of experiments made with minute care.

From the want of these elementary data, the formula at present in use, to determine the charges for different media, are necessarily empirical, and their results are to be relied on only within the limits in which they coincide with experiments. For most cases in practice, these approximations are near enough, and valuable as the only guides that the miner has to refer to.

732...The resistances which the gazes overcome are the weight of the volume of earth thrown from the crater, the tenacity of the medium, and the atmospheric pressure on the upper circle of the crater. The two first are proportional to the mass of earth thrown out, and the last to the upper surface of the crater. To express the ratio of these resistances to the charges, let us represent in any two mines by

$c\,c'$, the charges;

$r\,r'$, the radii of the craters;

$l\,l'$, the lines of least resistance;

$d\,d'$, the weight of the unit of volume of the two soils;

$n\,n'$, the constants, which, multiplied into the weights, will express the tenacities;

$h\,h'$, the heights of the atmospheric columns reduced to the densities as the soils.

Whatever may be the form of the crater, its volume can be expressed in terms of the surface of the upper circle, and some fractional part of the line of least resistance; so that if we represent by $\frac{l}{m}\,l$ and $\frac{l}{m'}\,l'$ this fractional part of the line of least resistance in the two cases, we shall have for the expression of the two volumes:

$$\pi r^2 \times \frac{l}{m}, \text{ and } \pi r'^2 \times \frac{l'}{m'};$$

and for their respective weights,

$$\frac{\pi r^2 l}{m} \times d, \text{ and } \frac{\pi r'^2 l'}{m'} \times d';$$

to express the tenacities we have,

$$\frac{\pi r^2 l d}{m} \times n, \text{ and } \frac{\pi r'^2 l' d'}{m'} \times n';$$

and for the weights corresponding to the atmospheric pressures,

$$\pi r^2 h d, \text{ and } \pi r'^2 h' d'$$

From these expressions we obtain the proportions

$$c : c' :: \frac{r^2 d}{m}\left[(n+1)l + mh\right] : \frac{r'^2 d'}{m'}\left[(n'+1) + l' m' h'\right].$$

For the same soil, as $m=m'$, $n=n'$, $d=d'$, and $h=h'$, this proportion becomes

$$c : c' :: r^2\left(l + \frac{m}{n+1}h\right) : r'^2\left(l' + \frac{m}{n+1}h'\right).$$

733...The relation between any two charges of mines in the same soil, expressed by this proportion, gives the means of obtaining the charge for any crater when, by experiment, the crater formed by any known charge has been found, provided the quantities n and h are known. Of the first, nothing definite is known but that it varies with the kind of soil. The second has been assumed equal to 11 feet. This want of definiteness in the value of these quantities has led to omitting them in the proportion, when used for practical purposes, in which case it takes the following form:

$$c : c' :: l r^2 : l' r'^2.$$

This is termed the *Miner's Rule*, as it is used for calculating tables of charges for different soils; and its results do not differ materially from those of experiments.

Making $l=l'$, the proportion becomes

$$c : c' :: r^2 : r'^2,$$

a proportion also differing but little from the results obtained within the ordinary limits of practice, when the lines of least resistance are the same for different charges.

734...Assuming, as is the case in common mines, that the craters are similar solids, then $l : l' :: r : r'$; hence,

$$c : c' :: l^3 : l'^3,$$

another form of the Miner's Rule, and the one used in calculating the tables of charges for similar mines.

The manner in which this rule is applied to calculate charges of common mines is as follows: the quantity of powder, q, in pounds, required to throw up one cubic yard of any species of soil, is found by experiment. As the solid contents of a truncated cone, like Fig. A, is equal to $\frac{11}{6}\ l^3$, l being the line of least resistance, the volume of the crater, whose line of least resistance is one yard, will be represented by $\frac{11}{6} \times (1^3)$ or $\frac{11}{6}$; this volume, multiplied by q, will give the charge in pounds for this crater, but from the proportion $c : c' :: l^3 : l'^3$, there obtains:

$$c : \tfrac{11}{6} q :: l^3 : 1^3, \text{ or } c = \tfrac{11}{6}\ q\ l^3,$$

for the charge for a crater whose line of least resistance is l. *To find the charge, therefore, for a given line of least resistance, cube this line, expressed in yards; take $\frac{11}{6}$ of the result and multiply it by the number of pounds required to throw out a cubic yard of the soil in question.*

The following table expresses the values of q:

	Lbs.	Oz.
Light sandy earth	1	13
Hard sand	2	00
Common earth	1	10
Wet sand	2	2
Earth mixed with pebbles	2	8
Clay mixed with loam	2	8
Rock	3	10

735...As the Miner's Rule is applicable only to common mines, resort must be had to some other to find the charges for overcharged and undercharged mines. The formula in most general use for these cases are those of Lebrun, a French engineer; which, although not based on any satisfactory hypothesis, nevertheless, coincide nearly in their results with those obtained by experiments within ordinary limits. The hypothesis assumed to obtain these formula is as follows: Suppose two craters, formed by two different charges, c and c', with the same line of least resistance, one giving a crater radius, r, equal to the line of least resistance, the other a crater radius, R, greater, the difference of the radii being $R—r$. Next, suppose the charge c' to belong to a common mine, of which the crater radius is r; $r'—r$, being the difference of the radii of two craters of the common mines of which the charges are c and c'; then the ratio of the two differences here expressed, arising from the same increase, c', of the charge c, will be constant under all circumstances of variation of soil, and of the lines of least resistance. Calling K this constant ratio, there obtains:

$$\frac{R-r}{r'-r}=K;$$

assuming $R=nr$, this formula becomes

$$\frac{r(n-1)}{r'-r}=K,$$

$$\text{or, } \frac{r'}{r}=\frac{1}{K}\times(n-1)+1;$$

but as r' and r belong to similar craters, the Miner's Rule gives $\frac{c}{c'}=\frac{r^3}{r'^3}$; from this there obtains,

$$c'=c\left[\frac{1}{K}(n-1)+1\right]^3.$$

The quantity, K, which enters into this expression must be ascertained by experiment, as indicated by the process followed in obtaining the formula. From a comparison of a number of experiments, the value of K gives

$$c'=c\left[0.91\,n+0.09\right]^3$$

736...The preceding method is also applied to find a formula for the charges of undercharged mines. In this case, R and r' being supposed less than r, $\frac{r-R}{r-r'}=K$, and hence $c'=c\left[1-\frac{1}{K}(1-n)\right]^3$ - - - (X).

The constant K in this case, is determined from a result of experiment; that if a certain charge of powder forms a common crater with a line of least resistance l, the same charge will not produce any external effect when the line of least resistance is increased to $1\frac{3}{4}\,l$ or $\frac{7}{4}\,l$: and, reciprocally, if a charge produces no external effect with a line of least resistance l, the same charge will form a common mine under a line of least resistance $\frac{4}{7}l$. If, then, the charge c', by supposition, does not produce any external effect under the line of least resistance l, it will produce a common mine under a line of least resistance $\frac{4}{7}l$; from this, by the Miner's Rule, there obtains

$$c' : c :: (\tfrac{4}{7}l)^3 : l^3,$$

or,

$$c' = c(\tfrac{4}{7})^3.$$

Now, substituting this value of c' in Eq. (X), and making $n=o$, its corresponding value for this of c'; there obtains $\frac{1}{K}=\frac{3}{7}$, which result, substituted in the same Eq. (X) it then becomes $c'=c\left[1-\frac{3}{7}(1-n)\right]^3$; hence $c'=c\left(\frac{3n+4}{7}\right)^3$, which is the formula for undercharged mines.

737...GALLERY FRAMES. Temporary galleries are made of framework covered in by plank, and are prepared but a short period before they are required for use.

738...The frames of temporary galleries consist of four pieces: two uprights termed *stanchions*, and two horizontal pieces, the one at top termed a *cap sill*, and the bottom piece a *ground sill;* Pl. 8, Fig. A, shows the connection between the parts of the frame.

The plank or boards which cover in the frames are termed *sheeting*. The top sheeting of the frames usually consists of boards from 3 feet 6 inches to 4 feet in length, from 7 to 12 inches in width, and from 1 to 1½ inches thick. The side sheeting may have the same length and breadth but need not be thicker than from ¾ to 1 inch. To set the frames up and retain them in their places, slips of plank termed *battens* are used, which are about 2½ inches wide and 1 inch thick.

The frames may be either of well seasoned oak or pine, the latter is preferable as lightest. The parts of each frame receive the dimensions in the annexed table:

Great gallery,.	.ground sill	6″×4″½.	stanchions	6×6″,	cap sill	7×6″,
Common gallery,	"	5×4,	"	5×5,	"	6×5,.
Half gallery,	"	4½×3½.	"	4½×4½,	"	5×4½,
Branches,	"	3½×3,	"	3½×3½,	"	4½×3½,
Small branches,	"	3×3,	"	3×3,	"	4×3.

739...Shaft Frames Pl. 8, Figs. 3, 4, 5. A shaft is a vertical pit, lined with sheeting on the outside of frames which are placed horizontally, and at suitable intervals apart.

The cross sections of shafts are either squares or rectangles; the dimensions of the sides of the section depending on the object of the shaft. When this is for driving a gallery from the bottom of the shaft, the dimensions of the shaft frames, in the clear, must be at least equal to that of the gallery, from out to out of its sheeting. A shaft, sunk for establishing a mine chamber simply, should usually be of the least dimensions, which, to allow the miner to work with facility, must not be less than 3 feet by 2 feet in the clear.

Two kinds of frames are usually requisite in sinking shafts: a *top frame*, Fig. 1, formed of four pieces, halved to fit each other, which, when put together, have the same dimensions in the clear as the shaft, each piece projecting beyond the side, or having an *over length* of 1½ to 2 feet; the other is termed a *side frame*, Fig. 2, and, also, consists of four pieces of smaller scantling than the top frame, halved at the ends to fit, its dimensions in the clear being the same as the other.

In very loose soil it may be necessary to use a temporary frame, *o*, Fig. 4, termed an *auxiliary frame*. This is somewhat larger in the clear than the preceding. Its uses will be explained farther on.

The opposite pieces of each frame are marked with a saw cut, termed a *score*, at their middle, on the upper side. The scores serve to fix the position which the frame should occupy when laid.

The scantling for top frames is usually 6 inches square; that of side and auxiliary frames 4½ inches, for a shaft over 4½ feet in the clear. For smaller shafts, the scantling may be of smaller dimensions.

740...Shaft Interval. The term *interval*, both in shafts and galleries, expresses the distance between two adjacent frames added to the thickness of the scantling of the frame, measured in the direction of the axis of the shaft, etc. With scantling and sheeting of the usual dimensions, the interval should not be greater than 3½ feet.

PROB., FIG. 3. *The depth of a shaft, and the height of a gallery to lead from the bottom of the shaft, being given, to estimate the shaft interval.*

Add together the height of the gallery frame from the top of its ground sill, the thickness of the top sheeting, and the thickness of the shaft frame; to this sum add 2 inches for free space between the gallery frame and the shaft frame next above it, to introduce the top sheeting. Subtract this sum from the depth of the shaft, and divide the remainder into any convenient number of equal or unequal intervals, each not greater than 3½ feet.

Let the depth of the shaft, for example, be 22 feet, and the height of the gallery 4′.6″ Then:

From ground sill to exterior of top sill...........	4′.11″
Top sheeting	0 1
Shaft frame..	0.4½
Free space.......	0 2
Total..	5 6½

This taken from 22 feet leaves 16′.5½″, which can be divided into four intervals of 3′.4″ each, leaving one interval of 3′.1½″, which may be placed either at top or bottom, but best in the latter position.

741...CONSTRUCTION OF SHAFT. To construct the foregoing shaft in a loose soil, there will be required a top frame; five side frames for the intervals above estimated; two for the remaining lower portion of the shaft; one auxiliary frame; four battens for each interval of the length of the interval added to the thickness of the shaft frame; from 12 to 20 square pickets about 18″ long; with the machinery and mining tools requisite for the operation.

742...The work is laid out by driving a picket to mark the axis of the shaft, and two others, which with the first are in the vertical plane containing the axis of the gallery. A level bed is then made for the top frame, the pieces of which are accurately laid and confined by pickets, one at the end of each piece; care being had to drive the two pickets of each piece together, so that its true position may be kept. Other pickets may be driven temporarily on the outside of the frame, at the angular points. After the frame is laid, the accuracy of its position is tested by seeing whether the distances from the centre of the central picket to the interior angular points, or, in other words, the *semi-diagonals*, are equal; if they are, the position is correct.

743...The excavation is now commenced, and, if the crumbling of the soil does not interfere, may be carried as far as the position of the first side frame; the sheeting boards, inserted between the soil and the exterior of the top frame, being gradually advanced with the excavation; here the first side frame is hung by four battens, two being nailed to each piece of the opposite sides of the top frame and to the two corresponding pieces of the side frame, the halvings of which are turned upward; after these pieces are adjusted by their scores and fixed, the other two pieces are laid on them, the halvings down, and secured by nails.

744...This frame being fixed, the ends of the sheeting of the next interval may be inserted between it and the sheeting of the first interval, and the excavation continued. The soil now becoming troublesome by its crumbling, measures must be taken to retain it firmly until the second frame is laid. For this purpose the auxiliary frame, Fig. 4, is introduced, and hung midway in the interval, like the usual frames. The sheeting which thus far has been gradually advanced with the excavation, is also inclined outward at bottom, to gain room for the auxiliary frame, by wedges inserted between the boards of the two intervals. After the auxiliary frame is fixed, the excavation and sheeting are carried on to the bottom of the interval, the next frame hung, and the sheeting for the new interval introduced. The auxiliary frame is now removed and placed in the next position, when reached by the excavation. The work will proceed in this order until the shaft is completed; when so, a picket is driven in the bottom, Fig. 5, to mark the central point.

REMARK. A sketch, made to a suitable scale, should be in hand for immediate reference in conducting such works. This is more particularly necessary for gallery work, the sketches for which should be very accurately drawn, referenced and numbered, as they serve not only for reference to guide the miner, but to determine positions and dimensions of some of the important portions.

745...COMBINATIONS OF TIMBER GALLERIES. A gallery which leads from another is termed a *return*, and is called *oblique* or *rectangular*, according to whether the projections of the axes of the two galleries make a right or an acute angle. The gallery from which the return is made is termed a *gallery of departure.* When the floor of the return rises or falls from that of the departure, the return gallery is termed *ascending* or *descending.*

746...WORKING PLANS. To make a working sketch of a combination of galleries, the projections of the axes are first laid out; their points of intersection marked; and the distances and referenee between all the points written. The half width of each gallery in the clear being next set off on each side of its axis, a line is drawn for it, then one parallel and exterior to it at the thiekness of the gallery frame, and, finally, a seeond to mark the exterior line of the sheeting.

The line $C D$, Figs. 6, 7, 8, is the axis of the gallery of departure, and $A B$ that of the return. The line $a b$ is the interior line of the gallery frames; $c d$ the exterior line of the same; $e f$ that of the sheeting. The corresponding lines for the remaining half of the gallery of departure, and those of the return, will be readily recognized. The frames m and m' bound the entrances to the returns; and those, u, v, of the auxiliary return, the entrance to the oblique return, Fig. 8.

The case of a change of direction in a gallery is shown in Fig. 9. Here, to obtain room for the miner to handle the sheeting, etc., an end of an auxiliary gallery is made off, on the salient angle of the break, just large enough for the object in view. Having set off these lines, the points of intersection of the exterior lines of the sheeting of the return with the exterior and interior lines of the frame of the gallery of departure are marked as follows, to determine the distance to be left between the two frames of the gallery of departure, between which the entrance to the return is placed: 1st, when the projections of the axes make a right angle, then the intersections of the exterior lines of the sheeting with the interior lines of the frames are marked; the entrance to the return will be equal to the distance between the exterior lines of the sheeting of the return; 2d, when the angle is between 45° and 90°, the intersection, *o*, of the exterior line of the sheeting of the return, which lies within the angle formed by the axes, with the exterior line, *c d*, of the gallery frames, and that, *o′*, of the other exterior line of the sheeting with the interior line of the same frames being marked, will give the points between which the frames of the gallery of departure must be placed to form the entrance; 3d, when the angle between the axes is less than 45°, the frames bounding the entrance to the return would fall too far asunder. It will, therefore, be requisite to make a rectangular auxiliary return from the gallery of departure, into which the oblique return will have its entrance. To determine the position of the rectangular return, Fig. 8, a line, *r s*, is first drawn exterior to the sheeting of the gallery of departure, and at a distance from it equal to the thickness of the frames to be used for the auxiliary return; the intersection, *o*, of the exterior line of the sheeting, which lies within the angle of the axes and the last line drawn, being marked, will give the point through which the inner line of the frames of the auxiliary return is to be drawn. This line being determined, all the other lines for this return can be readily set out. The rest of the problem will be treated as in the second case.

747...REMARKS. From an examination of the above cases, it will be seen that the object to be accomplished is so to place the two frames of the gallery of departure, which bound the entrance to the return, that the stanchions of these frames shall not be in the way of the miner when pushing forward the side sheeting; or, in other words, if the return were a box that could be pushed forward, like a drawer, in the direction of its axis, the stanchions in question should not hinder this movement.

Several other problems, of a like character, may present themselves in returns, and in changes of direction in galleries, which it will be unnecessary to treat here, as the illustrations above given will readily suggest the methods to be adopted for their solution.

748...DETERMINATION OF GALLERY AXES. Having set off all the lines on the working sketch, and marked the positions of the different frames, etc., at the junctions of the galleries, their forms, dimensions, and also their exact positions with respect to any fixed point, can be accurately determined from the scale of the sketch, and be written upon it for reference in conducting the work. For example: in Fig. 7, the determination of the points o and o', fix the positions of the gallery frames m and m', and the form, position and dimensions of the oblique frame q, of the return, where the galleries join. Having set off these parts, the point i, on the axis of the gallery of departure, equidistant from the points k and i, of the frame q, can be determined. This point, marked by a picket, serves to fix these points, and, with the picket at F, the direction of A B.

749...LANDINGS. The portion of the floor of the gallery between the frames that bound the entrance to a return, is termed a *landing;* as, for example, the spaces between the frames m, m', and u, v. The landing is in all cases horizontal, as well as that portion of an oblique return between the oblique frame q, and the one, x, next succeeding, which last should not be placed farther than an ordinary interval from the farthest point of q.

750...GALLERY INTERVALS. Having determined, by means of the working sketch, the landings and their frames with respect to the points of intersection of the axis of the gallery of departure with those of the returns, the intervals of this gallery can be calculated, and their positions marked out on the sketch. The manner of making this estimate will be best illustrated by the following example:

Let *A B*=118 feet, Fig. 10, be the total length of a gallery of departure, estimated horizontally along its axis, from the central picket of the shaft from which the gallery starts. At the point *C*, 44 feet from *A*, the axis of a rectangular return commences, and at *D*, 44 feet farther, that of an oblique one. The part *A C* of the gallery, Fig. 11, is to be a common great gallery; the part *C D*, Fig. 12, a common gallery; and the part *D B*, Fig. 13, a great branch. With these data, it is required to determine the intervals for the different portions of the gallery

To find the interval for the first portion, *A C*, subtract from the total distance, 44 feet, the following aggregate:

Half the width of the shaft in the clear...............2′.2″
The thickness of the lowest shaft frame.............. 0 4½
Half the width of the landing at *C*.....................2 0½
The thickness of a gallery frame at the landing......0.5

5′.0″

which leaves 39 feet to be divided into suitable intervals, which may be done by making twelve of them each 3 feet 3 inches.

The intervals of the portion *C D*, will be found as follows: from 44 feet take the following sum:

Half the width of the landing at *C*.....................2′.0½″
Thickness of the landing frame.........................0.5
The distance from *D* (as found from sketch) to the
landing frame beyond 0 9
Thickness of gallery frame at landing *D* 0.4½

3′ 7″

which leaves 40 feet 5 inches. This can be divided into nine intervals, each 3′ 1″, and four of 3′.2″ each.

To find the intervals for the part *D B*, from 30 feet take the following aggregate:

Distance from *D* to frame of landing beyond it...... 4′.5″
Thickness of landing frame beyond *D*................. 0.3½
Thickness of last frame at *B*....... .... 0.3½

5′.0″

This leaves 25 feet, which can be divided into six intervals of 3′.2″ each, and two of 3′

751...SLOPE-BLOCK. In setting the ground sills of frames in ascending or descending galleries, a small cubical block of wood, termed a *slope-block*, is used. This is a cubical block, the edge of which is equal to the difference of level between the ground sills of an interval. To determine the height of the slope-block for any portion of a gallery where the intervals are equal, or nearly so, the difference of level or of reference of the two extremities of the portion must be divided by the number of intervals. Thus, in the portion of the gallery from *A* to *C*, Fig. 10, there is an ascent of 5′, or 60″, and twelve intervals; the edge of the slope-block will, therefore, be $\frac{60}{12}''=5'$ In the portion from *C* to *D*, there is a fall of 4′.1,″ or 49″, and thirteen nearly equal intervals; the edge of the slope-block will, therefore, be 3″.7, nearly.

752...AUXILIARY FRAMES. In loose soils, besides the ordinary gallery frames, there is required, as for shafts in the same soils, an auxiliary gallery frame. This frame, Fig. 14. *o*, Fig. 15, is somewhat wider than an ordinary gallery frame, and somewhat lower than it. Its cap sill is rounded on top, and has two mortices on its lower side, to receive the tenons with which the two stanchions are finished. The mortices are a little longer than the tenons—the latter being confined in them by wedges when the frame is set up. To adjust the frame when set up, a pair of folding wedges are placed under each end of its ground sill. By these various contrivances, the frame can be readily set up or taken apart.

753...CONSTRUCTION OF GALLERIES. To explain, now, the practical operations in driving a gallery, let an example be taken where the soil is loose, and the floor of the gallery rises from the point of departure. In this case, the first frame of the gallery *o*, Fig. 16, must be set up within the shaft and against the shaft frames, on the side from which the gallery is to open. The ground sill of this frame being laid, the stanchions are secured to the intermediate shaft frames of the last interval by battens, and the top sill fastened. A horizontal beam, *c*, is then secured to the under side of the top shaft frame of the same interval, to preserve the proper slope for the top sheeting when inserted, wedges being placed between this beam and the sheeting board for this object. A like arrangement for the side sheeting may be made if necessary. The excavation of the gallery is now commenced at top, by forcing down with a crowbar the sheeting of the shaft, on the side of the gallery. The earth is removed gradually forward and downward, and the gallery sheeting advanced at the same rate. When the excavation has reached as low as the intermediate shaft frame, the piece of it that sustains the lower portion of the sheeting is removed, to allow the excavation to proceed. When, in this way, the earth is removed as far as the middle of the first interval, the auxiliary gallery frame, Fig. 15, is set up, to support the top and side sheeting until the second gallery frame is placed. To place this last frame, the position of the ground sill is first determined, Fig. 17, by placing the slope-block, *o*, on the ground sill first laid, and then, by a common mason s level, *A*, upon the side of which the interval is marked, laid upon the slope-block, bringing the top of the ground sill on the same level as that of the slope-block. The sill being adjusted and firmly secured, the stanchions are next set up, and secured by battens to the stanchions of the first frame, and the cap sill is secured in the last place. The adjustments of the stanchions and cap sills are made by an ordinary plumb-line, by means of which the edges of the stanchions are placed vertically, and the scores on the cap and ground sills brought into the vertical plane of the axis of the gallery

The battens are placed horizontally In a level gallery they are nailed, alternately, at 4 and 8 inches below the cap sill. In others, Fig. 17, they are nailed 4 inches below the lower of the cap sills of the two frames which they unite; this will bring them at 4 inches, added to the height of the slope-block, below the other.

The auxiliary frame is not taken down until wedges have been placed between the sheeting and the frame last placed, in order to introduce the boards for the next interval; and these last are kept in the proper direction, as the excavation is advanced, by wedges inserted between them and the sheeting of the interval finished.

754...BRANCH GALLERIES A LA HOLLANDAISE. These galleries are of the same dimensions as small branches; the frames are made of plank; they are placed touching each other, and serve at the same time both as frames and sheeting.

Each frame consists of four pieces; the stanchions have a tenon at each end, Fig. 18, fitting into notches cut in the cap sill and ground sill to receive them.

When the gallery is an ascending or descending one, the ends of the stanchions are cut obliquely, in order that their sides may always be vertical.

Fig. 19 is a plan and section of this description of gallery.

755...For the purpose of limiting the effect of explosion of mines upon the branches leading to them, and, at the same time, to enable the miner, acting on the defence, to push forward and open a new branch toward the crater, a portion of a branch leading toward the mine is made of heavy frames of the foregoing construction. The timber recommended for the purpose is oak, and the pieces of each frame are 12″ wide and 4″ thick. The portion of this strong framework, at the extremity, is solidly filled in with pieces of 4″ scantling, from 6 to 10 feet in length. For a branch 28″ high and 24″ wide, seven horizontal layers will be required, each layer consisting of 5 pieces. The centre piece of each layer may have a rope handle at its end to allow of its being drawn out readily. Filled in this way, and having earth well packed between the pieces, branches of this description will not be damaged by the explosion of mines of from 6 to 10 feet line of least resistance, even when the mines are within 4½ to 6 feet of the branch. From their chief object, these branches are termed by the French *rameaux de combat.*

756...SHAFTS A LA BOULE. These shafts are lined with frames made of plank, connected together as shown in Fig. 20.

In Fig. 21, a section of a shaft à la Boule is shown, which is sufficiently explanatory to render any other description unnecessary

This kind of shaft can only be used with advantage in favorable soil, on account of the difficulty of introducing the frames sufficiently near each other; they are commonly placed one foot apart, as shown in the figure. Large gabions, 6 feet long, and from 3 feet 6 inches to 4 feet in diameter, are sometimes used for lining shafts near the surface, smaller gabions being introduced as the work is proceeded with.

757...For the purposes of quickly establishing small camouflets and fougasses, a boring apparatus has been resorted to, the diameter of the boring tool being 4″ This machine is worked like ordinary tools of this kind. It is charged for explosion by inserting powder in cylindrical cartridges of somewhat less diameter than the shaft, which are well rammed forward; or, if a large charge is requisite, the end of the shaft can be enlarged by a tool with a joint, which will admit the tool to be so adjusted as gradually to increase the excavation at the end. Excavations made in this way are termed *artesian* shafts or branches.

758...CONSTRUCTION OF PERMANENT GALLERIES. When the floor of the gallery is not more than 10 or 12 feet below the surface, it will be generally best to open a trench for the work. The width of the trench at the bottom should be the same as the gallery from out to out. If the soil is very firm, the sides of the excavation may be made nearly perpendicular; at 6 feet above the bottom of the trench a berm 3 feet wide should be left, and at 6 feet above this another, and so on for every additional depth of 6 feet. These berms serve the place of scaffoldings, to pitch the earth out.

If the soil is very loose the slopes will require to be sustained by a sheeting to prevent the earth from caving in. After the masonry is completed, the excavated earth is carefully replaced.

759...When the construction is made entirely under ground, a wooden gallery is first formed, the width of which, between the frames, in the clear, Fig. 22, is equal to the width between the piers of the permanent gallery from out to out; its height being such that there will be 6 inches between the crown of the arch on the exterior and the cap sills. The top and side sheeting should lap about 8 inches.

When the gallery is completed, a new set of ground sills are laid alongside of those of the gallery, their length being equal to the width of the permanent gallery in the clear, Fig. 23. A new set of stanchions, *o*, *o*, are set up on these sills, to support a new set of cap sills of the same length as those of the gallery. Vertical boards, *a*, are placed alongside of stanchions of the wooden gallery, and are buttressed against the sheeting by two horizontal pieces of scantling, *c*, *c*, one near the top, the other near the bottom of the gallery. When this new arrangement is completed, the frames of the gallery first set up can be taken down and the masonry commenced.

The foundations of the piers, Fig. 24, are laid with an interior offset of 6 inches. The piers are then carried up, the lower horizontal buttress being gradually shifted up so as not to interfere with the work, and the lower courses of the side sheeting, which have now become unnecessary, being removed. When the piers are completed, the stanchions are taken down and replaced by props, *p*, *p*, resting on the outside of the tops of the piers.

When this change has been made, the way is clear for turning the arch. For this, four common centres, *A*, *A*, Figs. 25, 26, made of boards, will be requisite. Each of these centres is 18 inches broad, and is secured to a rectangular frame, *o*, of small scantling of the same breadth, and as long as the span of the arch. Each centre thus prepared rests upon a trestle, *q*, *q*, of sufficient height to bring the centre in its true position to receive the masonry.

The masons, to expedite the work, commence at the middle point of the gallery, where two of these centres are placed together, and close the arch over them; the other two centres are then placed alongside of these, and the arch in like manner is closed over them; the two first are then taken down, and removed to the outside of the two last set up, and the arch is thus carried on toward the two ends. The wood-work of the gallery is taken down as fast as the masonry supplies its place.

760...In the main galleries of communication, arched recesses are formed to serve as depôts, etc., for the implements of the miners. These recesses are from 6 to 12 feet in depth and usually of the same width, and may be placed at intervals of 15 or 20 feet from each other. Similar dispositions are made in the listening galleries for the magazines of earth required for tamping the mines; small portions of galleries, from 6 to 12 feet in length, are run out at right angles to the listening gallery for this purpose. A sufficient number of openings must also be left in the piers of the listening galleries, for the construction of the branches leading to the mine chambers.

761...In loose soils, and to give greater resistance to masonry galleries to globes of compression, it has been proposed to give them a cross section, of an oval form, instead of the one above given. Galleries of this form would be of more difficult construction and cost more than those of the usual form.

762...When several galleries branch off from the same

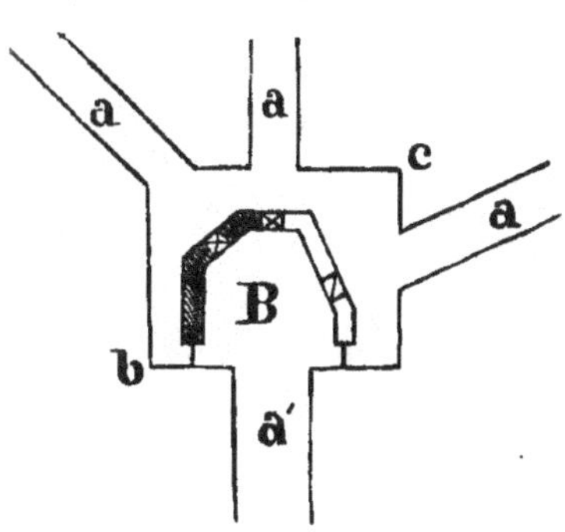

point, a large arched chamber of a square, or any polygonal form, is constructed, which serves for a depôt, and is also arranged with a crenated wall within it to defend the most advanced galleries. In the annexed figure, for example, if the galleries *a*, *a*, *a*, *a*, meet at a point, the square arched chamber, *b c*, is placed to connect them, and within this a space, *B*, is enclosed by a thin wall, constructed with loop-holes to fire in the direction of the most advaneed galleries, *a*, *a*, *a*.

763...The piers of the galleries are also arranged either with grooves or offsets, so that barriers may be made within them for defence against the enemy's miner when he penetrates into the gallery. In some cases a simple pit is dug across the gallery and covered by boards, which are taken up when the communication is required to be cut off.

764...MINE CHAMBERS. The chamber of a mine is a cavity, *A*, formed to receive the charge of powder, Fig. 27.

When the chamber is made at the end of a gallery, the centre of the chamber is placed on a level with the floor of the gallery. It is usually better to place the chamber at the end of a small branch return on one side. When the charge is not to be exploded immediately, or the ground is much saturated with moisture, it should be placed in a well pitched wooden case, or a good cask, or in a wooden case eovered with tarpaulin, or any like expedient adopted that may be at hand—the best receptacle is a water-tight tin case.

In dry ground, and when the charge is to be soon exploded, canvass bags will answer.

If the case to contain the powder is not more than 2 feet square, it may be introdueed into the chamber ready made; if of a greater dimension, it must be put together in the ehamber, the pieces to form the sides being arranged like the frames of branches *à la Hollandaise*.

An opening is left at the edge of the cover, about 4 inches square, for the introduction of the eharge, and a similar one in the side to receive the hose-trough.

The edge of a cubical case to contain a given charge is calculated on the supposition that 58.5626 pounds of powder are equal in bulk to a cubic foot; and 1,000 cubic inches will, therefore, contain 33.89 pounds. From this, if *P* represents the given number of pounds of powder, and *X* the side of the cubic sought in inches, then

$$33.89 : (10)^3 :: P : X^3,$$

$$X = 3.09 \sqrt[3]{P}.$$

That is, to obtain the edge of the cubical case in inches, extract the cube root of the given number of pounds of powder and multiply it by 3.09, or $3\frac{1}{10}$, nearly

From the bursting of guns, where the wad has not been pressed down on the powder, it has been thought that in charging mines a like increase of effect would be produced, by leaving a certain free space around the case. Experiments on this point have not been sufficiently decisive to lead to the adoption of this in practice.

765...HOSE TROUGHS. The hose trough is a small wooden channel, in which is placed a linen bag filled with powder, and termed the powder-hose, to fire the charge.

The bag should be of close texture and well sewed.

These troughs are made $1\frac{1}{2}$ inch square in the clear. The four pieces of which they are composed: the sill, sides and top, or cover, are from $\frac{1}{4}$ to $\frac{1}{2}$ inch each in thickness.

A trough should penetrate the powder case about 4 inches, and should exactly fit the opening left for it.

It is fastened to the floor of the branch by nails, through the sill, which enter small pickets driven to receive them. Sometimes the sides of the trough are confined by pickets to prevent its being disturbed.

The different lengths of the trough should be cut to fit exactly. Each portion of the trough should have its cover well fitted and secured with one peg only, in order that it may readily be removed to introduce the powder-hose.

The trough is said to make an elbow when it changes its direction. The pieces forming an elbow should be firmly yet simply connected; Figs. 28, 29, show the most common forms of elbows.

766...PROPORTIONING TRAINS. When several mines are to be fired at the same moment, it is necessary so to proportion their trains that, starting from the same point, the distances in time from that point to the charges may be all equal. The following cases show the manner of obtaining this result:

For two charges, Fig. 30, place a trough on the shortest

line from the one to the other, mark the centre of it, and let the principal trough join it in that point.

For three charges, Fig. 31, connect, as above, the two which are nearest. Let a trough from the middle point of this to the third charge, bisect the whole length of trough between this third charge and either of the others; then let the principal trough be joined to this last point.

For four charges, Fig. 32, first connect them two and two, then join the central points and proceed as above.

The elbows of a trough impede the eommunication of the fire, for which an allowanee must be made when proportioning the trains, each elbow being valued at 3 inches; thus, if on one side of the point where the principal trough connects is one elbow more than on the other, the principal trough should be placed 3 inches nearer to the eharge on that side, which is done by placing it $1\frac{1}{2}$ inches from the central point toward that side. Sqnare elbows impede somewhat more than oblique ones.

Experience has shown that two powder-hoses may be placcd within 18 inches of one another if covered with earth, and exploded separately without interference.

767...Tamping. Mines are tamped either with earth and sods, with earth and wood, or with sand-bags.

To tamp a branch with sods and earth, the miner first fills the branch with sods for a length of 3 feet, commencing at the chamber. The sods are piled in regular layers, the precaution being taken to throw loose earth over each layer, to fill the voids between the sods. When this length is finished, the miner fills in for an additional 3 feet with earth, which should be well packed. Another length of sods is laid of 3 feet, and so alternately through the entire branch.

To tamp with wood and earth, a stout shield of thick boards is first placed across the branch and firmly buttressed against the chamber, the branch is then filled with well packed earth, resting against the shield for a length of 3 fcet; billets of round or square timber are then packed across the branch for a length, likewise, of 3 feet; another length of earth of the same thickness is packed in against the wood, and so on for the entire length to be tamped; finally, at the end of the tamping another shield is set up and firmly buttressed.

Sand-bags, for tamping, are of the ordinary dimensions. To tamp with them, a shield is first placed against the chamber and well buttressed. The branch is then filled up with sand-bags laid in regular layers, loose earth being thrown over each layer to close the joints. This is the best kind of tamping, as it can be removed most speedily after the explosion.

The length of tamping is regulated by the line of least resistance of the mine; the part of the branch tamped equal to twice this line. This length must be measured in a right line from the chamber to the point of the branch where the tamping terminates, and not along the windings or elbows of the branch.

768...As tamping is a laborious operation, and requires considerable time to do it thoroughly, it has been proposed to insert a trough of 4″ or 5″ section, in the branch or shaft leading from the mine chamber to the main gallery, or branch, and then to tamp in the usual manner around the trough. Prepared in this way, the charge made into cylindrical cartridges, or else the powder placed in successive portions in a cylindrical vessel, attached by a joint at its bottom to the end of a rod, can be shoved forward through the trough and be thrown into the chamber in a very short time, and the mine be immediately afterward exploded.

769...METHODS FOR EXPLODING. The most common methods of firing mines, are by the use of the *monk* and the *box-trap*. These two methods require a powder-hose.

The monk is a bit of agaric, 1½ inches in length. The train to be fired by it is arranged as follows:

Stretch the extremity of the hose upon a sheet of paper, and sprinkle some dry, fine powder on it; cover this powder over with another sheet of paper, secured at its four corners with dry earth or stones; pass the monk through a hole in the upper sheet, and let it project half its length above it, its base being plunged in the powder on the bottom sheet; set fire to the monk at top with another piece of agaric, termed an *informer*, of the same dimensions and form as the first, and retire quickly.

The box-trap, Fig. 33, is a box 18 inches high and 6 inches wide in the clear. The bottom consists of a piece of plank 18 by 10 inches, and its cover is fixed at one side only with a wooden pin, about which it can be turned.

At 6 inches from the top of the box a horizontal slit is made in one of its sides, and grooves in the two adjacent to it, to receive a piece of board, which ought to slide freely in this arrangement. In the lower part of the box an opening is left on the side opposite the one cut for the slide, to admit the powder-hose.

To fire the train, place the box against the extremity of the tamping and secure it well; tie a string to the slide, and lead it along the stanchions of the gallery on pegs driven for that purpose; put the end of the hose into the box through the hole left for it, and spread on the top of it some dry fine powder; then put in the slide and close with earth, or rags of sand-bags, all communication between the lower part of the box and the branch; place a star-match of six or eight points, well lighted, on the slide; replace the cover, then pull the string and the star will fall below and fire the mine.

The two methods above described have the inconvenience of requiring a powder-hose, which, from its own explosion, poisons the galleries. They have also, and more particularly the monk, the defect of not producing the explosion always at the instant desired.

To avoid these inconveniences a galvanic current has of late been applied to fire mines, and with complete success. This method has been found particularly serviceable in firing charges under water.

A small rocket, Fig. 34, with a hemispherical head of wood, has, also, been tried successfully. To use it, a wooden trough with a smooth interior must be placed from the charge to the point where the rocket is to start; tin tubes have been recommended, but are found not to answer. The rocket is then placed in the end of the trough, the quick-match with which it is provided is lighted, and the rocket starts with very great velocity, penetrates the charge and fires it.

When the rocket has to pass elbows, or when it is desired to fire several mines at the same moment, a rocket is placed at each turn of the trough, with its quick-match secured round a nail; the first rocket arriving at the point where the other is placed fires it. In order the better to insure the first rocket firing the second, a quantity of powder ($\frac{1}{4}$ ounce) should be strown about the match of the latter, protected by a wedge-shaped slip of deal, nailed to the bottom of the trough; the rocket meeting this passes over the powder, which its rapid motion would otherwise disperse.

A rocket may be made to turn in a circular trough, when the radius of that part is not less than twice the length of the rocket.

In order to prevent the smoke of the charge penetrating the gallery through the trough, one or two small iron traps may be placed in the trough, which, being raised by the rocket, fall again by their own weight, and cut off all communication between the gallery and the charge.

A rocket 6 inches long will travel 100 yards, at least, and its velocity is so great that two rockets fired at the same moment, to run very different distances, leave no perceptible interval in the times of their arrival. This property of rockets renders it easy to proportion the trains of mines to be fired simultaneously, which with powder-hose requires great nicety.

The ordinary rocket for this service contains $\frac{3}{4}$ of an ounce of a composition formed $\frac{2}{5}$ of fine powder, $\frac{2}{5}$ of saltpetre, and $\frac{1}{5}$ of charcoal dust. These ingredients should be very carefully mixed, to make the rocket burn uniformly. Its usual diameter is nearly $\frac{3}{4}$ of an inch, and entire weight about $1\frac{1}{2}$ ounce. Rockets may be made much smaller when required.

770...The great advantages offered by galvanic batteries for exploding mines at considerable distances from the battery, either when isolated or combined in groups for simultaneous effects, have led to experiments which, from the uniform certainty of the results, besides other obvious advantages over any of the other methods above given, will, probably, cause the general adoption of this apparatus for military mines.

The method mostly adopted by the Continental engineers is the combination of Bunsen's battery with Ruhmkorf's apparatus for intensifying the current of induction. A copper conducting wire, which is insulated by one or two coats of gutta-percha, connects the charges with the galvanic apparatus. The charge is exploded by passing a spark through a very small portion of fulminate of mercury inserted between the ends of two copper wires, which are enclosed within a short tube of gutta-percha, coated within with sulphuret of copper. The wires are bent near the end of the tube, and twisted around each other. A little meal powder is thrown around the fulminate and the tube, which, with the tube and the bent part of the wire, is tightly closed in a small gutta-percha bag, to keep out moisture. To fire a single mine, one end of the twist is soldered to the conducting wire and the other inserted into the earth to complete the circle. For several mines, to be exploded at the same time, conducting wires connect the mines, and the ends of the twist are soldered one to each conductor except the end one, which has one of its ends inserted into the earth. By this combination, the series will be exploded without any sensible difference of time between the nearest and furthest mine.

771...BLASTS. Blasts are small chambers, or holes made in rock, or masonry, charged with powder. The forming of blast-holes requires the use of particular tools, called *borers*, *jumpers*, *scrapers*, *needles* and *tamping-bars*.

To form the blast-hole, two or three men are required; one holds the borer with both hands, while the head of it is struck with sledge-hammers by one or two others. The first turns the borer at each stroke so that the hole may be circular, and from time to time clears it out with the scraper.

When the hole required does not exceed 15 inches in depth, it may be excavated in the above manner; but if 20 inches or more deep, the jumper is generally made use of. The miner holds the jumper in both hands, raises it, and lets it fall in the hole, turning it continually; he also clears the hole with the scraper. When the stone is of a very hard description, it is usual to pour water occasionally into the jumper hole.

To load the hole, fill about one-fourth or one-third of it with powder, according to the nature of the stone. The charge for a depth of 18 inches is from 8 to 12 ounces.

To tamp and prime the blast-hole, the needle is first introduced, plunging it well into the powder and placing it on the smoothest side of the hole; then a layer of clay is laid on the powder, and is closely pressed down with the tamping-bar.

Other similar layers are then laid, or layers of brick reduced to small bits, the needle being turned repeatedly. It is usual to press down the first layers with a bar of wood—the helve of a tool, for instance—and the latter ones with the iron tamping-bar. When the hole is thus filled up, a small shell of clay is formed round the needle, which is then withdrawn, the hole left by it is filled with fine powder, and it is fired with a monk or a piece of port-fire.

The use of the needle is often dispensed with, in which case the priming is rolled up in a sheet of brown paper, or it is introduced in straw-stalks thrust into one another. This priming is placed in the hole at the same time as the charge, so that it may penetrate well into the latter. The tamping is then executed as before.

The use of the tamping-bar and the ordinary tamping may also be dispensed with, the hole being filled over the charge with very fine dry sand, poured in without any pressure.

The many accidents that have happened in priming

blasts have led to the invention of priming-fuses, which are made to burn somewhat in the same way as the fuse in the small Chinese fire-cracker. Their use is far safer than any of the former methods.

For blasts under water, the charge is inserted in a water-tight tin case, and fired either by a galvanic current or a priming-fuse, which is protected from the water by a small tube connected with the charge, and leading to the surface of the water.

The result of many experiments has shown that in blasting rock a large portion of the powder—nearly half—may be saved, by mixing with the remaining part fine dry saw-dust of elm or beech. In blasts exploded in this way, the effect is not the same as when the full charge of powder is used; the rock splits into fewer and larger pieces, and, to finish dividing them, a more frequent use of the sledge-hammer is required.

772...DEMOLITIONS. The charges of mines intended to overthrow masonry, are calculated as in a common soil, by using the proper quantities given in the preceding table for the different kinds of masonry to be destroyed.

773...TO BREACH A WALL. First ascertain, if practicable, the thickness of the wall, and then proceed thus:

First case. When the wall is from 2 to 3 feet thick, place one or two barrels of powder against the lower part of it, and fire them.

Second case. When the wall is from 5 to 6½ feet thick, place one or two charges under its foundations, plumb with the centre of the wall.

Third case. When the wall is from 9 to 12 feet thick, open at the foot of it, or about 12″ above the water level, a branch gallery, which must be driven to the centre of the wall; then make two perpendicular returns to this branch, and place the powder at their extremities, Fig. 35.

774...TO BREACH A WALL WITH A TERRACE. Open at the foot of the wall, or 12″ above the level of the water, a branch perpendicular to the direction of the revetement; drive it through the wall to the earth, then make, to the right and left, two other branches, following the back of the wall, and each in length equal to its thickness; place the charges at the end of these branches, so that the centre of each charge may be flush with the back of the wall.

775...DEMOLITION OF REVETEMENTS. When the revetement is without counterforts, or the counterforts are not more than 3 feet thick, several branches are driven perpendicular to the direction of the revetement, at equal distances apart. The charges used should produce craters that will cross each other a little.

When the wall has counterforts of the usual dimensions, the charges are placed, as far as practicable, in the lines of their axes and their junction with the revetement, Fig. 36.

When time presses, instead of making one branch for each pair of charges one is made for each charge; and the whole of the charges are placed at three-fourths of the thickness of the wall, and so regulated that their craters may slightly run into each other, Fig. 37

When galleries cannot be driven at the proper level for the charge, as in the demolition of wharves, etc., shafts are sunk behind the revetement, or at a short distance in the rear of it, Fig. 38, and branches are then driven to the positions for the charges; or, which is still better, because it is a more speedy operation, a shaft may be sunk for each charge.

The depth of the shaft must be sufficient to admit of a proper length of tamping.

If, at the same time with the wall, a mass of earth in the rear of it is to be destroyed, prolong the branches in the interior of the earth sufficiently to allow of the mines at the back of the wall exploding before those placed in the earth beyond, Fig. 39.

When there is a gallery, Fig. 40, at the back of the revetement, the charges should be placed along this gallery, excavating chambers for them in the revetement at distances apart equal to twice their line of least resistance, viz., at two lined intervals.

The portions of the gallery in the rear of the charges

are then tamped; at each end, the length of the tamping should be equal to twice the line of least resistance of the extreme charges.

The following method has been employed with success. Regarding as the line of least resistance the distance from the gallery to the surface of the wall, imagine a row of common mines placed at two lined intervals throughout the length and calculate the sum of their charges, to which add one-half for a great gallery; place the whole charge in several heaps, with strong trains leading from one to another. Then, tamp strongly and carefully the ends of the gallery, leaving the space intended to be demolished void. When the gallery is more than 2 yards wide and high, or if it have many issues difficult to tamp, the charge of powder must be farther augmented to produce the desired effect.

776...DEMOLITION OF TOWERS. If the interior diameter of the tower be 6 yards or more, Fig. 41, drive branches into a wall from the interior of the tower, and place charges so as to be a little nearer to the interior than to the exterior of the wall. When the tower is connected with walls, charges must be placed at their points of junction.

When the tower is but 4 or 5 yards in diameter, Fig. 42, sink a shaft to about the level of the bottom of the foundations, and place a charge there corresponding to the line of least resistance, measured from the centre of the charge to the foot of the wall outside.

Cover the floor of the tower with two rows of small beams, then lay upon them two beams crossing and halved into one another; and place upon these uprights abutting firmly against the masonry of the arch.

When a shaft cannot be sunk on account of water, and when the tower has loop-holes which prevent charges being placed in the walls, lay the charge on the floor of the tower, enclosed in a strongly constructed case, propped on all sides against the masonry.

When the tower is square, and has several floors or

stages, the charges may be placed at the four corners of the ground story, tamping the first floor.

777...DEMOLITION OF POWDER MAGAZINES. Place charges in the piers and gable ends, so that their craters may slightly cross each other.

When time presses, a charge is laid on the floor of the magazine, the doors are barricaded, and it is fired with a hose led outside.

To determine the quantity of powder required for the heap, calculate the number of common mines required to overturn a revetement of the same length and thickness as the walls of a magazine, including the piers; add one-half the sum of the charges thus found, and place the whole in one heap in the centre of the magazine.

The above method is only applicable to magazines of not more than 150 square yards surface. If of greater capacity, the quantity first found should be increased $\frac{1}{10}$ for every 15 square yards of additional surface, and be placed in two or more heaps, connected with powder-hose to fire them simultaneously.

778...DEMOLITION OF BRIDGES. To destroy a bridge, the piers of which are from 4 to 5 feet thick, place in one of the piers two charges of 130 to 160 pounds each, Fig. 43, and secure a plank to the bridge on which to place the powder-hose.

If the pier be from 6 to 10 feet thick, drive in the middle of it, parallel to its face, two small branches, at the ends of which place charges of from 200 to 230 pounds each, Fig. 44.

When there is not time to place charges in the interior of the piers, cut a trench over the key of the arch 18 inches deep, in which place 400 to 530 pounds of powder.

This quantity of powder has broken semicircular arches of 26 feet span, and 4½ feet thickness at the crown.

Another good method is to cut a trench in the form of a cross, Fig. 44, over the middle of the arch, each branch being about 10 feet long, and carried down to the extrados.

Place in each branch 200 pounds of powder for an arch $3\frac{1}{4}$ feet thick, and cover the charges with timber, earth, etc.

An arch may also be blown up by suspending an open trough under it with cords, and placing in it charges of powder similar to those already stated for trenches cut on the surface.

When the saving of powder is of consequence, sink a shaft down to one of the haunches, Fig. 45, and place the powder in one mass, unless the bridge be very wide. An arch of 18 inches, or 2 feet thickness of a bridge 20 feet wide, may thus be destroyed with 45 pounds of powder, if a loading can be applied over the charge, giving an equal resistance to the arch.

If the bridge is more than 20 feet wide, two shafts must be sunk, and charged as before described. When the side walls of the bridge above the piers are slightly built, and the loading of the arch is of loose rubbish, a small gallery should be driven about 5 or 6 feet from the arch stones, along the axis of the pier, as at *A*, Fig. 45; a return is then made toward the arch, and the charge is placed in contact with the extrados. Bridges of timber may be blown up by suspending barrels of powder under one or several bays.

779...Demolition of Houses. Begin by undermining the windows and doors, and cutting away the piers between them, so as to leave the building supported by a few piers only, nearly square. Place in each of the piers a charge of from 13 to 16 pounds of powder, tamping well with wood. Proportion the trains to the different charges, so that they may be simultaneously exploded. If pressed for time, resort to the same methods as for towers and galleries.

To destroy palisades, or gates, doors, etc., the best method is to suspend a leathern bag, filled with powder, either with a forked stick, a strong gimlet, or a stout copper nail, against the gate or palisade. The bag should have about an inch of port-fire firmly secured in one side of it, to communicate the fire to the charge. To throw down a strong palisade, from 30 to 50 pounds of powder should be used. To burst open a town gate, 60 or 70 pounds of powder will be required.

780...FOUGASSES. Mines are so called when placed at the bottom of small shafts, from 9 to 12 feet deep. The powder is lodged in one of the sides of the shaft, and it is fired from a secure spot by means of a powder hose, brought up one side of the shaft, and carried in a trough, parallel to the ground, 5 or 6 feet below the surface. When there is no occasion to fear that shells may fall on the part where the trough is laid, it will be sufficient to place it 2 or 2½ feet under the ground. The powder case and trough should be well pitched, the shaft tamped in the strongest manner, and the earth round about the shaft be dug over, that nothing may indicate to the enemy the position of the fougasse.

781...SHELL FOUGASSES. Shells may be buried singly, or in small heaps, and be made to burst either under the ground or on its surface.

If they are to burst under the earth, they must be sufficiently charged to produce a crater, through which the pieces are projected.

If they are to burst on the surface, the requisite quantity of powder to produce a crater and throw out the shells must be lodged under them, while these latter need only have a sufficient charge to burst them.

In all cases a box is used, Fig. 46, divided into two parts by a partition. The shells are placed in the upper part, their fuses project through the partition, and extend from ½ to 1 inch below it.

In the lower part, the hose only is placed when the shells are intended to produce their own crater; but powder sufficient to produce the crater is introduced when they are intended to burst on the surface of the ground.

The effects produced by common and shell fougasses are very limited, and only destructive near to their craters: consequently, they should not be exploded until the enemy is above them.

DESCRIPTION OF SHELL.	FULL CHARGE OF THE SHELL.		DEPTH AT WHICH THE FULL CHARGE PRODUCES A CRATER.	
	Lbs.	Oz.		
Calibre, 5½	1	0	2′	0″
" 8	2	9	2	10
" 10	5	0	3	6
" 13	11	0	4	7

782...CONDITIONS TO BE SATISFIED IN ARRANGING A SYSTEM OF MINES. As the galleries of a system of mines serve the purpose of underground communications, they should be subjected to the same conditions as other communications. A condition of primary importance is, that no combination shall be made which might compromise the safety of the enceinte. To this end, no gallery under the glacis should lead to the interior of the enceinte; for, should the enemy get possession of such a gallery, he might either penetrate into the work or else barricade the gallery and hold possession of it long enough to blow up the works under which it leads.

783...The galleries should not offer any facilities to the besiegers for carrying on their works. Those galleries, therefore, which, debouching in the ditches, might serve the besiegers for their descent of the ditch; also, a continued counterscarp gallery, which may not only facilitate the descent of the ditch of the besiegers, but, also, when in their possession, give them that of the whole system, and, besides, serve to protect their passage of the ditch, and to prevent sorties in it, should be rejected. A gallery behind a portion of the counterscarp not favorable to the enemy's works, is very useful as a depôt for the implements of the miners, and also as a communication.

784...A permanent system of mines should not be used, either for works that can be carried by storm or for covered-ways in a similar state; for the reason that the besiegers might easily get possession of the system before it could be brought into play.

785...The *débouché* of a system in the ditches must be revetted, to offer a sufficient obstacle to prevent the enemy from getting possession of the system by surprise; hence, a revetted counterscarp is a necessary condition in the establishment of the system.

786...The galleries should not be run out to any considerable distance beyond the covered-ways, both on account of procuring a good circulation of air, and because very advanced galleries are easily destroyed by the besiegers. The distance to which the galleries may extend should be so much the less, as the ground above them is well protected by the collateral works.

787...The soil must be suitable for the establishment of a system; wet, marshy ground, shifting sand, and hard rock, present almost insuperable obstacles; whereas, a dry, firm soil, soft rock, or ordinary earth under a thin superstratum of hard rock, are very favorable circumstances. If the sub-soil is wet, but presents a firm and dry superstratum 12 feet thick above the level at which the water collects, mines may still be placed with advantage.

788...Besides the above general conditions, there are certain special ones to be attended to in arranging the galleries and chambers.

The galleries should be placed as far below the surface as practicable, to withdraw them from the effect of the globes of compression of the besiegers. To drain the galleries they should have a slight inclination, about $\frac{1}{50}$, toward the ditches, or, if the ground descends toward a hollow, the inclination may be given in that direction.

789...The chambers, on the contrary, should be near the surface; by this arrangement the powder is economized, and all danger to the galleries from the explosion avoided, whilst the object of the mines, which is to destroy the enemy's works, can be as fully attained by small mines as large ones.

790...The galleries should not be placed nearer to each

other than twice the line of least resistance of the heaviest charged mines, and not much less than four times the line of least resistance of the smallest charges. This arrangement will admit of a combination of mines in two tiers, the line of least resistance of the lower being double that of the upper, the chambers of which may be so arranged that the explosions of one tier shall not affect either the galleries or the mines of the other. Twice the line of least resistance of the largest mines is the least distance that can be allowed between the galleries, in order that the mines of the lowest tier, which, being placed near one gallery, must destroy a part of it, shall not injure those parallel to it. By placing the galleries at this least distance apart, the branches for the service of the upper tier will be as short as possible, affecting thus a saving of time and labor, and from the same cause the galleries on any one point being as many as can be placed, there will be the advantage that some one of the galleries will be serviceable should others be injured by explosions.

791...The galleries and branches for the service of the different groups of mines, should be independent of each other, so that there may be no confusion in the service, and that no group may be rendered unserviceable by the destruction of the communications to another. The same principle should be attended to in combining the different groups of mine chambers.

792...The galleries and branches should never present their flanks or sides to the globes of compression of the besiegers. This rule leads to the rejection of enveloping galleries.

793...The systems of countermines proposed by most writers on this branch of the defence are generally of too complicated a character to admit of being executed at a reasonable cost, and they require for their service not only a large amount of powder but also a great number of miners.

The following arrangement, based on the general conditions just laid down, has been proposed, to meet in a simple and satisfactory manner the requisites of a subterranean defence:

Parallel to the capital of the demilune, four listening galleries are run out to a distance of from 50 to 80 yards beyond the salient of the covered-way. The interval between these galleries being twice the line of least resistance of the heaviest charged mines. If we take this line at 7 yards, or 21 feet, which is about the greatest for common mines, the interval of the galleries will be 15 yards. The dimensions of the listening galleries for about the first 20 yards may be those of a grand gallery, and the remaining part may be a common gallery. These galleries will depart from a transversal grand gallery, about 6 yards from the demilune counterscarp, which will serve as a communication between them, and also as a depôt. Other transversals of the size of half galleries or branches, will be made at different intervals for the purpose of ventilation. This group of galleries will have their outlet into the demilune ditch through two galleries, one leading from each extremity of the transversal grand gallery. To flank this group, other listening galleries will extend obliquely outward from the two outside parallel galleries. To serve the mines of this group, a series of ascending branches will lead from the galleries to chambers placed midway between the galleries, having a line of least resistance of 4 yards. This will place these chambers at about 8 yards from the two adjacent galleries. Smaller branches may lead, if necessary, from these last branches to other groups of chambers, having a line of least resistance of 2 or 3 yards. A series of chambers with lines of least resistance of 7 yards, will be established in juxtaposition with each listening gallery. From this arrangement it will be readily seen that ground over the galleries can be entirely broken up, and that the successive explosions of the mines of one group will destroy the branches and galleries which lead to them, without injuring those of other groups. The object of this disposition is to blow up by repeated explosions the ground over which the enemy must approach upon the demilune salient place of arms.

794...For the defence of the other portions of the glacis of the demilune covered-way, a counterscarp gallery of the dimensions of a grand gallery is placed between the two traverses next to the re-entering place of arms; a listening gallery extends from one extremity of this gallery in an oblique direction outward, and nearly parallel to the long branch of the covered-way crest between the two traverses, to within 20 yards of the foregoing arrangement. Other listening galleries, placed 15 yards apart, run out from the main one, about 20 yards, to menace every point of the glacis that can be occupied by the besieger's works. The groups of mines for these galleries may be arranged like those of the combination in advance of the demilune salient place of arms. The counterscarp gallery should have two outlets in the demilune ditch; but as these might compromise the safety of the whole arrangement, should the besiegers attack the covered-way by storm, they must be walled up when the third parallel is completed, and the communication with the galleries then kept up by a gallery leading to the main ditch. To supply the main listening gallery of this group with air, a branch should lead to it from a point of the demilune counterscarp under the traverse next to the one of the salient place of arms.

795...Groups of galleries and mines, similar to the one in front of the demilune salient place of arms, may be arranged for the defence of the bastion salient place of arms. And a gallery, leading from the counterscarp of the main ditch, may be made for the service of a group for the defence of the glacis of the re-entering place of arms.

796...To defend the breaches made in the demilune and its redoubt, a gallery may be made under the ditch of the redoubt, having its outlet in the main ditch; this gallery may divide into two branches, one leading under the demilune breach the other under that of the redoubt. Ascending branches may be made from the gallery leading to the demilune breach, for the service of a group of mines to blow up the demilune terreplein.

797...Finally, if the bastions are arranged with interior retrenchments, a disposition similar to the one made for the defence of the demilune may also be made for the defence of the bastion breach.

798...As the air in the galleries of mines is liable to become foul from various causes, some mechanical contrivances and chemical methods, by which the vitiated air can be removed and fresh air introduced, have to be resorted to for the purpose of enabling the miners to circulate through them with safety Air pumps, bellows, and artificial drafts procured by kindling a fire at one of the outlets of a system of galleries, are the ordinary expedients by which this object is attained.

799...The great pecuniary outlay requisite in establishing a system of permanent galleries, besides the large corps of experienced miners and the extra provision of powder demanded for their efficient service, when the system embraces any considerable extent of surface, has led engineers to consider whether the end proposed by subterranean means of defence might not be attained by some more simple expedients. Since the application of galvanic currents to exploding mines, and the facilities which it affords to effect this at very considerable distances, it has been proposed to substitute isolated shafts for galleries, placing them in positions most suitable to attain the besieger's works. These shafts, to give them a character of permanency, may be lined with masonry, and receive a stone or iron cover which may be concealed from view by placing it several feet below the surface. When wanted for service the shafts are charged and tamped in the usual manner, and connected with a galvanic battery by insulated wire conductors, laid sufficiently far below the surface of the ground to be without the sphere of the besieger's excavations and other accidents.

Attack & Defence of Permanent Works.

FRENCH MATERIALS.

1...Under this head are comprised the materials used by the besiegers for revetements and covers against the fire of the defences.

FASCINES. These are usually made 18′ long, and 9″ in diameter, and are afterward cut into suitable lengths for the purposes to which they are to be applied.

PICKETS. Those used for securing fascines are from 2′ to 4′ long, and from 1¼″ to 1¾″ thick; those for setting out or tracing the works are 18″ long and 1″ diameter.

SAP-FAGOTS. These are made, like fascines, of straight brush-wood at least 1″ in diameter. They are 2′ 9″ long, and 9″ in diameter. The centre stake should be from 1½″ to 2″ in diameter, and project 9″ beyond one end of the sap-fagot; this projecting portion is sharpened, to enable the sap-fagot to be planted firmly in the ground in an upright position.

GABIONS. The exterior diameter of these is 2′, and the height of watling is 2′ 9″ They are made with seven or nine stakes, which project 6″ above the watling at top, and are pointed.

At the siege of Sebastopol, the want of brush-wood for the watling of gabions led to the introduction of the common hoop-iron, for this purpose, which had served to secure the bales of hay. The number of pickets employed for each gabion was usually thirteen. It was found that these gabions could be constructed more readily than the ordinary kind; that they were not much heavier, more durable, and in all respects as serviceable. Since then, it has been proposed to use simple sheet-iron cylinders, of suitable dimensions, instead of the brush-wood gabion. For this purpose, rectangular sheets of iron, of suitable dimensions to form cylinders of the same height and diameter as the ordinary gabion, are prepared, with three or four holes punched near and parallel to the shorter sides of the sheet to secure these ends with wire when the sheet is bent into the cylindrical shape. Besides these, two other holes of larger size are punched toward the central portion of the sheet, so as to be diametrically opposite when the cylinder is formed, to receive a picket passed through them which serves as a handle in carrying the gabion. The advantages of this description of gabion are greater strength, lightness and durability than either of the others; offering great facility for distant transportation, and resisting better the blast of guns when used for revetting the cheeks of embrasures.

SAP-ROLLERS. This is a large gabion, 7′ 6″ in length, and 4′ 4″ exterior diameter. It requires for its construction fifteen stakes, each from 1¼″ to 2″ in diameter. After it is completed, it is stuffed compactly with fascines 7′ 6″ long. The sap-roller is sometimes made of two concentric gabions, the diameter of the smaller 2′ 6″ The space between the two is compactly stuffed with fascines.

SAND-BAGS. The sand-bag, for the revetement of batteries, when empty and laid flat, is 2′ 8″ long and 1′ 4″ wide; those used in the construction of the trenches are 2′ long 12″ wide.

BLINDAGE-FRAMES. These frames, Pl. 10, Fig. 1, are composed of two uprights, or stanchions, of 5″ scantling, each 8′ 6″ long, and pointed at both ends; and two horizontal pieces of the same sized scantling, each 3′ 4″ long. The horizontal pieces are notched upon the stanchions at 12″ from each end. The width of the frame from out to out is 3′ 4″; the distance between the horizontal pieces from out to out, 6′

An *auxiliary stanchion*, Fig. 2, with a projecting piece, is used in placing the blindage-frames.

GALLERY-FRAMES. The arrangement and dimensions of these are the same as those used in mining.

TRENCHES.

2...The term *trench* is applied to an excavation or ditch made by the beseigers, by means of which, and of the earth thrown from it, they are enabled to obtain speedy cover from the fire of the defences, and to approach them with security.

Trenches are divided into two principal classes—the *parallels* and the *approaches*. The parallels are designed as stations for troops to guard the trenches, and the workmen employed in their execution, from the sorties of the garrison. The approaches serve simply as covered communications which lead to the parallels, and toward the points of the defences upon which the attack of the besiegers is directed.

The general direction of the parallels is parallel to, or concentric with, the line connecting the most salient points of that portion of the defences attacked. The approaches are run in a zig-zag, or in a straight line, upon some or all of these points.

3...The trenches of the parallels, Pl. 10, Figs. 3, 4, 5, 6, receive a width at bottom of 10′; their depth in front is 3′, and in rear 3′ 6″ Two steps, each 18″ high and 18″ wide, lead from the bottom of the trench, on the front side, to the natural ground. The reverse of the trench receives a slope of 45°, or else, is also cut into two steps. The steps in front are alone revetted with fascines. The trenches of the approaches, Pl. 10, Figs. 7, 8, are 8′ wide at bottom, 3′ 6″ deep in front, and 4′ at the rear. The reverse receives a slope of 45° The front is usually made with a slope of 2′ base.

The earth from the trench is thrown to the front to form a parapet. The general height of this parapet is nearly 5′, its width at the base about 18′

4...SIMPLE TRENCH. When the parapet is formed of earth alone, Figs. 3, 4, 7, the trench is termed a *simple trench.* In this case the earth of the parapet is allowed to take its natural slope on the side toward the trench. The step, or berm, of 18″, between the foot of the parapet and the trench in the parallels serves as a banquette.

Portions of the parallels, Figs. 4, 6, from 20 to 30 yards in length, are arranged with steps, revetted with fascines, leading from the trench over the parapet, to enable the troops in the parallel to debouch from it against a sortie.

The direction of the trench is laid out by pickets, connected by white tape, which is marked off into lengths of 6′ by short pieces attached to it. The trench is executed by soldiers of the line; each man being furnished with a pick and shovel, with which he excavates 6′ in length of the trench, and as much of it to the rear as may be assigned to the relief, or working party, to which he belongs. After the trench has received its general width and depth, the slopes and steps are finished off with the assistance and under the direction of the engineer troops.

5...Flying Sap. When the trenches have been pushed forward to within destructive range of case shot, the construction by the simple trench has to be abandoned, and one which will afford more speedy shelter resorted to. This is effected, Figs. 5, 8, by placing a row of ordinary gabions in juxtaposition, along the direction of the trench; these being filled with the earth from the trench, the parapet is completed by throwing the remaining earth over and beyond them. This process is termed the flying sap, from the rapidity with which the work is done. It, also, is executed by troops of the line, each man bringing two gabions on the ground, which he is required to fill, and also to complete the portion of the trench, in the rear of them, assigned to the relief to which he belongs. The requisite height is given to the parapet either by heaping up the earth above the top of the gabions or by placing three ordinary fascines upon the gabions, two being in the bottom course and the other on top, and throwing up the earth at least as high as the top fascine.

In positions where the earth cannot be obtained in sufficient quantity to afford a speedy cover, as in a shallow stratum of soil on rock, etc., two rows of gabions, placed in juxtaposition, may be used for the flying sap.

The troops for constructing both this and the simple trench are divided into three parties, or reliefs. The first digs the trench to the requisite depth and to the width of 5′; the second widens it 4′ 6″; the third finishes what remains, giving the requisite slopes to the front and rear.

Remark. The dimensions and form given to the profiles of the parallels and boyaux in the preceding paragraphs are those used in our own and the English sapper practice. The French allow usually 3′ 3″ for the uniform depths of both, and 4′ 3″ for the height of parapet. This gives a cover of 7′ 6″ in the trench, which would seem ample, whilst it gives the parapet a more suitable height for the convenient delivery of the fire, if the troops stationed in the parallels are called upon to repel a sortie in this way.

6...Full Sap. The full sap, Figs. 9, 10, 11, is resorted to when the fire becomes so destructive that the flying sap cannot be used. The trench is opened and pushed forward by engineer troops alone; for this purpose a working party, termed a *brigade*, of eight sappers is requisite. The brigade is divided into two equal *sections;* the sappers of the first section dig the trench, and are numbered from 1 to 4, No. 1 leading. The other four are termed *assistants;* they bring forward the materials, and assist the first section in all the necessary operations.

The leading sapper, No. 1, is provided with a pick and shovel, and wears a musket-proof helmet and cuirass; he works on his knees, being covered, on his side toward the defences, by the parapet of the trench, from which he debouches, and in front by a sap-roller, which is placed perpendicular to the line of direction on which he is to work, and rests against the gabion he is filling, covering it one foot. The portion of the sap which he digs is 21″ wide at top and 21″ deep; it receives a slope of 4 perpendicular to 1 base on the front, and is vertical in the rear; and its length is 5′ So soon as this portion is finished, No. 2, who is protected in all respects like No. 1, commences to widen and deepen the trench 8″ at the point from which No. 1 started, and follows on after No. 1, keeping always 5′ in his rear. When No. 2 has pushed forward 5′, No. 3 commences and enlarges the trench in each direction 7″; he follows on also 5′ in rear of No. 2, but as the work thrown up by the sappers preceding him affords pretty good cover, he can work standing, taking the precaution to bend forward for greater security Finally, No. 4 begins when No. 3 has got on 5′, and deepens and widens 7″ As he is well covered, he can work in an unconstrained posture.

Besides the shelter given by the gabions, as they are successively filled, and the sap-roller, the further precaution is taken of driving sap-fagots along the berm, at the junction of the gabions; these are successively removed as they are no longer requisite. The trench fascines are placed upon the gabions by the assistants, and the remainder of the trench completed by working parties of the line, so soon as the brigade of sappers have proceeded far enough for the others to commence without hindrance.

7...DOUBLE SAP. This sap, Figs. 12, 13, consists of two heads of sap pushed forward by two brigades working abreast. Its object is to form a trench in a position exposed on both sides to fire. The head of the sap is covered by two sap-rollers placed end to end; a bag of wool, or a short sap-roller, being placed at their junction for additional security The distance between the two rows of gabions is 13′ The earth between the two lines of sap is removed by the usual working parties, as in the preceding case.

8...HALF-DOUBLE SAP. This is an ordinary line of full sap, Fig. 14, pushed forward in a position where it is necessary to give temporary cover on the reverse of the trench by gabions filled with sand-bags. The distance between the two rows of gabions, in this case, is only 5′ 6″; the single sap-roller covering in front this interval from enfilading fire.

9...DEFILEMENT OF TRENCHES. The position given to the

lines of the parallel, and the dimensions adopted for its trench and parapet, give ample cover to the troops in it from the plunging fire of works having anything like the usual command. But in the zig-zag approaches, or *boyaux*, as the line of the trench has to be directed toward the defences, it is necessary either to defile the trench, by giving it a direction such that the fire, coming over its parapet, will not have a plunge sufficient to attain a man standing in the reverse of it, or, when this cannot be done, by placing traverses along the line to be covered, which shall effect the proposed end.

In the usual cases of practice, the ground on which the approaches are run will be more or less uneven, and this inequality of surface, if quite appreciable, will demand a corresponding variation in the line of direction of an approach, where its defilement is to be effected by the position given to it with respect to the point from which it may be attained by the enemy's fire. In most cases, however, each portion of the line of the trench, corresponding to the changes in the surface, may, without any very great error, be regarded as lying either on a horizontal, or an inclined plane; and, in the latter case, the plane may either rise toward the dangerous point or descend in the same direction; there will, therefore, arise three cases of defilement, according to the position of the plane on which the trench is run with respect to the dangerous point.

To illustrate these cases, let the approach to be defiled, be a trench constructed with the flying sap. Now. whether the ground be horizontal or inclined, the relative position of the lines of the profile of the approach should be preserved as nearly as practicable. The vertical height of the top of the parapet—supposing the latter no higher than the top fascine—above the bottom of the trench, at the reverse side, Figs. 15, 16, 17, will then be 8′ 3″; and the horizontal distance between the same points 12′ Now, in order that a man standing at the reverse of the trench may be secure, the line of fire of the enemy should not have a greater plunge than 6′ 6″ above the bottom of the trench at this point. This will limit the inclination of the line of fire to the horizontal drawn through the top of the parapet to about 1 perpendicular to 7 base, or an angle of $\frac{1}{7}$. It will readily be seen from this that the line of the trench must not be run so near the dangerous point that the line of fire from it, passing through the top point of the parapet, and in the direction of the profile of the trench—that is, in a vertical plane containing the dangerous point, and perpendicular to the horizontal projection of the line of the trench—shall make a greater angle than $\frac{1}{7}$; and that, when the line of the trench satisfies this condition, it will be defiled by its position.

TO FIND THE DEFILED POSITION OF A TRENCH ON HORIZONTAL GROUND. Let *D*, Fig. 18, be the point of departure of an approach leading from a parallel, and *C* the most dangerous point of the defences for this approach, the height of which above the parapet of the approach is known. It is evident, from what has just been laid down, if the approach were continued on beyond the point *C*, and a line with an inclination of $\frac{1}{7}$ were drawn from *C* perpendicular to the direction of the approach and through the top of its parapet, that a man standing at the reverse of the bottom of the trench would not be attained by this fire: but as the top of the parapet, or interior crest of the approach, is horizontal, and the reverse of the bottom of the trench is parallel to it, it is farther evident that the plane which passes through the point *C* and the interior crest of the approach, will pass at the same height above every point of the reverse of the bottom of the trench that the line of $\frac{1}{7}$, through *C*, does above the point *G*, since this line lies in the plane; it, therefore, follows that, if the point *G* is defiled, every other point along the reverse of the trench will also be defiled. To construct the position of the line *D F* to satisfy this condition, describe from the point *C*, as a centre, with a radius equal to seven times the vertical height of *C* above the parapet of the approach, an arc of a circle, the tangent to this arc from *D* will be the required position.

NOTE. In Fig. 18, the dangerous point, *C*, is 18′ above the horizontal plane of the trench. The reference of this plane being (0), that of the point *C* is (18.0), and that of the interior crest of the approach is (4.25). The reference of the point *a* is (11.0); the declivity of the glacis planes $\frac{1}{21}$.

10...TO FIND THE DEFILED POSITION OF AN APPROACH ON INCLINED GROUND. Let, Fig. 18, two planes of a glacis intersecting in a ridge, *a b*, one of the planes rising in the direction of the dangerous point, *C*, and the other falling toward it, be taken as the ground on which the trenches are to be run; and let *A*, at the foot of the plane which ascends toward *C*, be the point of departure of the approach. Now, the plane being produced toward *C* may either pass above it, through it, or below it; in either of the two first positions it is evident, if the interior crest of the approach were directed on the point *C*, that the trench would be defiled; for no line of fire from *C* would, in either of these cases, have a plunge into the trench, and the same would hold true if the plane produced passed at a distance below it just equal to the height of parapet of the approach. In either of these cases, therefore, to defile the trench, it will only be necessary to direct its interior crest on the dangerous point, and this direction may be kept until the approach strikes the ridge at *B*.

11...At this point, as the plane of the glacis on which the prolonged branch of the trench is to be run descends toward *C*, and is seen in reverse by its fire, it will be necessary to change the direction of this branch so as to withdraw it from the plunging fire from C. This will be effected by giving this branch a direction such that a line of fire from *C*, having an inclination of $\frac{1}{7}$, and being contained in the profile plane of the trench which passes through *C*, shall clear the head of a man standing in the trench at the reverse side; and this will be the case if this line of $\frac{1}{7}$ passes through the interior crest of the parapet and 6′ 6″ above the bottom of the trench at the reverse. It is evident, in the first place, that this will be true for the profile plane through *C*. Now, since the line of the interior crest and the line of $\frac{1}{4}$ intersect, they will determine a plane which passes through *C*, and in which all the lines of fire from *C* which strike the interior crest are contained. As the reverse line of the bottom of the trench is parallel to the interior crest, and as the plane of fire in question passes at 6′ 6″ above that point of the reverse line of the bottom which is contained in the profile plane through *C*, it follows that this plane also passes at 6′ 6″ above every other point of this reverse line, and, therefore, that the direction of the trench which fulfils this condition will be defiled throughout from the fire coming from *C*.

To construct this position, let the point *C* be taken as the vertex of a right cone, the elements of which make an angle of $\frac{1}{4}$ with its base. The line of fire of $\frac{1}{4}$ will be an element of this cone. If the cone be intersected by a plane parallel to the one on which the approach is run, and at a distance above it equal to the height of the parapet, the interior crest of the approach must intersect the curve cut from the cone by this plane; and, to satisfy the conditions imposed, the point of intersection must be where the projection of the element of the cone is perpendicular to that of the interior crest, as these are the relative positions in projection of the line of fire of $\frac{1}{4}$ and of the approach. To construct the projection of the curve cut from the cone, it will only be necessary to intersect the cone and plane by equidistant horizontal planes, and to find the projections of the corresponding points of intersection of the lines cut from the two surfaces by these planes. To find the direction of the approach, join the point of its departure, *B*, with *C*, and on this line describe a semicircle; the point *X*, where this semicircle cuts the projection of the curve cut from the cone, will give the required direction, *B X*, of the approach.

A like construction would give the direction of an approach on an ascending plane, where the plane passes at a greater distance than the height of the parapet below the dangerous point.

12...It will be noted from what precedes that the approach is never directed *within* a dangerous point; for the obvious reason that, if so placed, it would be exposed to reverse fire from the point. If it should happen that the direction *B X*, found for the approach in the preceding case, would bring its prolongation within a dangerous point, *C′*, on the left of the ridge, toward which the plane ascends, it would then be necessary to change the direction *B X* to that of *C′ B X′*, and, as this would expose the trench to a plunging fire from *C*, it will be farther requisite either to deepen the trench, or to raise the parapet higher, to cover the reverse from this plunge.

13...It will be farther noted that, at the point of departure of an approach from a parallel, there will be a portion of the parallel, *o p q*, in the rear of the trench, which will not be fully covered by the parapet of the approach. This portion will be limited by the line of fire from *C* through *O*, where the reverse of the approach cuts the interior crest of the parallel, and by the reverse prolonged to *q*. To secure this portion, either the trench of the parallel must be deepened or that part of the parapet of the approach be raised, which is intercepted between the lines of fire from *C* on *p* and *q*.

14...Defilement by Traverses. When the defilement cannot be effected by the position given to the trench, resort must be had to traverses. Two cases present themselves under this head: one in which the reverse of the trench is exposed to a very slant fire; the other in which the trench is pushed forward between two dangerous points, and is, at the same time, exposed to an enfilading fire.

15...In the first case, Fig. 19, the trench is carried forward by means of the half-double sap. So soon as the head of the sap has been advanced the length of twelve gabions beyond No. 4, a short end of sap, termed a *wing traverse*, is commenced in a direction perpendicular to that of the trench, and run out until it intercepts the line of fire upon the point of departure at the distance of twelve gabions in its rear. When this end of sap is completed, the provisional parapet in its rear can be taken down and the trench enlarged to its proper width. In this way the trench is successively pushed forward and enlarged, until a position has been reached where it becomes necessary to place a traverse to cover the trench from both enfilading and reverse views. These traverses, *A*, *A*, are made by changing the direction of the trench perpendicular to that of the original line, and continuing in this new direction, by the full sap, the requisite length of the traverse; the original direction is then resumed, and continued, by the half-double sap, a sufficient distance to leave room for the width of the traverse and a trench of douple sap; another rectangular turn is then made, by the double sap, back to the line of gabions of the original trench, and the original direction is again taken up and carried forward by the half-double sap.

The traverses *A*, *A* are seven gabions, or about 14′ in width. Their length will depend on the position of the dangerous point, but they are seldom made over 30′ in length. Their distance apart will also depend on the command of the dangerous point. The portion of trench between any two traverses must be perfectly covered by the advanced traverse. As a practical rule, the traverses are not placed farther than 25 or 30 yards apart.

The portion of the trench, *B*, in rear of the end of the traverse is covered by extending sufficiently far to the rear of it an end of trench, *C*, forming a wing traverse, to intercept the line of slant fire.

16...In the second case, Fig. 20, the trench, *A*, is carried forward by the double sap, until the point of departure, *B*, is about being exposed to the fire coming in over the sap-rollers; a change of direction, *C*, at right-angles is then made by the full sap, to the right or left, and pushed forward the length of about fifteen gabions, when the original direction, *D*, by the double sap is resumed. A change of direction is sometimes made both to the right and left at right angles to the original direction, by the full sap, and pushed to the length of twelve or fourteen gabions. Then, from the extremities of these branches, a direction parallel to the original is taken up by the double sap, and pushed on until the point of departure is about being exposed, when a change of direction is made at right angles by the full sap, and the two branches are united on the original direction, *E*, which is resumed by the double sap.

17...TRENCH CAVALIER. This work consists of a parapet raised on a mound of earth, for the purpose of obtaining a plunging fire on the covered-way. The mound should, in all cases, be raised so high that the cavalier will have a command of $4\frac{1}{4}$ feet over the crest of the covered-way. The position of the cavalier is shown in the annexed Fig. When the trenches are advanced by the full sap nearly within reach of grenades thrown by hand, or about

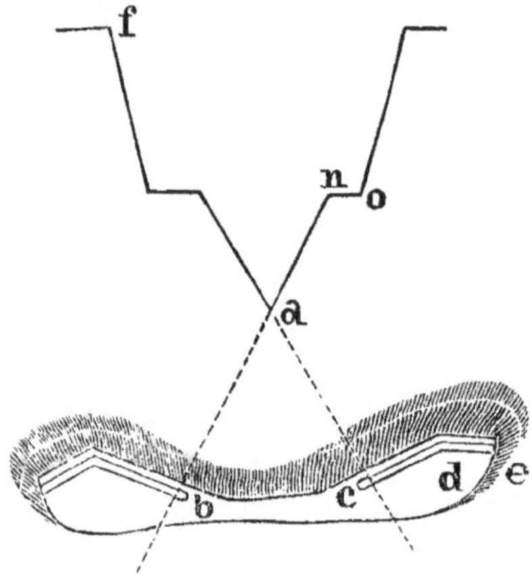

30 yards from the salient, *a*, of the covered-way, a circular portion of trench, *b c*, is formed, to embrace the production of the crests of the salient; from the extremities of this circular portion the sap is run perpendicular to the direction of the crests, to a distance, *c d*, of about 8 or 12 yards, so as to enfilade the covered-way; at the extremity, *d*, a *wing* or *return*, *d e*, is made to cover the part, *c d*, from the flank and reverse fire of the collateral works; this part, *d e*, may, in some cases, be arranged nearly parallel to the crotchets, *n o*, of the covered-way, so as to give a fire on them; but generally it serves only to cover the branch, *c d*, as has been explained.

18...There are two ways of forming the cavalier, depending on the nature of the soil. When the excavated earth is of such a nature that it can be easily made to stand at any slope, a profile, represented by Fig. 21, is preferred, as requiring less time and materials. After having laid out the position of the cavalier by the full sap, the sappers widen the trench 6′, and make a step at the bottom of the trench 22″ in height, and 5′ 6″ within the gabion of the parapet; this step serves as a platform on which the sappers mount to level the earth of the parapet even with the fascines on top of the first gabion, for the purpose of placing a second tier of gabions, which is placed 22″ beyond the first. This second tier is filled with earth, and crowned with two fascines, and the mound is raised to a level with the fascines, by widening the trench to the rear. The earth is now levelled even with the top of the fascines, and a third tier of gabions is placed just on the outside of the second; it is filled with earth, crowned with three fascines, and the mound is raised to a level with the upper fascine. This top tier forms the parapet of the work. Loop-holes are made by arranging sand-bags on top of the parapet, for the purpose of covering the heads of the men whilst in the act of firing. As the successive tiers of gabions are placed, steps, revetted with fascines, are made to lead to the top; these steps have a rise and tread of 22″; the top one serves as a banquette.

19...When the soil excavated is loose, a cavalier made in the manner just described would not be sufficiently firm. The following construction will in this case be used: After having traced out the cavalier by the full sap, a row of gabions, Fig. 22, is placed in the bottom of the trench, along the foot of the interior slope; this row is filled with earth, and crowned with two fascines, and earth is filled in between it and the interior slope, and brought to a level with the berm. A third tier of gabions is placed on this platform, alongside of the row forming the parapet of the trench; this tier is, in like manner, filled with earth, and crowned with two fascines. The second tier of the cavalier is commenced, by placing a fourth row of gabions over the joint of the two in the first tier; this is filled with earth, crowned with two fascines, and the mound is raised on the exterior to a level with this fourth gabion. A fifth row is next placed alongside of the two in the first tier, filled with earth and crowned with two fascines. A sixth is then placed alongside of the fourth, in the second tier, and arranged like the preceding. Finally, the parapet is formed on this second tier, by placing a gabion above the joint between those of the second tier, and arranging it as in Fig. 17 The steps are made to ascend to the top, by throwing up a mound of earth, on the interior, against the gabionade, and forming the surface into steps revetted with fascines, as in the last case.

DESCENTS OF THE COVERED-WAY AND DITCHES.

20...Blinded Descent. When a trench has to be pushed forward in a position where the command of the dangerous point is so great that it cannot be sheltered from the plunging fire by traverses, it is covered on the top and on the sides by fascines and earth supported by a framework, and is termed a *blindage*.

But this method of obtaining cover is principally requisite in trenches which descend toward the dangerous point; like the passages which lead from the trenches on the glacis into the covered-way, and to the bottoms of shallow ditches. The manner of forming the blindage, Figs. 23, 24, is to set up a row of blindage frames along each side of the trench or passage; to connect the two rows at top by like frames laid across the line of the trench; to cover the top frames by fascines and earth; and to fill in between the side frames and the sides of the trench with fascines. The trench is made by the double sap. Its width at bottom is 7′ 6″ The width between the frames, 6′ The frames and fascines of the blindage are gradually placed as the trench advances, the latter preceding the former about 5′ The work is begun by placing an upright frame on each side; the two are next connected by a frame on top, one side of which is lodged on the top cross pieces of the upright frames, and the other supported by two auxiliary frames until the next two upright frames are placed; the fascines are then thrown over the top frame to the depth of about 2′, and these are covered with earth or raw hides, to prevent their being set on fire. Fascines are at the same time placed in on the sides.

The slope given to the bottom of a blinded descent should not be greater than $\frac{1}{4}$ When the descent is to a covered-way, Figs. 23, 24, the bottom of it should debouch into the covered-way at 43″ below its terreplein; this will serve to determine the point of departure, the slope being fixed, which should be 5′ below the surface of the glacis, so that when the blindage is put up at this point the top of it shall not be above the level of the parapet of the trench. A horizontal landing about 8′ in breadth, is made at the entrance of the blindage; and this is connected with the bottom of the trench by two ramps of $\frac{1}{6}$.

The point selected for a blinded descent into a covered-way is usually at the end of a traverse: as the traverse will cover the outlet of the blindage from a plunging fire in front.

21...A descent to a ditch is usually by blindage, when the depth of the ditch does not exceed 10′ or 12′ For greater depths the commencement of the descent is by a blindage, Fig. 25, which is continued to a point where the bottom of the descent is about 9′ below the surface of the ground; here the blindage is terminated, and the remainder of the descent is made by gallery, as the depth of the earth above the gallery will be sufficient to allow the excavation to be carried on without trouble. In a firm soil, grand gallery frames are used for the descent; in a loose soil, common gallery frames. The construction of the gallery is the same as for a mine gallery.

The point of departure of a ditch descent is usually taken at only about 2′ below the bottom of the trench; the usual landing being made at this point. In a dry ditch, the bottom of the descent debouches at the usual depth of the full sap below the bottom of the ditch. In a wet ditch, it should come out about 15″ above the water level.

PASSAGES OF DITCHES.

22...DRY DITCH. The passage of a dry ditch is nothing more than a full sap, which leads from the outlet of the descent in the ditch to the bottom of the breach. From this point the trench and parapet are directed up the breach to the scarp wall, which forms the side of the breach toward the dangerous point. The only precaution necessary in making this passage is, to sink the trench at the outset to its full depth of 43″ to gain secure cover.

23...WET DITCH. The passage of a wet ditch is a perilous and difficult operation under any circumstances, but particularly so when a strong current can be produced, by the besieged, in the ditch. The methods usually recommended are to form a dike, or bridge of fascines and hurdles, laid in successive layers, and firmly connected by pickets. To form a footing for the dike, a grand gallery is excavated, directly behind the counterscarp wall, to a distance of 12′ or 15′ on each side of the descent, and the earth from it is thrown into the ditch, through the outlet of the descent. The dike, or bridge of fascines is gradually pushed forward from this point, being secured in the best way practicable to the earth thrown into the ditch. The sappers who carry forward the head of the dike are covered from the fire of the dangerous point by a musket-proof mask of fascines and boards, attached to a raft on which they work. The dike should be from 12′ to 15′ wide at top. A gabionade parapet is placed on it toward the dangerous side. It is formed of two tiers of gabions, filled with earth. The bottom one consists of two rows of gabions, each crowned with two fascines—the two rows being in juxtaposition; the top tier is a single row crowned with three fascines. The top of the dike is covered by a layer of earth, and the parapet with raw hides, to prevent the effects of incendiary compositions that might be thrown on them. Raft-bridges, on barrels, protected by a gabionade parapet, have also been proposed, particularly where a strong current is to be contended with.

BATTERIES.

24...ENFILADING AND COUNTER-BATTERIES. These batteries are used for destroying the artillery and silencing the fire of the defences. Positions are chosen for the first from which the terrepleins of the faces, that bear upon the ground on which the parallels and approaches are laid out, can be enfiladed; the second are so placed that they can bring a direct or a slant fire against the embrasures of the points to be silenced. The shot from the former is thrown with small charges, under angles of elevation of from 6° to 9°, so as to ricochet along the terrepleins, taking the guns of the defences in flank; the latter fire with full charges directly against the point to be attained.

25...As the effects of both direct and enfilading fire vary greatly with the range, positions should be chosen for these batteries as near the defences as they can be thrown up without too great a sacrifice of life. Positions which will give ranges between 300 yards and 700 yards, are the best; nearer than 300 yards, the workmen would be exposed both to the fire of musketry and case shot; beyond 700 yards, the fire upon the defences becomes very uncertain. The best points for these batteries are, therefore, on the zone of ground occupied by the first and second parallels; the former being at about 600 yards, and the latter about 300 yards, from the most salient points of the defences.

26...The batteries may be placed either within the parallel, in advance of, or in rear of it. The positions usually selected are from 20 yards to 30 yards in front of the parallel; because, if placed within it, there might be mutual interference between the service of the batteries and that of the parallel; and unless placed some distance in the rear of it, the parapet of the parallel might obstruct the shot of the battery, and the troops in the trench be annoyed by the fire.

The most effective positions for these batteries are in front of the second parallel; and unless the fire of the defences is very destructive, it will be best to place them there. If placed in front of the first parallel, it will be necessary to shift the most of them to the front of the second parallel soon after the latter is thrown up. For the third parallel, and the approaches leading to it from the second parallel, run the risk of being attained by shot from batteries at so great a distanee in their rear as the first parallel.

27...The site of the platforms of the batteries may either be on the surface of the natural ground or sunk below it. In the latter case, the battery is termed a *sunken battery*. In the former case, the parapet of the battery is obtained from a ditch in advance of it; in the latter, it is got from a trench in its rear. In the sunken battery, the labor of construction is less, and the men engaged in making it are placed more speedily under cover than in the other kind. Sunken batteries can only be used, however, when the trenches, or other elevated points, in advance of the batteries, whieh lie in their field of fire, will not intercept the shot; and, as a general rule, these batteries should be placed only in positions where their field of fire is completely unobstrueted by the trenches.

28...The interior crest of an enfilading battery should be nearly perpendicular to the prolongation of the line to be enfiladed; and be so placed that the shot from all the guns shall sweep the terreplein throughout its entire length. The position of a battery that will satisfy this last condition can be readily found, as it must evidently lie within the angle formed by producing to the exterior the diagonals of the terreplein to be swept. The best position of the guns will be to place one so that its line of fire shall be nearly on the prolongation of the interior crest of the line enfiladed, and the remainder on that side of this one on which the exterior line of the terreplein prolonged may fall.

29...In a counter-battery, the interior crest should be nearly parallel to the line to be counter-battered. A position somewhat oblique to the line, so that the shot of the battery may enter the embrasures obliquely, is also a good one for tearing away the cheeks of the embrasures, and exposing the guns of the defences.

30...Whenever a position has to be taken up for an enfilading or a counter-battery, in which the direction that can be given to the interior crest is very oblique to that which it ought to receive, it will be necessary to make the embrasures of the battery with a corresponding obliquity to the direction of the parapet; and, to avoid the inconvenience of these last, it will be farther necessary to break the interior crest into an indented line, to allow the muzzles of the guns to be run the requisite distance into the embrasures; placing one side of the indent perpendicular to the axis of the embrasure, and the other parallel to it.

31...Enfilading and counter-batteries are usually armed with 18 and 24-pounders, and 8-inch howitzers. The fire of the guns is mainly directed to destroy the artillery of the defences; that of the howitzers to sweep the covered-ways and ditches, to destroy the palisadings, and injure the traverses by the explosions of the shells that may lodge in them. As a general rule, there need not be more than seven pieces, nor should there usually be less than three in any one battery; the number depending upon the bearing which the artillery of the part to be silenced may have upon the ground on which the works of the besiegers must be placed. The batteries should be as far asunder as practicable, so as not to invite a concentration of the fire of the defences upon any point by the accumulation of a large number of pieces on it, and thus multiply the chances of loss both to the troops and *materiel*.

32...In computing the extent of front of a battery, Pl. 11, Fig. 26, an allowance of 18′, estimated along the interior crest, is made for each piece, and 6′ for each splinter-proof gabionade traverse, one of which is placed between every two guns, when there are more than three in a battery The flanks of the guns are covered by an epaulment thrown up on one, or both extremities of the parapet.

The length of the epaulment, measured along its interior crest, may be from 20′ to 30′ The direction of the epaulment with respect to the parapet will depend on that of the fire of the defences; as a general rule, the interior crest of the epaulment should make an angle of about 100° with that of the parapet. When the platforms are on the natural surface, the earth for the parapet, epaulments and traverses is taken from a ditch in front of the parapet and epaulments, and parallel to their respective directions. A narrow ramp, at the end of each epaulment, leads from the natural level to the bottom of the ditch, and serves for the convenience of the men whilst throwing up the battery. A trench, of the ordinary dimensions of an approach, and defiled from dangerous points, leads from each extremity of the battery to the parallel in its rear.

33...If the embrasures are so oblique as to require an indented parapet, the side or face of the indent, through which the embrasure is pierced, should be 22′, and perpendicular to the axis of the embrasure. The other side, or *flank* of the indent should be 25′, and parallel to the axis; a distance of only 7′ being left between these two last lines, to give all the thickness practicable to the portion of the merlon that forms the outer angle of the indent; for a like reason the face of the indent, at the extremity of the battery, should extend 21′ beyond the axis of the embrasure. These *data* will serve to estimate the total length of the parapet. Its thickness, estimated from the inner angles of the indents, is 18′

34...The profile of a battery will depend, both for its dimensions and form, on the command of the point from which it can be attained, and on the position of the surface of the ground, on which it is laid out, with respect to the defences.

Where the site of the battery is horizontal, and the command of the defences over it is within the usual limits of 20′ to 30′, the following forms and dimensions, Fig. 27, will afford ample cover to the men and *materiel* of the battery, when the platforms are on a level with the natural surface: Height of interior crest, 7′ 6″. Thickness of parapet, 18′ Interior slope, $\frac{4}{1}$. Superior slope, $\frac{1}{12}$. Exterior slope, the natural slope of the earth. The same dimensions and forms may be given to the epaulments, except the distance between their interior and exterior crests, which may be reduced to 12′ when the direction of the epaulment is quite oblique to that of the fire of the defences. In the contrary case, this distance should be 18′ The depth of the ditch is taken at 5′; its width will be regulated by the quantity of earth to be furnished for completing all the parts of the battery

35...The axes of the embrasures, Fig. 26, are 18′ apart, except at the points where splinter-proof traverses are placed—the requisite distance at these points being 24′, allowing 6′ for the width of the base of the traverse. The sill of the embrasure is 3′ 6″ above the platform for guns mounted on the ordinary siege carriage; its sole is parallel to the superior slope. The mouth of the embrasure is of a trapezoidal form, being 2′ wide at bottom and 3′ at top. The splay of the sole is obtained by giving the sides an inclination of $\frac{1}{10}$ with the axis. The top line of the check is obtained by setting off along the direction of the exterior crest, from the point where the side of the sole cuts it in projection, one-half the vertical distance between these two last lines, and joining the point thus found with the exterior point of the mouth at top.

Embrasures of howitzers may receive a counter-slope, giving the sole nearly the same inclination, from the sill upward, as the least angle of elevation under which it may be required to aim the piece.

36...The parapet of the battery and the embrasures are revetted either with gabions, fascines, or sand-bags; or with a combination of these

The epaulments need not be revetted, their interior slopes being made as steep as the earth will stand at. The gabion revetement is the firmest and most durable. When used for the parapet, two tiers will be requisite.

The requisite slope is given to the gabions of the first

tier by placing a row of fascines under them, along the foot of the interior slope. Another row of fascines is laid on top of the tier, along the interior slope, on which the gabions of the second tier rest. The requisite height is given to the parapet either by placing sods on the top tier or by earth alone. When sand-bags are used they are laid in single courses along the interior slope, and as headers and stretchers, the courses breaking joint. To give the bags greater durability, they should be impregnated with tar before being filled.

It has been found that raw hides will preserve the revetements of the cheeks from the effects of the concussion produced by the firing. For this purpose, the hide is folded with the hair inward. It is confined to the top of the cheek by pickets driven through it into the merlon; and at the mouth, and the other end of the cheek, by pickets driven into the revetement. The lower end is allowed to hang loose.

37...The splinter-proof traverses, Fig. 28, are formed of two tiers of gabions. The lower tier consists of two parallel rows of gabions, and is 5′ wide at the base; the rows of gabions are slightly inclined toward each other at top. The upper tier also consists of two rows, which rest on two rows of fascines, laid on the first tier, the gabions leaning against each other at top. The gabions and the space between them are well filled in with earth, which is heaped above the top tier. The traverse may be from 15′ to 18′ long. A passage-way of 2′ is left between the parapet of the battery and the end of the traverse.

38...The platforms are 10′ 6″ wide, 15′ long in the clear, and receive an upward slope of 7″ to 8″ from the hurter to the tail. They are composed of 5 sleepers, each 15′ long and 5″ on the side; of 12 planks, each 10′ 6″ long and 2″ thick; of 2 *ribands*, or *side-rails*, of the dimensions of the sleepers; and of a hurter. The sleepers are firmly imbedded in the ground, and secured by stout pickets at their ends. The planks are clamped between the side-rails and outside sleepers, these pieces being connected firmly either by screw-bolts and nuts or by rack-lashings.

39...In sunken batteries, the same length of interior crest is allowed for each gun as in the preceding case: but when the battery requires splinter-proof traverses, an allowance of 26′ is made for the distance between the axes of the guns separated by a traverse. The position and length of the epaulments are also determined as in the preceding case.

40...The trench of the battery, Fig. 29, when first excavated is 16′ wide at bottom, 3′ deep in front, and 2′ 6″ deep in rear. The front is cut down vertically in firm soil, and the reverse receives a slope of $\frac{1}{2}$. The interior crest of the parapet is 4′ 6″ above the natural surface; the parapet. 18′ thick; the interior slope, $\frac{4}{1}$; the exterior slope, $\frac{1}{1}$. A berm of 18″ is left between the parapet and the trench when first excavated.

41...As the dimensions above given to the trench will furnish earth only for the parapet, that required for the epaulment is taken from a ditch 5′ deep exterior to it; and a small portion of ditch is made exterior to the parapet, and opposite the position of each splinter-proof traverse, to provide the earth requisite for the traverse, and which is taken from the trench. The epaulment, if exposed only to an oblique fire, need not be thicker than 12′

42...The embrasures receive the same form, dimensions, etc., as in the preceding case.

43...The front of the trench is revetted with fascines. To put up this revetement, the trench is widened by cutting away the front, nearly to the width of the berm, and almost vertically. This will admit the muzzles of the guns to be run well into the embrasures.

To avoid the labor and expense of revetements, it has been proposed neither to revet the portion of the trench bordering the epaulment, nor the interior slope of the epaulment; but to leave a berm at this part, 3′ wide, when the trench is in course of construction, and, afterward, to give both to this portion of the trench and the interior of the epaulment as great a slope as the earth will stand well under.

44...When splinter-proof traverses are requisite, a portion of the ground, 6′ wide, on which the traverse is to stand, is left. The traverse is made by first placing two parallel rows of fascines at 5′ apart, on which a tier of gabions, also of two rows, rests; the gabions being so inclined as to touch at top. Earth is filled in the gabions and the void space between them, and heaped up above them to the same level as the interior crest. The sides of the trench bordering the traverse are cut to a suitable slope, and revetted with fascines. A passage of 2′ is left between the gabionade of the traverse and the interior slope of the parapet.

45...To provide against rainy weather, two or more holes should be dug at such points of the trench of the battery as may be found most convenient to receive the water that collects in the trench; and precautions should be taken to prevent water from being received into the trench, either through the trenches leading to it or from the natural surface.

46...The powder magazines should be at least 30′ in rear of the parapet of the battery. The ceiling of the magazine should not be more than a few inches above the natural level. The interior height need not be more than 5′ The width may be 6′, and the length 12′, in the clear. The sides of the magazine may be formed of frames and sheeting boards; or of a row of gabions crowned with two courses of fascines. The magazine is covered at top by splinter-proof timbers, 6″×9″, laid in juxtaposition, and covered with at least 3′ of earth, both on top and on the sides toward the parapet. A passage leads into the magazine, on the side from the parapet which is reached by one or two inclined trenches.

47...Mortar Batteries. There are two kinds of mortar batteries used in the attack: those for mortars throwing shells, and those for mortars throwing baskets of stones, or other like projectiles. Besides these, there is the Coehorn mortar, which, from its small size, may be placed in any unoccupied corner of the trenches. The first kind of batteries may be in front of the first and second parallels, or on any other points farther back. The positions chosen for them should be such as to bring as great a portion of the defences under the direction of their fire as practicable, to increase the chances of destructibility of each shell thrown. The second kind are placed in front of the third parallel, mainly with a view to annoy the covered-ways and parts adjacent.

48...The platforms of these batteries may be laid on the natural surface, in which case, the same forms and dimensions will be given to the parapet and epaulments of the battery as in gun batteries; but as the mortars must be set back from the parapet, to enable the shell to clear the interior crest by about 3′, a revetement will not be necessary, and the parapet may receive as great an interior slope as the earth can be made to stand under firmly.

49...The front of a mortar battery is estimated by allowing 15′ for each mortar, and 6′ for each splinter-proof traverse.

These batteries are, however, usually sunk below the natural surface, since several feet difference of level in the position of a mortar will have but little effect on the range or the trajectory. The profile suitable for such positions, under ordinary circumstances, is the following: Width of trench at bottom, 13′ 6″ Depth in front, 3′ 6″ Depth in rear, 4′ Reserve slope, ½. Front slope, 2′ base. Height of parapet, 4′ Thickness of parapet, 18′ Berm, 1′

50...The earth for the epaulment is taken from an exterior ditch; and, when splinter-proof traverses are required, portions of ditches are made opposite to their position, to furnish the requisite earth.

51...The platforms of mortars are 7′ 6″ long by 6′ 6″ wide. They are composed of two ground-sills, 7′ 6″ long and 6″ square; 5 sleepers, 7′ 6″ long and 6″ square; 2 side-rails, 7′ 6″ long and 4″ square; 8 planks, each 6′ 6″ long and 4″ thick. The ground-sills are laid horizontally, and firmly imbedded in the ground at 4′ 6″ apart, and transversely to the sleepers. Upon these the sleepers rest; each being confined by two stout pickets near each end. The planks are confined to the sleepers in the same manner as in gun platforms.

52...BREACH BATTERIES. Exposed revetements may be breached by heavy guns, at ranges from 400 to 600 yards, and batteries thrown up in such cases are in all respects like those for enfilading or counter-battering.

53...Where the revetements are covered from distant fire by the crest of the covered-way, the breach batteries must be either placed on the glacis or on the terrepleins of the defences, at points where no obstruction will intervene to prevent the fire of the guns from being directed at a point of the wall to be opened low enough to form a breach practicable to the ascent of an assaulting column.

In either of the latter cases the batteries must be sunk; the level chosen for the platforms being such as to subserve the object in view. The embrasures in these cases are usually cut out of the parapet, as an ordinary trench has generally to be first established as a preparatory step to commencing the battery. The forms and dimensions adopted for other sunken batteries will apply to these cases, with such modifications as may be demanded by the site of the battery, and the position of the point to be attained by the fire.

When a breach battery is established either on the glacis or upon the terreplein of a work, its guns will generally be exposed, both on their flank and rear, to the fire of dangerous commanding points, from which it will be necessary to cover them by traverses. The number of traverses and their position will depend upon the command and position of the dangerous points. To cover from the flank fire, if the command of the dangerous point is considerable, like that of a cavalier retrenchment, it may be necessary to place a traverse between every two guns, or even between each. The traverses used in such cases receive a thickness of 14′, or seven gabions, like those for covering an ordinary trench from an enfilading fire; their length will depend upon the relative positions of the dangerous point, and the exterior point of the battery to be covered; their height is usually not greater than the traverses for a trench.

When the reverse of the battery is exposed, it will generally arise from the salient position of some comparatively distant point, from which a slant fire may be brought to bear on this part of the battery; in which case it will generally be easy to cover the part exposed by running out, from the reverse of the battery, an end of trench, to form a wing traverse that shall intersect the lines of fire of the point upon every part exposed.

54...The guns of breach batteries should be so placed that the direction of their fire may be as nearly perpendicular as practicable to the line of wall to be breached; and where these lines are oblique to each other, the obliquity should not exceed 45°, otherwise the effect of the shot will be greatly diminished, and the operation retarded.

Besides the breach batteries, it will be necessary to place counter-batteries on the glacis. Their object will be to counter-batter and silence the artillery of those portions of the defences which can be brought to bear on the breach-batteries, or on the passages of the ditches. These batteries will usually be placed on the prolongation of the ditches of the defences. Their arrangement will be, in all respects, the same as that of the breach batteries.

SIEGE OPERATIONS.

55...The operations of a siege are usually divided into three epochs. In the first are comprised the investment, and other operations, preliminary to breaking ground against the work, or opening the trenches. The second comprises the labors from the opening of the trenches to the completion of the third parallel. The third, the subsequent operations to the reduction of the work.

First Period.

56...Investment. This is the first active operation of the besieging force; its object being to cut off all communication between the garrison and the exterior, to prevent succors of every kind from being thrown into the work, to sweep off everything in its vicinity that might in any way be serviceable to the garrison, and, finally, to cover a close reconnoissance of the defences by engineer and other officers.

For the successful attainment of these ends, the investing force, which is mainly, if not solely, composed of cavalry, should move upon the work with celerity and secrecy, and, after surrounding and securing all avenues to it, should send out detachments to scour the environs up to the very gates of the work, if practicable, and bring off with them, or destroy, all persons, cattle, provisions, etc., met with. A chain of posts and sentinels is in the meantime established in the best positions to prevent all access to the work, or egress from it; care being taken to select for the posts points which are not exposed to the artillery of the work, or are beyond its range. The posts occupied by the troops during the daytime, and termed the *daily cordon*, are shifted at dark, and points nearer the work are taken up, to form the *nightly cordon*, and hem it in more closely. The posts and sentinels for this purpose should be pushed as far forward as they can find shelters from the musketry of the defences; and under their protection the reconnoitering officers should spare no efforts to gain an exact idea of all the ground exterior to the work, and of the character of the defences.

57...Posting Besieging Force. The main body of the besieging army, with the engineer and artillery siege-trains, follows closely upon the investing corps, to prevent the line taken up by the latter, which, from its extent, is necessarily weak, from being forced either by the garrison or by strong detachments from without. The positions for the camps of the various corps are designated by the commanding general, after a careful reconnoissance. These are placed beyond the range of the heavy artillery of the work, with their color fronts facing from the work, and, as far as practicable, on points favorable to the health and comfort of the troops, and the defence. Whenever natural obstacles occur between the camps, they must be crossed by good lines of communication, so that no impediment may be offered to the speedy concentration of the troops upon any point threatened from without.

Besides the positions taken up for the camps, the besieging force will also occupy all points exterior to the camps, within cannon range, by which they are commanded, securing them by field-works of sufficient strength to subserve the end in view.

58...INTRENCHMENTS OF CAMPS. The front and the rear of camps are also secured by lines of field-works. The exterior works, termed the *Line of Circumvallation*, should form an unbroken line of intrenchments, composed of the most simple elementary parts, as tenailles, redans, etc., with a slight profile; its chief object being to prevent succors of small detachments from slipping into the place. The interior line, termed the *Line of Countervallation*, is composed of detached works, which, if the garrison is strong, should be in defensive relations. The main points which should be occupied by these works, are the principal avenues to the defences, and the positions selected for the parks of the siege train, to secure these points from the attempts of the garrison, and to render the entrance of large convoys into the defences impracticable.

These lines are placed about 200 yards in front and rear of the camps.

59...In the later sieges in Europe, lines of circumvallation, particularly, were seldom resorted to; the besiegers contenting themselves with occupying only the main points of their position by field-works, and giving the intervening space such protection as could be afforded by strong patrols and posts. This departure from former practice arose, in most cases, from the want of strength of the besieging force, and was frequently attended by the very events against which lines are chiefly effectual in guarding. As a field of battle against a succoring force of sufficient strength to cope with the besieging army, a position taken behind a line of circumvallation is, but in rare exceptions, eligible—a maxim that applies to all extended and weak lines; and in almost every case, where a serious effort has been made against such positions, it has proved successful, and has entailed heavy loss on the besiegers. But, it must be repeated, as this is not the object of these lines, they are not open to this objection; and, as they have been found serviceable for the sole purpose to which they should be applied, they ought to be thrown up in all cases where the means of the besiegers will admit of it.

60...Preparations for Opening the Trenches. Whilst the besieging force is occupied in arranging and securing their camps, a portion of it is employed in preparing the trench materials, establishing the parks, and getting everything in order preparatory to breaking ground against the defences. At the same time, close reconnoisances and careful instrumental surveys are made by the staff corps, to obtain *data* for a map of the defences and their environs, with a view of drawing up a plan of attack. With this object, the bearing and prolongations of the faces and capitals of all the defences should be carefully laid down; the character of the defences on every assailable point noted; that of the parts bearing on these points, and the nature of the ground over which they must be approached.

61...The parks, magazines of powder, and other *depôts*, are placed on the most secure points, beyond the range of the heavy artillery of the defences, and, if practicable, should be hidden from their view. The points selected, if not in the immediate neighborhood of the ground on which it is decided to open the trenches, should have avenues of easy access to it, for the transportation of whatever may be requisite in carrying forward the works of attack.

62...Point of Attack. After obtaining all the information that can be had from the reconnoisances, surveys and other sources, the next object is to decide upon the portion of the defences which it will be necessary to gain possession of to force the garrison to a surrender; this portion, usually embracing one or more fronts of the enceinté, with their outworks, and any advanced works that may be connected with them, and must be reduced before they can be assailed, is termed the *Point of Attack*. It is in the choice of this point—a decision which mainly rests with the commanding officer of the engineers—that the judgment and skill of this officer are shown. In making this selection, he must carefully weigh, not only the relative strength of the various points of the defences which are accessible, but the character of the site upon which the trenches and other works of the attack must be laid out, and the facilities of an easy communication between the parks, *depôts*, etc., and the point selected.

63...In considering the strength of the defences, those parts are regarded as unassailable by the ordinary measures of an attack, which border upon precipices, marshes, a water-course that cannot be forded, or are protected by works on inaccesible points, the fire from which sweeps in flank and reverse the ground over which the trenches must be run. Those parts, again, are considered as offering peculiar difficulties which present a series of works, in good defensive relations, which can only be carried in succession; or which are mined; or which have their ditches arranged for a play of water; or which have dry ditches of unusual depth; or, finally, where the works to be carried are displayed on a right line, embracing the same extent of front that the besiegers can take up with their trenches. The points which are looked upon as most advantageous to the attack are those in which the general combination of the works form a salient point with respect to the rest of the defences; as a point so situated can receive but little support from the collateral portions; can be enveloped by a line of trench of much greater extent than itself, along which positions can be obtained for enfilading and other batteries, the fire of which will be convergent upon that of the defences.

64...As regards the site on which the trenches and other works must be laid out, the difficulties presented to their construction by bare rock, marsh, or hard, stony ground, may be readily appreciated, as cover can only be had on the two first by bringing the earth from a distance to form the parapets, dikes, etc., and on the last from the labor requisite in digging the trenches, and the additional annoyance and injury to the troops from the fragments of stone scattered in all directions by the shot of the defences. But, besides these features, there are others less obvious which should be taken advantage of or be avoided, as favorable or otherwise to the construction of the works of the attack. A surface, for example, which slopes or falls away toward the defences, if commanded by them, is unfavorable both to the construction of trenches and batteries; as, to gain sufficient cover, both the parapet and trench will have to receive dimensions greater than under ordinary circumstances; and the defilement of approaches will also be less easily effected. A surface which rises toward the defences is very favorable, both for gaining cover speedily and for defiling with advantage the approaches; but is less so as a site for batteries if the slope is rapid. An undulating surface may offer, in some points, natural covers, and be at other points favorable as sites for batteries: this will depend upon the position of the undulation of the surface with respect to the fire of the defences. A ridge, for example, leading out from the defences, whilst it would present a cover to the works on one side of it from the fire of the defences on the other, would expose the trenches on the other side of it to a plunging fire from the same points.

A narrow valley, similarly placed, would be very unfavorable, as both of its sides would be exposed to a plunging fire.

Second and Third Periods.

65...Plan and Journal of the Attack. The plan of the attack is necessarily based upon the character of the defences of the point of attack, and of the site upon which the approaches and other works of the besiegers must be laid out; and by this term is understood both the means to be used at the successive stages of the operations, and the disposition given to the trenches and other works. The journal of the attack is a record of the daily operations of the besiegers; and is also a method in use among engineers to estimate the duration of a siege, from the opening of the trenches to the reduction of the work, on the supposition that the works of the attack can be carried on regularly, without interruption from unforeseen contingencies: a method of valuation which, as it is based on the time required to construct a given amount of work, as determined both from data furnished by actual sieges and the results of experiment in schools of practice, may be relied on as an approximation as close as the case admits; and, when applied in a spirit of fairness, may serve as a test of the comparative strength of different combinations or systems of permanent works.

66...The general disposition of the works of the besiegers is laid down on the map, made of the defences and environs, with as great accuracy as can be insured by surveys carefully made; and, from the results obtained in this way, the officers charged with this duty are enabled to set out on the ground the necessary points by which those charged with directing the construction of the works are guided.

67...As an illustration of the plan and journal of attack, we shall suppose the point of attack selected, Pl. 12, Fig. 1, to be an acute bastion with the two adjacent demilunes; and that the only collateral works, the fire of which bears on the ground over which the trenches must be run, are two collateral, obtuse bastions, the faces of which cannot be enfiladed, owing to their prolongations falling within the salients of the adjacent demilunes, and the two collateral demilunes; making in all one bastion and two demilunes, with their dependent outworks, which must be entered by breach or otherwise: and two bastions and two demilunes, with their dependent works, the fire of which must be kept under.

68....The approaches will be pushed forward in the direction of the capitals of the three first works; and the first and second parallels will embrace a sufficient front to include the prolongations of the faces of all the works bearing on the trenches, against which enfilading batteries will be requisite.

69...The first parallel will be laid out at 600 yards from the most advanced salients of the covered-ways, and parallel nearly to the line which connects these points. The approaches, which lead from it to the *depôts* of the trenches, will be run in zig-zags across the capitals, each not over 100 yards in length, and defiled from the most dangerous points within cannon range.

70...First Night. The position of the portion of the trenches upon which the besiegers are to break ground having been laid out, and the materials for the work having been placed in order for distribution, so as to avoid all unnecessary delay and confusion, the workmen are assembled at the depôts of the trenches before night-fall to receive their implements. The men selected for this duty are troops of the line, who usually take their arms with them. The men are divided into working parties, each of which is under the command of an officer of the line, and they are marched in single file by a flank and posted, after night-fall, where they are to work under the direction of the engineers.

The portion of the trenches opened this night are, usually, only the approaches that lead from the *depôts* of the trenches to the first parallel, and that portion of this parallel which embraces the capitals of the point of attack. To guard the workmen from sorties, as many battalions of the line as may be requisite, termed the *guards of the trenches*, are thrown forward about 30 paces in advance of and on the flanks of the men who open the first parallel. The flank companies of these battalions, divided into sections, cover the front of the battalions, and are posted about 30 paces from them; and each section posts two sentinels at about the same distance to its front. The sentinels keep a look out, kneeling on one knee; the remainder of the troops lie flat on the ground, to avoid the fire of the defences.

When the working parties are all posted, the men of each lying flat until all are ready to commence the work, the order is given to rise, ground their arms a few paces to the rear, and break ground.

The guards of the trenches keep their position until near dawn, when they are withdrawn and take post in the parallel, which, by this time, will be nearly excavated to its full width.

On the succeeding day all that remains to be done to the trenches opened is completed, and everything is got in readiness for the work of the coming night.

71...SECOND NIGHT. The parallel will be extended this night to embrace the prolongations of all the faces to be enfiladed, and some 100 or 150 yards beyond the extreme points so determined. A large square redoubt will be constructed at each extremity of the parallel, which will be armed with field pieces; and an epaulment for cavalry will be thrown up in the rear of each redoubt; the object of these works being to contain troops to act against sorties made on the flanks of the parallel.

The zig-zag approaches are pushed about 150 yards in advance of the parallel. The positions of these approaches are determined on the plan by setting off points on the first parallel at 30 yards on each side of the capital, and drawing lines from each of these points to corresponding points about 15 yards on the side of the capital, at the salient of the covered-way, then limiting the length of each zig-zag of these lines, the direction of each depending on its defilement. To cover more completely the reverse of each zig-zag, and secure it from positions that might be taken up, exterior to the defences, to enfilade it, the zig-zag in advance should be prolonged back beyond the limiting lines a distance of 10 or 12 yards to the rear of the one immediately behind.

72...REMARK. It may be observed here that by running approaches upon three capitals, we not only multiply the lines of communication between the parallels, but divide the attention of the besieged. The lines of the capitals are also the most suitable for these trenches on several accounts: first, they are the shortest lines between the parallels and the salients of the defences; second, the approaches along them, being within the angle formed by the prolongations of the faces, they are less exposed to the fire of the defences, and are less in the way of the fire of the besiegers than in any other position; third, in this position the approaches are more easily defiled from the collateral fire than in any other.

By confining the zig-zags within the lines drawn from the parallel, and converging toward the salients, the front of each approach is gradually contracted as it nears the salient, and offers less obstruction to the fire of the parallel.

73...The trenches and other works left incomplete at the end of the second night are finished on the following day; and this rule is followed throughout, as the trenches commenced by night are generally in a suitable state by dawn to give cover to the workmen and troops, and can be occupied, and what remains to be done to them be completed in safety by day.

74...THIRD NIGHT. The approaches are pushed forward 275 yards from the first parallel, and here the second parallel is commenced; a small portion of it only on each side of the approaches being opened, in which to lodge a few troops for the protection of the workmen.

This parallel is of less extent than the first, embracing only the prolongations of the faces of the point of attack. It is usually connected with the first parallel by a defiled line of trench at each of its extremities. Its distance from the first is determined from the consideration that the workmen employed on it must be protected by the guards of the trenches, who are still stationed in the first, and who, to afford this protection, should be posted where they can come to the aid of the workmen before the garrison can reach them in a sortie.

The rule here observed is also a general one. The trenches under construction never in any case being advanced so far that the guards in their rear cannot come up to their support before they can be reached by a sortie from the defences.

75...FOURTH NIGHT. The second parallel is entirely laid out on this night, and is completed on the following day The guard of the trenches takes post in the parallel as fast as a part of it is finished; a reserve equal to about one-third of the whole being left in the first parallel.

As the second parallel is at 325 yards from the salient of the place, the workmen are much exposed to the fire of grape shot; it will, therefore, be necessary to use the flying sap in its construction.

76...FIFTH AND SIXTH NIGHTS. Thus far the works of the attack have been pushed forward without the aid of artillery, but beyond the second parallel the fire of the defences becomes so destructive that further progress cannot be made, without great sacrifice of life, until it is silenced. To effect this, enfilading, mortar and counter-batteries are placed about 30 yards in front of the parallel. The number of guns in each battery will depend on the importance of the face to be silenced, and, according to this rule, the following distribution will be made:

A battery of 8 pieces will be erected against each face of the bastion of attack. A battery of 5 pieces against the right face of the demilune of attack and its covered-way, and one of 7 pieces against the left face, since the fire from the latter bears more directly on the approaches than that of the right face. As the two collateral bastions are supposed to be so obtuse that their faces cannot be enfiladed, it will be necessary to silence their fire by counter-batteries. As the left face alone of the bastion, on the right of the one of attack, has a direct action on the approaches, a counter-battery of 5 pieces is erected against it, and so placed as to obtain a slant fire into its embrasures. With regard to the collateral demilune on the same side, as its right face has but a slight bearing on the approaches, a battery of 3 pieces will prevent this face from being occupied by the besieged; but as the bearing of its left face is more direct, it will be necessary to establish a battery of 5 pieces against it; this last battery is placed in front of the first parallel. Two or three howitzers form a part of each battery, to sweep the covered-ways and ditches.

The mortar batteries are placed in positions where they will be most effective, which is usually about midway between the capitals of the works to be reached from them. About 4 mortars are placed in each battery, an allowance of 8 mortars being made for each front embraced by the trenches.

The mortar and gun batteries, the fire of which is not obstructed by the trenches in front of them, are sunk. The platforms of the others are on the natural surface of the ground.

Besides these batteries, which will be completed on the fifth and sixth nights, two or three zig-zags are pushed forward in advance of the parallel on the same nights, if the fire of the besieged is not too destructive.

77...SEVENTH NIGHT. As the enfilading batteries will be completed and armed on the sixth night, on the following morning they will all open their fire at the same moment, and by night the fire of the place will be nearly, if not entirely, silenced. The approaches are then pushed forward, and demi-parallels are established at from 100 to 150 yards in front of the second parallel. The demi-parallels may be from 100 to 200 yards in length, and have a return of 25 yards at their extremities to cover them on the flank. The length of the demi-parallel should be so regulated as not to obstruct the fire of the ricochet batteries. In some cases howitzers are placed in batteries established at the extremities of the demi-parallels, to enfilade the covered-ways; but as the demi-parallels are within good musket range of the covered-ways, it will generally be better to arm them with infantry, the top of their parapet being arranged with loop-holes made with sand-bags, to cover the marksmen whilst in the act of firing.

78...EIGHTH NIGHT. On this night the approaches are pushed forward by the flying and full sap, as opportunity may offer, and a portion of the third parallel is commenced when the approaches are within 60 yards of the most advanced salients.

79...NINTH NIGHT. The third parallel is completed. It should present a less development than the second, so as to be flanked by it, and will, therefore, usually embrace only the salients of the point of attack. Owing to this, and its having to receive the main body of the guard—the second parallel now containing only the reserve, whilst the first is used only as a depôt for the materials and to receive the wounded—the third parallel is made two or three feet wider than the other two.

80...REMARK. With the completion of this parallel begins the third and last period of the attack. At this point, the works of the besiegers are necessarily contracted to a very narrow front, and present but little more development than that of the point of attack. They are now upon the immediate ground of the defences, and within range of every means of annoyance. In pushing forward from this position the besiegers are, to a great degree, deprived of the assistance that they hitherto had from their enfilading and other batteries, as the position of their trenches on the glacis must obstruct this fire: they can no longer use the zig-zag approach, but have to gain ground by the double sap, and soon find themselves, as their works advance toward the re-enterings, the enveloped instead of the enveloping party, and liable at every moment to have their sappers cut off, and their labors stopped by sorties in small parties. It is at this stage, then, that more than ordinary precautions are requisite, not only to prevent retardation of the works, but to avoid unnecessary sacrifice of life; by preparing all possible means for insuring the success of each step, and by not advancing on one until the last taken is perfectly secure.

81...TENTH NIGHT. As the third parallel, Pl. 12, Fig. 1, from its position on the glacis, will mask the fire of the ricochet batteries against the covered-way, it will be necessary to establish new batteries in front of it, to dislodge the besieged from this outwork. For this purpose, stone-mortar batteries are found very effective. These batteries are placed at about 20 yards in front of the parallel, and are sunk. A battery of 4 or 6 mortars is placed on each side of the salients, nearly in the prolonged direction of the covered-ways. These batteries will be ready to commence their fire on the covered-ways on the morning after they are begun.

82...STORMING AND CROWNING THE COVERED-WAY. After the completion of the third parallel, preparations are made for crowning the covered-way, either by storm or by gradual approaches. In the former case, portions of the parallel are arranged with steps to enable infantry to sally from it on the covered-ways. The sappers, with all the necessary materials for crowning the covered-way, are collected in the parallel. At a preconcerted signal, a fire will be opened from the stone-mortar batteries, and all others that are still effective, against the covered-way and the other outworks. When it is perceived that the fire has produced its effect in clearing the outworks, at a preconcerted signal it will also cease; the troops will sally forth and carry the covered-way with the bayonet, and, after gaining possession of it, they will shelter themselves as they best can behind the traverse from the fire of the besieged. Whilst they, in this way, maintain possession of the covered-way, the sappers, who follow immediately in their rear, will open a trench about 4 or 5 yards from the crest of the glacis, around the salient place of arms, as far as its two traverses; when this trench will afford a shelter to the troops, they retire from the covered-way into it. This trench is afterward connected by suitable communications with the third parallel.

From the circumstances under which this operation is carried on, the probabilities are against its success and in favor of a great sacrifice of life in the attempt, if the besieged offer a vigorous resistance and make a skilful use of the means still at their disposal. With such chances, therefore, of failure, and the certainty of great losses even if successful, this mode of attack should only be resorted to in some contingency where the success of the siege depends on the time saved by it.

83...ELEVENTH NIGHT. When the covered-way is to be crowned by regular approaches, a constant fire is kept up from the stone-mortar batteries so as to render it untenable for more than a very few men. A trench, termed the *circular place of arms*, is now formed, by starting from two points of the parallel at 30 yards on each side of the capital, and pushing two branches of full sap to unite at about 15 yards from the parallel, on the capital. From this point a double sap is pushed along the capital, to within 30 yards of the salients of the demilune covered-ways. As the bastion covered-way is very retired, nothing more is done than to form the circular place of arms before it.

84...TWELFTH NIGHT. The trench cavaliers before the demilune salients are commenced, and the sap is pushed forward a few yards on the bastion covered-way

85...THIRTEENTH NIGHT. The trench cavaliers, which require from 36 to 48 hours for their completion, will be finished on this night, and an approach pushed from the stone-mortar batteries toward the re-entering place of arms.

86...FOURTEENTH NIGHT. The besieged being now driven from the covered-ways by the fire of the trench cavaliers, a double sap is pushed toward the salient of the demilune covered-way from the two extremities of the circular trench connecting the trench cavaliers. These two saps unite at 4 or 5 yards from the crest of the glacis.

The approaches toward the re-entering place of arms are advanced farther on.

87...FIFTEENTH NIGHT. The demilune covered-way is crowned as far as the second traverse. The approaches on the re-entering place of arms and the salient of the bastion covered-way are advanced.

88...A fourth parallel is begun on this night, commencing opposite the first traverses of the demilune covered-ways, and uniting the approaches pushed toward the re-entering places of arms.

89...SIXTEENTH NIGHT. The breach and counter-batteries around the salient place of arms of the demilune are completed and armed.

From 4 to 5 guns will be placed on each branch of the glacis of the salient place of arms, in the prolongations of the demilune ditch, to counter-batter the portions of the bastion faces which bear upon this ditch and the covered-way, and prevent this fire from retarding the lodgments about to be made on the terreplein of the salient place of arms and the passage of the ditch. About 4 guns are placed in a battery between the first and second traverses, to open a breach in the left face of the demilune. This breach should be from 20 to 30 yards in width, and not extend farther toward the salient than the position of the pancoupé, so as to expose as great an extent of the interior of the demilune as practicable.

The guns in these batteries will require cover in flank from the faces of the bastions and their cavaliers; and in rear from the most advanced salients of the works still occupied by the besieged.

The descent into the demilune covered-way, commenced on the fifteenth night, behind the first traverse, is finished; and the fourth parallel is completed. The width of the fourth parallel is the same as an ordinary approach, owing to the difficulty of defiling it.

These batteries will be completed and armed in 24 hours after the crowning is commenced. The breach will be practicable in 12 or 15 hours after the fire is opened.

90...SEVENTEENTH NIGHT. The approaches from the fourth parallel are pushed forward on the salients of the bastion covered-way and the re-entering place of arms. The crowning of the demilune covered-way is gradually advanced and a lodgment is made on the terreplein of the demilune salient place of arms, from which the demilune ditch can be swept by musketry

The descent into the demilune ditch is commenced on this night, behind the traverse of the salient place of arms.

91...In advancing the sap on the different salients of the covered-way, from the fourth parallel, care should be taken not to push forward one faster than the others, so as not to offer a temptation to the besieged to sally out on the head of the most advanced, to cut off the sappers. Moreover, the different brigades of sappers should be protected by a few picked men, stationed in short trenches that flank the direction of the double sap as it is pushed forward on the salients.

92...If, owing to the great width of the covered-way, or to the small breadth of the demilune ditch, or to the steepness of the glacis, by which the batteries placed along its crest would be very much exposed to a reverse fire from the collateral works, it should become necessary to place the breach and counter-batteries on the terreplein of the covered-way, they cannot be completed and armed before the seventeenth or eighteenth night. Although the batteries in this position would be well covered from reverse fire by the crest of the glacis, and from a flank fire by the traverses of the covered-way, still, they would require much more labor to establish them, and would be more exposed to the annoyance of grenades thrown from the demilune.

After the descent into the demilune ditch is commenced, it is steadily carried forward until it arrives at the point opposite the breach, where the opening into the ditch is to be made through the counterscarp wall. This opening should be pierced at night, and the precaution should be taken to run a small gallery along the back of the wall, on each side of the opening, so as to place a few men to fire through loop-holes made in the wall, for the purpose of defending the opening, and the sap pushed across the ditch to the breach.

93...Eighteenth, Nineteenth and Twentieth Nights. The approaches from the fourth parallel and the crowning of the covered-way are pushed forward and completed on these nights.

It will seldom be practicable to establish a trench cavalier against the bastion salient place of arms, owing to the reverse fire from the collateral demilunes. In such a case, if the besieged still occupy this work in force, so as to retard the progress of the sap, an attempt must be made to dislodge them by an open attack of a small party of picked troops, or else stone-mortar batteries may be placed in the position that would be occupied by the trench cavaliers, by means of which the besieged may be driven from this part of the covered-way.

So soon as the bastion covered-way is crowned, two descents are commenced into the main ditch, from the trench at the salient of the covered-way.

In very acute bastions, the breach and counter-batteries along the bastion covered-way might be completed on the twenty-first night. But, generally, before this can be done the demilune must be carried, as its fire would take these batteries so in reverse as to render their construction impracticable.

94...Twenty-fifth Night. The descent into the demilune ditch and passage of the ditch may be effected by this night at farthest.

Every precaution should be taken to prevent the besieged from interrupting this passage. The passage itself should be 4 or 5 yards wide at bottom, to afford a convenient place of arms for the troops, and it should be arranged with a banquette to sweep the ditch by a close musketry fire.

Besides making loop-holes in the counterscarp wall to flank the passage, it will also be well to push forward one or two zig-zags in the ditch itself, and place a small party of picked men in them to repel the sorties of the besieged.

95...The breach is gained possession of either by storm or by gradual approaches. The former will be resorted to when the besieged manifest a determination to keep possession of the demilune, in force, to the last extremity A few companies of picked men will be chosen for this service. All the materials will be collected at hand for crowning the breach, and, when everything is in a state of readiness, a warm fire will be opened on the breach and on all the works that in any way bear upon it. At a preconcerted signal the fire will cease, and the assaulting column, rushing through the breach, will drive the besieged from the demilune, and then, sheltering themselves as they best can from the fire of the other works, they will maintain possession of the breach until the sappers, who follow in their rear, can effect a lodgment on its top.

96...To make the lodgment by gradual approaches, the sappers will push forward a sap from the foot of the breach, over the ruins, giving it such a direction as to gain a shelter under the end of the wall that remains on the side of the breach which is exposed to the fire of the besieged. A few picked men will cautiously mount to the summit of the breach, occupying such sheltered points as may be found at hand, for the purpose of covering the sappers whilst at work. These men will be sustained by a detachment posted along the passage of the ditch.

97...Twenty-sixth Night. The lodgment on the breach of the demilune being effected on this night, the breach and counter-batteries along the bastion covered-way, and against the redoubt of the re-entering place of arms, can be completed and armed.

A breach battery of 4 guns will be placed along each crest of the bastion covered-way, as far from the salient as room can be had, for the purpose of opening as wide a breach as practicable at the bastion salient. A counter-battery, likewise of 4 guns, will be placed along the same crest, and in the best position to fire in the prolongation of the main ditch and silence the fire of the enceinte flanks opposite to them. A breach battery of 3 guns will also be placed against each of the redoubts of the re-entering place of arms, to open them on their faces that lie adjacent to the demilunes.

These batteries are covered in flank and rear in the same manner as those against the demilune.

To prevent the besieged from attempting to dislodge the besiegers from the demilune, it is well to construct a trench across its terreplein, from which the ditch of the demilune redoubt can be swept by a fire of musketry. This trench may be made on the twenty-seventh night.

98...So soon as the demilune breach is secured, a descent is commenced from the lodgment on it to the ditch of its redoubt.

This descent and the passage of the ditch of the redoubt will take until the thirty-second night.

In the meantime, zig-zags can be pushed forward in the demilune ditch toward the glacis of the single caponnière; and a double sap be formed in the parapet of the demilune itself, to overlook the ditches and to approach the cut in the demilune face.

A descent can also be made on or before the thirty-second night into the re-entering place of arms, and a lodgment be effected on its terreplein.

99.. On the thirty-second night, miners are set to work at the scarp wall of the demilune redoubt, and at the scarp and counterscarp walls of the cut. The mines may be completed and fired, and the lodgment be effected on the breaches by the thirty-fourth night; at which time the breach in the redoubt of the re-entering place of arms is also carried.

100...When a breach can be opened in the bastion face through the opening of the demilune ditch, the zig-zags in this ditch may be pushed forward nearly to the extremity of the ditch, and the passage of the main ditch opposite the breach in the salient be effected by the thirty-third night, so that the breaches in the body of the place, and those in the redoubts and the cut can all be carried on the thirty-fourth. But when a breach cannot be made in the face of the bastion through the demilune ditch, and it is deemed advisable to make one at this point, it will be necessary to carry the outworks first, and afterward to push forward the sap to crown the glacis of the single caponnière in the demilune ditch, where a breach battery of two guns may be established; at the same time, a lodgment is made behind the bastion covered face, and a breach battery of 4 guns is established there. These labors will require, for their completion, until the thirty-seventh night. In the meantime, lodgments are effected on the upper and lower terrepleins of the demilune redoubt, and in its parapet, to overlook the main ditch, the double caponnières and the tenailles.

The passages across the main ditch are also completed. the descent to the one nearest the shoulder angle being commenced from within the postern of the redoubt of the re-entering place of arms.

101...THIRTY-EIGHTH NIGHT. The lodgment on the breaches in the bastion will be effected on this night, and a descent be commenced from the top of the breach to the ditch of the cavalier.

102...THIRTY-NINTH AND FORTIETH NIGHTS. A lodgment will be effected on the bastion terreplein, and a breach battery of 4 guns be established against each face of the cavalier.

The breach in the cavalier and the descent into the ditch will be completed so that the final assault may be made on the forty-first night.

DEFENCE.

The object of this, like the preceding section, is to give a succinct detail of the operations of the garrison during the successive stages of the attack, supposing the works which they occupy provided with everything requisite for conducting the defence vigorously

103...During the investment, the garrison will resort to every means for cutting off parties of the investing corps which approach the work incautiously, and will particularly endeavor to prevent all attempts at reconnoitring. About one-third of the garrison will be kept on this duty, taking post around the work during the investment and as long after as they can maintain their position without too great danger.

104...As the defences at this period have no other danger to apprehend than a surprise, and nothing to annoy by a fire but reconnoitring parties, the artillery will be so posted as to be of most service in these cases. Two field guns, loaded with grape, should be placed in embrasure on each flank, and one or two more on the bastion faces to sweep the ditches of the demilunes with grape, to frustrate any attempt at a surprise; and two or three heavy guns, with long ranges, should be placed in barbette on each of the salients of the bastions and demilunes, to keep reconnoitring parties at a distance.

105...Whatever precautions may have been taken by the besiegers to deceive the besieged, relative to the point of attack and the time of opening the trenches, the latter, by keeping a strict watch on all the movements of the former, are usually enabled to ascertain both with tolerable certainty, and to prepare themselves accordingly. So soon as these points are known, the garrison, still keeping on the alert to frustrate all attempts at surprise, and without changing in any respect the artillery already in position, will place all the disposable pieces in reserve, in the best positions, on the fronts of attack and the collateral works, to do the most damage to the laborers and the guard of the trenches before they are placed under cover in the first parallel. Fire-balls will be thrown out every night to light up the ground and ascertain the position of the laborers and troops; and, so soon as they are discovered, a heavy fire of grape, etc., will be opened on them from all the guns that can be brought to bear on their position. At the same time, a few howitzers will keep up a ricochet fire in the direction of the capitals to annoy the workmen at the approaches.

After an interval of two or three hours, the parapet of the parallel will be proof against grape-shot, and then a fire of balls and hollow projectiles will be commenced, and directed both along the capitals and to take the guards and parallels obliquely

106...Unless the garrison is very strong, or the besiegers show a want of proper precaution in covering their laborers by a strong guard, sorties cannot be made at this period of the attack with much prospect of success, owing to the distance of the parallel from the defences. The most that ought to be attempted will be to make some charges of cavalry, to cause the laborers to stand to their arms, and thus retard, for a short time, their operations.

107...When, from the indications without, there is no longer any doubt respecting the real point of attack selected, all the disposable artillery will be brought forward and placed in barbette, in the best positions on this point and the collateral works, for sweeping the ground over which the trenches must be pushed. In the meantime, embrasures, platforms and traverses are prepared, on the most suitable positions to place the artillery under shelter so soon as the enfilading batteries are completed.

108...The following armament may be taken as a mean for this period of the defence: Eleven pieces in the bastion of attack, one of which is an 8-inch howitzer, firing in the direction of the capital, the others may be 18 or 24-pounders, five being placed on each face.

Seven or nine pieces of like calibre, and similarly disposed, may be placed in the cavalier of the bastion.

Eleven pieces will be placed in each demilune of the attack, one being an 8-inch howitzer to fire along the capitals, the others 12 or 18-pounders, six of which are placed on the face that bears on the ground opposite the bastion of attack; the other three on the other face.

Five pieces of heavy calibre on the faces of the two collateral bastions which bear most directly on the trenches: and their flanks which bear on the bastion of attack should each receive four pieces near the angle of the curtain.

In the collateral demilunes, six pieces are placed on the faces alone that bear on the trenches.

Besides the preceding, sixteen 8-inch howitzers should be placed in the covered-ways of the point of attack and of the two collateral fronts—two being in each place of arms, to fire in ricochet along the capitals. About twenty mortars should be distributed along the curtains, and in the demilune redoubts.

The pieces on the faces which are enfiladed should be covered by gabionade traverses, placing a traverse between every two pieces. The barbettes in the salients will be partly cut down, and the parapet be raised, to form merlons and embrasures for the guns at these points.

109...An uninterrupted fire should be kept up on the parts of the trenches in progress, particularly when the besiegers commence throwing up the enfilading batteries. The fire should be concentrated on a few of the principal batteries rather than scattered over all, because, by delaying the progress of these, the others, if the besieged act prudently, will not open their fire until all are ready.

110...If the approaches are not well defiled, or are directed too near the salients, works, termed *counter-approaches*, may be made from the covered-way to enfilade them. These works are usually small redan batteries, placed near the foot of the glacis to receive the artillery in reserve not required for the immediate defence of the work. They are connected with the covered-way by an ordinary trench. These batteries are kept armed only during the day, and are protected by small detachments of about 50 men, to secure them from surprise.

111...During this period, the engineer officers and workmen are employed in organizing the point of attack for a vigorous defence. The covered-ways are palisaded with care. Tambours, or block-houses, are established in the salient place of arms, and also in the re-entering places of arms, if there are no permanent redoubts. Similar arrangements are made in the demilunes which have no redoubts; and interior retrenchments, either of a temporary or permanent character, are made in the bastion of attack. Easy communications are established between all the works.

112...With regard to the portion of the garrison on daily duty, the greatest number will be posted in the defences more immediately threatened by the besiegers About 40 men may be posted in each salient place of arms of the point of attack, and 20 in the collateral salients: about 80 in each re-entering place of arms of the same point, and 40 in each of the collateral ones. Besides these, there should be a detachment of about 10 men in each demilune of the point of attack. The number and disposition of the daily guard will of course vary with circumstances. The main point to be attended to is, that no part of the work, of any importance, shall be left without a sufficient force to hold the besiegers in check, in case of surprise, until support can be obtained from the main body, which last should be so distributed as to be able to carry succor promptly to any part threatened or attacked.

113...So long as the besiegers are beyond musket range, the guards in the covered-way have only to keep on the alert, and to send forward in the daytime a few picked men, who take advantage of any shelter to approach the trenches, and fire on the workmen or guards who are exposed, and at night to keep out patrols to scour the ground around the work; to annoy the workmen when an opportunity offers, and to prevent the approach of reconnoitring parties. So soon as the trenches are pushed forward within musket range, an unintermitted warm fire of musketry is kept up on the workmen and guards that are exposed, some 8 or 10 good marksmen being placed in each salient for this service.

114...Sorties may be made with more chances of success when the besiegers commence the second parallel, as the guards of the trenches in the first parallel are not so near at hand to protect the workmen as during the construction of the trenches up to this point.

The detachment for the sortie, consisting of 3 or 400 infantry, will sally from the covered-ways to attack the second parallel on one or both flanks, and, if circumstances favor, in front. When the workmen are put to flight, instead of pursuing them into the first parallel, the detachment will form in battle order to cover a party of some hundreds of workmen, who follow in rear of the detachment whilst they are filling up the trenches, destroying the implements, and setting fire to the gabions. The working party will be covered on each flank by a detachment of infantry and all the disposable cavalry of the place. When the guards of the trenches appear in force to repulse the sortie the troops will retreat slowly, without compromising their safety, and will endeavor to draw the besiegers in the pursuit within short range of case shot, a fire of which will be opened on them so soon as the retreating troops are out of danger from it. This operation, if successful, may be repeated several nights in succession; the best moment is just before dawn, when the guards of the trenches are fatigued and sleepy with watching. Although the chances of success are greater at this stage than at the opening of the trenches, still, if the besiegers take proper precautions, the sortie will, in all probability, prove more prejudicial than advantageous to the besieged.

115...Before the besiegers open the fire of the enfilading batteries, the fire of the defences will be concentrated, as has been said, on the principal of these, and will be kept up against them until a marked effect is observed in the fire of the enfilading batteries. Only one gun will then be left between each traverse on the faces of the defences, the others are withdrawn and kept in reserve. The guns and howitzers kept in battery will fire steadily upon the heads of the approaches as they are gradually advanced.

116...After the third parallel is constructed, the howitzers may be replaced, with advantage, by stone and Coehorn mortars, firing from the covered-ways and the redoubts of the re-entering places of arms. Guns will be placed in embrasures, to fire in the direction of the ditches of the demilunes of attack against the crowning of their covered-ways.

117...At this stage, the musketry fire of the besiegers becomes very destructive to the artillerists whilst serving the guns. Strong oak musket-proof blinds should be arranged, to mask the mouths of the embrasures when the guns are not in battery Blinds, or covers of timber and earth, under which guns can be secured from projectiles that would reach them at top or in flank, will now be serviceable. A few guns covered in this way, and placed in the salients of the collateral works, to obtain a reverse view on the trenches constructed on the glacis, will prove a serious annoyance to the sappers, and will greatly retard their progress.

118...The troops in the covered-ways will keep up a warm fire of musketry against the heads of the sap, and on every exposed point. The men firing occupying points where they will be best sheltered and can best see the leading sappers. A few marksmen will also occupy the parapets of the demilunes and the redoubts, to keep up a fire from them, but only during the day, as at night this fire might injure the men in the covered-ways.

The greater part of the guards of the covered-way should now be withdrawn at night, and be posted in the demilunes and redoubts, so as to expose but few troops if an attack by storm is made.

119...Although sorties in large bodies will seldom prove successful after the second parallel is finished, those made by small detachments of 10, 20, or 30 men against the head of a sap, or other work, when the besiegers are advancing beyond the third parallel, will seldom fail if conducted with proper precautions.

This method of annoyance will be particularly serviceable during all the subsequent stages of the defence, as the besiegers cannot now have at hand a very large force.

120...The defence of the covered-ways will be regulated by the method pursued in the attack. When the latter is made by gradual approaches, the troops, with the exception of a few men who can find a shelter behind the short crotchets, will be withdrawn from the salient places of arms, so long as these are annoyed by the fire of the stone-mortars; when this fire ceases—which takes place when the sap is pushed forward from the third parallel—the troops again enter the salient places of arms, and renew their fire on the heads of the sap, directing it particularly against the sappers working at the trench cavaliers. When the trench cavaliers are completed and armed, the troops again retire from the salient places of arms, and occupy the traverses and short crotchets, where they maintain their fire, and throw hand grenades on the sap when it comes within their range. Stone and Coehorn mortars are also placed behind the traverses, to annoy the sap, etc.

121...If the besiegers are observed to be making preparations to attack by storm, no more troops than will be required to line the parapet of the covered-way should be posted in the more salient parts, and they should maintain their position no longer than is necessary to give the storming party one volley as they debouch from the third parallel; retreating immediately after to the main ditch, or to other designated points. A reserve of about 100 men is posted in each re-entering place of arms, to cover the retreat of those from the salients. All the other outworks are lined with troops, and such pieces as can still be brought to bear on the glacis, loaded with case shot, open, at the same time with the infantry, a deadly fire on the storming party, which is kept up until the assailants are either driven from the covered-ways or take shelter in the trenches constructed by the sappers along the crest of the glacis. A vigorous sortie, both on the front, the flanks, and the rear of the storming party, made from the collateral covered-ways, will, in such cases, be a judicious operation.

122...As the moment for crowning the covered-way approaches, the efforts of the besieged will be redoubled to retard the works of attack. Independently of the measures already laid down, the besieged will arm with artillery the flanks which bear on the point of attack, and will construct oblique embrasures in the curtains, to sweep the positions along the bastion covered-ways, where the besiegers are making the breach and counter-batteries. The guards of the covered-way will retire toward the re-entering as the crowning of the covered-way advances. disputing the ground foot by foot, and holding possession of each point until the besiegers are nearly in a situation to envelop it with their works. The stone and Coehorn mortars will be removed to the re-entering places of arms. or into some of the communications in the rear from which a fire can be kept up on the trenches. In fine, every possible means will be resorted to by which the sappers constructing the breach batteries and the descents can be cut off and their labors be retarded.

123...When the besiegers have established themselves so strongly on the glacis and the covered-way that sorties in small parties cannot be made without too great risk, a warm fire of musketry will still be kept up on the trenches from all the outworks, and the besieged will wait until the descent of the ditch debouches at the counterscarp before renewing the same game of sorties in small parties. A vigilant look-out will be kept, to ascertain this moment, and so soon as the sappers show themselves, every effort will be made to cut them off and destroy their work, by opening a fire, both of artillery and musketry, on the débouché, by sorties in small bodies, and by throwing loaded shells, grenades, etc., into the ditch.

124...In wet ditches, filled with stagnant water, the besieged will resort frequently to night attacks in boats on the dike or passage; and, in the case where water can be suddenly let into or be drawn from the ditch, chases of water will be used to sweep away the besieger's works.

125...In defending the breach of the demilune, the besieged will resort, not only to the fire of its redoubt, but will erect barricades on the right and left of the breach. across the demilune terreplein, from which a warm fire of musketry will be poured in on the besiegers whilst they attempt to gain possession of the breach either by gradual approaches or by storm. Small mines, or bomb fougasses, should be prepared at the summit of the breach, to be exploded so soon as the besiegers gain possession of it. The top of the breach will be strown with every possible obstacle that can retard the progress of the storming party, and grenades, thundering-barrels, etc., will be rolled over on the troops whilst mounting the breach.

126...The measures for the defence of the main ditch and of the breach in the bastion face, differ in nothing from those resorted to for the demilune. The besieged will make every effort to keep possession of the ditch to the last moment, by occupying the double caponnières and the tenailles, from each of which works a steady fire will be kept up on the besiegers whilst effecting the passage. Sorties of small bodies of picked troops will be frequently made under the protection afforded by the fire of the tenaille, etc. The posterns at this period require to be guarded with peculiar vigilance, to prevent the besiegers carrying them by surprise, and thus effecting an entrance into the interior of the work.

127...An assault of the breach in the bastion cannot be opposed by the bayonet without compromising the lines of the garrison, unless there exists a good interior retrenchment to cover the retreat from the breach; even in this case, to oppose the storming party with the bayonet will be an operation of great delicacy, for the besieged, if driven back, may not be able to effect their retreat without being so mixed up with the assailants as to render it impossible to prevent the latter entering with them into the retrenchments.

128...Finally, when the breach is effected in the interior retrenchment, the besieged may offer to capitulate, unless they are still able to protract the resistance a day or two by organizing temporary defences, and by placing the houses in the rear of the retrenchments in a defensive state, in which cases this breach should be disputed with the same obstinacy as those of the other works.

RELATIVE STRENGTH OF THE GARRISON AND BESIEGING FORCE.

As a permanent work should force an enemy to resort to an attack by regular approaches, its garrison should be at least of sufficient strength to prevent its being carried by a *coup de main*, or open assault. The largest garrison will depend upon the means provided within the work for lodging troops, and securing properly the munitions of war requisite for the number that can be accommodated during the presumed duration of the defence. Between these two limits the best military authorities estimate as a medium garrison, capable of making a good defence, 600 men per front, or bastion; this force being composed of the different arms of the service in the proper proportions for the duties required of them. When the defences comprise, besides the enceinte, some of the principal outworks, and it is intended to occupy them strongly, with a view to an active, vigorous defence, an allowance from 900 to 1,000 men should be made per bastion.

129...With respect to the quantity of artillery necessary for the armament of a permanent work, there is considerable discrepancy of opinion among military writers. A resolute garrison might preserve a work of tolerable strength from a *coup de main* without the aid of cannon; and an idea of the largest amount of artillery might be arrived at, by supposing each front to be armed with as many pieces as it can carry, with the addition of a suitable number of pieces in reserve to provide for casualties. But these are inadmissible extremes, and a medium estimate is to allow 3 heavy guns and one heavy mortar per front or bastion, with 60 heavy guns, 20 heavy mortars and 10 stone, or light mortars, for the armament of the point of attack.

In estimating the amount of ammunition, an allowance of 1,000 rounds is made for each gun, 800 rounds for each mortar, 100 musket cartridges per day for each soldier on guard; and 300 pounds of powder for each mine.

130...The strength of the besieging force is based upon that of the garrison. The usual estimate is to allow, for the daily duty of the trenches, at least as many troops as the garrison, including in this number the men employed in making the trenches. As the service of the besiegers is very onerous, the tour of duty in the trenches should not be more frequent than once in five or six days. Admitting this estimate, the besieging force, comprising all arms, should be at least five times as strong as the garrison.

131...In estimating the quantity of siege artillery, as many guns and mortars are allowed for the enfilading, counter and mortar batteries as the presumed armament of the point of attack; with an addition of 40 or 50 heavy guns for the breach batteries.

The medium allowance of ammunition for the artillery is 1,000 rounds for each gun, and 800 for each heavy mortar.

132...It is hardly necessary to observe that the above estimates are of a very general character, and are introduced here merely to give some idea of the relative proportions in question. Before undertaking the siege of a work, no pains should be spared to gain all the information possible respecting the state of its defences, and the probable difficulties to be encountered in its attack, and the estimates based on these data should be made on the supposition of the work being provided with all the means of a vigorous defence.

Remarks. In the preceding description of the methods of attack employed against permanent fortifications, the calculations for the extent and strength of the trenches and batteries have been based upon the range and effects of the artillery and small arms which were in general use in siege operations up to the recent important changes and improvements which have been made in the efficacy of arms and projectiles of every character. What corresponding changes in the methods of attack will be called for, arising from these improvements, special experiments and the experience derived from future sieges can alone determine.

From the very ample official records of the siege of Sebastopol, where the armament of the defensive works consisted, in a great measure, of the heaviest calibre of ships' guns, it would seem that no very marked deviations were made, either by the French or English, from the methods of attack used in previous sieges. The first parallels were commenced at about 700 to 1,000 yards from the positions of the defences, and the trenches were, for the most part, executed by the flying sap; the full sap being used by the French sappers alone, and only when they had approached very near to the defensive works. Owing to the peculiar difficulties presented by the character of the ground, the defensive armor prescribed for the leading sappers in executing the full sap was laid aside to enable the men to work more effectively.

In the construction of their batteries, the French appear to have deviated only in exceptional cases, arising from the nature of the site, from the dimensions and constructions which had been previously adopted by them. The English engineers, from their experience in this siege, are in favor of thicker parapets, and a greater extent of front for each gun for batteries, particularly for the heavy calibres of ships' guns with which some of their batteries were armed. These, with a few minor changes in the details of platforms and embrasures, are the only modifications in the siege works of any importance which the results of this memorable siege seem to have suggested.

In the defence of their trenches from the frequent sorties of the garrison, the French, after meeting with serious losses in the earlier stages of the siege, from the impetuosity of their troops in sallying upon the enemy beyond their trenches, finally adopted the safe rule laid down by Vauban of quietly withdrawing the guards from the portion of trenches upon which the sortie was directed, with the view of assailing the enemy so soon as they had got within them and whilst in a confused and broken condition. This plan met with full success, and was found most effectual in restraining the sorties.

In their defensive works, which were almost entirely of a temporary character, the Russians adopted for their parapets the ordinary dimensions for resisting the heaviest calibres. Although subjected to an incessant and terrible fire of the heaviest ships' guns, with which the besieger's batteries were armed, these parapets, with such daily care as could be given in repairing their damages, seem to have afforded ample cover to the garrison from the direct fire. For cover from vertical fire, resort was had to blindages, formed, in every sheltered nook, with the heavy timbers furnished by the dock-yards, which, being covered with a thickness of five or six feet of earth, seem to have answered completely their purposes as shelters from the shocks of the heaviest shells. To shelter the gunners from the embrasure shot of sharpshooters, the Russians converted the heavy ropes of their dismantled ships into a kind of matting, which was, in some cases, hung before the mouth of the embrasure; in other cases, this matting was made of a circular form, with a hole in the centre large enough to admit the chase of the gun, to which it was fastened as a screen for the men at the trail.

Owing to their ample garrison, the Russians were enabled to take up and fortify several strong, isolated positions, in advance of their continuous line of works, after the siege operations were well under way. They also used with great advantage small *troups-de-loup*, or pits for sharpshooters, in advance of their line, from which both the workmen at the trenches and the artillerists of the besiegers were greatly annoyed. These were in some cases connected and formed into a continuous trench of counter-approach, from which they were subsequently driven only after considerable loss to the besiegers.

CPSIA information can be obtained
at www.ICGtesting.com
Printed in the USA
LVHW100435110522
718424LV00003B/136